PRIZE STORIES 1985
The O. Henry Awards

D0816165

PRIZE STORIES 1985

The O. Henry Awards

EDITED AND WITH
AN INTRODUCTION
BY WILLIAM ABRAHAMS

DOUBLEDAY & COMPANY, INC.

GARDEN CITY, NEW YORK

1985

The Library of Congress has cataloged this work as follows:

Prize Stories. 1947–
 Garden City, N. Y., Doubleday.

   v. 22 cm.

 Annual.
 The O. Henry awards.
 None published 1952–53.
 Continues: O. Henry memorial award prize stories.
 Key title: Prize stories, ISSN 0079-5453.

 1. Short stories, American—Collected works.
PZ1.O11   813'.01'08—dc19   MARC-S
Library of Congress   ₁8402r83₁rev4

ISBN 0-385-19477-3
Library of Congress Catalog Card Number 21-9372

CONTENTS

PUBLISHER'S NOTE

This volume is the sixty-fifth in the O. Henry Memorial Award series.

In 1918, the Society of Arts and Sciences met to vote upon a monument to the master of the short story, O. Henry. They decided that this memorial should be in the form of two prizes for the best short stories published by American authors in American magazines during the year 1919. From this beginning, the memorial developed into an annual anthology of outstanding short stories by American authors, published, with the exception of the years 1952 and 1953, by Doubleday & Company, Inc.

Blanche Colton Williams, one of the founders of the awards, was editor from 1919 to 1932; Harry Hansen from 1933 to 1940; Herschel Brickell from 1941 to 1951. The annual collection did not appear in 1952 and 1953, when the continuity of the series was interrupted by the death of Herschel Brickell. Paul Engle was editor from 1954 to 1959 with Hanson Martin coeditor in the years 1954 to 1960; Mary Stegner in 1960; Richard Poirier from 1961 to 1966, with assistance from and coeditorship with William Abrahams from 1964 to 1966. William Abrahams became editor of the series in 1967.

In 1970 Doubleday published under Mr. Abrahams' editorship *Fifty Years of the American Short Story*, and in 1981, *Prize Stories of the Seventies*. Both are collections of stories selected from this series.

The stories chosen for this volume were published in the period from the summer of 1983 to the summer of 1984. A list of the magazines consulted appears at the back of the book. The choice of stories and the selection of prize winners are exclusively the responsibility of the editor. Biographical material is based on information provided by the contributors and obtained from standard works of reference.

INTRODUCTION

It has been almost twenty years since Doubleday, in the person of Samuel Vaughan, proposed that I become sole editor of this series in succession to Richard Poirier. I felt flattered and challenged by the invitation, and said yes. Thus began a commitment—to the O. Henry Awards and beyond that, to the short story—that continues to this day. The nineteen prize story volumes for which I have been responsible contain, I would like to believe, much of the best writing in the story that has been done in the past two decades. But I should add that when I began, I had no awareness that the commitment would prove so enduring—or so demanding.

Becoming editor of the series meant that I was transformed from an amateur to a professional reader. No longer could I leaf through an agreeable number of magazines—say, six—pausing to read an occasional story as my mood dictated. Instead, I would be required to read more than a thousand stories by American authors, published each year in more than a hundred magazines, many of which I hadn't known until then but which, as it proved, were to be an invaluable resource.

All in all it was a daunting commitment when looked at carefully, but at the beginning I felt it to be very much in the short run. I prepared myself for the moment when the boredom factor would set in. A California politician of that period, who later gained national prominence, once remarked of the giant redwood trees, "When you've seen one, you've seen them all." I assumed that eventually I would be saying the same thing about the stories. It turned out quite differently, however. Reading all the stories, year by year, I have been struck not by their resemblances but by their differences—in style, subject, and intention.

Indeed, it is the sense of variety—noticeable to anyone who reads widely—along with the refusal of writers to be categorized that makes reading contemporary stories so stimulating (one becomes addicted, not bored), and makes generalizations not only difficult, but often suspect. One story does not define a trend, nor does an overpublicized tendency intimidate writers who are indifferent to it and pursue a vision of their own.

The present collection will suggest something of the variety of the contemporary American story. Excellence, whatever the genre, has determined the choice: does a story fulfill its author's intention? Beyond that there are significant differences in the quality of what has been excellently achieved. Here we enter into regions of instinct, subjective judgment, one's personal taste—that last recourse of the harried editor. Obviously, I would prefer not to make generalizations; just as obviously, readers of a yearly collection such as this will be tempted to make them. Nothing I may say about the many other fine stories that for one reason or another have been omitted will deter them. Here are twenty-one stories, gathered from many places, and, as the authors may find to their discomfort, they are made to seem representative of this and that simply by being included in the collection.

If I can't deter generalizations, I can do my best to clear up some misconceptions that are frequently raised about the collection itself. To begin, the O. Henry Awards are not bestowed in a competition or contest. They are simply a recognition of merit. Writers do not "enter" their stories—manuscripts sent to the editor are returned unread. All that is required is that stories have had prior publication in a magazine—the size of its audience doesn't matter—during the calendar year from August 1 to August 1. As for magazines themselves, there is no need or wish for them to nominate stories. What is wanted is simple: that a magazine publishing stories will provide a complimentary subscription to the editor (for which he will certainly be grateful).

Simple, as is the whole process. Yet magazines don't always arrive on the editor's desk, unsolicited manuscripts do, so do *books* of stories (by the rules established for the collection, not eligible), and stories translated from foreign languages (again, *not* eligible, even if the translators are American).

Perhaps the most serious misconception is that stories are chosen to exemplify a theme or genre or magazine. If it is observed that many of the stories have to do with death, or aging, or sickness, or whatever theme emerges in a particular year, this is thought to happen because of the editor's predilection for death, et cetera. In fact, these are stories of exceptional worth that happen to have been published in one year. That so many stories should deal with the same theme may well suggest something about the period in which they were written. After all, writers for the most part live real lives in real worlds which are reflected, however obliquely, in what they write. But quality matters more than topicality in determining the worth of a story; and I try to approach it as a connoisseur, not a commissar.

Similarly, there are complaints that too many stories are "traditional," too many are "experimental," too many are drawn from the "little" magazines, too many are drawn from *The New Yorker* or *The Atlantic* . . . But, as I suggested earlier, excellence—transcending genre, theme, subject, and place of publication—is decisive.

Excellence takes many forms and there are excellent stories so different from each other that there is no profit in comparing them on the same scale. Certainly this is true of "Lily" by Jane Smiley and "Hot Ice" by Stuart Dybek, the two stories that this year share a jointly awarded First Prize. (There are no other prizes, except in the sense that *all* the stories are Prize Winners, arranged—not ranked—simply to show their individual qualities to best effect.)

Jane Smiley's "Lily" is the more immediately accessible in that it fits in the tradition of the well-made story. That tradition goes back at least as far as Maupassant. (It also, I add parenthetically, takes in O. Henry, for whom these awards are named, with no expectation that the stories chosen should be O. Henry-esque.) That is, the story will have a beginning, a middle or climax, and an end that comes logically if sometimes surprisingly in the light of what has preceded it. It will be short in terms of its time-scheme (if not in its length), and when it is over, we know as much as the author is willing to show us: that, we acknowledge, is all that we need to know.

Lily Stith, who has won "a prestigious prize," is awaiting the arrival of her friends Kevin and Nancy Humboldt for a two-day visit. Lily is beautiful, but to her, "her beauty seemed a senseless thing, since it gained her nothing in the way of passion, release, kinship, or intimacy. Now she was looking forward, with resolve, to making the Humboldts confess really and truly what was wrong with her—why, in fact, no one was in love with her." At the end of the story she has learned why, not from what the Humboldts have told her but from what, quite indifferently, they have allowed her to see of their lives. And the surprise of the story is that Lily is no longer dismayed by her predicament, but contentedly accepts it. Perhaps.

For there are more depths to the story than the incautious reader might assume. Everything is made to seem very plain and straightforward, the characters (as they present themselves) are altogether *ordinary*. And yet, if that is the case, why are we so startled, so taken aback, by what they do, which is, upon reflection, not less than extraordinary.

Lily is a poet and we can guess at the kind of poetry she must write, very like *her*, tidy, intelligent, with a grasp of how things are—up to a point. A lily floats on the surface of a pond; under the surface things happen. Ms. Smiley wonderfully pretends that surface is all—she allows us to see what Lily does not, that "the windowsills have not been vacuumed, and the leaves of the plants were covered with dust."

What gives the story its power is how we are gradually made aware of the depths under the surface, the truths that irony deflects but that gather force anyway. The Humboldts depart, Lily remains—we know to what future. Art, seemingly preoccupied with the commonplace, has brought to life something uncommon, funny, strange, and affecting.

Stuart Dybek's story is very different. It has a formal frame—the legend of a girl who was drowned and is thought to be preserved in an ice house—that recurs and is elaborated upon like a leitmotif in music. But the life it describes with amazing intensity goes on apart from the frame. What Dybek evokes is not only unfamiliar—people on the underside of society—but becomes the more powerful for being treated as though this were all the world possible—and indeed, for the boys and men about whom he is writing, that is true: as it has been, so it will be.

Dybek gathers into the contemporary story characters who have only infrequently been given a place in it, even as they are debarred from so much of life that is apart from them. But how he does so is unexpected in the tradition of naturalism to which his story might be thought to belong. His vision is poetic, in a way that, if Lily were writing about this milieu, would be unthinkable. Dybek's story proves the point that Lily suspected: ". . . life itself was to be found in dirt and disorder, in unknown dark substances that she was reluctant to touch."

"Lily" and "Hot Ice" represent opposite ends of the spectrum. Together they remind us of how much life, how much difference in life, the story can encompass. And the twenty-one stories in the present collection make the point not only inescapable, but inevitable.

—WILLIAM ABRAHAMS

PRIZE STORIES 1985
The O. Henry Awards

LILY

JANE SMILEY

Jane Smiley was born in Los Angeles, grew up in St. Louis, and studied at Vassar and at the University of Iowa, where she received her Ph.D. She now teaches at Iowa State University. She is the author of three novels: *Barn Blind*, *At Paradise Gate*, and *Duplicate Keys*. She lives in Ames, Iowa, with her husband, a historian, and their two daughters. She is presently at work on a novel about medieval Greenland.

Careering toward Lily Stith in a green Ford Torino were Kevin and Nancy Humboldt. Once more they gave up trying to talk reasonably; once more they sighed simultaneous but unsympathetic sighs; once more each resolved to stare only at the unrolling highway.

At the same moment, Lily was squeezing her mop into her bucket. Then she straightened up and looked out the window, eager for their arrival. She hadn't seen them in two years, not since having won a prestigious prize for her poems.

She was remarkably well made, with golden skin, lit by the late-afternoon sun, delicately defined muscles swelling over slender bones, a cloud of dark hair, a hollow at the base of her neck for some jewel. She was so beautiful that you could not help attributing to her all of your favorite virtues. To Lily her beauty seemed a senseless thing, since it gained her nothing in the way of passion, release, kinship, or intimacy. Now she was looking forward, with resolve, to making the Humboldts confess really and truly what was wrong with her—why, in fact, no one was in love with her.

A few minutes later they pulled up to the curb. Nancy climbed the apartment steps bearing presents—a jar of dill pickles she had made herself, pictures of common friends, a cap knitted of rainbow colors for the winter. Lily put it on in spite of the heat. The rich colors Nancy had chosen lit up Lily's tanned face and flashing teeth. Almost involuntarily Nancy exclaimed, "You look better than ever!" Lily laughed and said,

"But look at you! Your hair is below your hips now!" Nancy pirouetted and went inside before Kevin came up. He, too, looked remarkable, Lily thought, with his forty-eight-inch chest on his five-foot-nine-inch frame. Because of Nancy's hair and Kevin's chest, Lily always treasured the Humboldts more than she did her current friends. Kevin kissed her cheek, but he was trying to imagine where Nancy had gone; his eyes slid instantly past Lily. He patted her twice on the shoulder. She cried, "I've been looking for you since noon!" He said, "I always forget how far it is across Ohio," and stepped into the house.

That it had been two years—two years!—grew to fill the room like a thousand balloons, pinning them in the first seats they chose and forbidding conversation. Lily offered some food, some drink. They groaned, thinking of all they had eaten on the road (not convivially but bitterly, snatching, biting, swallowing too soon). Lily, assuming they knew what they wanted, did not ask again. Immediately Kevin's hands began to fidget for a glass to jiggle and balance and peer into, to turn slowly on his knee. Two years! Two days! Had they really agreed to a two-day visit?

Although the apartment was neat and airy, the carpet vacuumed and the furniture polished, Lily apologized for a bowl and a plate unwashed beside the sink. Actually, she often wondered whether cleanliness drove love away. Like many fastidious people, she suspected that life itself was to be found in dirt and disorder, in unknown dark substances that she was hesitant to touch. Lily overestimated her neatness in this case. The windowsills, for example, had not been vacuumed, and the leaves of the plants were covered with dust. She began to apologize for the lack of air-conditioning, the noise of cars and trucks through the open windows, the weather, the lack of air-conditioning again; then she breathed a profound sigh and let her hands drop limply between her knees.

Nancy Humboldt was moved by this gesture to remember how Lily always had a touch of the tragic about her. It was unrelated to anything that had ever happened, but it was distinct, always present. Nancy sat forward and smiled affectionately at her friend. Conversation began to pick up.

After a while they ate. Lily noticed that when Kevin carried his chest toward Nancy, Nancy made herself concave as she sidestepped him. Perhaps he did not exactly try to touch her; the kitchenette was very small. Jokes were much in demand, greeted with pouncing hilarity; a certain warmth, reminiscent of their early friendship, flickered and established itself. Conversation ranged over a number of topics. Nancy kept using the phrase "swept away." "That movie just swept me away!" "I live to be swept away!" "I used to be much more cautious than I am now; now I just want to be swept away!" Kevin as often used the word "careful." "I think you have to be really careful about your decisions." "I'm much more careful now." "I think I made mistakes because I wasn't careful." Lily listened most of the time. When the discussion became awkwardly heated, they leaped as one flesh on Lily and demanded to know about her prizewinning volume, her success, her work. Nancy wanted to hear some new pieces.

Lily was used to reading. Finishing the fourth poem, she wondered, as she often did, why men did not come up to her after readings and offer love, or at least ask her out. She had won a famous prize. With the intimacy of art she phrased things that she would not ordinarily admit to, discussed her soul, which seemed a perfectly natural and even attractive soul. People liked her work: they had bought more copies of her prizewinning volume than of any other in the thirteen-year series. But no one, in a fan letter, sent a picture or a telephone number. Didn't art or accomplishment make a difference? Was it all invisible? Lily said, "I think Kevin was bored."

"Not at all, really."

"I wasn't in the slightest," Nancy said. "They're very good. They don't have any leaves on them." Nancy grinned. She rather liked the occasional image herself.

Now was the time to broach her subject, thought Lily. The Humboldts had known her since college. Perhaps they had seen some little thing, spoken of it between themselves, predicted spinsterhood. Lily straightened the yellow pages and set them on the side table. "You know," she said with a laugh and a cough, "I haven't gone out in a month and a half. I mean, I realize it's summer and all, but anyway. And the last guy was just a friend, really, I—" She looked up and went on. "All those years with Ken, nobody even made a pass at me in a bus station. I didn't think it was important then, but now I've gotten rather anxious."

Kevin Humboldt looked straight at her, speculating. Yes, it must be the eyes. They were huge, hugely lashed, set into huge sockets. They were far more expressive and defenseless than anything else about her. The contrast was disconcerting. And the lids came down over them so opaquely, even when she blinked but especially when she lowered her gaze, that you were frightened into changing any movement toward her into some idle this or that. Guys he'd known in college had admired her from a distance and then dated plainer women with more predictable surfaces.

"Do you ever hear from Ken?" Nancy asked.

"I changed my number and didn't give him the new one. I think he got the message."

"I'll never understand why you spent—"

"Nine years involved with a married man, blah blah blah. I know."

"Among other things."

"When we were breaking up, I made up a lot of reasons, but now I remember what it was like before we met. It was just like it is now." Kevin thought of interrupting with his observation. He didn't.

"Everyone has dateless spells, honey," said Nancy, who'd had her first dateless spell after her marriage to Kevin. She had always attributed to Lily virginal devotion to her work. Nancy thought a famous prize certainly equaled a husband and three children. Love was like any activity, you had to put in the hours, but as usual Kevin was right there, so she didn't say this and shifted with annoyance in her chair. "Really," she snapped, "don't worry about it."

Kevin's jaws widened in an enormous yawn. Lily jumped up to find clean towels, saying, "Does it seem odd to you?" Kevin went into the bathroom and Nancy went into the bedroom with her suitcase. Lily followed her. "I have no way of knowing," she went on, but then she stopped. Nancy wasn't really listening.

In the morning Nancy braided and wound up her hair while Lily made breakfast. Kevin was still asleep. Nancy had always had long, lovely hair, but Lily couldn't remember her taking such pride in it as she was now, twisting and arranging it with broad, almost conceited motions. She fondled it, put it here and there, spoke about things she liked to do with it from time to time. She obviously cherished it. "You've kept it in wonderful shape," Lily said.

"My hair is my glory," Nancy replied, and sat down to her eggs. She was not kidding.

When Kevin staggered from bedroom to bathroom an hour later, Nancy had gone out to survey the local shops. Kevin looked for her in every room of the apartment and then said, "Nancy's not here?"

"She thought she'd have a look around."

Kevin dropped into his seat at the table and put his head in his arms. A second later he exclaimed, "Oh, God!" Lily liked Kevin better this visit than she had before. His chest, which had always dragged him aggressively into situations, seemed to have lost some of its influence. He was not as loud or blindingly self-confident as he had been playing football, sitting in the first row in class, barreling through business school, swimming two miles every day. Thus it was with sympathy rather than astonishment that Lily realized he was weeping. He wiped his eyes on his T-shirt. "She's going to leave me! When we get back to Vancouver, she's going to leave me for another guy!"

"Is that what she said?"

"I know."

"Did she say so?"

"I know."

"Look, sit up a second and have this piece of toast."

"He's just a dumb cowboy. I know she's sleeping with him."

She put food in front of him and he began to eat it. After a few bites, though, he pushed it away and put his head down. He moaned into the cave of his arms. Lily said, "What?"

"She won't sleep with me. She hasn't since Thanksgiving. She never says where she's going or when she'll be back. She can't stand me checking up on her."

"Do you check up on her?"

"I call her at work sometimes. I just want to talk to her. She never wants to talk to me. I miss her!"

"What do Roger and Fred say?" Roger and Fred were friends from college who also lived in Vancouver.

"They don't understand."

Lily nodded. Unlike Lily, Roger and Fred had wavered in their fondness for Nancy. Many times she had been selfish about certain things, which were perhaps purely feminine things. She thought people should come to the table when dinner was hot in spite of just-opened beers and half-smoked cigarettes or repair projects in the driveway. She had screamed, really screamed, about booted feet on her polished table. Roger and Fred especially found her too punctilious about manners, found her slightly shrill, and did not appreciate her sly wit or her generosity with food and lodging and presents (this liberality they attributed to Kevin, who was, simultaneously, a known tightwad). And they overlooked her capacity for work—willing, organized, unsnobbish bringing home of the bacon while all the men were looking for careers and worrying about compromising themselves. Lily and Kevin at least agreed that Nancy was a valuable article.

"Okay," Lily said, "who's just a dumb cowboy?"

"His name is Hobbs Nolan. She met him at a cross-country ski clinic last year. But he's not really outdoorsy or athletic; he just wears these pointy-toed cowboy boots and flannel cowboy shirts. Out there guys like him are a dime a dozen. . . ."

"You know him?"

"I've seen him. He knows people we know. They think he's a real jerk."

"You blame him for all of this, then?"

Kevin glanced at her and said, "No." After a moment he exclaimed "Oh, God!" again, and dropped his head on his arms. His hair grazed the butter dish, and Lily was suddenly repelled by these confidences. She turned and looked out the window, but Nancy was nowhere in sight. The freshness of the morning was gone, and the early blue sky had whitened. She looked at her watch. It was about ten-thirty. Any other morning she would already have sat down to her work with an apple and a cup of tea, or she would be strolling into town with her list of errands. She glanced toward the bedroom. The blanket was half off the bed and a corner of the contour sheet had popped off the mattress. Nancy's and Kevin's clothes were piled on the floor. They had left other items in the living room or the kitchen: Nancy's brush, a scarf, Kevin's running shoes and socks, two or three pieces of paper from Nancy's purse, the map on which they had traced their route. But hadn't she expected and desired such intimacy? He sat up. She smiled and said, "You know, you're the first people to spend the night here in ages. I'd forgotten—"

"I don't think you should worry about that. Like Nancy said, we all go through dry spells. Look at me, my—"

"Oh, that! I wasn't referring to that."

"My whole life was a dry spell before Nancy came along."

Lily sat back and looked at Kevin. He was sighing. "Hey," she said, "you're going to have a lot better luck if you lighten up a little."

"I know that, but I can't." He sounded petulant.

Lily said, "Well—"

"Well, now I'd better go running before it gets too hot." Kevin reached for his shoes and socks. But Nancy walked in and he sat up without putting them on. Nancy displayed her packages. "There was a great sale on halter tops, and look at this darling T-shirt!" She pulled out an example of the T-shirt Lily had seen on everyone all summer. It said, "If you live a good life, go to church, and say your prayers, when you die you will go to OHIO." Lily smiled. Nancy tossed the T-shirt over to Kevin, saying, "Extra extra large. I'm sure it will fit."

He held it up and looked at it and then said, glumly, "Thanks."

"Are you going for your run now?"

"Yeah."

But he didn't make a move. Everyone sat very still for a long time, maybe five minutes, and then Lily began clearing plates off the table and Nancy began to take down her hair and put it back up again. Kevin seemed to root himself in the chair. His face was impassive. Nancy glared at him, but finally sighed and said, "I got a long letter from Betty Stern not so long ago. She stopped working on her Chinese dissertation and went to business school last year."

"I heard that Harry got a job, but that it was in Newfoundland or someplace like that," Lily said.

"Who'd you hear that from?" Refusing even to look in Kevin's direction, Nancy combed her hair.

"Remember Meredith Lawlor? Did you know she was here? She's teaching in the pharmacy school here in Columbus. She raises all these poisonous tropical plants in a big greenhouse she and her husband built out in the country."

"Who's her husband?"

"She met him in graduate school, I think. He's from Arizona."

"I'd like to raise plants for a living. I don't know necessarily about poisonous ones." Nancy glanced at Kevin. Lily noticed that she had simply dropped her packages by her chair, that tissue paper and sales slips and the halter tops themselves were in danger of being stepped on. In college they had teased Nancy relentlessly about her disorderly ways, but Lily hadn't found them especially annoying then. Kevin said, "Why don't you pick that stuff up before you step on it?"

"I'm not going to step on it!"

"Well, pick it up anyway. I doubt that Lily wants your mess all over her place."

"Who are you to speak for Lily?"

"I'm speaking for society in general, in this case."

"Why don't you go running, for God's sake?"

"I'd rather not have a heart attack in the heat, thank you."

"Well, it's not actually that hot. It's not as hot as it was yesterday, and you ran seven miles."

"It's hot in here."

"Well, there's a nice breeze outside, and this town is very shady. When you get back we can have lunch after your shower. We can have

that smoked turkey we got at the store last night. I still have some of the
bread I made the day we left."

Kevin looked at her suspiciously, but all he said finally was, "Well, pick
up that stuff, okay?"

Nancy smiled. "Okay."

Still Kevin was reluctant to go, tying his shoes with painful slowness,
drinking a glass of water after letting the tap run and run, retying one of
his shoes, tucking and untucking his shirt. He closed the door laboriously
behind him, and Nancy watched out the window for him to appear on
the street. When he did, she inhaled with sharp, exasperated relief.
"Christ!" she exclaimed.

"He doesn't seem very happy."

"But you know he's always been into that self-dramatization. I'm not
impressed. I used to be, but I'm not anymore."

Lily wondered how she was going to make it to lunch, and then
through the afternoon to dinner and bedtime. Nancy turned toward her.
"I shouldn't have let all these men talk to you before I did."

"What men?"

"Kevin, Roger, Fred."

"I haven't talked to Roger or Fred since late last winter, at least."

"They think I ought to be shot. But they really infuriate me. Do you
know what sharing a house with Roger was like? He has the most rigid
routine I have ever seen, and he drives everywhere, even to the quick
shop at the end of the block. I mean, he would get in his car and drive
out the driveway and then four houses down to pick up the morning
paper. And every time he did the dishes, he broke something we got
from our wedding, and then he would refuse to pay for it because we had
gotten it for free anyway."

"Fred always said that being friends with Roger showed you could be
friends with anyone."

"Fred and I get along, but in a way I think he's more disapproving
than Roger is. Sometimes he acts as if I've shocked him so much that he
can't bear to look at me."

"So how have you shocked him?"

"Didn't Kevin tell you about Hobbs Nolan?"

"He mentioned him."

"But Hobbs isn't the real issue, as far as I'm concerned. Men always
think that other men are the real issue. You know, Roger actually sat me
down one night and started to tell me off?"

"What's the real issue?"

"Well, one thing I can't bear is having to always report in whenever I go somewhere. I mean, I get in the car to go for groceries, and if I decide while I'm out to go to the mall, he expects me to call and tell him. Or if I have to work even a half hour late, or if the girl I work with and I decide to go out for a beer after work. I hate it. I hate picking up the goddamned telephone and dialing all the numbers. I hate listening to it ring, and most of all I hate that automatic self-justification you just slide into. I mean, I don't even know how to sound honest anymore, even when I'm being honest."

"Are you—"

"No, most of all I hate the image I have of Kevin the whole time I'm talking to him, sitting home all weekend with nothing to do, whining into the phone."

"I think Kevin is mostly upset because you don't sleep with him."

"Well—"

"I really don't see how you can cut him off like that."

"Neither does he."

"Why do you?"

"Don't you think he's strange-looking? And everything he does in bed simply repels me. It didn't used to but now it does. I can't help it. He doesn't know how big or strong he is and he's always hurting me. When I see him move toward me, I wince. I know he's going to step on me or poke me or bump into me."

"Well, you could go to a therapist. You ought to at least reassure Kevin that you're not sleeping with this other guy."

"We did go to a therapist, and he got so nervous he was even more clumsy, and I am sleeping with Hobbs."

"Nancy!"

"Why are you surprised? How can this be a reason for surprise? I'm a sexual person. Kevin always said that he thought I was promiscuous until I started with him, and then he just thought that I was healthy and instinctive."

"Well, Nancy—"

"I have a feeling you aren't very approving either."

"I don't know, I—"

"But that's all I want. I realized on the way here that all the time I've known you I've wanted you to approve of me. Not just to like me, or even respect me, but to approve of me. I still like being married to Kevin, but all of us should know by now that the best person for being married to isn't always the best person for sleeping with, and there's no reason why he should be." She glanced out the window. "Anyway, here he comes." A moment later the door slammed open. Lily thought Kevin was angry, until she realized that he had simply misjudged the weight of the door. Sweat was pouring off him, actually dripping on the carpet. Nancy said, "Jesus! Go take a shower." Lily wanted to tell him not to drip over the coffee table, with its bowl of fruit, but said nothing. He looked at them with studied ingenuousness and said, "Four miles in twenty-five minutes. Not bad, huh? And it's ninety-three. I just ran past the bank clock."

"Great." Nancy turned back to Lily and said, "Maybe I should try to call Meredith Lawlor while I'm here. We were pretty good friends junior year. I've often thought about her, actually." Kevin tromped into the bathroom.

Washing lettuce for the sandwiches, Lily watched Nancy slice the turkey. It was remarkable, after all, how the other woman's most trivial mannerisms continued to be perfectly familiar to her after two years, after not thinking about Nancy or their times together for days and even weeks at a stretch. It was as if the repeated movement of an arm through the air or the repeated cocking of a head could engrave itself willy-nilly on her brain, and her brain, recognizing what was already contained in it, would always respond with warmth. In fact, although she did feel this burr of disapproval toward Nancy, and sympathy for Kevin, Kevin's presence was oppressive and Nancy's congenial. Nancy got out the bread she had made, a heavy, crumbly, whole-grain production, and they stacked vegetables and meat on the slices and slathered them with mustard and catsup. The shower in the bathroom went off and Nancy sighed. Lily wondered if she heard herself.

Lily remembered that the kitchen workers in the college cafeteria had always teased Kevin about his appetite. Certainly he still ate with noise and single-minded gusto. His lettuce crunched, his bread fell apart, pieces of tomato dropped on his plate and he wiped them up with more bread. He drank milk. Lily tried to imagine him at work. Fifteen months before, he had graduated from business school near the top of his class and had taken a risky job with a small company. The owner was impressed with his confidence and imagination. In a year he'd gotten four raises, all of them substantial. Lily imagined him in a group of men, serious, athletic, well-dressed, subtly dominating. Was it merely Nancy's conversation about him that made him seem to eat so foolishly, so dependently, with such naked anxiety? To *be* so foolish, so dependent?

When he was finished, Nancy asked him whether he was still hungry and said to Lily, "Isn't this good bread? I made up the recipe myself."

"It's delicious."

"I think so. I've thought of baking bread for the health-food store near us. In fact, they asked me to, but I'm not sure it would be very profitable."

"It's nice that they asked you."

"A couple of guys there really like it."

Kevin scowled. Lily wondered if one of these guys was Hobbs Nolan. Nancy went on, "I make another kind, too, an herb bread with dill and chives and tarragon."

"That sounds good."

"It is."

Lily was rather taken aback at Nancy's immodesty. This exchange, more than previous ones, seemed to draw her into the Humboldts' marriage and to implicate her in its fate. She felt a brief sharp relief that they would be gone soon. She finished her sandwich and stood up to get an apple. It was before one o'clock. More stuff—the towel Kevin had used on his hair, Nancy's sandals, Nancy's other hairbrush—was distributed around the living room. Lily had spent an especially solitary summer, with no summer school to teach and many of her friends away, particularly since the first of August. Some days the only people she spoke to were checkers at the grocery store or librarians. Her fixation on the Humboldts' possessions was a symptom that her solitary life certainly was unhealthy, that she was, after all, turning back into a virgin, as she feared. It was true that her apartment never looked "lived in" and that she preferred it that way. Suddenly she was envious of them; in spite of their suspicions and resentments their life together had a kind of chaotic richness. Their minds were full of each other. Just then Kevin said, with annoyance, "Damn!" and Nancy shrugged, perfectly taking his meaning.

"There's a great swimming pool here," Lily said. "I've spent practically the whole summer there. You must have brought your suits?"

Kevin had been diving off the high board steadily for at least forty-five minutes. At first, when Nancy and Lily had been talking about Kenneth Diamond and Lily's efforts to end that long relationship, Nancy had only glanced at Kevin from time to time. Lily remarked that she had slept with Ken fewer than twenty times in nine years. Nancy stared at her— not in disbelief but as if seeking to know the unfathomable. Then, for four dives, Nancy did not take her eyes off Kevin. He did a backward double somersault, tucked; a forward one-and-a-half lay-out; a forward one-and-a-half in pike position; and a double somersault with a half-gainer, which was astonishingly graceful. "I knew he dove in high school," she said, "but I've never seen this." A plump adolescent girl did a swan dive and Kevin stepped onto the board again. Other people looked up, including two of the lifeguards. Perhaps he was unaware that people were looking at him. At any rate, he was straightforward and undramatic about stepping into his dive. The board seemed to bend in two under his muscular weight and then to fling him toward the blue sky. He attempted a forward two-and-a-half, tuck position, but failed to untuck completely before entering the water. In a moment he was hoisting himself out and heading for the board to try again. Nancy said, "It's amazing how sexy he looks from a distance. All the pieces seem to fit together better. And he really is a good diver. I can't believe he hasn't practiced in all these years."

"Maybe he has."

"Maybe. I mean he looks perfect, and no older than twenty-one. That's how old he was when we first met—twenty-one. I was dating Sandy Ritter. And you were dating Murray Freed."

"I could have done worse than stick with Murray Freed. But he was so evasive that when Ken approached me in a grown-up, forthright way, I just gave up on Murray. He's got a little graphics company in Santa Barbara, and I hear he spends two or three months of the year living on the beach in Big Sur."

"Well, don't worry about it. I've always thought leisure and beauty were rather overrated, myself." She grinned. "But look at him! He did it! That one was nearly perfect, toes pointed and everything."

"I guess I'm sort of surprised that you think he's funny-looking. Everybody always thought he was good-looking in college."

"Did they? It's hard to remember what he looks like, even when I'm looking at him. I mean, I know what he looks like, but I don't know what I think about it. This diving sort of turns me on, if you can believe that."

"Really?" But Lily realized that she was vulnerable, too, and when Kevin came over, dripping and fit, toweling his hair and shoulders with Lily's own lavender towel, his smile seemed very white, his skin very rosy, and his presence rather welcome.

Actually, it was apparent that they all felt better. Lily had swum nearly half a mile, and Nancy had cooled off without getting her hair wet. Kevin was pleased with the dives he had accomplished and with Nancy's obvious admiration. All three of them had an appetite, and it was just the right time to begin planning a meal. "This is a nice park," Kevin said. "The trees are huge."

"We should get steak," Nancy said.

In the bedroom, putting on her clothes, Lily smiled to hear Nancy's laugh followed by a laugh from Kevin. Really, he was a good-humored sort of person, who laughed frequently. Although she could not have said how the visit had failed that morning, or why it was succeeding right then, she did sense their time filling up with possibilities of things they could do together. She heard Nancy say, "I think the coals must be ready by now," and the slam of the door. She pulled a cotton sweater over her head and went into the kitchen thinking fondly of the Humboldts' driving away the next morning with smiles on their faces and reconciliation in their hearts. She hadn't done anything, really, but something had done the trick. Kevin was sitting at the table wrapping onions and potatoes in foil. Lily opened the refrigerator and took out a large stalk of broccoli, which she began to slice for steaming. Kevin had put on a light-blue tailored shirt and creased corduroy slacks. His wet hair was combed back and he had shaved. He said, "Why did you stick with Diamond all those years? I mean"—he looked at her cautiously—"wasn't it obvious that you weren't going to get anything out of it?"

"I got a lot out of it. Ken's problem is that nobody thinks he's anything special but me. I do think he's quite special, though, and I think I got a good education, lots of attention, lots of affection, and lots of time to work. It wasn't what I expected but it wasn't so bad, though I wish there had been some way to practice having another type of relationship, or even just having dates."

"What did he think about your winning the prize?"

"I don't know. I broke up with him right after I applied for it, and I didn't read the letter he sent after I got it."

"Last night, when you were talking—" But the door opened and Nancy swept in. "The coals are perfect! Are these the steaks in here? I'm famished! Guess what? I got three big ears of corn from your neighbor, who was out in his garden. He's cute and about our age. What's his name? He was funny, and awfully nice to me."

"I've never even spoken to the guy," Lily said.

"What do you do? Cross the street when you see an attractive man?" Nancy teased.

"It's not that. It's that some curse renders me invisible. But Kevin was about to say something."

He shrugged.

"Put on you by Professor Kenneth Diamond, no doubt," Nancy said. She handed a potato back to Kevin. "Do that one better. The skin shows. Seriously, Lily"—Kevin took the potato back with a careful, restrained gesture—"you can't keep this up. It's impossible. You're the most beautiful woman anyone we know knows. You have to at least act like you're interested. I'm sure you act like you wouldn't go on a date for a million dollars. You don't prostitute yourself simply by being friendly." Kevin rewrapped the potato and handed it back to Nancy. Then he smiled at Lily and she had a brief feeling that something dramatic and terrible had been averted, although she couldn't say what it was. Nancy ripped the paper off the rib eyes and dropped it on the table.

The wine was nearly finished. Kevin had chosen it, a California red that he'd tried in Vancouver. He kept saying, "I was lucky to find this so far east. That isn't a bad liquor store, really." Lily hadn't especially liked it at first because of its harsh flavor and thick consistency, but after three glasses she was sorry to see the second bottle close to empty. She set it carefully upright in the grass. There was a mystery to its flavor that made her keep wanting to try it again. Nancy was talking about the play she had been in, as the second lead, with a small theater group in Vancouver. She had loved everything about it, she said. "The applause most of all," Kevin said, smiling. "She got a lot of it, too. The third night, she got more than anyone in the cast. She was pretty funny."

"I was very funny."

"Yes, you were very funny."

Nancy lay back on the chaise longue. "The director said that he thought I should take acting classes at the university. They have a very good program. I had never acted before, and they gave me the second lead. You know, there are tons of professional actors in Vancouver."

"It wasn't exactly a professional show. Only the two leads were getting paid, and the guy wasn't even an Equity actor," Kevin said.

"I know that."

Lily took a deep breath. Neither Kevin nor Nancy had changed position in the past five minutes. Both were still leaning back, gazing into the tops of the trees or at the stars, but their voices were beginning to rise. She said, "It must be lovely to live in Vancouver." She thought of it vividly, as if for the first time: thick vegetation, brilliant flowers, dazzling peaks, lots to eat and do, the kind of paradise teaching would probably never take her to.

"It's expensive," Nancy said. "And I've found the people very self-satisfied."

"I don't think that's true," Kevin said.

"I know you don't. Kevin likes it there just fine. But the university is good, and they send acting students off to places like Yale and England and New York City all the time."

"By the time you could get into acting school, you would be thirty-one at the very least." Kevin had sat up now, but casually. He poured the last of the mysterious-tasting wine into his glass.

"How do you figure that?"

"Well, frankly, I don't see how you can quit working for another two years, until I get established." He looked at the wine in the glass and gulped it down. "And maybe thirty-one is a little old to start training for a profession where people begin looking for work before they're out of their teens. And what about having kids? You can't very well have any kids while you're going to school full time. That play had you going eighteen hours a day some days. Which is not to say that it wasn't worth it, but I don't know that you would even want to do it six or eight times a year."

Nancy was breathing hard. Lily leaned forward, alarmed that she hadn't averted this argument, and put her hand on Nancy's arm. Nancy shook it off. "Kids! Who's talking about kids? I'm talking about taking some courses in what I like to do and what some people think I'm good at doing. The whole time I was in that play you just acted like it was a game that I was playing. I have news for you—"

"It was a community-theater production! You weren't putting on Shakespeare or Chekhov, either. And it's not as if Bill Henry has directed in Toronto, much less in New York."

"He's done lights in New York! He did lights on *The Fantasticks!* And on *A Chorus Line!*"

"Big deal."

Nancy leaped to her feet. "I'll tell you something, mister. You owe it to me to put me through whatever school I want to go to, no matter what happens to our relationship or our marriage. I slaved in the purchasing department of that university for three years so that you could go to business school full time. I lived with those crummy friends of yours for four years so we could save on mortgage—"

Lily said, "Nancy—"

Kevin said, "What do you mean, 'no matter what happens to our relationship'? What do you mean by that?"

"You know perfectly well what I mean! Lily knows what I mean, too!"

Lily pressed herself deep into her chair, hoping that neither of them would address her, but Kevin turned to face her. In the darkness his deep-set eyes were nearly invisible, so that when he said, "What did she tell you?" Lily could not decide what would be the best reply to make. He stepped between her and Nancy and demanded, "What did she say?"

"I think you should ask her that."

"She won't tell me anything. You tell me." He took a step toward her. "You tell me whether she still loves me. I want to know that. That's all I want to know." The tone of his voice in the dark was earnest and nearly calm.

"That's between you and Nancy. Ask her. It's not my business."

"But you know. And I've asked her. She's said yes so many times to that question that it doesn't mean anything anymore. You tell me. Does she still love me?"

Lily tried to look around him at Nancy, but seeing the movement of her head, he shifted to block any communication between them. "Does she?"

"She hasn't told me anything."

"But you have your own opinion, don't you?"

"I can't see that that's significant in any way."

"Tell me what it is. Does she still love me?"

He seemed, with his chest, to be bearing down on her as she sat. She had lost all sense of where Nancy was, even whether she was still outside. Wherever she was, she was not coming to Lily's aid. Perhaps she too was waiting for Lily's opinion. Lily said, "No."

"No, what? Is that your opinion?"

Surely Nancy would have stepped in by now. "No, it doesn't seem to me that she loves you anymore." Lily broke into a sweat the moment she stopped speaking, a sweat of instant regret. Kevin stepped back and Lily saw that Nancy was behind him, still and silent on the chaise longue. "Oh, Lord," said Lily, standing up and taking her glass into the house.

The Humboldts stayed outside for a long time. Lily washed the dishes and got ready for bed; she was sitting on the cot in the guest room winding her clock when Nancy knocked on the door and came in. "We had a long talk," she said, "and things are all right."

"Did you—"

"I don't want to talk about it anymore. This may be the best thing. At least I feel that I've gotten some things off my chest. And I think we're going to leave very early in the morning, so I wish you wouldn't get up."

"But I—" Lily looked at Nancy for a moment, and then said, "Okay, I won't. Thanks for stopping."

"You can't mean that, but I'll write." She closed the door and Lily put her feet under the sheet. There were no sounds, and after a while she fell asleep. She awoke to a rhythmic knocking. She thought at first of the door, but remembered that Nancy had closed it firmly. Then she realized that the blows were against the wall beside her head. She tried to visualize the other room. It would be the bed, and they would be making love. She picked up her clock and turned it to catch light from the street. It was just after midnight. She had been asleep, although deeply, for only an hour. The knocking stopped and started again, and it was irregular enough to render sleep unlikely for the time being. She smoothed her sheet and blanket and slid farther into the bed. Even after her eyes had adjusted, the room was dark: the streetlight was ten yards down, and there was no moon. Nancy and Kevin's rhythmic banging was actually rather comforting, she thought. She lay quietly for a moment, and then sat up and turned on the light. She felt for her book under the bed. The banging stopped and did not start again, and Lily reached for the light switch, but as her hand touched it, Nancy cried out. She took her hand back and opened her book, and Nancy cried out again. Lily thought of the upstairs neighbor, whom she hadn't heard all evening, and hoped he wasn't in yet. The bed in the next room gave one hard bang against the wall, and Nancy cried out again. Lily grew annoyed at her lack of consideration, and then, inexplicably, alarmed. She put her feet on the floor. Once she had done that, she was afraid to do anything else. It was suddenly obvious to her that the cries had been cries of fear rather than of passion, and Lily was afraid to go out, afraid of what she might see in the next room. She thought of Nancy's comments about Kevin's strength, and of Nancy's carelessness about Kevin's feelings. She opened the door. Lights were on everywhere, shocking her, and the noise of some kind of tussle came from their bedroom. Lily crept around the door and peeked in. Kevin had his back to her and was poised with one knee on the bed. All the bedcovers were torn off the bed, and Nancy, who had just broken free, was backed against the window. She looked at Lily for a long second and then turned her head so that Lily could see that her hair had been jaggedly cut off. One side was almost to her shoulder, but the other side stopped at her earlobe. The skein of hair lay on the mattress. Lily recognized it now. Seeing Nancy's gaze travel past him, Kevin set down a pair of scissors, Lily's very own shears, that had been sitting on the shelf above the sewing machine. Lily said, "My God! What have you been doing?"

Looking for the first time at the hair on the bed, Nancy began to cry. Kevin bent down and retrieved his gym shorts from under the bed and stepped into them. He said to Lily rather than Nancy, "I'm going outside. I guess my shoes are in the living room."

Nancy sat on the bed beside the hair, looking at it. It was reddish and glossy, with the life of a healthy wild animal, an otter or a mink. Lily wished Nancy would say that she had been thinking of having it cut anyway, but she knew Nancy hadn't been. She thought of saying herself that Nancy could always grow it back, but that, too, was unlikely. Hair like that probably wouldn't grow again on a thirty-year-old head. Lily picked up the shears and put them back on the shelf above her sewing table and said, "You were making love?"

The door slammed. Nancy said, "Yes, actually. I wanted to. We decided to split up, earlier, outside." She looked at Lily. "And then when I got in bed I felt happy and free, and I just thought it would be nice."

"And Kevin?"

"He seemed fine! Relieved, even. We were lying there and he was holding me."

"I can't believe you—"

At once Nancy glared at her. "You can't? Why are you so judgmental? This whole day has been one long trial, with you the judge and me the defendant! What do you know, anyway? You've never even lived with anyone! You had this sterile thing with Kenneth Diamond that was more about editing manuscripts than screwing and then you tell my husband that I'm not in love with him anymore! Of course he was enraged. You did it! You hate tension, you hate conflict, so you cut it off, ended it. We could have gone on for years like this, and it wouldn't have been that bad!"

"I didn't say I knew anything. I never said I knew anything."

Nancy put her face in her hands and then looked up and said in a low voice, "What do I look like?"

"Terrible right now—it's very uneven. A good hairdresser can shape it, though. There's a lot of hair left." Nancy reached for her robe and put it on; she picked up the hair, held it for a moment, and then, with her usual practicality, still attractive, always attractive, dropped it into the wastebasket. She glanced around the room and said, "Well, let's clean up before he gets back, okay? And can you take me to the airport tomorrow?"

Lily nodded. They began to pick things up and put them gingerly away. When they had finished the bedroom, they turned out the light in there and began on the living room. It was difficult, Lily thought, to call it quits and go to bed. Kevin did not return. After a long silence Nancy said, "I don't suppose any of us are going to be friends after this." Lily shrugged, but really she didn't suppose so either. Nancy reached up and felt the ends of her hair, and said, "Ten years ago he wouldn't have done this to me."

Had it really been ten years that they'd all known each other? Lily looked around her apartment, virginal again, and she was frightened by it. She felt a sudden longing for Kevin so strong that it approached desire, not for Kevin as he was but for Kevin as he looked—self-confident, muscular, smart. Her throat closed over, as if she were about to cry. Across the room Nancy picked up one of her hairbrushes with a sigh— and she was, after all, uninjured, unmarked. Lily smiled and said, "Ten years ago he might have killed you."

HOT ICE

STUART DYBEK

Stuart Dybek is the author of a book of poetry, *Brass Knuckles*, and a collection of stories, *Childhood and Other Neighborhoods*, which has won numerous prizes. He has had both NEA and Guggenheim fellowships, and is currently teaching creative writing at Western Michigan University.

SAINTS

The saint, a virgin, was incorrupted. She had been frozen in a block of ice many years ago.

Her father had found her half-naked body floating face down among water lilies, her blond hair fanning at the marshy edge of the overgrown duck pond people still referred to as the Douglas Park Lagoon.

That's how Eddie Kapusta had heard it.

Douglas Park was a black park now, the lagoon curdled in milky green scum as if it had soured, and Kapusta didn't doubt that were he to go there they'd find his body floating in the lily pads too. But sometimes in winter, riding by on the California Avenue bus, the park flocked white, deserted, and the lagoon frozen over, Eddie could almost picture what it had been like back then: swans gliding around the small, wooded island at the center, and rowboats plying into sunlight from the gaping stone tunnels of the haunted-looking boathouse.

The girl had gone rowing with a couple of guys—some said they were sailors, neighborhood kids going off to the war—nobody ever said who exactly or why she went with them, as if it didn't matter. They rowed her around to the blind side of the little island. Nobody knew what happened there either. It was necessary for each person to imagine it for himself.

They were only joking at first was how Kapusta imagined it, laughing at her broken English, telling her be friendly or swim home. One of them stroked her hair, gently undid her bun, and as her hair fell cascading over her shoulders surprising them all, the other reached too suddenly for the buttons on her blouse; she tore away so hard the boat rocked violently, her slip and bra split, breasts sprung loose, she dove.

Even the suddenness was slow motion the way Kapusta imagined it. But once they were in the water the rest went through his mind in a flash—the boat capsizing, the sailors thrashing for the little island, and the girl struggling alone in that sepia water too warm from summer, just barely deep enough for bullheads, with a mud bottom kids said was quicksand exploding into darkness with each kick. He didn't want to wonder what she remembered. His mind raced over that to her father wading out into cattails, scooping her half-naked and still limp from the resisting water lilies, and running with her in his arms across the park crying in Polish or Slovak or Bohemian, whatever they were, and riding with her on the streetcar he wouldn't let stop until it reached the ice house he owned, where crazy with grief he sealed her in ice.

"I believe it up to the part about the streetcar," Manny Santora said that summer when they told each other such stories, talking often about things Manny called *weirdness*, while pitching quarters in front of Buddy's Bar. "I don't believe he hijacked no streetcar, man."

"What you think, man, he called a cab?" Pancho, Manny's older brother asked, winking at Eddie like he'd scored.

Every time they talked like this Manny and Pancho argued. Pancho believed in everything—ghosts, astrology, legends. His nickname was Padrecito which went back to his days as an altar boy when he would dress up as a priest and hold mass in the backyard with hosts punched with bottle caps from stale tortillas and real wine he'd collected from bottles the winos had left on doorstoops. Eddie's nickname was Edwardo, though the only person who called him that was Manny, who had made it up. Manny wasn't the kind of guy to have a nickname—he was Manny or Santora.

Pancho believed if you played certain rock songs backwards you'd hear secret messages from the devil. He believed in devils and angels. He still believed he had a guardian angel. It was something like being lucky, like making the sign of the cross before you stepped in the batter's box. "It's why I don't get caught even when I'm caught," he'd say when the cops would catch him dealing and not take him in. Pancho believed in saints. For a while he had even belonged to a gang called the Saints. They'd tried to recruit Manny too, who, though younger, was tougher than Pancho, but Manny had no use for gangs. "I already belong to the Loners," he said.

Pancho believed in the girl in ice. In sixth grade, Sister Joachim, the ancient nun in charge of the altar boys, had told him the girl should be canonized and that she'd secretly written to the Pope informing him that already there had been miracles and cures. "All the martyrs didn't die in Rome," she'd told Pancho. "They're still suffering today in China and Russia and Korea and even here in your own neighborhood." Like all nuns she loved Pancho. Dressed in his surplice and cassock he looked as if he should be beatified himself, a young St. Sebastian or Juan de la Cruz, the only altar boy in the history of the parish to spend his money on different-colored gym shoes so they would match the priest's vestments—red for martyrs, white for Feast Days, black for requiems. The nuns knew he punished himself during Lent, offering up his pain for the Poor Souls in Purgatory.

Their love for Pancho had made things impossible for Manny in the Catholic school. He seemed Pancho's opposite in almost every way and dropped out after they'd held him back in sixth grade. He switched to public school, but mostly he hung out on the streets.

"I believe she worked miracles right in this neighborhood, man," Pancho said.

"Bullshit, man. Like what miracles?" Manny wanted to know.

"Okay, man, you know Big Antek," Pancho said.

"Big Antek the wino?"

They all knew Big Antek. He bought them beer. He'd been a butcher in every meat market in the neighborhood, but drunkenly kept hacking off pieces of his hands, and finally quit completely to become a full-time alky.

Big Antek had told Pancho about Kedzie Avenue when it was still mostly people from the Old Country and he had gotten a job at a Czech meat market with sawdust on the floor and skinned rabbits in the window. He wasn't there a week when he got so drunk he passed out in the freezer and when he woke the door was locked and everyone was gone. It was Saturday and he knew they wouldn't open again until Monday and by then he'd be stiff as a two-by-four. He was already shivering so bad he couldn't stand still or he'd fall over. He figured he'd be dead already except that his blood was half alcohol. Parts of him were going numb and he started staggering around, bumping past hanging sides of meat, singing, praying out loud, trying to let the fear out. He knew it was hopeless but he was looking anyway for some place to smash out, some plug to pull, something to stop the cold. At the back of the freezer, behind racks of meat, he found a cooler. It was an old one, the kind that used to stand packed with blocks of ice and bottles of beer in taverns during the war. And seeing it Big Antek suddenly remembered a moment from his first summer back from the Pacific, discharged from the hospital in Manila and back in Buddy's lounge on Twenty-fourth Street catty-corner from a victory garden where a plaque erroneously listed his name among the parish war dead. It was an ordinary moment, nothing dramatic like his life flashing before his eyes, but the memory filled him with such clarity that the freezer became dreamlike beside it. The ballgame was on the radio over Buddy's bar, DiMaggio in center again, while Bing Crosby crooned for the jukebox which was playing at the same time. Antek was reaching into Buddy's cooler, up to his elbows in ice water feeling for a beer, while looking out through the open tavern door that framed Twenty-fourth Street as if it were a movie full of girls blurred in brightness, slightly overexposed blondes, a movie he could step into any time he chose now that he was home; but right at this moment he was taking his time, stretching it out until it encompassed his entire life, the cold bottles bobbing away from his fingertips, clunking against ice, until finally he grabbed one, hauled it up dripping, wondering what he'd grabbed—a Monarch or Yusay Pilsner or Foxhead 400—then popped the cork in the opener on the side of the cooler, the foam rising as he tilted his head back and let it pour down his throat, privately celebrating being alive. That moment was what drinking had once been about. It was a good thing to be remembering now when he was dying with nothing else to do for it. He had the funny idea of climbing inside the cooler and going to sleep to continue the memory like a dream. The cooler was thick with frost, so white it seemed to glow. Its lid had been replaced with a slab of dry ice that smoked even within the cold of the freezer, reminding Antek that as kids they'd always called it hot ice. He nudged it aside. Beneath it was a block of ice as clear as if the icemen had just delivered it. There was something frozen inside. He glanced away, but knew already, immediately, it was a body. He couldn't move away. He looked again. The longer he stared, the calmer he felt. It was a girl. He could make out her hair, not just blond, but radiating gold like a candleflame behind a window in winter. Her breasts were bare. The ice seemed even clearer. She was beautiful and dreamy looking, not dreamy like sleeping, but the dreamy look DPs sometimes get when they first come to the city. As long as he stayed beside her he didn't shiver. He could feel the blood return; he was warm as if the smoldering dry ice really was hot. He spent the weekend huddled against her, and early

Monday morning when the Czech opened the freezer he said to Antek, "Get out . . . you're fired." That's all either one of them said.

"You know what I think," Pancho said. "They moved her body from the ice house to the butcher shop because the cops checked, man."

"You know what I think," Manny said, "I think you're doing so much shit that even the winos can bullshit you."

They looked hard at one another, Manny especially looking bad because of a beard he was trying to grow that was mostly stubble except for a black knot of hair frizzing from the cleft under his lower lip—a little lip beard like a jazz musician's—and Pancho covered in crosses, a wooden one dangling from a leather thong over his open shirt, and a small gold cross on a fine gold chain tight about his throat, and a tiny platinum cross in his right earlobe, and a faded India-ink cross tattooed on his wrist where one would feel for a pulse.

"He got a cross-shaped dick," Manny said.

"Only when I got a hard-on, man," Pancho said, grinning, and they busted up.

"Hey, Eddie, man," Pancho said, "what you think of all this, man?"

Kapusta just shrugged like he always did. Not that he didn't have any ideas exactly, or that he didn't care. That shrug *was* what Kapusta believed.

"Yeah. Well, man," Pancho said, "I believe there's saints, and miracles happening everywhere only everybody's afraid to admit it. I mean like Ralph's little brother, the blue baby who died when he was eight. He knew he was dying all his life, man, and never complained. He was a saint. Or Big Antek who everybody says is a wino, man. But he treats everybody as human beings. Who you think's more of a saint—him or the President, man? And Mrs. Corillo who everybody thought was crazy because she was praying loud all the time. Remember? She kneeled all day praying for Puerto Rico during that earthquake—the one Roberto Clemente crashed going to help. Remember that, man? Mrs. Corillo prayed all day and they thought she was still praying at night and she was kneeling there dead. She was a saint, man, and so's Roberto Clemente. There should be like a church, St. Roberto Clemente. Kids could pray to him at night. That would mean something to them."

"The earthquake wasn't in Puerto Rico, man," Manny told him, "and I don't believe no streetcar'd stop for somebody carrying a dead person."

AMNESIA

It was hard to believe there ever were streetcars. The city back then, the city of their fathers, which was as far back as family memory extended, even the city of their childhoods, seemed as remote to Eddie and Manny as the capital of some foreign country.

The past collapsed about them—decayed, bulldozed, obliterated. They walked past block-length gutted factories, past walls of peeling, multicolored doors hammered up around flooded excavation pits, hung out in half-boarded storefronts of groceries that had shut down when they were kids, dusty cans still stacked on the shelves. Broken glass collected everywhere mounding like sand in the little, sunken front yards and gutters. Even the church's stained-glass windows were patched with plywood.

They could vaguely remember something different before the cranes and wrecking balls gradually moved in, not order exactly, but rhythms: five-o'clock whistles, air-raid sirens on Tuesdays, Thursdays when the stockyards blew over like a brown wind of boiling hooves and bone, at least that's what people said, screwing up their faces, "Phew! they're making glue today!"

Streetcar tracks were long paved over; black webs of trolley wires vanished. So did the victory gardens that had become weed beds taking the corroded plaques with the names of the neighborhood dead with them.

Things were gone they couldn't remember, but missed; and things were gone they weren't sure ever were there—the pickle factory by the railroad tracks where a DP with a net worked scooping rats out of the open vats, troughs for ragmen's horses, ragmen and their wooden wagons, knife-sharpeners pushing screeching whetstones up alleys hollering "Scissors! Knives!" hermits living in cardboard shacks behind billboards.

At times, walking past the gaps, they felt as if they were no longer quite there themselves, half-lost despite familiar street signs, shadows of themselves superimposed on the present, except there was no present—everything either rubbled past or promised future—and they were walking as if floating, getting nowhere as if they'd smoked too much grass.

That's how it felt those windy nights that fall when Manny and Eddie circled the county jail. They'd float down California past the courthouse, Bridewell Correctional, the auto pound, Communicable Disease Hospital, and then follow the long, curving concrete wall of the prison back towards Twenty-sixth Street, sharing a joint, passing it with cupped hands, ready to flip it if a cop should cruise by, but one place you could count on not to see cops was outside the prison.

Nobody was there; just the wall, railroad tracks, the river and the factories that lined it—boundaries that remained intact while neighborhoods came and went.

Eddie had never noticed any trees, but swirls of leaves scuffed past their shoes. It was Kapusta's favorite weather, wild, blowing nights that made him feel free, flagpoles knocking in the wind, his clothes flapping like flags. He felt both tight and loose, and totally alive even walking down a street that always made him sad. It was the street that followed the curve of the prison wall, and it didn't have a name. It was hardly a street at all, more a shadow of the wall, potholed, puddled, half-paved, rutted with rusted railroad tracks.

"Trains used to go down this street," Manny said.

"I seen tanks going down this street."

"Tank cars?"

"No, Army tanks," Kapusta said.

"Battleships too, Edwardo?" Manny asked seriously. Then the wind ripped a laugh from his mouth loud enough to carry over the prison wall.

Kapusta laughed loud too. But he could remember tanks, camouflaged with netting, rumbling on flatcars, their cannons outlined by the red lanterns of the dinging crossing gates which were down all along Twenty-sixth Street. It was one of the first things he remembered. He must have been very small. The train seemed endless. He could see the guards in the turrets on the prison wall watching it, the only time he'd ever seen them facing the street. "Still sending them to Korea or someplace," his father had said, and for years after, Eddie believed you could get to Korea by train. For years after, he would wake in the middle of the night when it was quiet enough to hear the trains passing blocks away, and lie in bed listening, wondering if the tanks were rumbling past the prison, if not to Korea then to some other war that tanks went to at night; and he would think of the prisoners in their cells locked up for their violence with knives and clubs and cleavers and pistols, and wonder if they were lying awake, listening too as the netted cannons rolled by their barred windows. Even as a child Eddie knew the names of men inside there: Milo Hermanski, who had stabbed some guy in the eye in a fight at Andy's Tap; Billy Gomez, who set the housing project on fire every time his sister Nina got gang-banged; Ziggy's uncle, the war hero, who one day blew off the side of Ziggy's mother's face while she stood ironing in her slip during an argument over a will; and other names of people he didn't know, but had heard about—Benny Bedwell, with his "Elvis" sideburns, who may have killed the Grimes sisters, Mafia hitmen, bank robbers, junkies, perverts, murderers on death row—he could sense them lying awake listening, the tension of their sleeplessness, and Pancho lay among them now as he and Manny walked outside the wall.

They stopped again as they'd been stopping and yelled together: "Pancho, Panchoooooo," dragging out the last vowel the way they had as kids standing on the sidewalk calling up at one another's windows as if knocking at the door were not allowed.

"Pancho, we're out here, brother, me and Eddie," Manny shouted. "Hang tough, man, we ain't forgetting you."

Nobody answered. They kept walking, stopping to shout at intervals the way they had been doing most every night.

"If only we knew what building he was in," Eddie said.

They could see the upper stories of the brick buildings rising over the wall, their grated windows low lit, never dark, floodlights on the roof glaring down.

"Looks like a factory, man," Eddie said. "Looks like the same guy who planned the Harvester foundry on Western did the jail."

"You rather be in the Army or in there?" Manny asked.

"No way they're getting me in there," Kapusta said.

That was when Eddie knew Pancho was crazy, when the judge had given Pancho a choice at the end of his trial.

"You're a nice-looking kid," the judge had said, "too nice for prison. What do you want to do with your life?"

"Pose for holy cards," Pancho said, "St. Joseph my specialty." Pancho was standing there wearing the tie they had brought him wound around his head like an Indian headband. He was wearing a black satin jacket with the signs of the zodiac on the back.

"I'm going to give you a chance to straighten out, to gain some self-respect. The court's attitude would be very sympathetic to any signs of self-direction and patriotism, joining the Army for instance."

"I'm a captain," Pancho told him.

"The Army or jail, which is it?"

"I'm a captain, man, *soy capitan, capitan,*" Pancho insisted, humming "La Bomba" under his breath.

"You're a misfit."

Manny was able to visit Pancho every three weeks. Each time it got worse. Sometimes Pancho seemed hardly to recognize him, looking away, refusing to meet Manny's eyes the whole visit. Sometimes he'd cry. For a while at first he wanted to know how things were in the neighborhood. Then he stopped asking, and when Manny tried to tell him the news Pancho would get jumpy, irritable, and lapse into total silence. "I don't wanna talk about out there, man," he told Manny. "I don't wanna remember that world until I'm ready to step into it again. You remember too much in here you go crazy, man. I wanna forget everything like I never existed."

"His fingernails are gone, man," Manny told Eddie, "he's gnawing on himself like a rat and when I ask him what's going down all he'll say is I'm locked in hell, my angel's gone, I've lost my luck—bullshit like that, you know? Last time I seen him he says I'm gonna kill myself, man, if they don't stop hitting on me."

"I can't fucking believe it. I can't fucking believe he's in there," Kapusta said. "He should be in a monastery somewhere; he should of been a priest. He had a vocation."

"He had a vocation to be an altar boy, man," Manny said, spitting it out like he was disgusted by what he was saying, talking down about his own brother. "It was that nuns and priests crap that messed up his head. He was happy being an altar boy, man, if they'd of let him be an altar boy all his life he'd still be happy."

By the time they were halfway down the nameless street it was drizzling a fine, misty spray, and Manny was yelling in Spanish, *"Estamos contigo, hermano! San Roberto Clemente te ayudará!"*

They broke into "La Bomba," Eddie singing in Spanish too, not sure exactly what he was singing, but it sounded good: *"Yo no soy marinero, soy capitan, capitan, ay, ay Bomba! ay, ay Bomba!"* He had lived beside Spanish in the neighborhood all his life and every so often a word got through, like *juilota* which was what Manny called pigeons when they used to hunt them with slingshots under the railroad bridges. It seemed a perfect word to Eddie, in which he could hear both their cooing and the whistling rush of their wings. He didn't remember any words like that in Polish, which his grandma had spoken to him when he was little, and which, Eddie had been told, he could once speak too.

By midnight they were at the end of their circuit, emerging from the unlighted, nameless street, stepping over tracks that continued to curve past blinded switches. Under the streetlights on Twenty-sixth the prison wall appeared rust-stained, oozing at cracks. The wire spooled at the top of the wall looking rusty in the wet light as did the tracks as if the rain were rusting everything overnight.

They stopped on the corner of Twenty-sixth where the old ice house stood across the nameless street from the prison. One could still buy ice from a vending machine in front. Without realizing it, Eddie guarded his breathing as if still able to detect the faintest stab of ammonia, although it had been a dozen years since the louvered fans on the ice house roof had clacked through clouds of vapor.

"Padrecitooooo!" they both hollered.

Their voices bounced back off the wall.

They stood on the corner by the ice house as if waiting around for someone. From there they could stare down Twenty-sixth—five dark blocks, then an explosion of neon at Kedzie Avenue: taco places, bars, a street plugged in, winking festive as a pinball machine, traffic from it coming towards them in the rain.

The streetlights surged and flickered.

"You see that?" Eddie asked. "They used to say when the streetlights flickered it meant they just fried somebody in the electric chair."

"So much bullshit," Manny said. *"Compadre no te rajes!"* he yelled at the wall.

"Whatcha tell him?"

"It sounds different in English," Manny said. " '*Godfather, do not give up.*' It's words from an old song."

Kapusta stepped out into the middle of Twenty-sixth and stood in the misting drizzle squinting at Kedzie through cupped hands as if he had a spyglass. He could make out the traffic light way down there changing to green. He could almost hear the music from the bars that would serve them without asking for ID's so long as Manny was there. "You thirsty by any chance, man?" he asked.

"You buyin'?" Manny grinned.

"Buenas noches, Pancho," they hollered, "catch you tomorrow, man."

"Goodnight guys," a falsetto voice echoed back from over the wall.

"That ain't Pancho," Manny said.

"Sounds like the singer on old Platters' records," Eddie said. "Ask him if he knows Pancho, man."

"Hey, you know a guy named Pancho Santora?" Manny called.

"Oh, Pancho?" the voice inquired.

"Yeah, Pancho."

"Oh, Cisco!" the voice shouted. They could hear him cackling. "Hey baby, I don't know no Pancho. Is that rain I smell?"

"It's raining," Eddie hollered.

"Hey baby, tell me something. What's it like out there tonight?"

Manny and Eddie looked at each other. "Beautiful!" they yelled together.

GRIEF

There was never a requiem, but by Lent everyone knew that one way or another Pancho was gone. No wreaths, but plenty of rumors: Pancho had hung himself in his cell; his throat had been slashed in the showers; he'd killed another inmate and was under heavy sedation in the psycho ward at Kankakee. And there was talk he'd made a deal and was in the Army, shipped off to a war he had sworn he'd never fight; that he had turned snitch and had been secretly relocated with a new identity; or that he had become a trustee, and had simply walked away while mowing the grass in front of the courthouse, escaped maybe to Mexico, or maybe just across town to the North Side around Diversey where, if one made the rounds of the leather bars, they might see someone with Pancho's altar-boy eyes staring out from the makeup of a girl.

Some saw him late at night like a ghost haunting the neighborhood, collar up, in the back of the church lighting a vigil candle; or veiled in a black mantilla, speeding past, face floating by on a greasy El window.

Rumors were becoming legends, but there was never a wake, never an obituary, and no one knew how to mourn a person who had just disappeared.

For a while Manny disappeared too. He wasn't talking and Kapusta didn't ask. They had quit walking around the prison wall months before, around Christmas when Pancho refused to let anyone, even Manny, visit. But their night walks had been tapering off before that.

Eddie remembered the very last time they had gone. It was in December and he was frozen from standing around a burning garbage can on Kedzie, selling Christmas trees. About ten, when the lot closed, Manny came by and they stopped to thaw out at the Carta Blanca. A guy named Jose kept buying them whiskeys and they staggered out after midnight into a blizzard.

"Look at this white bullshit," Manny said.

Walking down Twenty-sixth they stopped to fling snowballs over the wall. Then they decided to stand there singing Christmas carols. Snow was drifting against the wall, erasing the street that had hardly been there. Eddie could tell Manny was starting to go silent. He would get the first few words into a carol, singing at the top of his voice, then stop as if choked by the song. His eyes stayed angry when he laughed. Everything was bullshit to him and finally Eddie couldn't talk to him anymore. Stomping away from the prison through fresh snow, Eddie had said, "If this keeps up, man, I'll need boots."

"It don't *have* to *keep up*, man," Manny snapped. "Nobody's making you come, man. It ain't your brother."

"All I said is I'll need boots, man," Eddie said.

"You said it hopeless, man; things are always fucking hopeless to you."

"Hey, you're the big realist, man," Eddie told him.

"I never said I was no realist," Manny mumbled.

Kapusta hadn't had a lot of time since then. He had dropped out of school again and was loading trucks at night for UPS. One more semester didn't matter, he figured, and he needed some new clothes, cowboy boots, a green leather jacket. The weather had turned drizzly and mild, a late Easter, but an early spring. Eddie had heard Manny was hanging around by himself, still finding bullshit everywhere, only worse. Now he muttered as he walked like some crazy, bitter old man, or one of those black guys reciting the gospel to buildings, telling off posters and billboards, neon signs, stoplights, passing traffic—bullshit, all of it bullshit.

It was Tuesday in Holy Week, the statues inside the church shrouded in violet, when Eddie slipped on his green jacket and walked over to Manny's before going to work. He rang the doorbell, then stepped outside in the rain and stood on the sidewalk under Manny's windows, watching cars pass.

After a while Manny came down the stairs and slammed out the door.

"How you doin', man?" Eddie said like they'd just run into each other by accident.

Manny stared at him. "How far'd you have to chase him for that jacket, man?" he said.

"I knew you'd dig it." Eddie smiled.

They went out for a few beers later that night, after midnight, when Eddie was through working, but instead of going to a bar they ended up just walking. Manny had rolled a couple bombers and they walked down the boulevard along California watching the headlights flash by like a procession of candles. Manny still wasn't saying much, but they were passing the reefer like having a conversation. At Thirty-first, by the Communicable Disease Hospital, Eddie figured they would follow the curve of the boulevard towards the bridge on Western, but Manny turned as if out of habit towards the prison.

They were back walking along the wall. There was still old ice from winter at the base of it.

"The only street in Chicago where it's still winter," Kapusta mumbled.

"Remember yelling?" Manny said, almost in a whisper.

"Sure," Eddie nodded.

"Called, joked, prayed, sang Christmas songs, remember that night, how cold we were, man?"

"Yeah."

"What a bunch of stupid bullshit, huh?"

Eddie was afraid Manny was going to start the bullshit stuff again. Manny had stopped and stood looking at the wall.

Then he cupped his hands over his mouth and yelled, "Hey! you dumb fuckers in there! We're back! Can you hear me? Hey, wake up niggers, hey spics, hey honkies, you buncha fucken monkeys in cages, hey! we're out here *free!*"

"Hey, Manny, come on, man," Eddie said.

Manny uncupped his hands, shook his head and smiled. They took a few steps, then Manny whirled back again. "We're out here free, man! We're smokin' reefer, drinking cold beer while you're in there, you assholes! We're on our way to fuck your wives, man, your girlfriends are giving us blow jobs while you jack-offs flog it. Hey man, I'm pumping your old lady out here right now. She likes it in the ass like you!"

"What are you doing, man," Eddie was pleading. "Take it easy."

Manny was screaming his lungs out, almost incoherent, shouting every filthy thing he could think of, and voices, the voices they'd never heard before, had begun shouting back from the other side of the wall.

"Shadup! Shadup! Shadup out there you crazy fuck!" came the voices.

"She's out here licking my balls while you're punking each other through the bars of your cage!"

"Shadup!" they were yelling and then a voice howling over the others, "I'll kill you motherfucker! When I get out you're dead!"

"Come on out," Manny was yelling. "Come and get me you piece of shit, you sleazeballs, you scumbag cocksuckers, you creeps are missing it all, your lives are wasted garbage!"

Now there were too many voices to distinguish, whole tiers, whole buildings yelling and cursing and threatening, *shadup, shadup, shadup,* almost a chant, and then the searchlight from the guardhouse slowly turned and swept the street.

"We gotta get outa here," Eddie said, pulling Manny away. He dragged him to the wall, right up against it where the light couldn't follow, and they started to run, stumbling along the banked strip of filthy ice, dodging stunted trees that grew out at odd angles, running toward Twenty-sixth until Eddie heard the sirens.

"This way, man," he panted, yanking Manny back across the nameless street, jumping puddles and tracks, cutting down a narrow corridor between abandoned truck docks seconds before a squad car, blue dome light revolving, sped past.

They jogged behind the truck docks, not stopping until they came up behind the ice house. Manny's panting sounded almost like laughing, the way people laugh sometimes after they've hurt themselves.

"I hate those motherfuckers," Manny gasped, "all of them, the fucking cops and guards and fucking wall and the bastards behind it. All of them. That must be what makes me a realist, huh, Eddie? I fucking hate them all."

They went back the next night.

Sometimes a thing wasn't a sin—if there was such a thing as sin— Eddie thought, until it's done a second time. There were accidents, mistakes that could be forgiven once; it was repeating them that made them terribly wrong. That was how Eddie felt about going back the next night.

Manny said he was going whether Eddie came or not, so Eddie went, afraid to leave Manny on his own, even though he'd already had trouble trying to get some sleep before going to work. Eddie could still hear the voices yelling from behind the wall and dreamed they were all being electrocuted; electrocuted slowly, by degrees of their crimes, screaming with each surge of current and flicker of streetlights as if in a hell where electricity had replaced fire.

Standing on the dark street Wednesday night, outside the wall again, felt like an extension of his nightmare: Manny raging almost out of control, shouting curses and insults, baiting them over the wall the way a child tortures penned watchdogs, until he had what seemed like the entire west side of the prison howling back, the guards sweeping the street with searchlights, sirens wailing towards them from both Thirty-first and Twenty-sixth.

This time they raced down the tracks that curved towards the river, picking their way in the dark along the junkyard bank, flipping rusted cables of moored barges, running through the fire-truck graveyard, following the tracks across the blackened trestles where they'd once shot pigeons and from which they could gaze across the industrial prairie that stretched behind factories all the way to the skyline of downtown. The skyscrapers glowed like luminescent peaks in the misty spring night. Manny and Eddie stopped in the middle of the trestle and leaned over the railing catching their breaths.

"Downtown ain't as far away as I used to think when I was a kid," Manny panted.

"These tracks'll take you right there," Eddie said quietly, "to railroad yards under the street, right by the lake."

"How you know, man?"

"A bunch of us used to hitch rides on the boxcars in seventh grade." Eddie was talking very quietly, looking away.

"I usually take the bus, you know?" Manny tried joking.

"I ain't goin' back there with you tomorrow," Eddie said. "I ain't goin' back there with you ever."

Manny kept staring off towards the lights downtown as if he hadn't heard. "Okay," he finally said, more to himself as if surrendering. "Okay, how about tomorrow we do something else, man?"

NOSTALGIA

They didn't go back.

The next night, Thursday, Eddie overslept and called in sick for work. He tried to get back to sleep, but kept falling into half-dreams in which he could hear the voices shouting behind the prison wall. Finally he got up and opened a window. It was dark out. A day had passed almost unnoticed, and now the night felt as if it were a part of the night before, and the night before a part of the night before that, all connected by his restless dreams, fragments of the same continuous night.

Eddie had said that at some point: "It's like one long night," and later Manny had said the same thing as if it had suddenly occurred to him.

They were strung out almost from the start, drifting stoned under the El tracks before Eddie even realized they weren't still sitting on the stairs in front of Manny's house. That was where Eddie had found him, sitting on the stairs out in front, and for a while they had sat together watching traffic, taking sips out of a bottle of Gallo into which Manny had dropped several hits of speed.

Cars gunned by with their windows rolled down and radios playing loud. It sounded like a summer night.

"Ain't you hot wearin' that jacket, man?" Manny asked him.

"Now that you mention it," Eddie said. He was sweating.

Eddie took his leather jacket off and they knotted a handkerchief around one of the cuffs, then slipped the Gallo bottle down the sleeve. They walked along under the El tracks passing a joint. A train, only two cars long, rattled overhead.

"So what we doing, Edwardo?" Manny kept repeating.

"Walking," Eddie said.

"I feel like doing *something,* you know?"

"We are doing something," Eddie insisted.

Eddie led them over to the Coconut Club on Twenty-second. They couldn't get in, but Eddie wanted to look at the window with its neon green palm tree and winking blue coconuts.

"That's maybe my favorite window."

"You drag me all the way here to see your favorite window, man!" Manny said.

"It's those blue coconuts," Eddie tried explaining. His mouth was dry, but he couldn't stop talking. He started telling Manny how he had collected windows from the time he was a little kid, even though talking about it made it sound more important to him than it was. Half the time he didn't even know he was doing it. He would see a window from a bus like the Greek butcher shop on Halsted with its pyramid of lamb skulls and make a mental photograph of it. He had special windows all over the city. It was how he held the city together in his mind.

"I'd see all these windows from the El," Eddie said, "when I'd visit my *busha,* my grandma. Like I remember we'd pass this one building where the curtains were all slips hanging by their straps—black ones, white ones, red ones. At night you could see the lightbulbs shining through the lace tops. My *busha* said gypsies lived there." Eddie was walking down the middle of the street, jacket flung over his shoulder, staring up at the windows as if looking for the gypsies as he talked.

"Someday they're gonna get you as a peeper, man," Manny laughed. "And when they do, don't try explaining to them about this thing of yours for windows, Edwardo."

They were walking down Spaulding back towards Twenty-sixth. The streetlights beamed brighter and brighter and Manny put his sunglasses on. A breeze was blowing that felt warmer than the air and they took their shirts off. They saw rats darting along the curb into the sewer on the other side of the street and put their shirts back on.

"The rats get crazy where they start wrecking these old buildings," Manny said.

The cranes and wrecking balls and urban renewal signs were back with the early spring. They walked around a barricaded site. Water trickled along the gutters from an open hydrant, washing brick dust and debris towards the sewers.

"Can you smell that, man?" Manny asked him, suddenly excited. "I can smell the lake through the hydrant."

"Smells like rust to me," Eddie said.

"I can smell fish! Smelt—the smelt are in! I can smell them right through the hydrant!"

"Smelt?" Eddie said.

"You ain't ever had smelt?" Manny asked. "Little silver fish!"

They caught the Twenty-sixth Street bus—the Polish Zephyr, people called it—going east, towards the lake. The back was empty. They sat in the swaying, long backseat, taking hits out of the bottle in Eddie's sleeve.

"It's usually too early for them yet, but they're out there, Edwardo," Manny kept reassuring him as if they were actually going fishing.

Eddie nodded. He didn't know anything about smelt. The only fish he ate was canned tuna, but it felt good to be riding somewhere with the windows open and Manny acting more like his old self—sure of himself, laughing easily. Eddie still felt like talking but his molars were grinding on speed.

The bus jolted down the dark blocks past Kedzie and was flying when it passed the narrow street between the ice house and the prison, but Eddie and Manny caught a glimpse out the back window of the railroad tracks that curved down the nameless street. The tracks were lined with fuming red flares that threw red reflections off the concrete walls. They were sure the flares had been set there for them.

Eddie closed his eyes and sank into the rocking of the bus. Even with his eyes closed he could see the reddish glare of the walls. The glare was ineradicable, at the back of his sockets. The wall had looked the same way it had looked in his dreams. They rode in silence.

"It's like one long night," Eddie said somewhere along the way.

His jaws were really grinding and his legs had forgotten gravity by the time they got to the lake front. They didn't know the time, but it must have been around four and the smelt fishers were still out. The lights of their kerosene lanterns reflected along the breakwater over the glossy black lake. Eddie and Manny could hear the water lapping under the pier, and the fishermen talking in low voices in different languages.

"My Uncle Carlos would talk to the fish," Manny said. "No shit. He'd talk to them in Spanish. He didn't have no choice. Whole time here he couldn't speak English. Said it made his brain stuck. We used to come fishing here all the time—smelt, perch, everything. I'd come instead of going to school. If they weren't hitting he'd start talking to them, singing them songs."

"Like what?" Eddie said.

"He'd make them up. They were funny, man. It don't come across in English: *'Little silver ones fill up my shoes. My heart is lonesome for the fish of the sea.'* It was like very formal how he'd say it. He'd always call this the sea. I'd tell him it's a lake but he couldn't be talked out of it. He was very stubborn—too stubborn to learn English. I ain't been fishing since he went back to Mexico."

They walked to the end of the pier, then back past the fishermen. A lot of them were old men gently tugging lines between their fingers, lifting nets like flying underwater kites, plucking the wriggling silver fish from the netting, the yellow light of their lamps glinting off the bright scales.

"I told you they were out here," Manny said.

They killed the bottle sitting on a concrete ledge and dropped it into the lake. Then they rode the El back. It was getting lighter without a dawn. The El windows streaked with rain, the Douglas Avenue station smelled wet. It was a dark morning. They should have ended it then. Instead they sat at Manny's kitchen table drinking instant coffee with Pet milk. Eddie kept getting lost in the designs the milk would make, swirls and thunderclouds in his mug of coffee. He was numb and shaky. His jaw ached.

"I'm really crashin'," he told Manny.

"Here," Manny said. "Bring us down easier, man."

"I don't like doing downers, man," Eddie said.

"Ludes," Manny said, "from Pancho's stash."

They sat across the table from each other for a long time, talking, telling their memories and secrets, only Eddie was too numb to remember exactly what they said. Their voices—his own as well as Manny's—seemed *outside*, removed from the center of his mind.

At one point Manny looked out at the dark morning and said, "It still seems like last night."

"That's right," Eddie agreed. He wanted to say more, but couldn't express it. He didn't try. Eddie didn't believe it was what they said that was important. Manny could be talking Spanish; I could be talking Polish, Eddie thought. It didn't matter. What meant something was sitting at the table together, wrecked together, still awake watching the rainy light spatter the window, walking out again, to the Prague bakery for bismarcks, past people under dripping umbrellas on their way to church.

"Looks like Sunday," Manny said.

"Today's Friday," Eddie said. "It's Good Friday."

"I seen ladies with ashes on their heads waiting for the bus a couple days ago," Manny told him.

They stood in the doorway of the Prague, out of the rain, eating their bismarcks. Just down from the church, the bakery was a place people crowded into after mass. Its windows displayed colored eggs and little frosted Easter lambs.

"One time on Ash Wednesday I was eating a bismarck and Pancho made a cross on my forehead with the powdered sugar like it was ashes. When I went to church the priest wouldn't give me real ashes," Manny said with a grin.

It was one of the few times Eddie had heard Manny mention Pancho. Now that they were outside, Eddie's head felt clearer than it had in the kitchen.

"I used to try and keep my ashes on until Good Friday," he told Manny, "but they'd make me wash."

The church bells were ringing, echoes bouncing off the sidewalks as if deflected by the ceiling of clouds. The neighborhood felt narrower, compressed from above.

"I wonder if it still looks the same in there," Manny said as they passed the church.

They stepped in and stood in the vestibule. The saints of their childhood stood shrouded in purple. The altar was bare, stripped for Good Friday. Old ladies, ignoring the new liturgy, chanted a litany in Polish.

"Same as ever," Eddie whispered as they backed out.

The rain had almost let up. They could hear its accumulated weight in the wing-flaps of pigeons.

"Good Friday was Pancho's favorite holiday, man," Manny said. "Everybody else always picked Christmas or Thanksgiving or Fourth of July. He hada be different, man. I remember he used to drag me along visiting churches. You ever do that?"

"Hell yeah," Eddie said. "Every Good Friday we'd go on our bikes. You hada visit seven of them."

Without agreeing to it they walked from St. Roman's to St. Michael's, a little wooden Franciscan church in an Italian neighborhood; and from there to St. Casimir's, a towering, mournful church with twin coppergreen towers. Then, as if following an invisible trail, they walked north up Twenty-second towards St. Anne's, St. Pius, St. Adalbert's. At first they merely entered and left immediately, as if touching base, but their familiarity with small rituals quickly returned: dipping their fingers in the holy-water fount by the door, making the automatic sign of the cross as they passed the life-sized crucified Christs that hung in the vestibules where old women and school kids clustered to kiss the spikes in the bronze or bloody plaster feet. By St. Anne's, Manny removed his sunglasses, out of respect the way one removes a hat. Eddie put them on. His eyes felt hard boiled. The surge of energy he had felt at the bakery had burned out fast. While Manny genuflected to the altar, Eddie slumped in the back pew pretending to pray, drowsing off behind the dark glasses. It never occurred to Eddie to simply go home. His head ached, he could feel his heart racing, and would suddenly jolt awake wondering where Manny was. Manny would be off—jumpy, frazzled, still popping speed on the sly—exploring the church as if searching for something, standing among lines of parishioners waiting to kiss relics the priest wiped repeatedly clean with a rag of silk. Then Manny would be shaking Eddie awake. "How you holding up, man?"

"I'm cool," and they would be back on the streets heading for another parish under the overcast sky. Clouds, a shade between slate and lilac, smoked over the spires and roofs; lights flashed on in the bars and *taquerias*. On Eighteenth Street a great blue neon fish leapt in the storefront window of a tiny *ostenaria*. Eddie tried to remember exactly where it was. They headed to St. Procopius where, Manny said, he and Pancho had been baptized, along a wall of viaducts that schoolchildren had painted into a mural that seemed to go for miles.

"I don't think we're gonna make seven churches, man," Eddie said. He was walking without lifting his feet, his hair plastered with a sweat-like drizzle. It was around 3 P.M. It had been three p.m.—Christ's dark hour on the cross—inside the churches all day, but now it was turning 3 P.M. outside too. They could hear the ancient-sounding *Tantum Ergo* carrying from down the block.

Eddie sank into the last pew, kneeling in the red glow of vigil lights that brought back the red flicker of the flares they had seen from the window of the bus as it sped by the prison. Manny had already faded into the procession making the Stations of the Cross—a shuffling crowd circling the church, kneeling before each station while altar boys censed incense and the priest recited Christ's agony. Old women answered with prayers like moans.

Old women were walking on their knees up the marble aisle to kiss the relics. A few were crying, and Eddie remembered how back in grade school he had heard old women cry sometimes after confession, crying as if their hearts would break, and even as a child he had wondered how such old women could possibly have committed sins terrible enough to demand such bitter weeping. Most everything from that world had changed or disappeared, but the old women had endured—Polish, Bohemian, Spanish, he knew it didn't matter; they were the same, dressed in black coats and babushkas the way holy statues wore violet, in constant mourning. A common pain of loss seemed to burn at the core of their lives, though Eddie had never understood exactly what it was they mourned. Nor how day after day they had sustained the intensity of their grief. He would have given up long ago. In a way he had, and the ache left behind couldn't be called grief. He had no name for it. He had felt it before Pancho or anyone was lost, almost from the start of memory. If it was grief, it was grief for the living. The hymns, with their ancient, keening melodies and mysterious words, had brought the feeling back, but when he tried to discover the source, to give the feeling a name, it eluded him as always, leaving in its place nostalgia and triggered nerves.

Oh God, he prayed, I'm really crashing.

He was too shaky to kneel, so he stretched out on the pew, lying on his back, eyes shut behind sunglasses, until the church began to whirl. To control it he tried concentrating on the stained-glass window overhead. None of the windows that had ever been special for him were from a church. This one was an angel, its colors like jewels and coals. Afternoon seemed to be dying behind it, becoming part of the night, part of the private history that he and Manny continued between them like a pact. He could see night shining through, its neon and wet streetlights illuminating the angel on the window.

LEGENDS

It started with ice.

That's how Big Antek sometimes began the story.

At dusk a gang of little Mexican kids appeared with a few lumps of dry ice covered in a shoe box as if they had caught a bird. *Hot ice*, they called it, though the way they said it sounded to Antek like *hot eyes*. Kids always have a way of finding stuff like that. One boy touched his tongue to a piece and screamed *"Aye!"* when it stuck. They watched it boil and fume in a rain puddle along the curb, and finally they filled a bottle part way with water, inserted the fragments of ice they had left, capped the bottle and set it in the mouth of an alley waiting for an explosion. When it popped they scattered.

Manny Santora and Eddie Kapusta came walking up the alley, wanting Antek to buy them a bottle of rum at Buddy's. Rum instead of beer. They were celebrating, Kapusta said, but he didn't say what. Maybe one of them had found a job or had just been fired, or graduated, or joined the Army instead of waiting around to get drafted. It could be anything. They were always celebrating. Behind their sunglasses Antek could see they were high as usual, even before Manny offered him a drag off a reefer the size of a cigar.

Probably nobody was hired or fired or had joined anything; probably it was just so hot they had a good excuse to act crazy. They each had a bottle of Coke they were fizzing up, squirting. Eddie had limes stuffed in his pockets and was pretending they were his balls. Manny had a plastic bag of the little ice cubes they sell at gas stations. It was half-melted and they were scooping handfuls of cubes over each other's heads, stuffing them down their jeans and yowling, rubbing ice on their chests and under their arms as if taking cold showers. They looked like wild men— shirts hanging from their back pockets, handkerchiefs knotted around their heads, wearing their sunglasses, their bodies slick with melted ice water and sweat; two guys in the prime of life going nowhere, both lean, Kapusta almost as tan as Santora—Santora with that frizzy beard under his lip, and Kapusta trying to juggle limes.

They were drinking rum using a method Antek had never seen before and he had seen his share of drinking—not just in the neighborhood—all over the world when he was in the Navy, and not the Bohemian Navy either like somebody would always say when he would start telling Navy stories.

They claimed they were drinking Cuba Libres, only they didn't have glasses so they were mixing the drinks in their mouths, starting with some little cubes, then pouring in rum, Coke, a squeeze of lime, and swallowing. Swallowing if one or the other didn't suddenly bust up over some private joke, spraying the whole mouthful out, and both of them choking and coughing and laughing.

"Hey Antek, lemme build you a drink," Manny kept saying, but Antek shook his head no thanks, and he wasn't known for passing up too many.

This was all going on in front of Buddy's, everyone catching a blast of music and air-conditioning whenever the door opened. It was hot. The moths sizzled as soon as they hit Buddy's buzzing orange sign. A steady beat of moths dropped like cinders on the blinking orange sidewalk where the little kids were pitching pennies. Manny passed around what was left in the plastic bag of ice, and the kids stood sucking and crunching the cubes between their teeth.

It reminded Antek of summers when the ice trucks still delivered to Buddy's—flatbeds covered with canvas, the icemen, mainly DPs, wearing leather aprons, with Popeye forearms that even in August looked ruddy with cold. They would slide the huge, clear blocks off the tailgate so the whump reverberated through the hollow under the sidewalks, and deep in the ice the clarity shattered. Then with their ice hooks they'd lug the blocks across the sidewalk trailing a slick, and boot them skidding down the chute into Buddy's beery-smelling cellar. And after the truck pulled away, kids would pick the splinters from the curb and suck them as if they were ice-flavored Popsicles.

Nobody seemed too interested when Antek tried to tell them about the ice trucks, or anything else about how the world had been, for that matter. Antek had been sick and had only recently returned from the VA hospital. He returned feeling old and as if the neighborhood had changed in the few weeks he had been gone. People had changed. He couldn't be sure, but they treated him differently, colder, as if he were becoming a stranger in the place he had grown up in, now, just when he needed the most to belong.

"Hey Antek," Manny said, "you know what you can tell me? That girl that saved your life in the meat freezer, did she have good tits?"

"I tell you about a miracle and you ask me about tits?" Antek said. "I don't talk about that anymore because now somebody always asks me did she have good tits. Go see."

Kids had been trying for years to sneak into the ice house to see her. It was what the neighborhood had instead of a haunted house. Each generation had grown up with the story of how her father had ridden with her half-naked body on the streetcar. Even the nuns had heard Antek's story about finding the girl still frozen in the meat freezer. The butcher shop on Kedzie had closed long ago and the legend was that after the cops had stopped checking, her body had been moved at night back into the ice house. But the ice house wasn't easy to break into. It had stood padlocked and heavily boarded for years.

"They're gonna wreck it," Eddie said. "I went by on the bus and they got the crane out in front."

"Oh-oh, last chance, Antek," Manny said. "If you're sure she's in there maybe we oughta go save her."

"She's in there," Antek said. He noticed the little kids had stopped pitching pennies and were listening.

"Well, you owe her something after what she done for you—don't he, Edwardo?"

The kids who were listening chuckled, then started to go back to their pennies.

"You wanna go, I'll go!" Antek said loudly.

"All right, let's go."

Antek got up unsteadily. He stared at Eddie and Manny. "You guys couldn't loan me enough for a taste of wine just until I get my disability check?"

The little kids tagged after them to the end of the block, then turned back bored. Manny and Eddie kept going, picking the pace up a step or two ahead of Antek, exchanging looks and grinning. But Antek knew that no matter how much they joked or what excuses they gave, they were going like him for one last look. They were just old enough to have seen the ice house before it shut down. It was a special building, the kind a child couldn't help but notice and remember—there, on the corner across the street from the prison, a factory that made ice, humming with fans, its louvered roof dripping and clacking, lost in acrid clouds of its own escaping vapor.

The automatic ice machine in front had already been carted away. The doors were still padlocked, but the way the crane was parked it was possible for Manny and Eddie to climb the boom onto the roof.

Antek waited below. He gazed up at the new Plexiglas guard turrets on the prison wall. From his angle all he could see was the bluish fluorescence of their lighting. He watched Manny and Eddie jump from the boom to the roof, high enough to stare across at the turrets like snipers, to draw a level bead on the backs of the guards, high enough to gaze over the wall at the dim, barred windows of the buildings that resembled foundries more than ever in the sweltering heat.

Below, Antek stood swallowing wine, expecting more from the night than a condemned building. He didn't know exactly what else he expected. Perhaps only a scent, like the stab of remembered ammonia he might have detected if he were still young enough to climb the boom. Perhaps the secret isolation he imagined Manny and Eddie feeling now, alone on the roof, as if lost in clouds of vapor. At street level, passing traffic droned out the tick of the single cricket keeping time on the roof —a cricket so loud and insistent that Manny didn't stop to worry about the noise when he kicked in the louvers. And Antek, though he had once awakened in a freezer, couldn't imagine the shock of cold that Manny and Eddie felt as they dropped out of the summer night to the floor below.

Earlier, on their way down Twenty-sixth, Manny had stopped to pick up an unused flare from along the tracks, and Antek pictured them inside now, Manny, his hand wrapped in a handkerchief, holding the flare away from him like a Roman candle, its red glare sputtering off the beams and walls.

There wasn't much to see—empty corners, insulated pipes. Their breaths steamed. They tugged on their shirts. Instinctively, they traced the cold down a metal staircase. Cold was rising from the ground floor through the soles of their gym shoes.

The ground floor was stacked to the ceiling with junked ice machines. A wind like from an enormous air-conditioner was blowing down a narrow aisle between the machines. At the end of the aisle a concrete ramp slanted down to the basement.

That was where Antek suspected they would end up, the basement, a cavernous space extending under the nameless street, slowly collapsing as if the thick, melting pillars of ice along its walls had served as its foundation. The floor was spongy with waterlogged sawdust. An echoing rain plipped from the ceiling. The air smelled thawed, and ached clammy in the lungs.

"It's fucken freezing," Eddie whispered.

Manny swung the flare in a slow arc, its reflections glancing as if they stood among cracked mirrors. Blocks of ice, framed in defrosted freezer coils, glowed back faintly like aquarium windows from niches along the walls. They were melting unevenly and leaned at precarious angles. Several had already tottered to the sawdust where they lay like quarry stones from a wrecked cathedral. Manny and Eddie picked their way among them, pausing to wipe the slick of water from their surfaces and peer into the ice, but deep networks of cracks refracted the light. They could see only frozen shadows and had to guess at the forms: fish, birds, shanks of meat, a dog, a cat, a chair, what appeared to be a bicycle.

But Antek knew they would recognize her when they found her. There would be no mistaking the light. In the smoky, phosphorous glare her hair would reflect gold like a candle behind a frosted pane. He was waiting for them to bring her out. He had finished the wine and flung the pint bottle onto the street so that it shattered. The streets were empty. He was waiting patiently and though he had nowhere else to be it was still a long wait. He could hear the cricket now, composing time instead of music, working its way head first from the roof down the brick wall. Listening to it, Antek became acutely aware of the silence of the prison across the street. He thought of all the men on the other side of the wall and wondered how many were still awake, listening to a cricket, waiting patiently as they sweated in the heavy night.

Manny and Eddie, shivering, their hands burning numb from grappling with ice, unbarred the rear door that opened onto the loading platform behind the ice house. They pushed out an old handcar and rolled it onto the tracks that came right up to the dock. They had already slid the block of ice onto the handcar and draped it with a canvas tarp. Even gently inching it on they had heard the ice cracking. The block had felt too light for its size, fragile, ready to break apart.

"It feels like we're kidnapping somebody," Eddie whispered.

"Just think of it as ice."

"I can't."

"We can't just leave her here, Edwardo."

"What'll we do with her?"

"We'll think of something."

"What about Antek?"

"Forget him."

They pushed off. Rust slowed them at first, but as the tracks inclined towards the river they gained momentum. It was like learning to row. By the trestle they hit their rhythm, speed became wind—hair blowing, shirts flapping open, the tarp billowing up off the ice. The skyline gleamed ahead, and though Manny couldn't see the lake, he could feel it stretching beyond the skyscrapers. The smelt would have disappeared to wherever they disappeared to, but the fishermen would still be sitting at the edge of the breakwater, their backs to the city, dreaming up fish. He knew now where they were taking her. They were rushing through waist-deep weeds crossing the vast tracts of prairie behind the factories, clattering over bridges and viaducts. Below, streetlights shimmered watery in the old industrial neighborhoods. Shiny with sweat, with the girl already melting free between them, they forced themselves faster, rowing like a couple of sailors.

IN THE WHITE NIGHT

ANN BEATTIE

Ann Beattie was born and raised in Washington, D.C., and now lives in Charlottesville, Virginia. Her new novel, *Love Always*, will be published this spring by Random House.

"Don't think about a cow," Matt Brinkley said. "Don't think about a river, don't think about a car, don't think about snow. . . ."

Matt was standing in the doorway, hollering after his guests. His wife, Gaye, gripped his arm and tried to tug him back into the house. The party was over. Carol and Vernon turned to wave goodbye, calling back their thanks, whispering to each other to be careful. The steps were slick with snow; an icy snow had been falling for hours, frozen granules mixed in with lighter stuff, and the instant they moved out from under the protection of the Brinkleys' porch the cold froze the smiles on their faces. The swirls of snow blowing against Carol's skin reminded her—an odd thing to remember on a night like this—of the way sand blew up at the beach, and the scratchy pain it caused.

"Don't think about an apple!" Matt hollered. Vernon turned his head, but he was left smiling at a closed door.

In the small, bright areas under the street lights, there seemed for a second to be some logic to all the swirling snow. If time itself could only freeze, the snowflakes could become the lacy filigree of a valentine. Carol frowned. Why had Matt conjured up the image of an apple? Now she saw an apple where there was no apple, suspended in midair, transforming the scene in front of her into a silly surrealist painting.

It was going to snow all night. They had heard that on the radio, driving to the Brinkleys'. The Don't-Think-About-Whatever game had started as a joke, something long in the telling and startling to Vernon, to judge by his expression as Matt went on and on. When Carol crossed the room near midnight to tell Vernon that they should leave, Matt had quickly whispered the rest of his joke or story—whatever he was saying—

into Vernon's ear, all in a rush. They looked like two children, the one whispering madly and the other with his head bent, but something about the inclination of Vernon's head let you know that if you bent low enough to see, there would be a big, wide grin on his face. Vernon and Carol's daughter, Sharon, and Matt and Gaye's daughter, Becky, had sat side by side, or kneecap to kneecap, and whispered that way when they were children—a privacy so rushed that it obliterated anything else. Carol, remembering that scene now, could not think of what passed between Sharon and Becky without thinking of sexual intimacy. Becky, it turned out, had given the Brinkleys a lot of trouble. She had run away from home when she was thirteen, and, in a family-counselling session years later, her parents found out that she had had an abortion at fifteen. More recently, she had flunked out of college. Now she was working in a bank in Boston and taking a night-school course in poetry. Poetry or pottery? The apple that reappeared as the windshield wipers slushed snow off the glass metamorphosed for Carol into a red bowl, then again became an apple, which grew rounder as the car came to a stop at the intersection.

She had been weary all day. Anxiety always made her tired. She knew the party would be small (the Brinkleys' friend Mr. Graham had just had his book accepted for publication, and of course much of the evening would be spent talking about that); she had feared that it was going to be a strain for all of them. The Brinkleys had just returned from the Midwest, where they had gone for Gaye's father's funeral. It didn't seem a time to carry through with plans for a party. Carol imagined that not cancelling it had been Matt's idea, not Gaye's. She turned toward Vernon now and asked how the Brinkleys had seemed to him. Fine, he said at once. Before he spoke, she knew how he would answer. If people did not argue in front of their friends, they were not having problems; if they did not stumble into walls, they were not drunk. Vernon tried hard to think positively, but he was never impervious to real pain. His reflex was to turn aside something serious with a joke, but he was just as quick to wipe the smile off his face and suddenly put his arm around a person's shoulder. Unlike Matt, he was a warm person, but when people unexpectedly showed him affection it embarrassed him. The same counsellor the Brinkleys had seen had told Carol—Vernon refused to see the man, and she found that she did not want to continue without him—that it was possible that Vernon felt uncomfortable with expressions of kindness because he blamed himself for Sharon's death: he couldn't save her, and when people were kind to him now he felt it was undeserved. But

Vernon was the last person who should be punished. She remembered him in the hospital, pretending to misunderstand Sharon when she asked for her barrette, on her bedside table, and picking it up and clipping the little yellow duck into the hair above his own ear. He kept trying to tickle a smile out of her—touching some stuffed animal's button nose to the tip of her nose and then tapping it on her earlobe. At the moment when Sharon died, Vernon had been sitting on her bed (Carol was backed up against the door, for some reason), surrounded by a battlefield of pastel animals.

They passed safely through the last intersection before their house. The car didn't skid until they turned onto their street. Carol's heart thumped hard, once, in the second when she felt the car becoming light, but they came out of the skid easily. He had been driving carefully, and she said nothing, wanting to appear casual about the moment. She asked if Matt had mentioned Becky. No, Vernon said, and he hadn't wanted to bring up a sore subject.

Gaye and Matt had been married for twenty-five years; Carol and Vernon had been married twenty-two. Sometimes Vernon said, quite sincerely, that Matt and Gaye were their alter egos, who absorbed and enacted crises, saving the two of them from having to experience such chaos. It frightened Carol to think that some part of him believed that. Who could really believe that there was some way to find protection in this world—or someone who could offer it? What happened happened at random, and one horrible thing hardly precluded the possibility of others happening next. There had been that fancy internist who hospitalized Vernon later in the same spring when Sharon died, and who looked up at him while drawing blood and observed almost offhandedly that it would be an unbearable irony if Vernon also had leukemia. When the test results came back, they showed that Vernon had mononucleosis. There was the time when the Christmas tree caught fire, and she rushed toward the flames, clapping her hands like cymbals, and Vernon pulled her away just in time, before the whole tree became a torch, and she with it. When Hobo, their dog, had to be put to sleep, during their vacation in Maine, that awful woman veterinarian, with her cold green eyes, issued the casual death sentence with one manicured hand on the quivering dog's fur and called him "Bobo," as though their dog were like some circus clown.

"Are you crying?" Vernon said. They were inside their house now, in the hallway, and he had just turned toward her, holding out a pink padded coat hanger.

"No," she said. "The wind out there is fierce." She slipped her jacket onto the hanger he held out and went into the downstairs bathroom, where she buried her face in a towel. In time, she looked at herself in the mirror. She had pressed the towel hard against her eyes, and for a few seconds she had to blink herself into focus. She was reminded of the kind of camera they had had when Sharon was young. There were two images when you looked through the finder, and you had to make the adjustment yourself so that one superimposed itself upon the other and the figure suddenly leaped into clarity. She patted the towel to her eyes again and held her breath. If she couldn't stop crying, Vernon would make love to her. When she was very sad, he sensed that his instinctive optimism wouldn't work; he became tongue-tied, and when he couldn't talk he would reach for her. Through the years, he had knocked over wineglasses shooting his hand across the table to grab hers. She had found herself suddenly hugged from behind in the bathroom; he would even follow her in there if he suspected that she was going to cry—walk in to grab her without even having bothered to knock.

She opened the door now and turned toward the hall staircase, and then realized—felt it before she saw it, really—that the light was on in the living room.

Vernon lay stretched out on the sofa, with his legs crossed; one foot was planted on the floor and his top foot dangled in the air. Even when he was exhausted, he was always careful not to let his shoes touch the sofa. He was very tall, and couldn't stretch out on the sofa without resting his head on the arm. For some reason, he had not hung up her jacket. It was spread like a tent over his head and shoulders, rising and falling with his breathing. She stood still long enough to be sure that he was really asleep, and then came into the room. The sofa was too narrow to curl up on with him. She didn't want to wake him. Neither did she want to go to bed alone. She went back to the hall closet and took out his overcoat—the long, elegant camel's-hair coat he had not worn tonight because he thought it might snow. She slipped off her shoes and went quietly over to where he lay and stretched out on the floor beside the sofa, pulling the big blanket of the coat up high, until the collar touched her lips. Then she drew her legs up into the warmth.

Such odd things happened. Very few days were like the ones before. Here they were, in their own house with four bedrooms, ready to sleep in this peculiar double-decker fashion, in the largest, coldest room of all. What would anyone think?

She knew the answer to that question, of course. A person who didn't know them would mistake this for a drunken collapse, but anyone who was a friend would understand exactly. In time, each of the two of them had learned to stop passing judgment on how they coped with the inevitable sadness that set in, always unexpectedly but so real that it was met with the instant acceptance one gave to a snowfall. In the white night world outside, their daughter might be drifting past like an angel, and she would see this tableau, for the second that she hovered, as a necessary small adjustment.

THE QUARRY

HELEN NORRIS

Helen Norris has spent most of her life in Alabama, and now makes
her home in Montgomery. She has had three novels published. The
University of Illinois Press will publish a collection of her short fiction
this year. This is her second story to be included in this series.

They were always moving, she and Jake and Sam and Luke. They followed the heavy cranes and bulldozers wherever the monsters paused to
nose the earth. This time the four of them had settled near a quarry in a
rough, abandoned shack. The men were brothers, all with great arms and
reddish hair and eyes like gray chinks in a rusty wall. Carrie was married
to one of them, to Jake. It almost didn't matter to her which one, they
were so alike. Luke had a scar the length of his face where he had fallen
from the crane. Sam had lost a finger in one of the machines and mangled another. But unless she was looking at Luke from the left or hand-
ing Sam the bread, she could easily mistake the one for the other. Jake,
who was the oldest, was heavier than the rest. He had a slope to his
shoulders and the freckles on the back of his neck came together. But
she noticed that only because they were married.

She cooked and washed the same for all of them. They wore each
other's clothes. They treated her the same, hardly seeing her at all but
holding her somehow imprisoned in their will. She felt it as a pressure, a
crowding together of her senses and her flesh, as if the three of them had
jammed her into a corner. It even had the rank and pungent smell of
tobacco they liked to chew when they tore into the earth.

When she lay beside Jake at night she could hear across the room the
breathing of the others settle into his. On the nights when he would pull
her roughly toward him, it was as if they all together held her for a time,
and let her go. She was worn out with the weight of them. Then their
will for her relaxed and she felt herself adrift in the room as if she lost
her way. It was strange how they could have her so in thrall and yet not

think of her. As if they had dredged her up from some pond or quarry they were digging long ago and then had forgotten her.

If there was money for it they liked to drink beer after supper. They took the radio to the porch and listened to country music for a while. Then they raised their voices, banging words together above the words of the songs. Their laughter had the sound of stones breaking loose and thumping down a hill.

She had learned the trick of standing aside from their laughter, of living prisoned in their realm and hardly knowing it. But it wrapped her up somehow away from the world. Now and then when she was baking bread, the oven smell would free her a little and she could settle in the window with her chin between her knees, her bare feet cautious of the splinters in the wood, and feel all the pressure of the clouds and the crows, the pressure of the leaves and the towhees in the tangle of the jimson weed and the shells of tiny eggs that were caught in the web that billowed from the sill. It was all of it a mothering hand on her skin. It went away when she thought of the men.

The ruined house they lived in was so near the quarry that from the yard a few feet from the kitchen she could see the jagged edge of it. When they left off grinding, roaring, blasting for the day, rocking her fragile cage with senseless thunder and she had finished with the food and cleaning, the men unbridled her a little and left her to settle in the amber quarry dust that covered all the house. There was a captive softness in her. She was like a talking bird repeating in her mind the words they gave her: "Hell, no . . ." "You got any notion what kinda trouble that is?" . . . "Godamighty, man . . ." She heard their words so much their roughness wore away. There were never any words that were her own.

One day after supper she walked past them on the porch and sat on the slowly rotting steps outside. The house was far gone, with decaying, splintered boards. The floor of it sagged. They must be out of it by winter. The wind would take it over. Once they had eaten, the men would never see her. Their will for her went slack and she was free to sit till bedtime, shelling peas for tomorrow or drawing in the dust with the toe of her sandal, listening to the katydids or listening to the music, with now and then a hoot owl breaking through like a far-off string of a guitar. She could hear them talking up above her with their chairs rocked back, feet propped against the flimsy pillars of the porch. Sam had heard about a convict just escaped from the penitentiary in the county next to theirs. They tried to find the news of it on the radio. "Hell, it ain't no more'n twenty miles away . . ." "Well, if it was me I'd take off into Walker. You know one a them wells we dug up around Jasper . . ." "Hell, Sam, they find you in half a day." "Naw, naw, I'd get in one a them dry wells we covered up and I'd hide out in one a them wells. Hell, they covered up with vines . . ." "Hell, Sam, them dogs can find a well. Them dogs has got a smell a you. Hell, Sam thinks all he got to do is take his socks off . . ."

With the laughter their will for her relaxed a little more, like a rope eased out and dropped along the ground. She left the steps and picked her way slowly toward the quarry. She had never been there before, only walked a little from the house while the bread was baking and looked down upon it where it lay half under her, obscured by the scrub oaks, the rocks, and the willows, but here and there a yawning emptiness that frightened her a little. She had turned away from it before.

Now she wanted to get away from the talk of the men. As she walked she found herself surrounded by the breath of pines and the screams of katydids. The path grew so steep that she was almost running, and it seemed to her, as she settled into the motion, that she ran to meet the quarry because it had a will for her. Abruptly she came out on the other side of the wood and the quarry was almost there at the foot of the hill before her.

She picked her way down slowly, clinging to the bitterweed and stripping as she crept the dried and bitter blooms. The small rocks stumbled after her. The pine cones from above bounced before her down the slope, and stones were in her sandals till she pulled them off, and tears were in her eyes from dust that plumed around her. She dragged the hillside with her and her cage world with her, while her life rushed downward to the edge and paused. The flow of all her days was halted at the edge.

Even before she came to it she seemed to see inside that it was empty like herself and had no speech of its own when the man thunder stopped. And like herself it waited to be given words. Breathless at the rim, she saw the giant hollow blood and orange mouth with broken teeth and down inside a band of coral clay, a raw and helpless tongue. . . .

She could not see the machines until she leaned far over the ragged willows caught in the corner of the mouth, and there they were beneath her standing docile like cattle in the barn, almost invisible from the red and orange dust that caked their patient bodies.

It was all so quiet. The mouth before her waited speechless. She had no words of her own, but after a time to try its echo she gave it bits of words that had been given her. She heard it swallow them and spit them up.

Then it was quieter than any grave. Till suddenly just below her some rocks were loosened from the wall and went tumbling downward out of hearing. She leaned far over the edge, and through the willows she saw the man on a small, narrow ledge eight or ten feet below. He was lying on his side, body facing the wall, with his head twisted upward. He was dressed in white. She thought at first he was dead. But she looked into his face, which was stubbled with beard, and his eyes that were startled out of sleep. She knew at once it was the convict.

She was not afraid. She looked at him simply with a kind of question. He was still as a rock. She drew back briefly and looked out across the quarry and into the sunset that was striping the sky and into the lonely field beneath and the wood beyond.

Slowly, clinging to a rock for support, she leaned again to see him through the willows below. He had not changed his position. The afternoon light made shadows of leaves on his face and his clothes. Along the sleeve of his shirt was a reddish brown stain that looked to her like blood. She found herself looking straight into his eyes. And they had no will for her. No will at all. They seemed instead to wait upon her will for him. She drew back quickly. Slowly she grew aware of being adrift.

She picked up her sandals and began the heavy climb without looking back. The pine wood was full of night, noisy with frogs and insects. She guided herself by the voices of the men. When she reached the house she put on her sandals and walked straight past them and went to bed. . . . All night she slept below the willows on the ledge.

On the following day, as she went about her work, it was she who lay unmoving along the ledge, hidden from the men in her nest of willows. They would come into the quarry from the farther side where a road had been cut for the truck to maneuver. If she lay stone-still they would hardly see her burning slowly in the sun. But she shrank from knowing what it must be like when the earth around her shuddered with the grinding and the blasting and the red and yellow dust rose to choke her very breath.

In the late afternoon when the men had released her, she took some strips of fried pork fat she had saved from breakfast and buried them in the fresh corn bread from supper. She wrapped them in a leaf from the sycamore tree and put them in her pocket. She walked past the men sitting dazed with their music. In the weeds near the rusty pump she found the jar she kept there for drinking, and she filled it with water. She pumped a long time to make the water come cold. When the sun was almost down she went again to the quarry, running through the pine wood, sliding down the hill, clutching at the bitterweed, careful of the jar.

She stopped above the ledge. She listened for a time to the great troubled silence that sprang like a gray cat up from the quarry. The shadow below her smelled of rock and ash. When she narrowed her eyes she could see the stubbled earth that swept away to the wood as if it were pasture land, low and grassy, where the cows were grazing in the fields of her childhood. Then she leaned far over, and the convict was there.

He was sitting upright with his back against the wall. She saw his legs in the white pants and his feet in heavy socks and the top of his head with its curling black hair full of red quarry dust and twigs from the willows and a place near the crown where the hair had gone thin. She wound the neck of the jar with a vine she had pulled from a pine in the wood and knotted it and lowered it over the edge, slowly to keep it from banging the rocks, till she felt it caught and jerked like a fishing line. At once she let it go and dropped to her knees, while she clutched at a willow to lean above the ledge.

The stain on his shirt was darker than before and caked with dirt. He held the jar without looking up, as if he had known all along she would come. He drank steadily and deeply. Above him her own throat flooded with cold as if they drank together.

Then from her pocket she took the bread and meat wrapped in the sycamore leaf and dropped it beside him. He picked it up quickly and turned from the wall to look into her face. His eyes were red and haunted with the day-long torment of the quarry and his hunger and thirst. She could see how young he was, almost a boy. The cheeks that bloomed from the dark stubbled jaw were flushed with sunburn. Below his temple was a bruise that twisted downward like the scar on Luke's face. Without taking his eyes from her own, he ate what she had brought him in a trance of relief. And when he had finished he frowned at the sky and squeezed his eyes shut. She saw that he was looking again into her face, groping at her will for him as on the day before.

She said to him softly, "You hurt real bad?"

He gave no sign. She could taste his weariness like rust on her tongue. She felt herself falling and clung to the willow with both her hands. She lowered her voice. "You better leave here tonight. You hear, now."

He looked at the sky and back to her face. The arms that were bracing her began to tremble and the shudder passed into her shoulders and breast. For a moment she felt herself falling against him, and out of the fear and the rapture of falling she said to him softly, "You kill somebody?" She could see the evening gnats swarming about him and settling like dust on the stain of his shirt.

At once she drew back and fell on the sand and sucked in her breath and rubbed the quivering ache in her arms. The gnats swirled up from the ledge like smoke. When her arms grew quiet she crooned to herself, "You hear, now, you better leave here tonight."

She did not trust herself to look at him again. Her limbs were like water. She stood up slowly and returned to the men.

On the next day she went as before with the food and the water. The convict was gone. The tightness went out of her chest and her throat. She sat on the rim of the quarry and ate with mounting hunger the bread and strips of pork she had wrapped in the leaf. She drank from the glass jar slowly and deeply as the convict had done. And with a kind of happiness she thought of him moving through the wood like a motherless child but growing stronger, moving far away. . . .

Then she climbed the hill. The voices of the men growing happy, then quarrelsome, sifted down upon her, but the words were confused. As she neared the words they rounded into shapes that were familiar to her. "Hell, no, Sam . . ." And to her deep amazement they were talking about her. Never in all her life with Jake had she overheard them talking about her. She had to strain to hear above the shrill of the katydids. Sam, it seemed, had found a girl in town. "Hell, Sam, what would we do with another woman?" said Jake. "Two women . . . !" "Well, we gotta think ahead, Jake. Now, how old is Carrie? Well, how old is she, Jake? Hell, ol' Jake don't have the least notion how old Carrie is." She could hear their laughter. The moon had risen behind the wood and was shining all around her.

After they had gone to bed she lay beside Jake. She let the baby she had lost long ago come into her now. She felt it sleeping with the men and waiting to be born. She alone was awake and drifting in her mind over all the room. She got up and by the light of the full moon she looked at herself in the old dresser mirror that was spackled and cracked from all their moving around. She rubbed the circles underneath her eyes. She smoothed her hair still brown with just a little gray. She undid the knot of it and combed it about her neck and over her shoulder the way she used to wear it when Jake would come to call nearly twenty years ago.

At noon when she was serving them the food at the table, leaning over Jake with a bowl of peas, she said to them suddenly: "If you don't know it . . . I'm thirty-eight."

They all stopped chewing and looked at her in mute surprise. Sam and Luke looked at Jake. They went on chewing, their eyes on the food.

At the moment she had said it she felt their will for her relax. But then they chewed her back into it. She went and stood in the doorway. She never ate with the men.

The long quarry summer was turning into autumn. The evenings were cooler and night came soon. Each day at sunset when she crept along the gaping mouth, the quarry and the sky would bay at one another in the same howling color till it hummed in her throat. And she waited till at last they swallowed one another. Sometimes she tossed them a little of the man talk that had followed her through the wood, and something in the sky-earth would swallow up the words. She would sit there mourning in the coolness, hugging her arms, dozing a little, and dreaming the words. Before going home she always looked down upon the ledge where the convict had been.

Her life with the men became a faraway thing. She cooked and cleaned as if the three of them were dreaming all her motions. Sometimes she dropped things flat up on the floor.

Once Jake yelled when she tipped and broke the bowl with the greens. "What's got into you, Carrie? Seems like ever thing you touch you break!"

She stared deep into the rust of his face. "What d'you mean ever thing?"

"I mean what I said."

"You talkin' about the baby?"

"The baby! What baby? There ain't no baby!"

"There was," she said.

"We never had nary baby. Get it outa your head. You cain' call a baby somethin' don't live."

Sam and Luke got up and went to the porch. She could hear them coughing and spitting in the weeds. Jake went after them.

She followed him and stood against the frame of the door. She let the splinters slide through the flesh of her arm. "You tryin' to tell me we didn't have no baby that lived a whole day?"

"Shut up," he said.

She walked to the quarry each day in a dream. Nothing but the quarry belonged to her now. The joe-pye weed was blooming near the edge of the wood. A little farther on, the goldenrod was budding up and down the slope. It was sweeter in the sunlight than anything she knew. But she wanted the goldenrod to leave her alone. None of it was given her to touch in her dream. She began to grow afraid when she thought of the convict.

But once when she was kneeling at the quarry's brink the red and orange valley blew toward her like a flame. A weakness came upon her. She flung herself backward to keep from falling in. Her breath was knocked away and then it filled with sky. In her mouth was a syllable and then another with the green taste of reed along a river's edge. For the first time of all she made a word of her own. She made it out of childhood and the dust in her throat and the rank bitter smell of her hands in the weed. She made it out of nothing the way the world was made. . . .

As soon as she had made it, it fell into the quarry out of hearing, out of mind. She only knew it for a word full of power, and a testing word. A word that could free her to pick up her things and walk away down the road.

Her mind stopped thinking for a while after that. She gathered little rocks and made a circle on the ground. A brown thrasher chirped. He was lost in the weeds. When she raised her eyes, chips of cloud were burning-red and behind them the sky was blooming with the purple of ironweed. Then her mind came back and saw herself walking again down the road. She would walk for a while in her own sweet will and then give it over to the will of the road, to the call of the crows, to the whisper of moss in the forks of the trees. She could see herself walking through low-branching trees as the convict had done.

She covered her face with her bitter-smelling hands. She must make herself strong. Stronger than men. Through the bars of her fingers she saw the quarry below her deeper than hell and broken open and running with blood. It was like herself and had no speech of its own when the man thunder stopped. It lay beneath her helpless as the convict had lain. It looked into her face and seemed to ask her will for it, as the convict had done.

She lay with her face in the sand and the rocks and cried for a little and thought and cried again. Things were born in her mind till the tears at last swept everything away but the quarry helpless and wordless before her, and how it was like her life with Jake and the rest. She must use it for the testing and the proving and the greening of her will. She must make her whole life and the quarry fall down, fall down, whichever one first she didn't care.

Each day she came to it she clung to a willow branch and leaned far over with the testing word. "Fall," she said. "Fall down. Fall down." It swallowed up the sound of her. She would not stop. She repeated the word till her voice was shriller than the katydids behind her in the wood above.

One day when she spoke a small rock loosened from the wall and plunged downward. It was hardly a thing at all. No larger than a hickory nut. She laid her face against the sand and wept for joy.

She stayed away the next day for fear it wasn't so, that her word had moved the rock. After supper Sam went into town and came back with beer. The girl he had brought was out in the pick-up. Carrie heard them laugh. "Is Sam aimin' to marry her?" she said to Jake.

"Hell, no," he said. "We got no place to put 'er."

"Is that the onliest reason?"

He cut across her face with his metal gray eyes. "Hell, you know Sam."

She waited for a while. "Is she purty, Jake? Well, what she like?"

"Cut it out, Carrie."

"Would he be marryin' if I was to leave?"

"If you was to leave and go where?" he said.

In the night she heard the laughter of Sam and the girl. They were on the porch. And then they were quiet. Jake heard their silence and dragged her against him. He smelled of their will for her—stale tobacco, strong and rank. He smelled of the quarry. He poured all the dust of it into her flesh.

Afterwards the rain came down through the roof. And Luke yelled, "HOO!" in the dark. "I'm wet." She heard the bed being dragged and banged. She felt it in her body and drew herself into a hard, tight ball. Through the window she smelled the wet of the sand. A hoot owl called in the sycamore tree. She thought of the quarry gone soft in the rain. The willows were moist and feathered with rain. The stone she had loosened lay cold at the foot of the broken wall.

On the next day she went to the quarry. She filled her mouth with sky and then she called to the earth and the rocks of the earth that circled the pit: "Fall down. Fall down . . ." Her voice was full and gathered to a greatness. She hardly knew it for her own. And this time across from her the great rim tore in a tiny movement of the earth. If she had not been looking directly at the spot she would never have noticed a differ-ence in the land. Suddenly it was there, a little winding crevice no bigger than the stem of a fern in the piney wood behind her, running back into the field, disappearing in the weeds, and down into the crater for the length of her hand.

She sat very still with her heart on fire. It was the way she had felt long ago at the church when they said she was saved and the songs of praise were sung and the arms embraced. But it was far away, almost like another country ago. Each time they moved they seemed to move a little farther from those praising songs. But then she had felt a power in her throat and a singing in her hands. . . .

She sat with her eyes upon the crevice till the light was gone.

All the following day she wandered through the red and amber dusty hours. Morning and afternoon the great machines were tearing at the mouth below and shaking her cage. She placed herself inside the smell of baking bread, saving her substance for the work of the evening.

When it was time to go she walked through the piney wood gathering the fern. At the rim she spread the fern down, mounding it neatly to make a place for her to kneel. After she had knelt, she leaned far over, looking down upon the ledge where the convict had been. Intently she thought of him moving far away—in a big city now, walking between the buildings and into the stores and never looking back and no one ever knowing. He was eating something. It seemed to her an apple. She thought of him with gladness.

She tore bits of fern and rolled them in her hands till she smelled of greenness, and she filled her lungs with the green smell of fern. And then she whispered to the ledge to fall. The breath of her whisper was green and free. "Fall . . . fall . . . fall . . . ," she chanted slowly, her green voice rising. The ledge beneath her shimmered. A tiny bit of earth broke free of the edge. "Fall . . . fall . . ." The willows shuddered. The ledge began to sway. "Fall . . . fall." It crumbled slowly with a sigh and fell without sound upon the tongue of coral clay.

She lay on the fern and turned her face to the sky. She thought of the very first night with Jake, the night of their marriage when they were all alone . . . before they began to follow the machines . . . and how they lay in bed and didn't sleep all night, how he kissed her throat. Now she could see the moon above the pines. She touched her hair and took out the pin that held it in a knot. She kissed it and combed it with her fingers and braided it over a piece of the fern.

When she reached the house they had gone to bed. She stood in the doorway. It was as if the house had been empty without her, and as soon as she entered it she filled it brimful with the shadows of herself. She was in the moonlight on the bed with Jake. She could feel their will for her a sleeping thing, but she was not adrift as she had been before. Even in the darkness was a path for her feet. She took off her clothes and lay beside Jake and listened to his breathing and the breathing of the others that melted into his. She thought of the baby long ago that had been born too soon and how she heard its breath in the night long after it was taken and buried near the church.

Then she saw herself walking behind the convict in the city. He turned into a street. She was turning with him. When he threw away the apple she picked it up and took out the seeds and held them in her mouth. She thought she would plant them at the quarry's rim.

After that she took to doing something that she could not explain. When she married, her mother had given her some yellow dishes. Most of them were broken with moving from place to place. Only one cup and five saucers were left. Now each morning while the men were tearing at the crater, she took a single saucer and buried it deeply in the trembling earth beside the old well where the ground was soft. It gave her pleasure to dig in the yielding ground, to place in the hole the saucer which she had wrapped in several layers of paper, then replace the earth. She pressed her hands against the little new grave. The grains of sand were live with the movement in the hill. She felt herself alive with the movement in the sand.

The morning she was burying the last one of all, Luke came up from below for water. The sweat was running down the valley of the scar across his face. He stood without a word and looked down upon her. She felt how he called up the will of the others and joined it with his and coiled it around her. She knelt without looking up. She stopped her digging. In her mind she placed her will in the hollow of her hand and then she placed her hand in the hollow of his scar, which was whiter than the rest of him and weaker than the rest. She was almost sorry that she had to do it. He drank a long time from the mouth of the pump, and some of the water splashed onto her hair. Then he washed his arms and his throat and face. But her hand in his scar never washed away. At last he went away from her without a word.

She fell across the little yellow dish she had wrapped in a bit of paper sacking from the crossroads store. Now she knew exactly why she had to bury it and bury the other dishes in the graves nearby. There must be nothing left in the house that was hers from the long ago time, nothing of her own they could catch in their will. Only the yellow teacup was left in the house. It had a chip on the rim. . . . She lay across the dish in the warm, damp ground that moved, even swayed to the digging below.

She fastened her will to the churning machines till it was moving the earth. The earth broke sobbing at her command. She was full of its torment, and full of the child inside her that was crying to be born and would come too soon.

That evening she wrapped the yellow cup in her apron and took it with her to the quarry. It was hard not to drop it as she slid down the hill. When she reached the bottom she sat by the quarry and unwrapped her cup. She filled it with sand and poured the sand slowly down through the willows where the ledge had been. With her eyes on the wood beyond the stubbled field, she thought of the convict and how she would bring him all the water he could wish. He would drink from the cup, and the child she had lost long ago would be his. "You watch out, now," she would say, "there's a chip on the rim . . ." She stared at the chip and knew without looking that a chip of earth fell from the rim of the crater. She stood up slowly and moved away from the edge. Her will was from the sky and the mountain behind and all the minutes of the years of her life she had waited. She put the cup to her lips and whispered across the rim of it: "Fall . . . fall down."

At once from top to bottom the quarry shuddered. The willows tossed and spun. Pebbles at the rim skittered down and downward into mother-naked earth. Bitterweed was ripped away and tumbled in. The pines above her shrieked. She had a swift glimpse of the coral tongue of clay, how it twisted and rose. The bleeding mouth tore and fell in upon itself.

The red and orange dust hid the face of the sun and the face of the moon that waited in the wood.

When she reached the house she rolled her things into a roundness and bound them and wound them with a string she had saved. And when it was daylight she walked away.

LUST

SUSAN MINOT

Susan Minot grew up in Manchester-by-the-Sea, Massachusetts, and now lives in New York City. She received a Bachelor of Arts degree at Brown University and a Master of Fine Arts at Columbia. Her stories have appeared in *Grand Street, The New Yorker,* and *The Paris Review,* and also in the *Pushcart Prize IX* collection and *The Best American Short Stories 1984.* Susan Minot's first book, *Monkeys,* will be published by E P Dutton in 1985.

Leo was from a long time ago, the first one I ever saw nude. In the spring before the Hellmans filled their pool, we'd go down there in the deep end, with baby oil, and like that. I met him the first month away at boarding school. He had a halo from the campus light behind him. I flipped.

Roger was fast. In his illegal car, we drove to the reservoir, the radio blaring, talking fast, fast, fast. He was always going for my zipper. He got kicked out sophomore year.

By the time the band got around to playing "Wild Horses," I had tasted Bruce's tongue. We were clicking in the shadows on the other side of the amplifier, out of Mrs. Donovan's line of vision. It tasted like salt, with my neck bent back, because we had been dancing so hard before.

Tim's line: "I'd like to see you in a bathing suit." I knew it was his line when he said the exact same thing to Annie Hines.

You'd go on walks to get off campus. It was raining like hell, my sweater as sopped as a wet sheep. Tim pinned me to a tree, the woods light brown and dark brown, a white house half-hidden with the lights already on. The water was as loud as a crowd hissing. He made certain comments about my forehead, about my cheeks.

We started off sitting at one end of the couch and then our feet were squished against the armrest and then he went over to turn off the TV and came back after he had taken off his shirt and then we slid onto the floor and he got up again to close the door, then came back to me, a body waiting on the rug.

You'd try to wipe off the table or to do the dishes and Willie would untuck your shirt and get his hands up under in front, standing behind you, making puffy noises in your ear.

He likes it when I wash my hair. He covers his face with it and if I start to say something, he goes, "Shush."

For a long time, I had Philip on the brain. The less they noticed you, the more you got them on the brain.

My parents had no idea. Parents never really know what's going on, especially when you're away at school most of the time. If she met them, my mother might say, "Oliver seems nice" or "I like that one" without much of an opinion. If she didn't like them, "He's a funny fellow, isn't he?" or "Johnny's perfectly nice but a drink of water." My father was too shy to talk to them at all, unless they played sports and he'd ask them about that.

The sand was almost cold underneath because the sun was long gone. Eben piled a mound over my feet, patting around my ankles, the ghostly surf rumbling behind him in the dark. He was the first person I ever knew who died, later that summer, in a car crash. I thought about it for a long time.

"Come here," he says on the porch.

I go over to the hammock and he takes my wrist with two fingers. "What?"

He kisses my palm then directs my hand to his fly.

Songs went with whichever boy it was. "Sugar Magnolia" was Tim, with the line "Rolling in the rushes/down by the riverside." With "Darkness Darkness," I'd picture Philip with his long hair. Hearing "Under my Thumb" there'd be the smell of Jamie's suede jacket.

We hid in the listening rooms during study hall. With a record cover over the door's window, the teacher on duty couldn't look in. I came out flushed and heady and back at the dorm was surprised how red my lips were in the mirror.

One weekend at Simon's brother's, we stayed inside all day with the shades down, in bed, then went out to Store 24 to get some ice cream. He stood at the magazine rack and read through MAD while I got butterscotch sauce, craving something sweet.

I could do some things well. Some things I was good at, like math or painting or even sports, but the second a boy put his arm around me, I forgot about wanting to do anything else, which felt like a relief at first until it became like sinking into a muck.

It was different for a girl.

When we were little, the brothers next door tied up our ankles. They held the door of the goat house and wouldn't let us out till we showed them our underpants. Then they'd forget about being after us and when we played whiffle ball, I'd be just as good as them.

Then it got to be different. Just because you have on a short skirt, they yell from the cars, slowing down for a while and if you don't look, they screech off and call you a bitch.

"What's the matter with me?" they say, point-blank.

Or else, "Why won't you go out with me? I'm not asking you to get married," about to get mad.

Or it'd be, trying to be reasonable, in a regular voice, "Listen, I just want to have a good time."

So I'd go because I couldn't think of something to say back that wouldn't be obvious, and if you go out with them, you sort of have to do something.

I sat between Mack and Eddie in the front seat of the pickup. They were having a fight about something. I've a feeling about me.

Certain nights you'd feel a certain surrender, maybe if you'd had wine. The surrender would be forgetting yourself and you'd put your nose to his neck and feel like a squirrel, safe, at rest, in a restful dream. But then you'd start to slip from that and the dark would come in and there'd be a cave. You make out the dim shape of the windows and feel yourself become a cave, filled absolutely with air, or with a sadness that wouldn't stop.

Teenage years. You know just what you're doing and don't see the things that start to get in the way.

Lots of boys, but never two at the same time. One was plenty to keep you in a state. You'd start to see a boy and something would rush over you like a fast storm cloud and you couldn't possibly think of anyone else. Boys took it differently. Their eyes perked up at any little number that walked by. You'd act like you weren't noticing.

The joke was that the school doctor gave out the pill like aspirin. He didn't ask you anything. I was fifteen. We had a picture of him in assembly, holding up an IUD shaped like a T. Most girls were on the pill, if anything, because they couldn't handle a diaphragm. I kept the dial in my top drawer like my mother and thought of her each time I tipped out the yellow tablets in the morning before chapel.

If they were too shy, I'd be more so. Andrew was nervous. We stayed up with his family album, sharing a pack of Old Golds. Before it got light, we turned on the TV. A man was explaining how to plant seedlings. His mouth jerked to the side in a tic. Andrew thought it was a riot and kept imitating him. I laughed to be polite. When we finally dozed off, he dared to put his arm around me but that was it.

You wait till they come to you. With half fright, half swagger, they stand one step down. They dare to touch the button on your coat then lose their nerve and quickly drop their hand so you—you'd do anything for them. You touch their cheek.

The girls sit around in the common room and talk about boys, smoking their heads off.

"What are you complaining about?" says Jill to me when we talk about problems.

"Yeah," says Giddy. "You always have a boyfriend."

I look at them and think, As if.

I thought the worst thing anyone could call you was a cockteaser. So, if you flirted, you had to be prepared to go through with it. Sleeping with someone was perfectly normal once you had done it. You didn't really worry about it. But there were other problems. The problems had to do with something else entirely.

Mack was during the hottest summer ever recorded. We were renting a house on an island with all sorts of other people. No one slept during the heat wave, walking around the house with nothing on which we were used to because of the nude beach. In the living room, Eddie lay on top of a coffee table to cool off. Mack and I, with the bedroom door open for air, sweated and sweated all night.

"I can't take this," he said at 3 A.M. "I'm going for a swim." He and some guys down the hall went to the beach. The heat put me on edge. I sat on a cracked chest by the open window and smoked and smoked till I felt even worse, waiting for something—I guess for him to get back.

One was on a camping trip in Colorado. We zipped our sleeping bags together, the coyotes' hysterical chatter far away. Other couples murmured in other tents. Paul was up before sunrise, starting a fire for breakfast. He wasn't much of a talker in the daytime. At night, his hand leafed about in the hair at my neck.

There'd be times when you overdid it. You'd get carried away. All the next day, you'd be in a total fog, delirious, absent-minded, crossing the street and nearly getting run over.

The more girls a boy has, the better. He has a bright look, having

reaped fruits, blooming. He stalks around, sure-shouldered, and you have
the feeling he's got more in him, a fatter heart, more stories to tell. For a
girl, with each boy it's like a petal gets plucked each time.

Then you start to get tired. You begin to feel diluted, like watered-
down stew.

Oliver came skiing with us. We lolled by the fire after everyone had
gone to bed. Each creak you'd think was someone coming downstairs.
The silver-loop bracelet he gave me had been a present from his girlfriend before.

On vacations, we went skiing, or you'd go south if someone invited
you. Some people had apartments in New York that their families hardly
ever used. Or summer houses, or older sisters. We always managed to
find someplace to go.

We made the plan at coffee hour. Simon snuck out and met me at
Main Gate after lights-out. We crept to the chapel and spent the night
in the balcony. He tasted like onions from a submarine sandwich.

The boys are one of two ways: either they can't sit still or they don't
move. In front of the TV, they won't budge. On weekends they play
touch football while we sit on the sidelines, picking blades of grass to
chew on, and watch. We're always watching them run around. We shiver
in the stands, knocking our boots together to keep our toes warm and
they whizz across the ice, chopping their sticks around the puck. When
they're in the rink, they refuse to look at you, only eyeing each other
beneath low helmets. You cheer for them but they don't look up, even if
it's a face-off when nothing's happening, even if they're doing drills
before any game has started at all.

Dancing under the pink tent, he bent down and whispered in my ear.
We slipped away to the lawn on the other side of the hedge. Much later,
as he was leaving the buffet with two plates of eggs and sausage, I saw
the grass stains on the knees of his white pants.

Tim's was shaped like a banana, with a graceful curve to it. They're all
different. Willie's like a bunch of walnuts when nothing was happening,
another's as thin as a thin hot dog. But it's like faces; you're never really
surprised.

Still, you're not sure what to expect.

I look into his face and he looks back. I look into his eyes and they
look back at mine. Then they look down at my mouth so I look at his
mouth, then back to his eyes then, backing up, at his whole face. I think,
Who? Who are you? His head tilts to one side.

I say, "Who are you?"

"What do you mean?"

"Nothing."

I look at his eyes again, deeper. Can't tell who he is, what he thinks.

"What?" he says. I look at his mouth.

"I'm just wondering," I say and go wandering across his face. Study the chin line. It's shaped like a persimmon.

"Who are you? What are you thinking?"

He says, "What the hell are you talking about?"

Then they get mad after when you say enough is enough. After, when it's easier to explain that you don't want to. You wouldn't dream of saying that maybe you weren't really ready to in the first place.

Gentle Eddie. We waded into the sea, the waves round and plowing in, buffalo-headed, slapping our thighs. I put my arms around his freckled shoulders and he held me up, buoyed by the water, and rocked me like a seashell.

I had no idea whose party it was, the apartment jam-packed, stepping over people in the hallway. The room with the music was practically empty, the bare floor, me in red shoes. This fellow slides onto one knee and takes me around the waist and we rock to jazzy tunes, with my toes pointing heavenward, and waltz and spin and dip to "Smoke Gets in Your Eyes" or "I'll Love You Just for Now." He puts his head to my chest, runs a sweeping hand down my inside thigh and we go loose-limbed and sultry and as smooth as silk and I stamp my red heels and he takes me into a swoon. I never saw him again after that but I thought, I could have loved that one.

You wonder how long you can keep it up. You begin to feel like you're showing through, like a bathroom window that only lets in gray light, the kind you can't see out of.

They keep coming around. Johnny drives up at Easter vacation from Baltimore and I let him in the kitchen with everyone sound asleep. He has friends waiting in the car.

"What are you crazy? It's pouring out there," I say.

"It's okay," he says. "They understand."

So he gets some long kisses from me, against the refrigerator, before he goes because I hate those girls who push away a boy's face as if she were made out of Ivory soap, as if she's that much greater than he is.

The note on my cubby told me to see the headmaster. I had no idea for what. He had received complaints about my amorous displays on the town green. It was Willie that spring. The headmaster told me he didn't care what I did but that Casey Academy had a reputation to uphold in the town. He lowered his glasses on his nose. "We've got twenty acres of woods on this campus," he said. "If you want to smooch with your boyfriend, there are twenty acres for you to do it out of the public eye. You read me?"

Everybody'd get weekend permissions for different places then we'd all go to someone's house whose parents were away. Usually there'd be more boys than girls. We raided the liquor closet and smoked pot at the kitchen table and you'd never know who would end up where, or with whom. There were always disasters. Ceci got bombed and cracked her head open on the banister and needed stitches. Then there was the time Wendel Blair walked through the picture window at the Lowe's and got slashed to ribbons.

He scared me. In bed, I didn't dare look at him. I lay back with my eyes closed, luxuriating because he knew all sorts of expert angles, his hands never fumbling, going over my whole body, pressing the hair up and off the back of my head, giving an extra hip shove, as if to say *There.* I parted my eyes slightly, keeping the screen of my lashes low because it was too much to look at him, his mouth loose and pink and parted, his eyes looking through my forehead, or kneeling up, looking through my throat. I was ashamed but couldn't look him in the eye.

You wonder about things feeling a little off-kilter. You begin to feel like a piece of pounded veal.

At boarding school, everyone gets depressed. We go in and see the housemother, Mrs. Gunther. She got married when she was eighteen. Mr. Gunther was her high-school sweetheart, the only boyfriend she ever had.

"And you knew you wanted to marry him right off?" we ask her.

She smiles and says, "Yes."

"They always want something from you," says Jill, complaining about her boyfriend.

"Yeah," says Giddy. "You always feel like you have to deliver something."

"You do," says Mrs. Gunther. "Babies."

After sex, you curl up like a shrimp, something deep inside you ruined, slammed in a place that sickens at slamming, and slowly you fill up with an overwhelming sadness, an elusive gaping worry. You don't try to explain it, filled with the knowledge that it's nothing after all, everything filling up finally and absolutely with death. After the briskness of loving, loving stops. And you roll over with death stretched out alongside you like a feather boa, or a snake, light as air, and you . . . you don't even ask for anything or try to say something to him because it's obviously your own damn fault. You haven't been able to—to what? To open your heart. You open your legs but can't, or don't dare anymore, to open your heart.

It starts this way:

You stare into their eyes. They flash like all the stars are out. They look at you seriously, their eyes at a low burn and their hands no matter what starting off shy and with such a gentle touch that the only thing you can do is take that tenderness and let yourself be swept away. When, with one attentive finger they tuck the hair behind your ear, you—

You do everything they want.

Then comes after. After when they don't look at you. They scratch their balls, stare at the ceiling. Or if they do turn, their gaze is altogether changed. They are surprised. They turn casually to look at you, distracted, and get a mild distracted surprise. You're gone. Their blank look tells you that the girl they were fucking is not there anymore. You seem to have disappeared.

BREAD AND BUTTER QUESTIONS

CLAUDE KOCH

Claude Koch is a Professor of English at La Salle University. He conducts workshops in fiction and verse, and has won fiction fellowships from Dodd-Mead, the *Sewanee Review,* and the Rockefeller Foundation. Born in 1918, Mr. Koch lives in Philadelphia. He has had four novels published.

Marty McCann, the Bishop's man. That was the prophetic tag in the seminary. It isn't very charitable of me to say that I never liked him.

I never liked him.

Or to say that he was not very bright in quests of the heart. In charity, he was dense. Ten years and a continent away, and I still resented his Herodian presence.

Lock up the children, Martin's about!

His letter came to me at the North American College, Casa Sancta Maria, Via dell' Umilata 30, Rome, on the Feast of the Holy Innocents, and I resented it. Not because he was the Bishop's Secretary and the youngest Monsignor in the diocese, but because he had risked nothing to get where he was and would probably risk nothing the rest of his life.

I buttoned his letter in my cassock and walked off my annoyance in the winter sunset with the vesper bells of Rome sweeping clean the evening air, and with strokes like a tongue in cotton patiently summoning the evening star. By the time I reached the Spanish Steps the west was burning, and if I were back in the Sem and innocent again I might say it burned like a Sacred Heart. It certainly burned like the subject of Martin's letter, little Cos Estime of those seminary days, with a fire that made all things new. I wondered if it burned so in the dust of the Via Flaminia. That is where one would have found Cos were he in Rome instead of El Salvador, a child among the obscurities of things that were, and that were imagined. One Epiphany set his steps in the poor streets forever.

Not solemnly, you understand, but abruptly, with the bizarre insistence of a vaudeville routine. Martin, who had charmed his way up the ecclesiastical ladder, could not comprehend this. So he wrote to me. Hadn't I known Cos best? But that was years ago. *Yet he must be investigated. Radicalized, you see . . . And wants to give up his citizenship and be incardinated there. Don't think that there is not sympathy in the Chancery Office . . .*

Ah, Martin, Martin, he might have saved you. He almost saved me, and may yet if I hear again from you.

You never knew him. You were one year out of the Sem and already sharing your cloak with the New Money at Old St. Madeline's on the Main Line when he had his revelation, and it was in no paddy field or coffee plantation, but the rambunctious environs of Widdershins Pike that all of us seminarians avoided like sin. That was where he lost his innocence. (It all sounds like the theatricals he used to star in.)

I walked till midnight. The stars went out over Ara Coeli, and it was cold. Martin was judging Cos, but Cos was judging me.

Once Cos said: "Do you think the Twelve took just a sip on that last night? It's a bread and butter question." He was never irreverent, but had he lived in another age he might have been a Fool. No, Martin, you never knew him.

You remember, there were nicknames in the Sem. You were Torquemada, didn't you know? Cos was "Orphan Annie." He had eyes like saucers, like compendious oceans. Looking into them, one could believe in miracle, youth pop-eyed in wonder at the world. You know people like that: they wear all through their lives the badge of childhood; just around the corner, for them, the angel makes his visitation. Sometimes just because of them we say "Lord I believe, help Thou my unbelief." They drag us after them, and once or twice, through their eyes, we are teased by mystery; they invite its presence. That was Cosmo Estime then, a deacon in his third year in theology and out that year for his internship at St. Stanislaus Kostka's. Perhaps the chancery sent him there because his name sounded foreign, I don't know. You see how little faith I have left in the formal procedures. Actually, we saw him only twice that term, once just before his Epiphany sermon, and once just after.

You remember those cherished moments in the Sem when we gathered around the carved oak tables in the refectory of an evening, the dishes cleared away, and some accomplished mimic from the class above to bring back tales of pastors and parish shenanigans, of pomposity and piety, from the Great World that we would soon venture out to save. Otherwise it reached us only through the sirens, the fire and violence transmuted to sound, barely heard through the mullioned windows of the refectory, that fragmented everything, really, light and form, so that we saw nothing whole.

We believed in the quest, our own manifestation to the Gentiles. Legends abounded, and we were eager to perpetuate them. Even the tables on which we leaned were legendary: Doveston, Bird and Hull, Manchester, 1877, shipped from the old world when the first Ordinary had dreams of a second Avignon or Port Royal along the Delaware. But, except for the sirens, the world arrived by messenger, like Cosmo.

Cosmo a guerrilla? They would have shot him for mocking them. He was more than a mimic. He was an artist, and he might well have created for us a St. Stanislaus Kostka's that never was. He had his master's for which he'd translated and annotated a fourteenth century manuscript of John of Hildersheim, *The Three Kings of Cologne*, but to see him there at the head of the refectory table you'd think he was a visiting high school kid all fired up to a vocation. *Non angli sed angeli* his aunt had said when she gave him the keys to a Volkswagen for his parish work, *non angli sed angeli*. She had attended Miss Shipley's school on Philadelphia's Main Line, and her teeth locked on the Latin.

He came back for the first time that term on the third night after Christmas, the Feast of the Holy Innocents, his face glowing like an old communion plate before Vatican II. We could warm ourselves by little Cos in that echoing barn of a room, floor to ceiling in great walnut panels that were more daunting than the Rector's presence or the gloom of the Prefect of Discipline. He had what we used to call in those days "a devotion" to the Three Kings, and his good news was that he'd been asked to deliver the Epiphany sermon at St. Crispian's, that sedate Anglo-Catholic parish far across town.

Cos in his dog collar (for no one entered the refectory in those days who did not wear the cassock) contained multitudes; and the accents of the fading world of St. Stanislaus Kostka, its pastor, and its housekeeper were a part of our revels that evening. It was good and innocent fun.

Now there is a K-Mart where St. Stanislaus school and convent used to be and, under Canon 1184 *("Conversio ad usum profanum non sorditum")* the church, converted to profane but not sordid uses, serves as a Salvation Army haven for homeless men.

But you must imagine Cos before all of that, there at the head of the table, spinning out of himself a sweet, comic love for his fellow man, and the sense of merry peace it gave us, and quiet, like entering a warm room where the intricate webs hang undisturbed in the sun. A raw season on the outside, but the refectory windows were leaded and translucent, and save for the minatory sirens the rippled glass kept it at a distance.

Martin, Martin, the hand-made glass of the Refectory, how pleasantly it distorted, how comfortingly it excluded! Do you know that Cos once put his fist through it? In sorrow.

Well . . . Cos Estime's pastor at St. Stanislaus Kostka's was a wraith of a man ("You had to look twice," Cos said; "he was too short to be a Pole."), but given to moments of unexpected firmness when his Sign of the Cross developed into a featherweight's uppercut. One of his Deacon's innocent pleasures was to bewilder the old man with his alligator turtle neck, or his guitar, or his soft leather shoes, all those perks of Vatican II.

"Led me see yur fud, now," Fr. Tumaz would say, or "Wad beast is dad?" Or so Cosmo heard him, with an innocent ear more tuned to vaudeville than to accents. Tumaz had been a superb Latinist, but the New Church had left him with little to do with that tongue. And his English had suffered a sea change, to our delight and the delight of little Cos. Enough said. A Polish dialect needs a Master's hand. I'll save it for the punch line.

They liked each other, the Pastor and the Deacon, and Cosmo preened himself mildly with the conviction that he alone brought the Great World beyond the walls to the vast, windy rectory; for, more and more, the old priest confined himself to wandering the four cavernous floors and the draped and tenebrous rooms under whose Edwardian swags and moldings five assistants had once bustled.

What was Fr. Tumaz tracking down? Cos didn't know. Sometimes his footfall, jarring a loose board over the back parlor, distorted the picture on the housekeeper's T.V. and swung the *podlaznik* that hung point down from her ceiling, and swayed the chandelier-like *pajaki* whose ingenious designs of paper and straw draped by the large Christmas evergreen. Cosmo sampled the apples and nuts and *swaity* with delight, and practiced getting his tongue around the old peasant terms.

"I'm doing to Polish what he does to English," he'd say. All his life Tumaz had served in an ethnic parish: sermons in Polish, and, after Vatican II, the Mass in the Old Tongue. All over now; the financial city had moved in like Herod against the children and left little room for poor parishioners. Cosmo told it tenderly, so that one could believe in the Children of God.

Like a dutiful son, the Deacon, who had no father of his own, strove each Sunday to be back at St. Stanislaus rectory by six-o-five, because, just as the great Angelus bell ceased to shake the empty church, the Pastor would be bent over his supper plate, his hand, so large for such a gnomish body, within inches of the dinner bell. And in the kitchen the mad housekeeper would strain to descend upon them with unpronounceable Eastern European dishes. Yet it was a nice accommodation: Cosmo Estime's Sunday afternoons were free, and he had discovered Ecumenism. So just about the time Fr. Tumaz' hand reached the bell, he'd be inside the scored oak doors of the Rectory after a defensive drive along Widdershins Pike from St. Crispian's evensong far across town. How hazardous this was on a nose-bitten, frosty St. John's Eve within the octave of Christmas, he'd try to tell the Pastor.

"But you got home," and Tumaz blew on the seat before he sat in order not to crush a soul that might be lodging there. "Good, now we eat." He hardly sounded like that, of course; and there was always a pause while Cos transliterated. Then: "You have no idea, Father. That street is a Comanche Trail. People signal left and turn right; they pop up from nowhere and you can't see them. It's an allegory of the world, perversity run wild."

"Then stay home. One place's good's another. It's St. Vitus dance."

"No, no, Father. You should get out and get around. Come to St. Crispian's some day. Believe me, they use more incense than the Vatican. They'll be led by the nose into the Church." Cosmo enjoyed his own humor perhaps more than anyone else. "It's time for a change; change is in the air." He had some news to break slowly: "Why not invite the Canon over some Sunday? I tell you, change is in the air."

"Hah. Like when the Quakers got the ACLU after us for bingo in the firehouse." Fr. Tumaz settled behind his cigar and blew smoke out of his ears. "Some 'Friends.' That's ecumenism."

Cosmo took the plunge: "They've asked me to give the Epiphany sermon at Evensong."

The featherweight came through: "Yes? You got permission?" Fr. Tumaz was sometimes obsidian; perhaps it was the eyes.

"Of course, Father, it all depends on you, but I didn't think you'd mind."

"Why not?" The old priest went back into his shell. "Nothing to do here." Then the housekeeper came in, and during the protracted exchange in Polish the Deacon dreamed of a triumph on Epiphany at Crispian's. It was that anomalous conjunction of Vatican II and

Anglican tradition that charmed him—an apostle to the Gentiles, indeed.

"You heard it?" Father Tumaz's question was ambiguous. "Another rumor. They're building a K-Mart." So had the Gentiles eaten away at the old man's parish. "Pretty soon, all *kaput.*"

"Cheer up, Father," Cosmo said; "look at London, the parishioners move out, but then the Church serves the businessmen. You catch them on the fly." Cosmo had never been closer to London than Hackensack, but he had his ear to the ground at Crispian's. "Not to worry."

"They closed St. John Kanty's." Fr. Tumaz shrunk still farther behind his plate and raised smoke against all optimism. "It's getting cold here."

And late that night the Deacon could hear the Pastor's unsteady footsteps, poking by tactile memory into the dark and vacant upstairs rooms, and the tumult of ancient plumbing. As Cosmo told it, his face, as fresh and open as a spring meadow awaiting the plow, would cloud over. "There's a fatalism, a peasant patience about him that breaks my heart sometimes. I'm not used to the sorrows of old men."

But we moved away from that thought quickly enough; it was hardly meet for the festive season, and uncharacteristic of Cosmo. He was on firmer ground with the housekeeper.

The housekeeper was surely mad, or possessed. It pleased Cos to be undecided. She appeared and disappeared, Cos said, and her actual location in the great house was frequently a matter of doubt. Sometimes she sulked with a cantankerous calico cat before the television; sometimes she harangued Cos in phrases vaguely translatable from the Women's Liberation Movement. Her progresses through the bleak corridors were tempestuous; she seemed a distracted angel, a fury, to whom deacons were, indeed, a lower order. She might have unsheathed a Sword of Fire before the gates of innocence. Cos anticipated her intermittent appearances with a fascinated unease—it was so comforting when she left. She essayed just enough English to fix her in the Deacon's mind as an unreconstructed alien. Her name was Hilda Wardzinski.

"Hay, Misder," she'd say, "yur spoiled. You doan ead yur puddin," or "Misder, you ged home fur subber or you doan ead." She was a shepherd of repasts. Seldom did her conversation not revert to this. She cajoled and threatened by beet and bean, so that when she appeared at his parlor door on the Eve of St. Stephen, Cosmo's immediate thought took him back to his orphaned but affectionate rearing by the maiden aunt, and youthful questions concerning uneaten spinach and greens. And yet, to be chided and reproved, and wanted and cared for again . . . ! But Hilda Wardzinski's commitment was to Fr. Tumaz alone.

But there she was, at his door, and perhaps it was the matter of the Epiphany sermon on which he labored that led him to perceive her biblically, her hair raised as though moved by a current of fire, and the mop in her hands like St. Michael's sword at rest.

"He's donstairs," she said. "He painds sacred hards on wadges."

Cos sorted that, digested it, and came up with a reasonable response: "Yes?"

"He wands to taug."

"He wants to sell me a watch?"

"He wands to sell you a car."

"It's a mistake. Tell him to go away."

"Misder," her mop divided the threshold, "he painds . . ."

"I know. Sacred hearts on watches. I still don't need a car, Mrs. Wardzinski."

Sometimes, on the facades of Gothic cathedrals, such admantine intensity was captured in the sculptured pose of sibyl or prophet: "You bedder listen. You be sorry . . ."

Cosmo Estime closed the door politely. Mrs. Wardzinski and her mop receded like all our yesterdays beyond the door.

The house creaked like a ship. Cosmo thought of partings and journeys. He heard the ancient oil furnace go on, and there was the clap of expanding tin in the air vent. He felt deliciously alone.

So detached from the blundering world, in such a mood, one could contemplate the Magi: how elegant and fastidious Kings of the East journeyed in separate and jeweled silence to an Herodian land, swayed to sleep on the camels' backs that rose and fell like the pulsing of Time itself. Until they met, those strangers, at a place where three roads joined, and their alien languages were reconciled as a single prophetic tongue of leaping flame. *That* struck just the right note. There was a tap on his door.

"Please, Mrs. Wardzinski," he said. But the corridor was dark, save for a pale night light hanging like a scarcely materialized emanation outside the Pastor's room down the hall. Cosmo was not tall, but he saw with ease above the silhouette on his threshold. Perhaps his eyes were strained from bending too assiduously over the Eastern globe. The Pastor was a peel of shadow or of dark glass.

"Let me in."

"Of course, Father." Cosmo hurried a rocking chair over by the hot air vent. "It's late for you."

"It's *Swiete Wieczory*, it's the Holy Evenings." Fr. Tumaz blew on his chair. "God Himself walks the earth." The Pastor's legs did not reach the floor. "A Guest in the house is God in the house. She is upset. You should go down."

And Cosmo, the mimic, would shrink behind the table in the refectory as he told of Mrs. Wardzinski's distress, until we could believe that it was Fr. Tumaz explaining it all: how one waited for the guests on the Holy Evenings; how scarce they were in these latter days; how in the Old Country it might be God Himself (and Cosmo's mimicry would strike the incredulous note) painting Sacred Hearts on watches or selling used cars. The laughter was joyous, and not mocking.

"I'll apologize, Father. I did not know the custom. Anyhow, I've got a car. Why should he call on me?"

"Zoltan Sleveck. Every year he comes on the Holy Evenings," the Pastor arced his large hand back and forth: "Business and pleasure. I don't drive; you drive." He bent forward to get a start, and rocked like a child, gaining momentum. His gaze withdrew under clumps of his white eyebrows, like stones under snow, and he seemed to be traveling. Cosmo waited patiently. Finally: "At home, on Christmas Eve, the animals talk in human voices; only the innocent hear them." Then: "Bells ring under water, and the springs turn to wine and honey." He rocked forward until his feet touched the floor; "It's too late now."

Cosmo caught the priest's arm as he lurched forward: "Father, can I get you some tea? Let me get you something."

"It's too late."

Later, as Cosmo put a period to his sermon, the snow wind against the shutters almost rose above those hesitant steps that rattled the loose joists overhead. He heard the Pastor fretting with the weary grandfather's clock in his room: the chimes ran together, and then all the hours struck at once.

Ah, Marty, Marty . . . I hear the bells, the minatory bells of Rome. It's 3 A.M., and they summon to an accounting. You shall have it, because in judging Cos you pass judgment upon me. *Cos's Casual Comedy* shall we call it? It's like a fiction I have lived, and I no longer am sure what, in its essentials, belongs to Cos's imagination and what to my own, and what has no part in the imagination but poses the "bred and budder quesdions" that old Fr. Tumaz debated through the grim white-sheeted Edwardian rooms of St. Stanislaus Kostka.

Epiphany came and went, and it wasn't that long ago, was it, Marty? But a choiring time, when more than the Magi seemed to wear their plates of gold. Cos came back to the seminary on February 2, Candlemas Day. He was too late for supper, but the refectory was warm from the recent meal. "Our Lady of the Candles," he said. He sat without taking off his coat. "That's what *they* call it. There were five old women in the procession today. No one else. A candle went out."

We tried to comfort him: "You must be cold. Have some coffee."

"No." Though he mimicked no one, he seemed physically diminished behind the table. He did not look at us with the untranslatable eye of Fr. Tumaz or the exaltation of his possessed housekeeper; he fixed upon the distorting panes of refectory glass as though there were some answer there. Then: "What do you think they really did with . . ." He dipped his head toward us with the expression of a child caught with his hand in the cookie jar: ". . . with the gold, the frankincense, and the myrrh?" Was he acting again? "And the cold . . . God, how cold it must have been . . ."

Perhaps he was leading, straight-faced, into a joke. "Come on, Cos, what's new? What are you up to? Tell us about the sermon." We could wait for the punch-line. "Tell us about Epiphany."

His hair had always been his one vanity. It framed his face like a medieval courtier's. "An angel," his aunt had said when he preached his first sermon, "an angel by Carlo Crivelli." *Non angli sed angeli.* And often, in his laundry, she packed an angel cake, sly wit of a doting aunt, and absolutely against The Rule.

"It's ten-thirty," his barber had said. Was it later than he thought on that Epiphany? "No, that's the charge."

It wasn't a bit like the movies. The man made absolutely no concession to the Cloth, and Cos was in his dog collar. *Nova Cuts* the sign read, banging after him in the intermittent sleet and the morning wind.

The Pastor's voice had scarcely risen above the knockings in the radiators under the painted glass of St. Stanislaus' lancet windows that morning, and the public address system had long ago failed. After Mass, the score of old parishioners left the church a shell and appeared at the rectory door, bearing gifts. Fr. Tumaz introduced them, one by one: "They come like the Kings," he said. "Pretty soon, where do they go? It's a bread and butter question." Cos sat still, then lapsed into the old man's dialect: "Id's a bred and budder quesdion." Perhaps it was true.

"We were in the seminary together," the Pastor said of the Cardinal, "but it's getting late." To the Pastor, Cos said, the closing of St. Stanislaus would be like interdicting the stable at Bethlehem; perhaps it was easier for the Cardinal—his ethnic roots lay under carefully cultivated urban sod.

Such melancholy reflections accompanied the Deacon as he set out for St. Crispian's. The morning had broken from night like a husk, the core of night was still there, and heavy clouds scraped shag across the bulk of St. Stanislaus' tower. Behind the wrought iron gates of the parish churchyard one forlorn railroad tree had pushed up through the brick, and snow unseasonably logged with water was a sulky residue by the first pastor's cenotaph. What would they do with those old bones when the Cardinal finally put his foot down? Perhaps it was the threat of winter lightning, the sullenly charged air, but Cos felt at a loss, as, when a child, the bleachers filled on Fathers' Day at Prep, and there was no one to applaud his play. He teetered at the church steps, uncertain of past or future, and hugged his sermon to him like a security blanket. A police car rocked by, its siren pulsing, the rotating web of flashing light a fiery wheel that Ezekiel might have seen. It was too dismal a day for visions. A tall man in a dark overcoat, swinging an umbrella like a scythe, caught his arm as he passed. The St. Crispian sermon slipped to the ground, fluttering in front of the stranger, who stepped upon it.

"Sorry, Father, but I couldn't tell whether you were coming or going." The envelope was wet, a fine start for the day. Cos was bewildered enough to say: "But I'm not a priest."

The air brakes of a trolley clattering past the rectory burned darkly. It should have been a clear day, with sounds far away, and a fresh snow making all things new—it should have been a day for children, he thought. But the fumes of traffic lay close to the ground, and he backed his Volkswagen from the rectory driveway into resentful horns. How could one evoke those gaudy and alien kings on such a day?

He pulled up to a drugstore for a box of cigars, Italian stogies banded in gold, the Pastor's last comfort. "Gift wrap, please," he said. The clerk deducted ten percent: "Have a good day, Father." Epiphany brightened, and momentarily the January wind rinsed the air of middle earth. He drove toward Widdershins Pike. Over the ragged city skyline, huge shapes emerged in the Eastern sky. Were the Magi preceded by sirens? The winter lightning arrayed and disarrayed great dark cloud heads in tiaras of gold. Plated armor rose and fell, and caravans moved, ominous and stately, across the element. His Epiphany sermon unfolded there above the traffic, like a toy panorama of his childhood. "The Unexpected Majesty," the title came to him like a revelation. A camel's hump filled the horizon; and as he watched it whisk away he turned into Widdershins Pike, where the festive season had long since lost its energy. No Christmas wrappings blew along the gutters there in the diminished light. No streamers hung from pole to pole or draped boarded and ravaged facades that had no place in his vision. He looked up from jaywalking pedestrians, but the vision was gone. The car lurched.

It was a flat, no doubt of it. Talk about coming down to earth, Cos said. He limped to the curb and stepped out into a scattering of broken glass. He sighed, gathered his sermon and shook out the dampness, packed the cigars under his arm, locked the car, turned down his scarf ostentatiously so that his dog collar showed, and set out in a mode of transportation as unfamiliar to him as to the Magi. It was characteristic of Widdershins Pike that gas stations had gone the way of drugstores. He would have to abandon the caravan. He walked.

Drab black figures shuffled past, Arab shapes of Galilean Jews cluttering the shabby ways along which his Magi searched? Something to remember if lesser lines were blotted. Yet he was not prepared for—a mullah's lament from a tower? *Drop-kick me, Jesus, through the goalposts of life . . .*" He was certain he had heard it, unlikely as that seemed. Such charismatic chants were not to be anticipated on Widdershins Pike; he'd gathered that from simply driving through. It blared from a storefront, and he was shoved toward it, caught between a supermarket cart ridden by a disreputable black child and propelled by a black girl in her teens, and a hunched black man carrying a two-by-four that whacked the Deacon between his shoulder blades. He recoiled. He might have been a king of Tarshish, lost on Broadway, there was such a contrived, theatrical quality to the moment.

The Holy Rock Evangelical Apostolic Church—behind the panel of the storefront and framed by plastic representations of stained glass, the Gothic lettering identified the source of bedlam. A black man of uncommon tallness, propped in the doorway, balanced to one ear the radio from which issued the theological directive. Long of face and long of hand, he exposed a range of teeth as white as his ecclesiastical collar. His hair hung in disconcerting dreadlocks.

"Come in, Man," he said; "come in, Reverend. It's de house of de Lord."

As he told it, Cos's dialect faltered. He seemed to relive the emergency, with which he was totally unprepared to cope. "What . . . ?" he said; "what . . . ?" And so it came to pass that, like the guest without the wedding garment and summoned precipitously from the byways, he was ushered firmly through the open door.

"We brothers, Man," the large man adroitly unshouldered the radio and thrust a card into his hand. Fingers reached around the lintel and the radio vanished. There was that inescapable pressure on his arm, and a voice in his ear: "Ah kin tell yo' a man of vision . . ." Then he was propelled into a room against a blast of sound that reduced Jesus and the goalposts of life to a whisper.

"Come on, Cos," I remember saying; "it *was* Epiphany, the time of the unexpected? That's a Twelfth Night tradition . . ." But he kept his solemn face, and we awaited the droll moment so cleverly withheld.

"That's me." *The Reverend Antipater Slim* the card read, *Rector and Proprietor—The Holy Rock Evangelical Apostolic Church.* And Cos pulled the card from his overcoat pocket and laid it on the table. "Who yo', Brother?"

Cosmo was crushed. He mumbled "St. Stanislaus," swallowed, and looked wildly about. "We *co*-religionists," the Rev. Slim said, "*co*-religionists."

In the cave of fantasy behind the storefront he grew aware of incongruous things. There was an altar, surely, but was that a television set perched upon it? And was that *The Secret Storm* competing with radical lyrical blasts from The Second Coming, who spoke from a stereo on the epistle side? Crowding the television was a tabernacle, and atop the tabernacle a monstrance.

"Beautiful, Man," the Reverend Antipater Slim swept a hand in appreciation; "dem Brothers of St. Bardolph sold out dere *re*-dundant chapel: *re*-dundant, dey said, *re*-dundant." He squeezed Cos's arm: "We got a lot in common, Brother."

Strobe lights complicated the television screen and whirled volleys of shooting stars on stereo and monstrance. Cos was aware of snufflings nearby, and his own urgent need to decamp.

"Join in a prayer to de Lord, Man," the Reverend Slim was actually pressing him to his knees, "a prayer to de Lord." Cos was still a man of many voices, and we smiled at his doleful tone. "A-men . . . A-men . . . ," and sleepy confirmation arose unenthusiastically from the dark under the strobe lights. Time passed as in an enchanter's cave.

It would not be injudicious to say that Cos Estime left that place in a state of shock. Sounds unnatural to the human ear followed him up

Widdershins Pike: "Y'all come back, hear!" Antipater Slim waved from the doorway the hand not engaged with the retrieved radio.

Cos was sufficiently modern to know that miracles are ceased, and wonders officially the property of Disneyland. Yet there was still room for nightmare. His eyes were wide to the wonders of the imagination, but not to the improbabilities of fact. Was this a joke he was springing on us?

The sidewalk seemed a freeway for children riding pilfered supermarket carts as wagons, and he barely escaped the press before a state liquor store that could have been composed of hands reaching for the Pastor's gift cigars. It was altogether a missionary experience and quite beyond the call of duty. Meanwhile, through a vision and a dream, dark figures flitted, balancing huge radios. They were real indeed, for though the noise level did not change, the endlessly repeated refrains occasionally did. He arrived, exhausted, before a drugstore and blessed the window, festive with deodorants, depilatories, and toothpaste, that told him he had safely managed Widdershins Pike. He bought himself a bottle of aspirin.

At St. Crispian's, the Deacon's hosts remarked to each other upon his bemused air, and attributed it to piety. Candlelight wavered across polychrome statues and gothic bosses, the atmosphere of a proper English village church. He mounted the pulpit in a state of ecclesiastical abstraction, still carrying his peace offering to Fr. Tumaz, and his sermon. To his ecumenical congregation, the gift-wrapped box was appropriate and symbolic—they needed no explanation. Cos became aware of it himself with some confusion. He extracted his sermon from its envelope and spread it on the lectern. In a silence that left him curiously deprived, he turned to his text.

"Ah, yes . . . ," he began, with the air of one who has entered a scene *in media res*, "the manifestation to the Gentiles . . . One can see them, these comfortable men, having arrived in state, after the star, in their garments of green and gold, startled to find themselves . . . to find themselves . . . ," his voice faltered, the ink had run, the high style was leveled, and one word was as illegible as another. Yet he could not stop; he carried on, extemporaneously, from some unsuspected spring, with the surprise of one who has stumbled on the denouement of a detective story: "What had they to do, these comfortable men, with peasants, with the lowest rung of the social ladder? How unearthly the choiring must have seemed! Sounds hardly fit for the ear of man, engendering dreams and nightmares for years to come!"

He lingered over that, as though listening for an echo of what he had said, as though for confirmation that he had said it. A sigh escaped the congregation: *Non angli sed angeli!* "Why," he said, still in that attitude of listening, "why should this epiphany, this revelation, this grotesque majesty be shown to such unlikely persons, the comfortable, the kings of the earth? Oh, the things that can happen . . . That can *still* happen," he said. "You have no idea." And in a gesture of wonder, or despair, he spread his arms, scattering his useless homily like chaff. Exhaled breaths fluttered from rapt dowagers in the choir. *Quel geste!* "The *things* I could tell you . . . that go on in the world . . ." It was not what he said, but the transfigured voice, as though he spoke with tongues. "There are revelations every day . . . *re*-dundant revelations," and he waved Fr. Tumaz' cigars. In the shocked silence that followed, he realized that he had simply been scared out of his wits and slow in recovering. But to the congregation of St. Crispian's, this wild-eyed visitation on one sedate evensong hinted at levels of meaning. Whatever he subsequently said Cos Estime could not recover; but sidesmen and churchwardens quite agreed that Epiphany had never, at St. Crispian's, been more thrillingly shadowed forth.

Afterward, in the parsonage, Cos gulped down a sherry.

"Do you mean," Canon Anstruther said, "That you're parked down *there?*" His wife proffered the decanter.

Six sherries later, Cos was feeling himself again, he could not resist: "It's Epiphany. It's Twelfth Night. Everything at sixes and sevens. Lord of Misrule. Festivity. . . . High jinks . . ." Cos could do the six sherry voice well.

"Well, I'm delighted that you can take it so lightly." Canon Anstruther tendered another sherry: "Can you change that tire?"

"Just get me there." The sherry was as good as adrenaline. "Greater miracles have happened." Through the gothic windows of the parsonage the afternoon was flushed and enriched. It had actually been a triumph.

"I don't mind telling you," the Canon said, "this neighborhood is not my cup of tea."

"Let me out here. It's just around the block. I'll walk."

"If you say so. I'm glad to help, but I don't even like to turn into Widdershins, I never feel that the drivers have licenses." The Canon laid a restraining hand on Cos's knee: "Here. Your box. It was all quite effective. You have a future as a preacher."

When Cos turned the chill corner he saw the odd cant to his Volkswagen down the Pike. He attributed it to a flat tire and sherry. But a figure whose dreadlocks hung like a threat rose from beside the car and rolled a wheel up and into The Holy Rock Evangelical Apostolic Church. "What!" Cos cried. "What!" and tumbled over yet another child and another supermarket cart.

It was a fact. There was his viper-green Bug, three-wheeled and with the front axle up on wooden blocks, while around it rocked and crashed and throbbed alien sounds, piped through the open door of Reverend Slim's establishment.

"I roared," Cos said; "it was the sherry." One would have given much to hear Cos roar. Bewilderment and outrage warred within his breast, and he was through the door of The Holy Rock Evangelical Apostolic Church and tripping over a recumbent figure before he came to his senses.

"Reverend." A hand lifted him bodily, and a voice close to his ear overcame The Grateful Dead. "Ah knew yo'd come back to de Lord's House. We do thank yo' fo' you contribution."

"What . . . ! What . . . ?" Cos blinked at the strobe lights, and there was a heavy odor of something not sherry.

"Doan worry, Man," the Reverend Slim said, "give us yo' key. I goin' put yo' *ex*-trey wheel on right dis minute."

"My extra . . . ? My what . . . ?"

"Who needs a *ex*-trey. The good Lord gives *ex*-treys fo' dese folks." The large hand turned purple and rose and green and gold as it waved across recumbent figures on the floor and huddled shapes in chairs against the wall, who in their turn underwent vivid transformation. "Dey in fo' de night. Fo' de night," he repeated, an octave higher.

Again, Cos Estime felt himself propelled and overcome, bewildered as St. Paul on the road to Damascus. Antipater led him stumbling over grunting, multicolored forms and across in front of the altar to the protests of alcoholic voices. "Dis my sacri*sty*," the Reverend Slim spoke proudly; he opened the door and Cos's wheel rolled out. He flipped a switch. Bereft of speech, Cos looked upon the spoils of the Church: supermarket carts, automobile tires and wheels, strings of outdoor Christmas lights, three municipal flares and assorted garden furniture, two park benches, and a dog house. "*Ex*-treys," the Reverend Slim said; "we gets *ex*-treys for de po' folk out dere. Des money in *ex*-treys." He pointed to a wood stove in the corner on which a great laundry pot steamed: "Soup. Y'all hungry?"

"Hungry . . . ?"

"Fantastic. Give me yo' key. I put on de *ex*-trey wheel. Yo' have soup." He released Cos's arm: "Close de doah. Jes relax."

Cos gathered his shattered resources while the Reverend picked his way back over recumbent figures. He closed the door; but still, through it, breathed and huffed inarticulate mutterings as of a multitude of beasts.

There are moments that press upon us a reconsideration of things as they are. Cos implied that this was one of them. "I tested the soup," he said. "I didn't know what else to do. Then I counted the strings of lights. Slim must have dismantled the decorations of a city block. That would have been difficult to do, a triumph of a kind, also." Cos finally shed his coat; his suit was rumpled as though he had been sleeping in it. "It was a point of view that had never occurred to me, with calculation, that is." There was silence in the refectory as he fixed his eyes on each of us in turn. "Then I began to think of the gold, the frankincense, and the myrrh, where had it come from, where did it end up . . . ?" He was engaged with such unsettling thoughts, seated on a park bench and sipping soup, when the Reverend Antipater Slim returned.

"Done, Brother," Slim spoke at the top of his lungs from the doorway. "Better 'n new. Y'all been charitable, too!" He thoughtfully removed Cos's wheel from his path as he guided him from the room.

Cos was well away from the curb before he realized that the Reverend Slim was waving with the Pastor's cigars: "Y'all come back, hear!"

Cos pulled up at the rectory in another snow flurry.

"Huh," Mrs. Wardzinski stepped aside from the door unwillingly, "you not late for a change."

"Where's the Pastor?"

"Don't bother him. He's setting the clock. It don't work."

Supper corresponded with the Angelus. Some things, at least, were predictable.

"You don't eat?" Fr. Tumaz said. "Big party over there?"

"No," Cos said. He played with his spoon. "I . . . well, I had something on the way home."

Silence. Then:

"Father, what do you think happened to the gold, the frankincense, and the myrrh?"

"What a question!"

Mrs. Wardzinski held Cos's empty plate dangerously over his head. "Not good enough?" She left the room, breathing Polish.

"Fader . . . ," Cos caught himself, "Father, I'm serious."

Tumaz' eyes could be like gunstones: "Are you having a crisis of faith?"

"Why do you say that?" But before Tumaz could reply, Mrs. Wardzinski put her head through the drapes.

"He's there. He wants St. Stanislaus." She pointed maliciously to Cos. "That's you, he says."

"Wait . . . , please," Cos said to Fr. Tumaz.

The Rev. Antipater Slim relaxed on a chair by the door. "A fine *establishment*," he said. "All *right!*"

Cos had not a mean bone in his body, but he could not resist: "Where's your radio?"

The Reverend held out the gift box of cigars:

"Not *ex*-treys. Yo' got a fine place here, Brother," he said.

"Yes," Cos said. "It's not mine. I work here. Thank you. Good*bye.*"

"Right, Brother. But yo' come see me. We gonna build."

Cos asked even as he came back through the drapes: "Why did you say that?" As he told his story then, we knew he had left us. He was back at St. Stanislaus Kostka's. I think he is still at St. Stanislaus Kostka's, no matter where *you* place him, Marty.

"Id's a bred and budder quesdion." I remember his mimicry, but there were tears, not humor, in it. "Dey cause trouble. Stig to mystery, id's safer." The old priest's eyes softened: "Wad you god dere?"

Cos came over beside him, Tumaz was such a little man, and his physical reach was short: "Id's for you, Fader," he said.

Tumaz held his hand over the cigars: "You gud. Doan worry aboud gold, abod myrrh. Abod where id goes." He teetered to his feet. "Come wid me, son. Help me stard de clog again."

He took Cos by the arm, and they went upstairs. All that night Cos lay awake, listening to the hours they had set right between them, and thinking about the imminence of certain questions in Bethlehem, and at St. Stanislaus Kostka's.

We sat quietly, not knowing quite what to say, not sure that a point had been made. Cos pushed himself to his feet: "He believes in the Kings," he said. "He believes in the Spirits that sit on the chairs on the Holy Evenings. What protection are they for him now?"

He settled his coat around his shoulders like a cloak, as though he were cold, and walked to the window. I felt for him, Master of Arts, Comedian, Translator of John of Hildersheim. Mimic Extraordinary, young

Deacon. He was tapping at a loose pane in the leaded glass when I put my arm about his shoulders.

"Come on, Cos. It's only a legend. You know that. Where would we be without legends?"

"Where am I now?" he said. "Where am I now that I know the question?" He looked at me with those orphaned eyes of his, and smiled his half-moon, clown's smile. "Fr. Tumaz has no *ex*-treys in all this great Church. I think I must go out and get a park bench or two, or a dog house; I think I am too proud to unstring the municipal ornaments."

"Look here, Cos." Perhaps I was too attentive to my own gestures, but I did not see the blow; and when I looked up Cos was sucking on his knuckles, and the wail of a siren seemed appropriate to the broken pane.

"It's what they don't tell us that matters," he said. "That's what I'll do, when I know enough. I'll preach a sermon on the Wise Men and the *Ex*-treys . . ." He poked at a sliver of glass: "How will I explain this?"

I don't know how he did, but I think you have the explanation, Martin. I wonder, will you someday be investigating me? Only faith prevents one's asking the bred and budder quesdions, Martin, but I think that only the questions prove the faith.

GLIMPSE INTO ANOTHER COUNTRY

WRIGHT MORRIS

Wright Morris was born in Central City, Nebraska. *A Cloak of Light*, the third volume of his memoirs, is being published this year.

Hazlitt's wife carried a broom to ward off the neighbor's dogs as she walked with her husband down the drive to the waiting taxi. Too old now to attack, the dogs barked hoarsely from behind a screen of bushes. "I'll outlive them if it kills me," she remarked, and she stooped for the morning paper, flattened by the garbage pickup. "No ethnic food," she told Hazlitt. "You hear me? You remember what happened in Phoenix." From his shoulders, as he stooped to kiss her, she removed the gray hairs.

Hazlitt was reluctant to fly, anywhere, but he wanted something in the way of assurance—of life assurance—that he hoped to get from a specialist in New York. "If that's what you want," his own doctor, in San Francisco, had advised him, "and you can afford it, go get it." Could he afford it? He had that assurance from his wife. "You're worth it," she said.

She had made considerable fuss to reserve Hazlitt a seat at one of the plane's windows, which turned out to be near the center of the right wing. A stewardess helped him out of his coat, and held it while he felt through the pockets for his glasses. A woman with quick searching eyes came along the aisle to stop at his row, then turned to hiss at her companion. The habit of hissing at people had always dismayed Hazlitt.

The woman's hair looked as if she had just blow-dried it. The man with her, by appearance a cultivated person, wore a smart suède cap and carried their coats. His rather abstracted manner led Hazlitt to feel he might be a teacher, off to an academic meeting. As he reached her side, the woman slipped between the seats to the one beside Hazlitt, without glancing at him. She registered his presence, however, as she would a draft from the window, by shifting in the seat toward her companion. She wore knit gloves. With one hand she clutched a paperback book.

Hazlitt had not flown enough to know if her indifference to him was part of the etiquette of plane travel, where so many strangers were jammed in together: why start up something with a person who might well prove to be tiresome? He himself was guarded even with his colleagues at the university. The woman at his side had an appealing intactness, and her profile seemed intelligent. A perfume, or it might be a powder, was faintly scented with lilac.

Advised to buckle his seat belt, he observed that the palms of his hands were clammy. At the takeoff he faced the window with closed eyes. Perhaps the tilted wing spared him the vertigo that might have been part of the lift-off, and as the plane set its course he caught glimpses of the far blue horizon. The woman beside him browsed in a copy of the New York *Times*, picked up in the airport. Her interest seemed to be in the ads. At one point, he was screened off behind the paper but able to check the market quotations on his side. Finished with the paper, she stuffed it between the seats on her left, away from Hazlitt. He thought that rude, since he made it a point to share newspapers with his travelling companions. As she relaxed for a moment, closing her eyes, he was able to appraise her profile further—a little sharp to his taste, but attractive. From the pink lobes of her ears he received faintly erotic signals.

Suddenly, perhaps feeling his gaze, she turned to look directly past him, as if someone had tapped on the window. Now she would speak, he thought, but she didn't. She turned away, with a birdlike quickness, and leafed through the pages of her paperback book. Idle riffling—the sort of thing Hazlitt found irritating. At the back of the book, she paused to read a few words about the author, then turned to read the book's concluding page. That done, she read the next-to-last page, then the one before it. As she read, she nibbled at the corner of her lip.

Hazlitt was flabbergasted. He had discovered that the book she chose to read backward was "The White Hotel." He could not fully believe what he had seen, yet there was no question he had seen it. She did manage to read most of the final chapter before turning the book back to its opening page, which she placed face down in her lap. What did she want now? Something to drink. Her husband raised his hand to signal one of the stewards.

Surely a more worldly traveller than Hazlitt would not have been so appalled by what he had witnessed. How justify this scanning of a book in reverse? Could it not be argued that a sensible person, of a sensitive nature, might want to know what was in store before making a full commitment? Perhaps, but the practice was new to Hazlitt, a sworn and outspoken enemy of speed-reading.

At the announcement that they were passing over Lake Tahoe, the woman leaned toward the window as if she might see it. Her seeming unawareness of Hazlitt had a calming effect on him. He made way for her. He was at pains not to be there. Leaning forward, she had crushed several pages of her book, but this, too, was a matter of indifference to her. She put the book aside to accept, from her companion, a news magazine. She leafed through the pages, then stopped to consider an article on crime, with illustrations.

"Oh, my God!" she exclaimed, crumpling the page, and turned to fix Hazlitt with an intense, green-eyed stare. Did she think him a criminal? It seemed to him that her eyes moved closer together. "There's no place to go!" she cried. "Just imagine!" She had ignored Hazlitt; now he felt cornered by her. "Where would *you* go?" she barked.

His lips were dry. He wet them, and said, "My wife and I were recently in Oaxaca—"

"*Mexico?* Are you crazy?" She saw that he might be. "There is *nowhere* . . ." Her voice trailed off. Her husband had placed his hand on her lap to calm her.

"I was at a party in the forties—" Hazlitt began.

"In the forties!" she cried. "Who lives in the forties?"

Fortunately, he divined her meaning. "The *nineteen*-forties—the party was in the East Seventies. Musicians, writers, composers, and so on. Do you remember Luise Rainer?" Clearly she did not. "At the time," he continued, "she was an actress—"

"You write?" she asked him.

Hazlitt did write scholarly articles; he asked himself if she considered that writing. "I was with a friend," he said, "a painter. We all agreed there was nowhere to escape to. The war was everywhere, or soon would be. Then one of them said, 'You know what? There *is* no *where*. All the wheres have vanished.' "

Perhaps the woman felt there was more to the story. Her lips parted, but she said nothing.

"We have friends in Buenos Aires," he went on, "but I would never go so far as to recommend it."

"It's like no *air*. That's what it's like. It's like there's less air."

"As a matter of fact—" began Hazlitt, but she had turned from him to her crumpled magazine. Carefully, as if she meant to iron it, she smoothed it out on her lap. "That book you were reading," he continued. "I've met the author. A very respectable chap." (Everything he was saying was the purest hogwash.) "I know that he would consider it a personal favor if you read his book as it was printed, from the front to the back."

What had come over him? In her green, unblinking stare he caught the glimpse of a chill that might excite a lover. She turned from him to lean on her companion, who peered over her frizzly hair at Hazlitt. The man wore tinted bifocals. His expression was mild. "My wife said you had a question?"

Returning his gaze, Hazlitt knew he had been a fool. "It's just that I happen to know the author, and took the liberty of speaking for him."

"He's crazy," said the wife. "Don't rile him."

Calmly the man removed his glasses and polished the lenses with a fold of his tie. Unmistakably, Hazlitt recognized one of his own kind. A physicist, perhaps, with those hairy fingers. Or a member of a think tank. "Theoretically," the man said, breathing on a lens, "there is something in what you say, but, as a practical matter, having bought the book my wife is free to read it as she pleases, or to ignore it. Wouldn't you agree?"

Particularly galling to Hazlitt was the way the fellow had turned the tables on him. It was usually he who was the cool one, the voice of reason in the tempest, the low-keyed soother of the savage breast. Worse yet, this fellow was about half his age.

"Of course! Of course! Stupid of me. My apologies to Mrs.—"

"Thayer. I'm Dr. Thayer."

Across the lap of Mrs. Thayer, who shrank back to avoid him, Hazlitt and Dr. Thayer clasped hands, exchanged the glances of complicit males. If there was a shred of solace in it for Hazlitt, it lay in Mrs. Thayer's full knowledge of this complicity.

"Take the filthy book!" she said, thrusting it at him. "And read it any way you like!"

Hazlitt let it fall to the floor between them. He fastened his gaze on the glare at the window. Some time later, the stewardess, serving his lunch, had to explain to him how to pull out the tray from the seat in front of him, and pry the lid from his salad dressing.

Hazlitt would say for this woman—when he discussed it with his wife —that she maintained to the last his nonexistence. He remained in his seat until the plane emptied, then wandered about the airport. He caught a glimpse of Dr. Thayer, on one of the escalators, helping his wife into her coat. The sharpness of her elbows troubled Hazlitt. Thin and intent as a cat, she reminded him of someone. Was it his wife? She groped in her purse for a piece of tissue, pressed it to her nose.

In the taxi to Manhattan, Hazlitt was moved to chat a bit with the driver, but the Plexiglas barrier between them seemed intimidating. Through the tinted windshield, as they approached the city, the October evening skyline was like the opening shot of a movie. Hazlitt had often told his wife that if the sun never rose he might like city living. In the car lights the streets glittered like enamel. It pleased him to note, as they drew near the Plaza Hotel, the horse-drawn hacks lined up along the curb. One of the drivers was a young woman with pigtails, frail as a waif. She held a leather feed bag to the muzzle of her horse, whose pelt shone like patent leather where the harness had worn off the hair.

The hotel porter, elderly himself, took a proprietary interest in Hazlitt. He led him into the bathroom to explain that the knobs on the faucets might confuse him if he got up at night for a drink of water: they turned contrary to the usual directions. A sign of the times, Hazlitt thought.

He thanked the porter, then stood at the window listening to the sounds of the street. A warm, moist breeze stirred the curtains. The tooting horns put him in mind of the radio plays of the forties. Turning to phone his wife, he saw his reflection in the mirror on the closet door. Something about the light, or the mirror, altered the impression he had of himself. A pity his wife couldn't see it. He would call her later; it was early still in California, and such talk could make her uneasy. What she feared the most when he travelled without her was that he might do something foolish, if not fatal, and end up hospitalized where she could not get at him. As he washed his hands—taking care with the faucets— he remembered her final caution: not to walk the streets at night, but if he did, not to be caught without money. She had given him a hundred dollars in twenties on the understanding he was not to spend it, so that when the muggers looked for money they would find it.

Hazlitt meant to stroll a bit—he needed the exercise—but when he left the hotel the young woman with the pigtails and her black spotted horse were still there. Frequent tosses of the horse's head had spread oats on the street and sidewalk. Jovially, Hazlitt inquired, "This rig for hire?"

"That depends where you're going." She spoke to him from her perch in a tone of authority.

"Bloomingdale's," he said, "before it closes."

"That's where I'm headed," she replied, ignoring his playful tone, and

watched him climb into the cab. Hazlitt must have forgotten the leisurely pace of a weary horse. He leaned forward in the seat as if that
might urge it along. As they approached Bloomingdale's, he saw that
peddlers had spread their wares out on the sidewalks.

The girl stopped the horse so that the hack blocked the crosswalk, and
a stream of pedestrians swirled around it. As Hazlitt arose to step down
from the cab, it teetered slightly, and he peered about him for a helping
hand. One of the peddlers—a tall, swarthy fellow wearing a pointed hat
made of a folded newspaper—had taken a roll of bills from his pocket to
make change for a customer. This person, lights reflected in her glasses,
peered up at Hazlitt with a look of disbelief. Did he seem so strange? A
moment passed before he recognized Mrs. Thayer. She wore tinted,
horn-rimmed glasses, and a babushka-like scarf about her hair, tied beneath her chin. To take her change, while holding her purse, she gripped
one of her knit gloves between her teeth, where it dangled like a third
hand. The sight of Hazlitt had, in any case, left her speechless. He could
think of nothing better to do than slip one hand into his coat front and
strike the comical pose of a public figure welcomed by an admiring
throng. The tilt of the carriage may have led him to misjudge the step
down to the street. He toppled forward, both arms spread wide, and
collapsed into the arms of the peddler, knocking off his paper hat. Over
the man's broad shoulder he caught a glimpse of Mrs. Thayer, her hand
clamped to her mouth now in either astonishment or laughter. She was
gone by the time Hazlitt's feet were firmly planted on the street.

The peddler, after recovering his hat, was remarkably good-humored
about it. "She knows you, eh?" he said, giving Hazlitt a leer as he
smoothed the rumpled front of his coat. Hazlitt pondered the query as
he selected, from the peddler's display, a French-type purse for his wife,
a woman reluctant to buy such things for herself.

"Don't you worry!" the peddler added. "She'll be back. I still got her
three dollars!" From his wad of bills he peeled off several and passed
them to Hazlitt, giving him the smile of a collaborator. "You O.K.?" he
said, and steadied the older man's arm as he stepped from the curb.

In Bloomingdale's foyer, where the doors revolved and Hazlitt felt
well concealed by the darkness, he paused to spy on the peddler. There
was something familiar about him—a big, rough fellow who turned out
to be so gentle. In his sophomore year at college, Hazlitt had been
intrigued by a swarthy, bearded giant, wearing a faded orange turban and
a suit coat over what appeared to be his pajamas, who used to cross the
campus directly below the dormitory window on his way to a shack in

the desert wash. He walked with a limp, and carried a sack of groceries over his shoulder. As he passed beneath Hazlitt's gaze he would crook his head around, revealing his dark, hostile expression, and then beam directly at him the wide-eyed, toothy smile of a child beholding a beloved object. These extremes of temperament were like theatrical masks of contrary humors slipped on and off his face. Hazlitt learned that the man was a Sikh, one of a sect of fiercely independent warriors in India. What had brought him to California? Everything about him was out of scale and seemed disconcerting—even his smile. There were rumors that he kept his wife captive, that he trapped and ate coyotes. But what did all of that have to do with Hazlitt spying on a peddler from Bloomingdale's foyer so many years later?

Nevertheless, the incident had aroused him, agreeably. This state, he thought, might be what his younger colleagues called "having a buzz on" —an expression that had previously mystified him. He wandered about the store's crowded aisles. In the cosmetic section, the customers and the clerks chattered like birds in an aviary. They leaned to peer into mirrors as if uncertain who they were. Hazlitt paused at a counter displaying bracelets set with semiprecious stones. A young woman with dark bangs to the edge of her eyes spoke to him. She opened the case to lift out several of the items. In her opinion, they cost practically nothing—a special purchase at seventy-nine dollars. He would have guessed a price a third of that, but he showed no surprise. One by itself was very nice, she advised him, but two or more enhanced their beauty. To illustrate, she placed two about her broad wrist, above a hand with blunt fingers and cracked nails.

"Very well," Hazlitt said, feeling nothing at all, and waited as she wrote up the order. Was it cash or card? Card, he replied, and searched it out in his wallet.

"Oh, I'm so sorry," she said, "but we don't take Visa."

Hazlitt's astonishment was plain. He wondered if it might be a cunning revenge of the East on California. Would they accept his check? Of course. As he filled one out, his wife's face materialized suddenly, then receded. He wrote so few checks that she had cautioned him to make certain he did it correctly.

His driver's license was also needed, the clerk told him. Ah, he was from San Francisco? She had spent a summer with a friend in Carmel, where she nearly froze. Hazlitt explained that the summers might run cooler than the winters, which was why some people found it so attractive. She did not follow his reasoning, her attention being on other matters. "I've got to get this O.K.'d," she said. "Would you just like to look around?"

Hazlitt looked around. Having already spent so much money, he could do without further temptations. To get out of the crowded aisles he wandered into an adjoining department. Against a pillar he saw a canvas chair, apparently meant for the lover of horses: it was made with stirrups, bridles, bits and strips of harness leather. He sagged into it. Nearby, a TV screen glowed like the sun at a porthole. He made out the image of a dense throng of people moving about in a large, dimly lit building. The flowing garments of the women, the density of the crowd suggested it was somewhere in India. As his eyes adjusted, Hazlitt saw that the floor seemed to be strewn with bodies, to which the passing crowd was indifferent. Some were alone. Others were gathered in crumpled heaps. The milling of the figures among these fallen creatures gave the scene an unreal, dreamlike aspect. Were they dead? No, they were sleeping. The film gave Hazlitt a glimpse into a strange country where the quick and the dormant were accustomed to mingle. Perhaps, he thought, it was not the walkers but the sleepers who would range the farthest in their travels.

He was distracted by a stream of jabbering, excited people, most of them young, who hurried down the store aisles toward the front exit. Then, rather suddenly, the place was quiet. He delayed a moment, expecting further excitement, then came out of the shadows and returned to the jewelry counter. The clerk was not there. Other departments also appeared to be abandoned. Through the glass doors of a side entrance he saw hurrying figures and flashing lights. A young man in shirtsleeves, with a perplexed expression, ran toward Hazlitt, waving a flashlight. He took him by the arm and steered him down the aisle. "Out! Out!" he cried. "We're emptying the building!"

"The clerk still has my driver's license," said Hazlitt, but in his agitation the man ignored him. He urged him along through the empty store to where several policemen stood at the exit.

"The clerk has my driver's license!" Hazlitt repeated.

"Don't drive," the man replied. "Take a cab."

Police vans and patrol cars blocked off the street. He stood for some time under one of the awnings waiting for something dramatic to happen. The revolving beacons on the cars lit up the faces of the crowd like torches. Several men in helmets and olive-drab uniforms entered the building carrying equipment. Hazlitt heard someone call them a bomb squad. The awareness that he had no driver's license, no positive identification, touched him with an obscure elation. He strolled along with a noisy group of young people who had just exited from a movie, and they seemed to take his presence for granted. When someone asked him the time, he said, "Nearly nine," and was reminded that he had not yet called his wife. "You won't believe this," he would say, knowing she would.

To get his call so early in her evening startled her. "Where are you?" she cried. It was his custom to report the events of the day—or the non-events, if so they proved to be—and this time he really had a story to tell. But, hearing the note of concern in her voice, he changed his mind. Any mention of the bomb scare would disturb her rather than amuse her.

He explained—feeling the need to be explicit—that he was in his hotel room, seated on the bed, facing the partially opened window. A cool breeze stirred the curtain. He asked her if she could hear the car horns in the street below. If she had been with him, he said, they would have gone to a play—she loved the theatre. As she spoke to him—how well he saw her—she would be seated at the kitchen table, behind the lazy Susan, with its clutter of vitamin bottles, and several of the squat candle glasses set out in anticipation of the first seasonal storms and blackouts. Hazlitt knew so exactly just how it all was that he could hear the sound of the wall clock—stuffed with a towel to mute the ticking—and he could read the pressure (falling) on the barometer at her shoulder. He continued to talk, in a way that soothed her, about his short ride in the horse-drawn hack (a thing they had done together), and about the swarthy peddler selling his wares on the Bloomingdale's corner—for some reason, he avoided mention of Mrs. Thayer—until she spoke up to remind him that he was phoning from New York, at his own expense, and not from his office at the college. Before he replied she had hung up.

He was aware, with the lights switched off, how the sounds at the window seemed magnified. In the play of reflections on the ceiling he glimpsed, as through a canopy of leaves, the faraway prospect he had seen on the Bloomingdale's TV—bustling figures swarming soundlessly among the bodies strewn about a station lobby. Somehow the spectacle was full of mystery for him. None of this was a dream—no, he was awake; he heard the blast of the horns below his window—but the dreamlike aura held him in its spell until those sleeping figures arose to continue their journey.

In the doctor's waiting room the next morning, Hazlitt faced a wall of brightly colored children's paintings, goblin-like creatures with popped eyes, short stumpy arms, stilt-like legs. It was his wife who once remarked that this was probably how most children saw the world—like specimens under the lens of a microscope. In the suspended time that Hazlitt sat there, he held and returned the gaze of a purple-faced goblin, preferring it to the pale, ghostly image of the old man reflected in its covering glass.

The specialist's assurance, spoken at Hazlitt's back between thumps on his rib cage, drew more from its offhand manner than from what the man said: he showed little real concern. Every hour, Hazlitt gathered, the doctor saw patients more deserving of attention. His assistant, a well-coiffed matronly woman with sinewy legs and the profile of a turkey, shared with Hazlitt her opinion that "a reprieve is the best one can expect, at our age."

He was down in the street, flowing north with the current, before he sensed that he was free of a nameless burden, and seemed lighter on his feet. He crossed to Park Avenue for a leisurely stroll through the Waldorf lobby, for the pleasure of its carpet and the creak of expensive Texas luggage. Approaching Bloomingdale's again, he paused to reconsider the previous evening's scene: Hazlitt himself teetering in the hack, the dark-skinned peddler in his paper hat, and Mrs. Thayer reaching for her change, with one of her knit gloves still dangling from her teeth.

Back at Bloomingdale's jewelry counter, he found that the girl with the bangs had the morning off. In her place, an older and more professional clerk requested some further identification before she could give him his license back with the bracelets. She reminded him that one couldn't be too careful. Last night's bomb scare—a telephone call from the Bronx—proved to be without foundation, but the entire building had had to be vacated. What was this country coming to, she asked him.

Before Hazlitt could reply his attention was distracted by a display in the case he was leaning on—a short strand of pearls on a headless bust. Was it some trick of the lighting that made them seem to glow? "These are real?" he asked the saleswoman. They were real. Would he like to see something less expensive? Her implication piqued him, because it was accurate. She took the strand from the case and let him hold it. He knew nothing about pearls, but he was dazzled. He saw them on his wife—he saw her wide-eyed astonishment, her look of disbelief. "If it's not too inconvenient," he said, "I'd like to return the bracelets and take the pearls."

He had not troubled to ask the price, and the clerk gave him a glance of puzzled admiration. "We'll just start all over," she said, "but I'm afraid I'll have to ask you once more for your driver's license."

Right at that point, Hazlitt might have reconsidered, but he did not. From his wallet he removed a second blank check, and waited for the woman to present him with the bill. The sum astounded but did not shock him. Writing the numbers, spelling the sum out gave him a tingling sense of exhilaration. Again he saw his wife, seated across the table from him, gaze at him openmouthed, as she would at a stranger.

"This will take a few minutes," the clerk said, and went off into the crowded aisles.

Hazlitt's elation increased. He drummed his nails on the case as he peered about him. One might have thought that he had propositioned the clerk, that she had accepted and gone off to pretty up a bit and get her wrap. His exhilaration persisted as he moseyed about. In the bakery department, he flirted with the clerk who served him a croissant he could eat on the spot.

Back at the jewelry counter, he found everything in order. Was there anything else? His wife kept her jewels in pouches, he said—would they have a small pouch? The woman found one, of a suède-like material, into which the pearls nestled.

He was out of the building, under an awning that dramatized his own reflection in the shopwindow, before he again remembered the incident with the peddler on Fifty-ninth Street. He wanted to ask him if Mrs. Thayer had come back for her change, but the fellow was not there.

In the early years of their marriage, while he was doing his graduate work in the city, Hazlitt had loved to walk up Fifth Avenue with his wife for lunch at the Met. The museum itself confused and tired her; she did not like mummies, or tombs, or religious paintings. But Hazlitt liked to watch the people as they strolled about looking at objects, the stance they assumed when contemplating an art work. Secret transactions were encouraged there, he felt, and a burden of culture was enlarged or diminished. An hour or so of this spectacle always left him so fatigued he was eager for the comforts of the dim Fountain Court lunchroom, the buzz of voices, and the splash of water.

Heading for the museum now, Hazlitt was already at Seventy-eighth Street before he was aware of the almost stalled bumper-to-bumper traffic. Passengers riding downtown in the buses and cabs made no faster progress than those who were walking. Some waved and exchanged remarks with the pedestrians. Hazlitt sauntered along, hardly caring that it had started to drizzle. Puddles had formed on the steps of the Met, and the sleeves and shoulders of his coat were wet. He checked the coat, then strolled about in a crowd like that in Grand Central Terminal. Just off the lobby, to the right, a new book department was jammed with shoppers. Hazlitt was attracted by the displays and the brilliant lights. On one of the tables, someone had opened, and left, a large volume—Fauve paintings, as bright as Christmas candy. Across the table another browser, sniffling slightly, her face partially veiled by the hood of a transparent slicker, had paused to dip into a collection of van Gogh's letters. She read the last in the book, which she seemed to like; she tried the next-to-last, then the next. Her slicker clearly revealed the unfortunate S-curve of her posture, and the purse that she clutched to her forward-thrusting abdomen. She pressed a wad of tissue to her nose as she sneezed.

Hazlitt wore a tweedy wool hat that concealed, his wife insisted, his best features. Mrs. Thayer passed so close behind him that he felt and heard the brush of her slicker. Was it possible that she found his reappearance as unsurprising as he found hers? Then he saw her at a distance, looking at cards, and her cheeks appeared flushed. It troubled him that she might have a fever. The short-sleeved dress she wore under her transparent raincoat exposed her thin arms. Later, in one of the admission lines, he watched her remove one of her knit gloves by gripping the tips of the fingers with her teeth, then tugging on them like a puppy. Hadn't her husband explained to her about germs?

Although it was still early, and Hazlitt was not fatigued, he made his way toward the Fountain Court lunchroom. He was standing at the entrance for a moment or two before he noticed the renovation. The dusky pool and its sculptured figures were gone. The basin was now a mere sunken pit, of a creamy color without shadows, and it was already bustling with diners crowding its tables. Instead of the refreshing coolness and splash of the water, there was the harsh clatter of plates and cutlery. Hazlitt just stood there, until he was asked to move. There was a bar to his right—he could have used a drink—but the flood of creamy light depressed him. He backed away, and out of long habit found the stairway that led down to the basement.

The dark and cool lavatory in this wing of the building used to be one of Hazlitt's regular stops. The high windows were near a playground, and he could often hear the shrill cries of the children outside. He thought he heard them again now as he opened the door, but the babble stopped as he entered the washroom. Six or seven small boys of assorted colors and sizes, their arms and faces smeared with gobs of white lather, stood facing the mirror at the row of washbowls. Their wide-eyed, soapy faces seemed to stare at Hazlitt from an adjoining room. The stillness, like that of a silent movie, was broken only by the sound of lapping water. A thin film of water covered the tiles at Hazlitt's feet.

As if he found this circumstance more or less normal, he crossed the room to the nearest booth and pushed open the door. A youth, older than the others, was crouched on the rear of the fixture with his feet on the bowl's edge. With the thumb of his right hand he depressed the handle. The water spilled evenly from the rim of the clogged bowl to splash on the floor.

In the dark of the booth, Hazlitt saw little but the cupped whites of the boy's eyes. The youth raised his free hand slowly to his face as if to wipe away a lingering expression. Something in this gesture, like that of a mime, revealed to Hazlitt that the boy was stoned. In the deep void of his expanded pupils was all the *where* that the world was missing. The eyes did not blink. Hazlitt turned from him to face the mirror, and the boys, who had formed a circle around him. One had opened his shirt to expose his torso, creamy with lather. With the light behind them, all Hazlitt saw was the patches of white, like slush on pavement. Still, it pleased him to have their close attention.

The smallest boy thrust a hand toward him, its wet palm up. "Trick or treat," he said gravely. Two of those beside him hooted like crows.

"Well, let's see," Hazlitt said, and drew some coins from his pocket. He exposed them to the light, the silver coins glinting, just as the boy gave his hand a slap from the bottom. The coins flew up, scattering, then fell soundlessly into the film of water.

"Hey, man, that's no treat!" the boy scoffed, and he rolled his eyes upward.

From the pocket of his jacket Hazlitt withdrew the suède pouch; he loosened the noose and let the string of pearls fall into the boy's coral palm. How beautiful they were, as if just fished from the deep! The boy's hand closed on them like a trap; he made a movement toward the door as one of the others grabbed him. Down they both went, slippery as eels, with their companions kicking and pulling at them. They thrashed about silently at Hazlitt's feet like one writhing, many-limbed monster. He was able to leave unmolested and track down the hall in his squishy shoes.

In the gift shop off the lobby he bought a pin, of Etruscan design, that he felt his wife would consider a sensible value. Carrying his coat—the drizzle had let up, and the humid air seemed warm—he walked south under the trees edging the Park to the Seventy-second Street exit. Held up by the traffic light, he stood breathing the fumes of a bus and listening to the throb of its motor. At a window level with his head, one of the riders tapped sharply on the glass. Hazlitt was hardly an arm's length away, but he saw the woman's face only dimly through the rain-streaked window. What appeared to be tears might have been drops of water. The close-set green eyes, as close together as ever, were remarkably mild, and gave him all the assurance he needed. As he stared, she put a wadded tissue to her nose, then raised her gloved hand, the palm toward him, to slowly wag the chewed fingertips. Its air brakes hissing, the bus carried her away.

SAINT MARIE

LOUISE ERDRICH

Louise Erdrich grew up in Wahpeton, North Dakota, and is the author
of *Tacklight*, a book of poems, and *Love Medicine*, a novel, both published by Holt, Rinehart, and Winston. She lives in New Hampshire
with her husband and literary collaborator, Michael Dorris, and their
five children.

So when I went there, I knew the dark fish must rise. Plumes of radiance
had been soldered on me. No reservation girl had ever prayed so hard.
There was no use in trying to ignore me any longer. I was going up there
on the hill with the black-robe women. None were any lighter than me. I
was going up there to pray as good as they could, because I don't have
that much Indian blood. And they never thought they'd have a girl from
this reservation as a saint they'd have to kneel to. But they were going to
have me. And I'd be carved in pure gold. With ruby lips. And my
toenails would be little pink ocean shells, which they would have to stoop
down off their high horse to kiss.

I was ignorant. I was near age fourteen. The sky is just about the size
of my ignorance. And just as pure. And that—the pure wideness of my
ignorance—is what got me up the hill to the Sacred Heart Convent and
brought me back down alive. For maybe Jesus did not take my bait, but
them Sisters tried to cram me right down whole.

You ever see a walleye strike so bad the lure is practically out its back
end before you reel it in? That is what they done with me. I don't like to
make that low comparison, but I have seen a walleye do that once. And
it's the same attempt as Sister Leopolda made to get me in her clutch.

I had the mail-order Catholic soul you get in a girl raised out in the
bush, whose only thought is getting into town. Sunday Mass is the only
time my father brought his children in except for school, when we were
harnessed. Our souls went cheap. We were so anxious to get there we
would have walked in on our hands and knees. We just craved going to

the store, slinging bottle caps in the dust, making fool eyes at each other. And of course we went to church.

Where they have the convent is on top of the highest hill, so that from its windows the Sisters can be looking into the marrow of the town. Recently a windbreak was planted before the bar "for the purposes of tornado insurance." Don't tell me that. That poplar stand was put up to hide the drinkers as they get the transformation. As they are served into the beast of their burden. While they're drinking, that body comes upon them, and then they stagger or crawl out the bar door, pulling a weight they can't move past the poplars. They don't want no holy witness to their fall.

Anyway, I climbed. That was a long-ago day. A road for wagons wound in ruts to the top of the hill where they had their buildings of brick painted gleaming white. So white the sun glanced off in dazzling display to set forms whirling behind your eyelids. The face of God you could hardly look at. But that day it drizzled, so I could look all I wanted. I saw the homelier side. The cracked whitewash, and swallows nesting in the busted ends of eaves. I saw the boards sawed the size of broken windowpanes and the fruit trees, stripped. Only the tough wild rhubarb flourished. Goldenrod rubbed up their walls. It was a poor convent. I know that now. Compared with others it was humble, ragtag, out in the middle of no place. It was the end of the world to some. Where the maps stopped. Where God had only half a hand in the Creation. Where the Dark One had put in thick bush, liquor, wild dogs, and Indians.

I heard later that the Sacred Heart Convent was a place for nuns that don't get along elsewhere. Nuns that complain too much or lose their mind. I'll always wonder now, after hearing that, where they picked up Sister Leopolda. Perhaps she had scarred someone else, the way she left a mark on me. Perhaps she was just sent around to test her sisters' faith, here and there, like the spot-checker in a factory. For she was a definite hard trial for anyone, even for those who started out with veils of wretched love upon their eyes.

I was that girl who thought the hem of her black garment would help me rise. Veils of love, which was only hate petrified by longing, that was me. I was like those bush Indians who stole the holy black hat of a Jesuit and swallowed little scraps of it to cure their fevers. But the hat itself carried smallpox, and it was killing them with belief. Veils of faith! I had this confidence in Leopolda. She was different. The other Sisters had long ago gone blank and given up on Satan. He slept for them. They never noticed his comings and goings. But Leopolda kept track of him and knew his habits, the minds he burrowed in, the deep spaces where he hid. She knew as much about him as my grandma, who called him by other names and was not afraid.

In her class, Sister Leopolda carried a long oak pole for opening high windows. On one end it had a hook made of iron that could jerk a patch of your hair out or throttle you by the collar—all from a distance. She used this deadly hook-pole for catching Satan by surprise. He could have entered without your knowing it—through your lips or your nose or any one of your seven openings—and gained your mind. But she would see him. That pole would brain you from behind. And he would gasp, dazzled, and take the first thing she offered, which was pain.

She had a string of children who could breathe only if she said the word. I was the worst of them. She always said the Dark One wanted me most of all, and I believed this. I stood out. Evil was a common thing I trusted. Before sleep sometimes he came and whispered conversation in the old language of the bush. I listened. He told me things he never told anyone but Indians. I was privy to both worlds of his knowledge. I listened to him but, still, I had confidence in Leopolda. For she was the only one of the bunch he even noticed.

There came a day, though, when Leopolda turned the tide with her hook-pole.

It was a quiet day, with all of us working at our desks, when I heard him. He had sneaked into the closets in the back of the room. He was scratching around, tasting crumbs in our pockets, stealing buttons, squirting his dark juice in the linings and the boots. I was the only one who heard him, and I got bold. I smiled. I glanced back and smiled, and looked up at her sly to see if she had noticed. My heart jumped. For she was looking straight at me. And she sniffed. She had a big, stark, bony nose stuck to the front of her face, for smelling out brimstone and evil thoughts. She had smelled him on me. She stood up. Tall, pale, a blackness leading into the deeper blackness of the slate wall behind her. Her oak pole had flown into her grip. She had seen me glance at the closet. Oh, she knew. She knew just where he was. I watched her watch him in her mind's eye. The whole class was watching now. She was staring, sizing, following his scuffle. And all of a sudden she tensed down, poised on her bent kneesprings, cocked her arm back. She threw the oak pole singing over my head. It cracked through the thin wood door of the back closet and the heavy pointed hook drove through his heart. I turned. She'd speared her own black rubber overboot where he'd taken refuge, in the tip of her darkest toe.

Something howled in my mind. Loss and darkness. I understood. I was
to suffer for my smile.

He rose up hard in my heart. I didn't blink when the pole cracked. My
skull was tough. I didn't flinch when she shrieked in my ear. I only
shrugged at the flowers of hell. He wanted me. More than anything he
craved me. But then she did the worst. She did what broke my mind to
her. She grabbed me by the collar and dragged me, feet flying, through
the room and threw me in the closet with her dead black overboot. And
I was there. The only light was a crack beneath the door. I asked the
Dark One to enter into me and alert my mind. I asked him to restrain
my tears, for they were pushing behind my eyes. But he was afraid to
come back there. He was afraid of her sharp pole. And I was afraid of
Leopolda's pole, too, for the first time. I felt the cold hook in my heart.
It could crack through the door at any minute and drag me out, like a
dead fish on a gaff, drop me on the floor like a gutshot squirrel.

I was nothing. I edged back to the wall as far as I could. I breathed the
chalk dust. The hem of her full black cloak cut against my cheek. He had
left me. Her spear could find me any time. Her keen ears would aim the
hook into the beat of my heart.

What was that sound?

It filled the closet, filled it up until it spilled over, but I did not
recognize the crying wailing voice as mine until the door cracked open, I
saw brightness, and she hoisted me to her camphor-smelling lips.

"He *wants* you," she said. "That's the difference. I give you love."

Love. The black hook. The spear singing through the mind. I saw that
she had tracked the Dark One to my heart and flushed him out into the
open. So now my heart was an empty nest where she could lurk.

Well, I was weak. I was weak when I let her in but she got a foothold
there. Hard to dislodge as the months passed. Sometimes I felt him—the
brush of dim wings—but only rarely did his voice compel. It was between Marie and Leopolda now, and the struggle changed. I began to
realize I had been on the wrong track with the fruits of hell. The real
way to overcome Leopolda was this: I'd get to heaven first. And then,
when I saw her coming, I'd shut the gate. She'd be out! That is why,
besides the bowing and the scraping I'd be dealt, I wanted to sit on the
altar as a saint.

To this end, I went on up the hill. Sister Leopolda was the consecrated
nun who had sponsored me to come there.

"You're not vain," she had said. "You're too honest, looking into the
mirror, for that. You're not smart. You don't have the ambition to get

clear. You have two choices. One, you can marry a no-good Indian, bear his brats, die like a dog. Or two, you can give yourself to God."

"I'll come up there," I said, "but not because of what you think."

I could have had any damn man on the reservation at the time. And I could have made him treat me like his own life. I looked good. And I looked white. But I wanted Sister Leopolda's heart. And here was the thing: Sometimes I wanted her heart in love and admiration. Sometimes. And sometimes I wanted her heart to roast on a black stick.

She answered the back door, where they had instructed me to call. I stood there with my bundle. She looked me up and down.

"All right," she said finally. "Come in."

She took my hand. Her fingers were like a bundle of broom straws, so thin and dry, but the strength of them was unnatural. I couldn't have tugged loose if she had been leading me into rooms of white-hot coal. Her strength was a kind of perverse miracle, for she got it from fasting herself thin. Because of this hunger practice her lips were a wounded brown and her skin was deadly pale. Her eye sockets were two deep, lashless hollows. I told you about the nose. It stuck out far and made the place her eyes moved even deeper, as if she stared out of a gun barrel. She took the bundle from my hands and threw it in the corner.

"You'll be sleeping behind the stove, child."

It was immense, like a great furnace. A small cot was close behind it.

"Looks like it could get warm there," I said.

"Hot. It does."

"Do I get a habit?"

I wanted something like the thing she wore. Flowing black cotton. Her face was strapped in white bandages and a sharp crest of starched cardboard hung over her forehead like a glaring beak. If possible, I wanted a bigger, longer, whiter beak than hers.

"No," she said, grinning her great skull grin. "You don't get one yet. Who knows, you might not like us. Or we might not like you."

But she had loved me, or offered me love. And she had tried to hunt the Dark One down. So I had this confidence.

"I'll inherit your keys from you," I said.

She looked at me sharply, and her grin turned strange. She hissed, taking in her breath. Then she turned to the door and took a key from her belt. It was a giant key, and it unlocked the larder, where the food was stored.

Inside were all kinds of good stuff. Things I'd tasted only once or twice in my life. I saw sticks of dried fruit, jars of orange peel, spices like cinnamon. I saw tins of crackers with ships painted on the side. I saw pickles. Jars of herring and the rind of pigs. Cheese, a big brown block of it from the thick milk of goats. And the everyday stuff, in great quantities, the flour and the coffee.

The cheese got to me. When I saw it my stomach hollowed. My tongue dripped. I loved that goat-milk cheese better than anything I'd ever eaten. I stared at it. The rich curve in the buttery cloth.

"When you inherit my keys," she said sourly, slamming the door in my face, "you can eat all you want of the priest's cheese."

Then she seemed to consider what she'd done. She looked at me. She took the key from her belt and went back, sliced a hunk off, and put it in my hand.

"If you're good you'll taste this cheese again. When I'm dead and gone," she said.

Then she dragged out the big sack of flour. When I finished that heavenly stuff she told me to roll my sleeves up and begin doing God's labor. For a while we worked in silence, mixing up dough and pounding it out on stone slabs.

"God's work," I said after a while. "If this is God's work, then I've done it all my life."

"Well, you've done it with the Devil in your heart, then," she said. "Not God."

"How do you know?" I asked. But I knew she did. And I wished I had not brought up the subject.

"I see right into you like a clear glass," she said. "I always did."

"You don't know it," she continued after a while, "but he's come around here sulking. He's come around here brooding. You brought him in. He knows the smell of me and he's going to make a last-ditch try to get you back. Don't let him." She glared over at me. Her eyes were cold and lighted. "Don't let him touch you. We'll be a long time getting rid of him."

So I was careful. I was careful not to give him an inch. I said a rosary, two rosaries, three, underneath my breath. I said the Creed. I said every scrap of Latin I knew while we punched the dough with our fists. And still, I dropped the cup. It rolled under that monstrous iron stove, which was getting fired up for baking.

And she was on me. She saw he'd entered my distraction.

"Our good cup," she said. "Get it out of there, Marie."

I reached for the poker to snag it out from beneath the stove. But I had a sinking feeling in my stomach as I did this. Sure enough, her long arm darted past me like a whip. The poker landed in her hand.

"Reach," she said. "Reach with your arm for that cup. And when your flesh is hot, remember that the flames you feel are only one fraction of the heat you will feel in his hellish embrace."

She always did things this way, to teach you lessons. So I wasn't surprised. It was playacting anyway, because a stove isn't very hot underneath, right along the floor. They aren't made that way. Otherwise, a wood floor would burn. So I said yes and got down on my stomach and reached under. I meant to grab it quick and jump up again, before she could think up another lesson, but here it happened. Although I groped for the cup, my hand closed on nothing. That cup was nowhere to be found. I heard her step toward me, a slow step. I heard the creak of thick shoe leather, the little *plat* as the folds of her heavy skirts met, a trickle of fine sand sifting somewhere, perhaps in the bowels of her, and I was afraid. I tried to scramble up, but her foot came down lightly behind my ear, and I was lowered. The foot came down more firmly at the base of my neck, and I was held.

"You're like I was," she said. "He wants you very much."

"He doesn't want me no more," I said. "He had his fill. I got the cup!"

I heard the valve opening, the hissed intake of breath, and knew that I should not have spoken.

"You lie," she said. "You're cold. There is a wicked ice forming in your blood. You don't have a shred of devotion for God. Only wild, cold, dark lust. I know it. I know how you feel. I see the beast . . . the beast watches me out of your eyes sometimes. Cold."

The urgent scrape of metal. It took a moment to know from where. Top of the stove. Kettle. She was steadying herself with the iron poker. I could feel it like pure certainty, driving into the wood floor. I would not remind her of pokers. I heard the water as it came, tipped from the spout, cooling as it fell but still scalding as it struck. I must have twitched beneath her foot because she steadied me, and then the poker nudged up beside my arm as if to guide. "To warm your cold-ash heart," she said. I felt how patient she would be. The water came. My mind was dead blank. Again. I could only think the kettle would be cooling slowly in her hand. I could not stand it. I bit my lip so as not to satisfy her with a sound. She gave me more reason to keep still.

"I will boil him from your mind if you make a peep," she said, "by filling up your ear."

Any sensible fool would have run back down the hill the minute Leopolda let them up from under her heel. But I was snared in her black intelligence by then. I could not think straight. I had prayed so hard I think I broke a cog in my mind. I prayed while her foot squeezed my throat. While my skin burst. I prayed even when I heard the wind come through, shrieking in the busted bird nests. I didn't stop when pure light fell, turning slowly behind my eyelids. God's face. Even that did not disrupt my continued praise. Words came. Words came from nowhere and flooded my mind.

Now I could pray much better than any one of them. Than all of them full force. This was proved. I turned to her in a daze when she let me up. My thoughts were gone, and yet I remember how surprised I was. Tears glittered in her eyes, deep down, like the sinking reflection in a well.

"It was so hard, Marie," she gasped. Her hands were shaking. The kettle clattered against the stove. "But I have used all the water up now. I think he is gone."

"I prayed," I said foolishly. "I prayed very hard."

"Yes," she said. "My dear one, I know."

We sat together quietly because we had no more words. We let the dough rise and punched it down once. She gave me a bowl of mush, unlocked the sausage from a special cupboard, and took that in to the Sisters. They sat down the hall, chewing their sausage, and I could hear them. I could hear their teeth bite through their bread and meat. I couldn't move. My shirt was dry but the cloth stuck to my back and I couldn't think straight. I was losing the sense to understand how her mind worked. She'd gotten past me with her poker and I would never be a saint. I despaired. I felt I had no inside voice, nothing to direct me, no darkness, no Marie. I was about to throw that cornmeal mush out to the birds and make a run for it, when the vision rose up blazing in my mind.

I was rippling gold. My breasts were bare and my nipples flashed and winked. Diamonds tipped them. I could walk through panes of glass. I could walk through windows. She was at my feet, swallowing the glass after each step I took. I broke through another and another. The glass she swallowed ground and cut until her starved insides were only a subtle dust. She coughed. She coughed a cloud of dust. And then she was only a black rag that flapped off, snagged in barbed wire, hung there for an age, and finally rotted into the breeze.

I saw this, mouth hanging open, gazing off into the waving trees.

"Get up!" she cried. "Stop dreaming. It is time to bake."

Two other Sisters had come in with her, wide women with hands like paddles. They were smoothing and evening out the firebox beneath the great jaws of the oven.

"Who is this one?" they asked Leopolda. "Is she yours?"

"She is mine," said Leopolda. "A very good girl."

"What is your name?" one asked me.

"Marie."

"Marie. Star of the Sea."

"She will shine," said Leopolda, "when we have burned off the dark corrosion."

The others laughed, but uncertainly. They were slow, heavy French, who did not understand Leopolda's twisted jokes, although they muttered respectfully at things she said. I knew they wouldn't believe what she had done with the kettle. So I kept quiet.

"Elle est docile," they said approvingly as they left to starch the linens.

"Does it pain?" Leopolda asked me as soon as they were out the door.

I did not answer. I felt sick with the hurt.

"Come along," she said.

The building was quiet now. I followed her up the narrow staircase into a hall of little rooms, many doors, like a hotel. Her cell was at the very end. Inside was a rough straw mattress, a tiny bookcase with a picture of Saint Francis hanging over it, a ragged palm, and a crucifix. She told me to remove my shirt and sit down on her mattress. I did so. She took a pot of salve from the bookcase and began to smooth it upon my burns. Her stern hand made slow, wide circles, stopping the pain. I closed my eyes. I expected to see the docile blackness. Peace. But instead the vision reared up again. My chest was still tipped with diamonds. I was walking through windows. She was chewing up the broken litter I left behind.

"I am going," I said. "Let me go."

But she held me down.

"Don't go," she said quickly. "Don't. We have just begun."

I was weakening. My thoughts were whirling pitifully. The pain had kept me strong, and as it left me I began to forget, I couldn't hold on. I began to wonder if she had really scalded me with the kettle. I could not remember. To remember this seemed the most important thing in the world. But I was losing the memory. The scalding. The pouring. It began to vanish. I felt that my mind was coming off its hinge, flapping in the breeze, hanging by the hair of my own pain. I wrenched out of her grip.

"He was always in you," I said. "Even more than in me. He wanted you even more. And now he's got you. Get thee behind me!"

I shouted that, grabbed my shirt, and ran through the door, throwing the shirt on my body. I got down the stairs and into the kitchen, but no matter what I told myself, I couldn't get out the door. It wasn't finished. And she knew I would not leave. Her quiet step was immediately behind me.

"We must take the bread from the oven now," she said.

She was pretending nothing had happened. But for the first time I had gotten through some chink she'd left in her darkness. Touched some doubt. Her voice was so low and brittle it cracked off at the end of her sentence.

"Help me, Marie," she said slowly.

But I was not going to help her even though she calmly buttoned my shirt up and put the big cloth mittens in my hands for taking out the loaves. I could have bolted then. But I didn't. I knew that something was nearing completion. Something was about to happen. My back was a wall of singing flame. I was turning. I watched her take the long fork in one hand, to tap the loaves. In the other hand she gripped the black poker to hook the pans.

"Help me," she said again, and I thought, "Yes, this is part of it." I put the mittens on my hands and swung the door open on its hinges. The oven gaped. She stood back a moment, letting the first blast of heat rush by. I moved behind her. I could feel the heat at my front and at my back. Before, behind. My skin was turning to beaten gold. It was coming quicker than I had thought. The oven was like the gate of a personal hell. Just big enough and hot enough for one person, and that was her. One kick and Leopolda would fly in headfirst. And that would be one millionth of the heat she would feel when she finally collapsed in his hellish embrace.

Saints know these numbers.

She bent forward with her fork held out. I kicked her with all my might. She flew in. But the outstretched poker hit the back wall first, so she rebounded. The oven was not as deep as I had thought.

There was a moment when I felt a sort of thin, hot disappointment, as when a fish slips off the line. Only I was the one going to be lost. She was fearfully silent. She whirled. Her veil had cutting edges. She had the poker in one hand. In the other she held that long sharp fork she used to tap the delicate crusts of loaves. Her face turned upside-down on her shoulders. Her face turned blue. But saints are used to miracles. I felt no trace of fear.

If I was going to be lost, let the diamonds cut! Let her eat ground glass!

"Old she-devil bitch!" I shouted. "Kneel and beg! Lick the floor!"

That was when she stabbed me through the hand with the fork, then took the poker up alongside my head and knocked me out.

I came around maybe half an hour later. Things were so strange. So strange I can hardly tell it for delight at the remembrance. For when I came around this was actually taking place. I was being worshiped. I had somehow gained the altar of a saint.

I was lying back on the stiff couch in the Mother Superior's office. I looked around me. It was as though my deepest dream had come to life. The Sisters of the convent were kneeling to me. Sister Bonaventure. Sister Dympna. Sister Cecilia Saint-Claire. The two with hands like paddles. They were down on their knees. Black capes were slung over some of their heads. My name was buzzing up and down the room like a fat autumn fly, lighting on the tips of the tongues between Latin, humming up the heavy, blood-dark curtains, circling their swaddled heads. Marie! Marie! A girl thrown in a closet. Who was afraid of a rubber overboot. Who was half overcome. A girl who came in the back door where they threw their garbage. Marie! Who never found the cup. Who had to eat their cold mush. Marie! Leopolda had her face buried in her knuckles. Saint Marie of the Holy Slops! Saint Marie of the Bread Fork! Saint Marie of the Burnt Back and Scalded Butt!

I broke out and laughed.

They looked up. All holy hell burst loose when they saw I was awake. I still did not understand what was happening. They were watching, talking, but not to me.

"The marks . . ."

"She has her hand closed."

"Je ne peux pas voir."

I was not stupid enough to ask what they were talking about. I couldn't tell why I was lying in white sheets. I couldn't tell why they were praying to me. But I'll tell you this. It seemed entirely natural. It was me. I lifted up my hand as in my dream. It was completely limp with sacredness.

"Peace be with you."

My arm was dried blood from the wrist down to the elbow. And it hurt. Their faces turned like fat flowers of adoration to follow that hand's movements. I let it swing through the air, imparting a saint's blessing. I had practiced. I knew exactly how to act.

They murmured. I heaved a sigh and a golden beam of light suddenly broke through the clouded window and flooded down directly on my face. A stroke of perfect luck! They had to be convinced.

Leopolda still knelt in the back of the room. Her knuckles were crammed halfway down her throat. Let me tell you, a saint has senses honed keen as a wolf's. I knew that she was over my barrel now. How it had happened did not matter. The last thing I remembered was that she flew from the oven and stabbed me. That one thing was most certainly true.

"Come forward, Sister Leopolda." I gestured with my heavenly wound. Oh, it hurt. It bled when I reopened the place where it had begun to heal. "Kneel beside me," I said.

She kneeled, but her voice box evidently did not work, for her mouth opened, shut, opened, but no sound came out. My throat clenched in the noble delight I had read of as befitting a saint. She could not speak. But she was beaten. It was in her eyes. She stared at me now with all the deep hate of the wheel of devilish dust that rolled wild within her emptiness.

"What is it you want to tell me?" I asked. And at last she spoke.

"I have told my sisters of your passion," she managed to choke out. "How the stigmata . . . the marks of the nails . . . appeared in your palm and you swooned at the holy vision . . ."

"Yes," I said, curious.

And then, after a moment, I understood.

Leopolda had saved herself with her quick brain. She had witnessed a miracle. She had hid the fork and told this to the others. And of course they believed her, because they never knew how Satan came and went or where he took refuge.

"I saw it from the first," said the large one who had put the bread in the oven. "Humility of the spirit. So rare in these girls."

"I saw it too," said the other one with great satisfaction. She sighed quietly. "If only it was me."

Leopolda was kneeling bolt upright, face blazing and twitching, a barely held fountain of blasting poison.

"Christ has marked me," I agreed. I smiled a saint's smirk in her face. And then I looked at her. That was my mistake.

For I saw her kneeling there. Leopolda with her soul like a rubber overboot. With her face of a starved rat. With her desperate eyes drowning in the deep wells of her wrongness. There would be no one else after me. And I would leave. I saw Leopolda kneeling within the shambles of her love.

My heart had been about to surge from my chest with the blackness of my joyous heat. Now it dropped. I pitied her. I pitied her. Pity twisted in my stomach as if that hook-pole were driven through me at last. I was caught. It was a feeling more terrible than any amount of boiling water and worse than being forked. Still, still, I couldn't help what I did. I had already smiled in a saint's mealy forgiveness. I heard myself speaking gently.

"Receive the dispensation of my sacred blood," I whispered.

But there was no heart in it. No joy when she bent to touch the floor. No dark leaping. I fell back onto the white pillows. Blank dust was whirling through the light shafts. My skin was dust. Dust my lips. Dust the dirty spoons on the ends of my feet.

Rise up! I thought. Rise up and walk! There is no limit to this dust!

DA VINCI IS DEAD

R. C. HAMILTON

R. C. Hamilton was born in Mansfield, Ohio, and currently resides on
a family sheep farm in the Laurel Hills area of western Pennsylvania.
He has received training and certification as a shearer, and also breeds
and raises Shetland Island Sheep Dogs on the farm. In his spare time
he plays various instruments in a Scottish/Irish traditional folk music
band in various local bars. He and his wife have one child, Sam, named
for Sam Hamilton in Steinbeck's *East of Eden*. Hamilton is employed
at a university library as an evening/weekend supervisor.

He sat in the room with the curtains drawn, waiting for Mrs. Lolliard.
She would come in perhaps five minutes. . . . Long experience had
taught him that protesting was useless. In the choice between the two
evils, he'd decided upon the path of least resistance. The swim was
tiring, usually boring, but he had found that escaping Eunice Lolliard
was a bit more tiring, more boring. So again, he would go.

Sounds from the pool drifted in through the windows, splashing, the
murmur of small talk, and occasionally, the clank and rattle of the diving
board. Jay Milton would come with her, and the mindlessness of their
chatter would inevitably begin. They'd spread their towels, three in a
line, and Morento would be held captive, compelled eventually to stand,
"spellbound" with Eunice, as Jay mounted the diving tower and plunged
through his stiff and semi-graceful swan dive. And then Milton would
surface, flash his dentures, and cry, "See Morento, nothing to it." "Oh
yes do, John," Mrs. Lolliard would say, "dive John, please."

Was it so necessary, really, in what were probably the last decades of
their lives, for them to still be going through the procedures of character
assassination? Try as he would, their needling him about a dive would
always get to him, hurt him. Nowadays, of course, the real resentment
had left him—probably a lucky thing too. He was uncertain of how his
body would take a dive from the tower. When he was a child, while in a
study room at school, a boy—a bully, really—had once found it necessary

to sit behind him every day, and for the entertainment of the other schoolchildren, reach up and flick and flick at his ears until they turned red. It went on, every day, for weeks. Finally then, finally, anger had come—he had turned around and, without a word, he'd slapped the boy. The room grew quiet, expectant, but, taken by surprise, the bully too was silent. When the bell rang, he, Morento, arose, and without turning, left the room. Now, however, anger like that did not come. In their late sixties and seventies, he had always supposed, people would be dignified, wise, worldly. There would no longer be the need to prove oneself, to demonstrate one's abilities, to assert one's individuality. But no, the people were still behaving like schoolchildren. Unfortunately, perhaps, he no longer felt the obligation to justify his actions, either. And so he would be hurt, but not act. How to account for it? It was not easy.

One was required to take a shower before entering the pool. He would take his early—in his room, then dry, and change into his trunks, and wait for Mrs. Lolliard and Milton. The five-minute wait made it worthwhile. It *was* hot, and the showering refreshed him, stimulated him. The rug under his bare feet felt wonderfully clean and soft, and the wind in the curtains and the splashes and cries from the pool soothed him. After the swim—the afternoon passed, he would return alone to his room and feel amazingly clean, and it nearly always would be after five o'clock then and the better part of another day would have been seen through. The swimming, too, exhausted him, and he slept well.

Having a room next to the pool *was* a stroke of luck—it lent a certain validity to his reluctance to use the men's shower room. He wondered about certain of the men who used the room. People reacted differently to the difficulties of dealing with age and sex. Some apparently retained an active interest, and possibly this explained some of the posturing and coquettishness that so tenaciously held sway. But he wondered about the old homosexuals—no doubt there were some—and their reactions to the whole process. Once, his room had been in the northwest complex, across Sullivant Avenue, and rather than walk across that hot street, undignified, on display for twenty-year-old van drivers and the pitying middle-aged housewives in his baggy, saggy, pitiful swimming trunks, he chose to use a locker in the shower room provided near the pool. The room was a strange place, the old men would cruise and totter about in their white, naked bodies like odd fishes swirling through dim waters. Some of them stayed in there for hours, completely naked, showering, sitting bedraggled on the benches, smoking and muttering. Some of them stared at you outright—and it was this that made Morento curious about the old homosexuals. Did they retain their active interest in sex? Did they find an aesthetic pleasure in the crumpled old bodies, or did they dream—Apollo, Theseus? It was hard to tell. One strange person, as a joke—or what—had inscribed the word "fuck" on a green wall in the locker room. "Fuck," and that was all. Morento often wondered if he had meant it as a command. If so, the artist was in charge of a haggard army. Well, no. It was a stereotype, and there was a great deal of promiscuity, all things considered, at Redwood. Closing doors. Whispered conversations in the hallway during the dead of the night. He was not sad not to be a part of it. Perhaps that was it. Secure within himself. It was not necessarily a companion of aging, but a presence, nonetheless.

Clank, and thud, rattle. Morento waited for the splash, but it was indistinguishable among the general wet sounds coming in the windows. He tried to imagine that the sounds were those of rain, but then realized that he preferred thinking in terms of the truth. A sunny, hot day, a swimming pool just outside his room. The curtains were pulled shut, and the room was dim and green, and he was sitting on the bed in his swimming trunks, waiting for Milton and Mrs. Lolliard. His toes explored in the pile of the carpeting. It was a blessing, having had his room changed. The previous occupant had died—thrombosis? And in the fathomless workings of the Redwood mechanism, he had been shuffled from the northwest complex to here. A blessing.

It was there, at his first room, that he had first met Mrs. Lolliard— Eunice—quite by accident. She was a parody, no, an epitome really, of the aged hostess. He remembered thinking how awful a trait it seemed. In middle age she'd probably been the epitome of the aged debutante. Before that? Perhaps the epitome of the aged spoiled child. The circle spiraled down to her birth. Then what? He'd been directed, by mistake, to her room upon admission. The door had been ajar, and, assuming an orderly had been along and had left it open for him, he'd stepped in. At first, a curious sound had come to him—mechanical, rhythmic, but soft —plopping and bubbling. He'd searched the dim room for its source, waiting for his eyes to adjust. So strange. Then he saw Mrs. Lolliard, sitting, silhouetted against the window, sobbing. She looked out over a little courtyard of trees, and held a handkerchief to her mouth. Morento had made a motion to leave, assuming, correctly, that there'd been some mistake, but before he could slip away she'd looked up, and their eyes had met. They'd stared at one another meaninglessly, as one might stare at a slice of pickle on another diner's plate. And then he'd left. The orderly had come up with his bags, and together, the two of them had found the proper room.

And so. What about that little incident, that sobbing? Was it over something real, or imagined? Some trifle—perhaps a harsh word from a friend, a confused romance? Or was it darker? More ominous? The last decades of one's life. The last of the moments for looking out over courtyards, seeing insects, flowering trees, the sun. She had come over that evening as one of a group formally welcoming him to their floor. Their eyes had met and had conveyed no messages. Strangers, as if they had never seen one another before. Nor had she ever mentioned it since, even alluded to it obliquely. The matter had been left unfinished, undisturbed. Mrs. Lolliard had sobbed, and apparently she would not sob again. At any rate, he felt certain that the matter was a bond—he would always be curious, knowing that there was probably more to her than she revealed. At least he kept his end of the shallow association going. As for her? What *was* her motive for befriending him, including him in her activities, finding things for him to do? Perhaps it was embarrassment over the sobbing incident. Rather than avoiding him, she confronted him. Or perhaps—and this was something Morento feared—perhaps it was pity. Poor old homeless, friendless man. No relatives, no place to go. Her confused role as hostess. Actually, he had a daughter on the West Coast, in Portland, and he in fact had an open invitation to live there. It was a big house, full of pianos—her husband was an instructor at a university. They all got along together well, even respected one another. But Morento refused to clutter her life. He was active now, and reasonably independent—a retirement fund, the installments still arriving from the sale of his business. They had drifted apart, and he preferred to keep it so. The thought of the invalid, the credulous old relative-boarder, the vegetable—it appalled him. There was no telling how it would be as he grew still older. But, provide, provide. He had at least provided for himself. Still, what if Mrs. Lolliard had, did, misjudge his motives for staying at Redwood, did really believe him friendless, homeless, lonely? The truth was much different. It was simply, he supposed, that he knew his place. He was an old man, and however much an educated society might try not to, it would treat him as such, supply him with the sorts of options it imagined an old man would prefer. He could not work, he was past retirement. He was not independently wealthy, or exceptionally well known. He was not exactly an artist, or a statesman. He had no private concern left of his own. And his choices, therefore, were two: to quietly, cheaply live alone, or to live so with others like him. And he would live, do thus, until he died. In fact, he *had* lived alone, for two and a half years. He'd taken a small, pleasant room across the street from the Public Library in the midst of a cluster of squares undergoing an urban renewal project. He had visited the library often, reading voraciously, reading of things he had never known he held an interest in. The Bog People—they were Iron Age humans found beautifully preserved in Danish bogs, complete, down to their fingerprints. Or about musical instruments of the middle and high Renaissance—the pochette, the hautbois, the chitarronne. On warm days, he would sit on the stone benches on the library lawn, close his eyes to slits, and soak in the sun. He had seen cats, in rooms like dim aquariums, lie so in a beam of sun, luxuriating. As he remembered it now, it *did* seem pleasant. But there were unpleasant things, hopeless battles with depression, and then the urge to lose himself too often in alcohol. He'd found, too, that he might strike up and carry on a pointless conversation with a total stranger on the library steps—an annoying, unpleasant thing he had seen so many old men do, something he hated doing, and hated himself for doing. It was unaccountable, foolish. He knew, someday he would probably need a home anyway. Redwood really was that, underneath the ultra-modern brick and glass facade. One quadrant in the south was precisely that, in fact—a place exclusively for the invalids, the poor souls who had lost control of their bowels, or their muscles, or their minds. The rest was just a holding zone, a corral, despite the swimming pool, the yoga classes. Morning activities, Tuesday the 29th. Billiards, cards, shuffleboard, mosaics 9:30–12:00, bowling, New Olympic Lanes, Terrarium 10:00–11:00. Shopping trip scheduled for 1 P.M. Morento shunned the organized activities. They appalled him, the rigidity, the shallowness. Instead of succumbing to them he read, wandered the halls, went to the theater. Always, as often as was possible, he kept to himself. He did not deceive himself, he needed human company. But mostly just the presence of others was enough. One especially needed the presence of others one's own age. That was, he supposed, the point of these centers. It *did* tend to relieve the sense of isolation. And always, always, there was someone worse off than oneself.

One winter Morento had paced the halls when suddenly, faintly, he had caught a strain of banjo music. He had traced it to a large, dim, empty auditorium. In the front row center seats a lone man played the tenor banjo. Morento did not particularly like the tenor banjo, although he was aware that he was monstrously ignorant of the instrument, as of so many other things. But the man's playing was superb. The acoustics, the emptiness of the auditorium, gave the banjo a haunted, faraway ring. He stood, unnoticed, in the back, listening. For some reason he imagined being in a long, pitch-black tunnel, or in the cellar of a bombed-out building during the Second World War, and hearing the unaccountable and out-of-place music—"Waitin' for the Robert E. Lee," "You're a Grand Old Flag"—who was playing those songs in this cellar, and why? It was ghastly, and yet utterly lovely. When the man stopped suddenly, Morento shook himself out of his bizarre thoughts. "Bravo," he said, into the echoes.

The man was Billy Shandy. He was eighty. He had, as it turned out, a kind of arthritis that was progressing in such a way as to rob him gradually of his muscular control. Even so, his banjo playing was marvelous. He once had been a virtuoso player in a novelty band in the forties and fifties. But tastes in music constantly change, and even an audience concerned with the esoteric had drifted away from Dixieland and ragtime. "Music doesn't evolve," Billy had told him, "in the sense of an evolution to a higher or better form. It's a foolish misconception to think that way about any art form." Music developed, it trended, it was influenced. But it did not evolve. They talked for hours. The taste for Dixieland had diminished. That was that. He had found himself on the streets. It was ludicrous. "In other ages, instruments would pretty much be developed that could produce the sounds a people wanted to hear. But now? Too much diversification, too much specialization, too much commercialism. One tended to get lost in the crush." Morento wasn't sure if this was strictly true. They argued the point for days, weeks. Billy Shandy progressively lost the use of his hands. That was two years ago. Then, one night Billy had died in his room—an unsuspected aneurism. The argument, they never resolved. And so, true, it was true, there was always someone there worse off than oneself.

There was a knock on the door and Morento started, his feet jerking up off the soft rug on the floor. "John?" he heard. It was Mrs. Lolliard. "John dear, are you there? Ready for a swim? The water's waiting, John."

He slowly got to his feet and walked toward the door. "Coming, Eunice, I'm coming."

The sunlight, unexpectedly, hit him like a fist. It stunned him, blinded him. He could make out her straw hat and a row of projecting teeth. Milton, he sensed, was standing somewhere off to the right.

"Ah, there you are, there you are. We simply have to hurry, John, it's absolutely crushing in this heat. I think I'll just sit down in the shallow end and just sit and sit there for hours like an alligator or something. Don't you think so, Jay? Won't that be about the only thing we can do in this awful heat?" Jay Milton was silent, ignoring her, then chose to talk to Morento instead. "Are you all right, Morento? You look unhappy about something." He chuckled, sounding uneasy.

"It's the light, I think," Morento said to them. "It caught me by surprise as I came through the door. I should have put on some sunglasses." The two of them studied him, and then Eunice turned abruptly, and started across the concrete walkway to the pool. "Light, heat, these blistering days . . . it's horrible, isn't it?" she said. "And yet sunglasses won't be much help against the heat now, will they, John? Not a bit."

Curiously, Morento did not feel the heat at all. Even in that first flash of brilliance he had felt no heat. He was blinded. Milton and Mrs. Lolliard were wavering shapes ahead of him, moving through pane after pane of shattering glass, of fragmenting slivers and crystals. It wasn't the heat, he knew. Blood sugar. He *knew* that's what it was. Glucose. Like a hangover, except the body wasn't dehydrated. It affected the central nervous system. There was a drink now, a concoction, for athletes, football players—it was nearly pure glucose. That, or a glass of wine, would clear this up immediately. He looked up. Ragged slivers that looked like broken fiberglass covered the trees.

"Hot, hot, hot," Mrs. Lolliard was repeating, inanely. He followed along behind, taking careful steps, almost like a shying horse. When they reached the pool, the light flashing up from the water left circles on his retinas like popping flashbulbs. "Eunice, Jay," he said, "I'll be with you in just a minute. Just going over for a candy bar at the little stand. Don't let me hold you up. Go on in, why don't you?"

"Oh John," he heard her say, disapproval in her voice, and then, "well, all right, if you must. But don't be long will you? We'll leave our things near the shallow end. See? My orange towel?"

Morento smiled. The only thing he seemed to be able to see was her straw hat. "Yes, yes, I'll be along," he said. Her orange towel. He wondered if they had guessed. No, it was a slightly inappropriate illness for an old man. High blood pressure might have been a more suitable affliction. They might have enjoyed knowing though—the conversational possibilities were endless. One could hardly have done better with a broken hip. He walked stiffly to the confection stand and asked the white-suited attendant there for a chocolate bar. It would take longer, but the candy bar would probably work. A doctor had once prescribed raisin bread as an aid, and mild exercise. Morento was incredulous, insulted that therapy might consist of something so absurd as raisin bread. "Raisin bread," he had asked, "what on earth has this to do with raisin bread?" But the doctor had insisted.

He felt like an eccentric, still, a lunatic, buying loaf after loaf of raisin bread at the bakery on the next block. Apparently, the baker believed him obsessed. "This single-minded fixation for raisin bread. This erratic old man again. Senile." Was there no understanding anywhere?

He'd exercised with the doctor. Behind Redwood, a large, untouched field nestled between the freeway and Sullivant Avenue. They'd hit hollow plastic golf balls back and forth. One day the field was covered with dandelions and they'd spent an afternoon hitting the heads of the dandelions instead of the golf balls.

They spoke of the war. The doctor had been with the American Navy in the Mediterranean and he told of fishing Italian sailors out of the water after his ship had blown up the Italian vessel. "One man," he said, "came aboard with a pistol and shot a medic from Texas through the head. There was some confusion. He aimed the gun again and again, firing, missing—a lieutenant knocked him back into the water, and he somehow drowned." The doctor lopped another dandelion. The noise of the distant traffic came to them faintly. Morento knew that the doctor found the two moments insoluble. One failed to define the other. Standing quietly in the field of dandelions lent no meaning to the craziness of the war.

"Are all the events of life thus," the doctor would be thinking, "one giving no meaning to another, a childhood having no bearing on middle age, lunch having no real relation to dinner? Was the craziness relative? Not limited to war? Are we madmen?" Morento could see the thoughts flash past in the doctor's eyes. Then, lop, another dandelion sailed into the air. Morento had no answers for him. The field was green, the dandelions yellow, the sky overhead, blue. When the sun went down, ending their conversation, the sun was red. The doctor later was transferred to Atlanta, yet Morento continued to buy raisin bread. Perhaps he *was* obsessed.

He sat down on a bench and began to eat his candy bar. And, mercifully, in perhaps a minute's time, his vision began to clear. To his left, he saw a chess match in progress, and after staring at the pieces intently, he realized that it would probably be black's game. Morento knew the man who played white, and felt a sudden spasm of pity, although he attempted to control these things. Pity for others, he knew, felt too often

—and perhaps too often uncalled for—was ultimately merely disheartening. But this man playing white oppressed him. There are things in life the mind does not want to be subjected to. He had seen a dog once, struck by a car, slide under a parked delivery van and die. The brain would cower away from various events. One involved this man. One October he had wandered down to the main entrance, ostensibly in order to buy a newspaper. In fact, as he remembered it, he *did* buy a newspaper—pointless act. As he rose from the vending box, some bustle, some movement at the door made him glance up. Two young people were entering, a man and a woman, and between them, draped in a pathetically oversized black overcoat, walked this man. In an instant, the situation was clear to Morento. The man and woman both wore expressions of guilt, grief, but there was some measure of relief flashing about their eyes. The old man, a short, thin, monkey-faced man, had a smile glazed on his face, exposing round, gray teeth. His eyes were like those of a child on his way to school for the first time. He smiled, smiled incessantly, insanely, and looked about in apprehension and horror. The young ones—the children, of course—need not have felt guilty, for there was no resentment flashing in the monkey man's eyes. The ordeals of convincing, confrontation, even of packing—they were over now. Any anger the little man might have felt was surely swallowed up now by his fear. In a lifetime, so, the emotion, once called up, had neither changed nor dulled—the first day at school, the first day at dancing class, the first day in a new neighborhood, a new job—age had neither compensated nor helped this man adjust to what stole through his darting eyes. The minute Morento saw him, he knew. The first day in the home for the aged. He carried two bags—his life's belongings, and they weighted his arms down to his sides and caused him to walk with a curious, awkward bobbing—he looked up to Morento hopefully, a new friend perhaps, smiling, almost mechanical-looking, bobbing, monkey-faced, fearful, and as he came closer, Morento had fallen back in his own palpable horror. He'd attempted a smile that surely must have looked like a grimace to them, and had fled from the reception hall, stung, cowering, a madman. He'd fled to his own room in order to hide, to escape the vision of the monkey man shuffling in to be committed to the hands of utter strangers. (Insane strangers, his children must surely have thought, after witnessing Morento's singular retreat.) And Morento had sputtered on the way, had begun some effort at an expression of his bitterness, some recrimination. But it had died. Things, memories, flashed through his mind during all of his crucial moments, and then something in him would die. It was a kind of resignation. Perhaps a form of death itself. The shaking of the head, the shrugging. "What's the use?" Now, so full of fear, wary of rejection, here sat this monkey man, playing white, losing, being rejected. It was a kind of a circle, the kind Morento had grown weary of seeing. You can't teach an old dog new tricks. Actually, the saying went, "you just can't teach a dog tricks, whatever the age." For the myth, the stereotype of the dignity or worldliness that accompanied old age was as overblown as the myths about sex or senility. Children of the aged would always have to confront their own capacity for heartlessness, just as their monkey men would always have to feel damaged and insecure. Well, that all might be something he and Billy Shandy could have argued over anyway. He wasn't sure if it was exactly true. You might teach a dog a series of very strong habitual motions. Billy would have been slightly more optimistic, at any rate.

Unexpectedly, the monkey face rose up suddenly from the chessboard and grinned at Morento anew. "Hello, John," the little man said, "quite the weather we're having, isn't it?"

Morento was dumbfounded. He stared at the monkey man in bewilderment. How had he known his name? There had been no introductions that Morento could recall. And yet here he sat, smiling at him with his round, gray teeth, having called him "John." Just for an instant, Morento faltered. Was it possible that there *had* been an introduction, something which he had forgotten? The prospect of a weakening memory was a particularly ugly one. Sometimes he would consider it with a certain sense of waiting, as if in anticipation of an inevitable breakdown in some household appliance or an automobile. When, exactly, would the first lapse occur? He tried, once more, to remember. *Had* there been a meeting, formal introductions? Nothing definite would seem to clarify for him. He became suddenly aware of the fact that the little man was still staring at him, his face beginning to fall just slightly. Morento made a hurried decision to opt for an approximation of the truth. He always *had* been an impossible one for names and faces.

"I'm sorry," he would say, "I seem to have forgotten. . . ."

But before Morento could speak, the monkey man's opponent, the fellow playing black, interrupted. "Oh, for Christ's sakes, Phillip," he said, in a voice loud enough for several surrounding sunbathers and chess players to hear. "Don't bother trying to patronize Morento. You know how he is. Rather wander with his nose in a book than give a man the time of day. Forget him, Phil, come on, just play the game."

Morento had turned to this second man with a sense of growing confusion. He knew him vaguely, recognized him well enough, anyway, to be able to pick the face from a crowd. *You know how he is.* The invective surprised Morento. "No," he thought to ask, "how am I?" And yet long habit of remaining guarded restrained him.

"My God, Morento," the man said suddenly, angrily, "as talkative as you are you should have gone to a monastery, do you know that? Or else maybe to a cave somewhere you could practise your asceticism sitting naked on a pallet. You come nosing around here, scrutinizing our game as if you've got even a mild interest in the real world for a change, and Phil here is nice enough to extend you an opening line, and what do you do but stare at him emptily, as if he were only a spot on the wallpaper. You've got your nerve, Morento, that's all I can say. Is there something *wrong* with you?"

White moved, and made an error which Morento saw immediately would prove fatal. He could not seem to get his eyes away from the pieces on the board. He was, he realized, utterly embarrassed. And yet what was there to say? Small wheels of a certain, recognizable panic had begun to turn in his brain. "Was there something wrong with him?" The question was probably entirely appropriate. He *did* come off as reclusive, detached. He could not deny it. Perhaps he *had* been introduced to these two men already, at some nameless social function, and perhaps he *had*—even selectively—forgotten all about it. He wondered briefly just how pervasive the characterization might be. Old Morento. That surly, nervy old coot.

At last, he forced his gaze up away from the chessboard, and confronted the two old men before him with upraised palms. "You must excuse me," he told them, "I was . . . reminiscing. I didn't mean to intrude. The heat. I've . . . been . . . somewhat tired."

The fellow playing black stared back at him grimly, while Morento marveled at the lameness of the explanation, at his own utter inability to simply tell these two perfectly cognizant fellow human beings precisely what he'd meant and had been thinking. The monkey man smiled at him apologetically, his face full of understanding and forgiveness.

"Within three moves," Morento could not restrain himself from thinking, "you will be hopelessly checkmated, you poor old fool." And, without another word, he arose and walked hurriedly off across the cement terrace toward the pool. Behind him he heard, or at least thought that he heard, a single, not particularly well-suppressed guffaw, and his ears, he knew, were burning.

"Never mind, Phil," Black's voice said, "never mind. Let's play."

Distraught now, Morento wondered what it was that was so endlessly difficult about simple human understanding. For all of our lives we tried, each saying, "I *am*, I think, this is what I saw." And yet toward the end came the prospect of everlasting silence, and the barriers were still just as real, just as high, just as difficult to overcome. He hated himself, suddenly, for his own stupidity. We were hopelessly tormented animals, given the glimpse of communion with our languages, only to find both our words and minds inadequate. "Is there something wrong with you?" "A mild interest in the real world for a change."

The ground beneath him was a patchwork of soft towels, radios, and sunglasses. The sweet vegetable scent of tanning lotion pervaded the air. Tanning old skin. The candy *had* helped, for Morento could see clearly now, in the focal plane, although the edges of his vision were still encased in a swirling fog. Orange towels lay everywhere, and for a brief instant, the entire situation made him feel frustrated, even angry. But of *course* communication was a farce, when even everyday living was cluttered with muddled thinking. What did Black expect? How could Morento, in just one small example, be expected to find Mrs. Lolliard's orange towel in such a sea of vapid uniformity? Was he psychic? The people played chess calmly while death stole upon them. Could they think of nothing better to do after so many hard-won years? They were buffaloes, they were asses. The silliness, the irony of it, prompted him to shrug. Mrs. Lolliard was certainly an ass, that much was clear. The point in her case at least wasn't that she'd spent her life as little more than a shallow poseur—such judgments lacked meaning, semantically, objectively, in terms of the galaxy Andromeda. The truth of the matter, really, lay in the ecumenical fact that Mrs. Lolliard was simply an ass. Now there was something a man could believe in, something he could take with him to his grave.

He sat down at the edge of the pool and lowered his feet into the cool water. Between the soft rug in his apartment and the water, his feet, he admitted, were having a pleasant day. But what a fool he was. "You know how he is."

He looked out, observing the bobbing faces. Several old men were insisting upon diving from the tower. Complete idiots, of course. In his younger days, he might have called them something worse. One barrel-chested fellow would do a flipping sort of a dive designed to send up towers of spray and create a small tidal wave. Morento watched one wave cross the entire pool until it welled up around his legs. Da Vinci, he remembered, had become interested in the motions of waves in his last years. Shortly before his death he'd left the cryptic note, something like, "My life has been spent observing the wrong things, seeing in the wrong ways." What had he seen so suddenly in those waves, Morento had often wondered. An enigma, perhaps. Life's enigma.

"John, John, John!" The fact that someone had been calling his name broke through his thought. "John." It was Mrs. Lolliard's voice, and he finally located her, sitting in the shallow end and waving her arms wildly in the air. "John, yoo-hoo, John!" He sighed. Yes, there was the world. Mundane, tinged with disappointment, predictability, embarrassment. He waved back, and smiled, deciding to be dense. It was only when he saw her pointing that he realized she didn't want him to join her after all. She pointed vigorously, like a child, directing his attention back to the tower. He perceived, in a forlorn way, what was happening. Mrs. Lolliard had once somehow gotten wind that he, Morento, had been a diver in college. Of course, Jay Milton, too, had received this information. And ever since, motivated by something obscure and ominous, she had been trying to get him to jump from the tower. Milton, in a tangled, sick way, kept trying to make it into a challenge, a contest. Well, damn them, he *had* been a diver in college, but it had been a fiasco. He had nearly knocked himself unconscious once in practice, and in his only meet he had finished dead last. At critical moments during his dives, an odd thing would happen—his mind would wander. This would break his concentration, interrupt an act that really should have been performed by the reflexes alone. Now, periodically, perhaps once in two weeks, Milton would make his ritualized challenge. And Mrs. Lolliard, an avid, probably bloodthirsty accomplice, would cheer them on.

A dive will last for seconds, fractions of seconds. Yet somehow during those moments the mind was able to wander. Of course all thoughts were similar insofar as they were nearly instantaneous—or were they? Yet, at any rate, his mind would seem to fly from his head the instant he left the board, then try to scramble back before he splashed into the pool. He would usually hit too soon. He would think of odd things, fearful things. He had been a night watchman once in a foundry. Across a river a freight train chugged by, agonizingly slow. In an empty boxcar leaned a figure in a white shirt. The person spit. Then splash, he was under the surface. He rode in a car along a highway, passed a cattle truck. A pig stared at him with a beady eye. It was bound for the slaughterhouse. Then, again, he was hitting the water and the dive was ruined. It was a fantastic experience, he had no control over it. Inexplicable. This all had happened when he was a young man, in his twenties.

Now, an old man, a duffer, an old body, what could he expect to do in a dive except to kill himself?

He saw Milton climb to the top of the tower and walk out to the edge. Mrs. Lolliard waved frantically and Milton turned to her, gracious, and nodded, then waved over at Morento. Would it be a swan dive, a flip? A cut-away? Was there no end to the thrills life had to offer? Milton left the board, swinging through the low arc of a swan dive. Typical. It was probably what you would call his "best" dive. Then, a moment later, sure enough, the bobbing head came up and the arm was extended in a lazy wave. The sunlight flashed from the water and burned into Morento's eyes with a new intensity. He pulled his legs from the pool and stood up. He would certainly have to get sunglasses, heat or no heat. He walked along the sidewalk surrounding the pool to the shallow end where Mrs. Lolliard wallowed, still wearing her hat.

"John," she called, "John, won't you dive for me—please, someday?" She was pouting. He smiled, looking down at the grass that grew in the cracks of the cement. Water trickled there like estuaries of the Amazon. This he could see. This famous dive. He would walk to the tower, set his hands and feet upon the aluminum ladder. Some time ago, it would occur to him, some faceless foundryman had cast this ladder, while wondering idly, instantaneously, whose feet might someday climb the rungs. Countless feet, thousands of slapping feet, belonging to old men and women, people as dull as buffaloes. Asses. Then, he, Morento, would arrive and think idly, instantaneously, of the anonymous workman who had made the thing. But already he would be on his way up, the person forgotten, as he himself had been forgotten. Glass would shatter and cascade around him, patches of fog as thick as spun sugar would drift at the corners of his eyes. He would step onto the board—it has a sandpapery surface not unlike sharkskin—his feet would carry him to the edge. And he would stand there, wavering, unsure of his balance, not sure even of what dive he could do. And then he would look at the water below and know that he would never dive. The height would appall him, he would sink to one knee. "I am an old man," he would think, "I am too old. I will die." And so, slowly, agonizingly, he would make his way back to the ladder, then down. Yes, this he could see well. His stupendous dive, his answer to the challenge. Then? Then he would walk across the courtyard, disgraced. There was no dignity in age. He would feel the same, useless, wasted emotions. Shame. Embarrassment. Humiliation. He would have been forever unable to rid himself of the need to try to command the respect of others. He would understand clearly that he associated with people he pretended to disdain. And he would know with crushing certainty: he is lonely. I am lonely. I will die.

Yes, yes, Morento thought, shaking himself slightly, that is what the thing reduced itself to. Loneliness, death. It was true, he must be honest. The prospect drove him to Redwood, drove him to Mrs. Lolliard and Milton. Books notwithstanding, travel, a lifetime of unusual work. There had been Billy Shandy. . . . Morento had considered learning the banjo. But then, what had happened to Billy's instrument? And Billy dead. Of *course* he liked Eunice, in his begrudging, detached way. He appreciated her inconsistencies, even her childishness. And Milton wasn't a bad sort, well intentioned. They *were*, innocently enough, only trying to include him, when it came right down to it. And yet who was there left, honestly, to genuinely *talk* to? The doctor in Atlanta? The people on the steps of the library? "Pardon me, sir, I must tell you of an important event from my past. . . ." And what if he *should* suddenly die, without having explained certain things? Was the sum of one's life, one's experience, only to be wasted in final silence?

"Is there something *wrong* with you?" Black had asked, and suddenly Morento knew. Of *course* there was something wrong with him. He was an old man. An isolate. Full, still, of some nameless expectation in life, which neither he nor the people surrounding him could ever supply. And all of their lives were full up now, with the sum of their experiences, and they had not learned, had not triumphed. Morento was just as guilty as the rest. Life was simply going on in them, carrying them along with biomechanics, and they were little more than stupefied clocks, waiting to run down. The compensation of any human understanding between them was a fabled myth. The process of aging itself was virtually synonymous with resignation, entrenchment. The living experience had escaped them, and they had let it go willingly, one and all. And now there was left only the loneliness, and in time, of course, merely death.

"John," Eunice was saying, "John, are you all right? John?" He had been standing, staring down at his feet, at the Amazon trickling between his toes.

In the distance, the barrel-chested man jumped from the tower once more and sent a small wave rippling out toward them across the water. It advanced and grew, filling Morento with sudden, inexpressible dread. Even Da Vinci was dead, he realized. His mind left him momentarily, fleeing to some indefinable place beyond understanding. The shouts, laughter, slop of the water, all seemed to fade to vague buzzings, and the wave diminished as it approached, it became indistinguishable, lost. "Da Vinci is dead," he told her, then turned abruptly, and hurried through the scattered towels, and, "John?" she said, "John?" she kept calling after him, "John?"

DAUGHTER OF THE REVOLUTION

JOSEPH MCELROY

Joseph McElroy was born in Brooklyn, New York, in 1930. He is the author of six novels, including the forthcoming *Women and Men*. His stories have appeared in *The New Yorker*, *Antaeus*, *Grand Street*, and other magazines. He lives in New York City.

In the old sense of the word, Maureen seemed so sternly "gay" when we met at a swing in my building in late '75, so determined to say what she wanted you to do, and how and where and how fast and for how long—and again exactly how—since even moment-to-moment sex, let alone parenthood, takes planning nowadays—that her quite real tenderness hid itself away somewhere. It was like a spray of Baby's Breath that at first you hardly notice in a white room I remember—you, I—in a white china vase near white curtains, and in summertime. Her tenderness strangely rested inside the seeming strength of all that up-front explicitness and the strict feminist *management* of personal power equaling *discovery* of personal power—isn't that how her Leader's doctrine went? A spray of Baby's Breath was what she had in her hand in the elevator one morning, ensconced in dark-green tissue, and I didn't yet know this lovely girl with a beautiful leather knapsack on her back; and though she stood foursquare, doctrinally balanced on both feet—for, as I learned, she was into Kung Fu two evenings a week—her airy way kept her very light and she was scarcely in touch with the floor of the elevator rising, but "it" promised tenderness, what "it" was. She must have been taking those tiny buds of white bloom to her Leader, unless she was taking them for herself, to be with her while she was with her friend.

No doubt about how she came into my apartment the first time, the tenderness at last if not at first. She asked if my body was anesthetized. She found my giant Spanish table with the abandoned treadle built into its lower structure; and she found the brass bed (worth twelve hundred dollars) halfway polished as it stayed for two months; and she found the barstools at the breakfast nook, and found "all these books, Luce!" and found a square, delicate Harvard chair my father bought years after he had graduated and six months before he died, and a tall, noble Windsor chair my mother when she visits from Santa Fe sits in resolutely as if she would take it back, instead of me. Yes, Maureen came in and found my whole godawful history wound up between my shoulder and the root of my strong neck, when I was "dying" of cigarettes, smoking, *not* smoking. Tenderness? It lived in her fingertips when her mind was dreaming. Other times, hardly to be seen when she was talking power, her tenderness might have been nestling in the arms of her Leader.

Oh well, the German word is too close, and her Leader was even less fascist than some of those who are casually called fascist nowadays. When you've had a lover who was a political economist—a real love— you get fussy about such things. But who was more fussy than Maureen? —though I don't mean the sound of her voice coming, nor her saying not quite softly, "Go round and round in a very small circle, that's all, and then I'll tell you what happens after that." I mean about words: like "discrimination" could never mean deciding subtly between ideas; and "energy" could never be questioned, I mean as a word, because we all knew what it meant.

She showed me all over again that I had nipples. She found my feet as if I had lost them in their charge of tension. She told me how she had felt at ten wearing a T-shirt to school in Florida and getting sore. I mean she would talk about her body, the quality of her gums if she went a day without eating a grapefruit, the number of days she might go without taking a shit, how to brush your teeth (though one day when I thought What the hell, we'll talk about this, then—why she closed the subject as soon as I opened my mouth); the hint of past surplus along her lower back, the power feel of pubic hair growing back in, how her insteps felt when she came with a man, with a woman, or alone; or—but orgasm was good or better because of how *you* managed things. It came from the Leader's talk, though Maureen went always a bit further. I had known that I had nipples and in a sense I did not need to be reminded, and I speak of it here because sex for all the talk and activity in those years when the War was winding down and our aging parents, retired beyond climatic change, would rather not think about what was going on in our lives, and Mr. N. (wasn't it?) was in the Situation Room taping crises (though I have been told there are no situations, only people!), what I found coming for me from Maureen was not mainly sex, and so the lullaby of her hand on my chest—my breast—seemed mostly deeply loving, though it also turned me on.

I put this down in a notebook helter skelter like a letter, and why write words after all if not *to* somebody? Your other self, like another sex.

And if you believe, and even if the revolution had already happened, why not take your position with regard to other people: it may not mean they will take your advice, but they won't go running all over you—right, Maureen, dear? And so Maureen, in the last days of this that I am getting to, would urge me to take a workshop; would even tell me her adored Leader had advised the same, while I added that there are no neutral messages and why was Maureen carrying messages from that star-quality teacher (whom I already knew) to me?

Once I stayed in Maureen's apartment overnight—not what she wanted from me or from sex—and when I left early in the a.m. finding brief instructions on where to find a bag of whole-grain cereal and to drink from one of the jars of juice in the refrigerator rather than operate the juicer myself (as if I ever would have), I gave in to some silly tenderness of mine and left Maureen a note saying just, "Thanks, Maureen. You're lovely. I loved being here." And later in the day wondered if that was going too far.

In public the twice I involved myself in all that supposed openness, she was so noisy when she came, so joyfully hard in her spasmodic calls that she could have been being raped—it was like work, or it was too much like the high of a lunatic hooked on to what wasn't in the end known, though not the *un*known. But then with me one time she did come, came in all those quick breaths like contraction-control, then some soft long breaths even before she let go that last private wonder and laughed and I did, too, but I knew it was real and I had felt it in the muscles of her buttocks that must have been drained of all fatty tissue by lecithin or God knows what recent compound. But it wasn't me supposedly; it was her being (as the Leader said) responsible for her orgasm. Yet the Leader was something else, and I would not pretend to sum her up except that she enjoyed her life enormously and if she, as she used to say in her own famous words, "ran the fuck" (with whoever), and if it was a little on the olympic side of lust, she was fun and had preferred a long-distance variety of body-trips to the usual.

I put this down in a notebook but why write words after all if not *to* someone? Which is anesthesia? Which is waking truth? There came a day when I thought all I wanted was Maureen's well-being. She came in to see me on her way home, for she was by then living in the building—

not because I lived there, but because her Leader did. And she said she had had a date with this guy out in Brooklyn—well, the Heights, which is not "out" so much as over the Bridge—and he had lived there since his mother had dropped him out of the carriage on his head on a curb of Garden Place in about 1935; and when I said, Did it go okay, and Maureen said, I gave him what *he* wanted, and he gave me what he was *able* to, I laughed and said, But that happens with women, too. But Maureen said, Oh Luce, you take things too personally, you work too hard, you're afraid of Pleasure, you're work-addicted, you go so far but not far enough.

I know, I know, I said, I've heard all that before, but you can't see that work's a chosen pleasure, because you and your mother-superior have discovered that some people get baffled and anxious when they're having a ball.

Maureen got mad, called me compulsive, work-addicted—

—That's *you*, I said.

—compulsively lazy, she said—and I felt close but left out, then. And it came to me as if I had left it and come back to it—an idea as solid as a silver money-clip (we do not (we have decided not to) carry bills in our wallets any more)—that what I wanted from Maureen was her well-being.

But in the excitement of those days, I did not shrug off all that blind talk of addiction, and though Maureen might say I was work-addicted and, as with my nipples and my recently very hard-rubbed scalp, had not yet begun to discover my body, I would hook into the provincial evangelism of their thinking and remonstrate angrily that addictions were not all the same, and being in love was not a cocaine habit (which Maureen's Leader did not have but used—can you use a habit?—experimenting with that eight-foot-tall snuff ground out of that particular hard-to-capture mountain of our mind first thing in the morning to test its effect on her work, which I tried (pissed off) to point out to Maureen apparently did not come under the category of addiction). And before she could take the chance to speak, I went on, as if I didn't want to keep her on the spot, and said Freedom was the issue of course but addiction was such a third-rate way to reduce it, and she should let some of the poets tell her "Isn't it time our loving freed/us from the one we love."

Because there had to be some use in my having had a brief horrendous affair with a young German writer who wrote obliquely about New York City taking liberties with the street-geography on the north margin of the Pan American Building, but spoke to me unforgettable lines of German poetry as courteously in translation as generous toward the English translators; amazingly generous, if you think about it. Meanwhile, Maureen told me that I should not put myself down calling my talk confused except that sometimes I did not answer the question with the information asked for, which was partly not Sharing (I capitalize it in my mind), and partly not loving myself enough to keep my attention on the thing asked for.

But once I found in a scrap of diary of Maureen's those very lines written as prose and ascribed admiringly to *me*, so that I could have added what "happens" next except I would have gained only the honesty of admitting I'd been here reading her stuff, which was mostly second-hand from her beloved workshop-Leader who had changed Maureen from (I'd seen the photos) a fulsome Miss America catatonically walking through boyfriends and boozy hotel clubs with dark rustling dancefloors —to anyway someone who was physically a marvel and mentally at least determined to save herself, if side by side with her Leader, who was herself changing before *my* eyes though I could never easily speak of that woman to Maureen—except admiringly.

I have written down what she looked like, and my words are surprisingly good, though no more worth recalling than a hundred details attended to in the course of my week administering a hospital, or a vital part of its work, going round in circles yet despite the relation of nurse to doctor a strong feminist fiber there in the strength of the women, so many women, working there, even if too often administering dubious medications prescribed as simply as a springy intern-priest accepts his relation to a tough, middle-aged nurse-nun—nephew to aunt in the ongoing patriarchy.

Maureen was definitely beautiful in the clothes she made for herself— right down to a lovely pale suede suit (almost Western) and linen shirts sewn so invisibly you could find the patterns of that instinctive knowledge in the thoughtfulness of Maureen's hands touching yours or folding together to brace herself when she did a magical headstand that made the room all except me fall away, the walls opening but not into the other apartments of the building.

Her face, even when some blood beneath it paled, could carry forth saffron perfume of color, half faintly tanned, half flowering coral, half in turn recalling childish freckles that might have begun beneath the light of one summer's sun but scarcely took hold. The eyes were like the cheekbones, don't ask me how, some width of hope and freshness stunned toward a fixity of purpose adopted from outside herself. Tall, narrow, leaner and leaner, with the softest wide mouth and the most dynamically drawn feet, arched inward and upward, toes somewhat spaced as if she went barefoot, and she would ask, actually, to have her big toe rubbed and rubbed in a circular motion—her model and guide and Leader used other people's big toes to give herself an orgasm.

I have written down what Maureen looked like. Her eyes were brown with blue flecks; her hair, never dyed like that of her Leader, but for months shorn to the bone so it reminded you not of someone getting into touch with a living and beautiful head but of a model I saw strolling the autumn streets of Napoleon's birthplace in Corsica totally bald with, evidently, a lover, who looked like a male model, yet in that sculptured skull a victim and later I thought, "A victim of the century in general."

Maureen said, "Power," when I asked her what she wanted. Over whom, I asked—over which Indians? I asked, cornily remembering her Peace Corps work and her trips back to the Southwest where she had once been an Army child and might speak now of how the padres had practically halved the population of the Pueblo Indians by bringing in measles, no wonder they needed those mission churches to get those poor, measles-ridden, smallpoxed native Americans in out of that powerful light.

I knew Maureen when she worked for a bank, a giant bank, *the* bank (if such a structure has a name) (Oh Luce, you're living in your head again!) (Oh God, Maureen—) (Oh Goddess, Luce, okay?) (Okay, Oh Goddess, Maureen, you're the one living inside your head, I'm just a person) (Oh, there you go again, Luce, saying "just" to minimize yourself). Her immediate superior called her in. And soon after she was promoted to a position of considerable responsibility handling Eurodollar accounts, called her in to "discuss" the garlic smell that came like smoke signals all morning from her breath. Garlic *therapy*, garlic *therapy*, and did you read about the old nut whose five-mornings-a-week bus driver wouldn't take him anymore and he sued the company, it was in New Jersey, so it isn't just women.

And in not quitting for twelve more months, Maureen later said she had not been in touch with her anger (I smiled) or with the fascist implications of (Listen, dear, the garlic is Good, your problem is you're not high enough up in the bank and probably not even a man could ever be that high) (You're doing a smoke-screen number on me, Luce, did you know that?) (No, honey, you got to get up into the abstract, that's the echelon where garlic don't matter no more) but a tear came into my eye because I thought, People matter, and the clients matter even if they turn away and don't dig the odor of garlic because their nosebuds spent too long in the smokehouse and never felt deep earthsmoke, and Maureen matters, Maureen matters.

She was the girl, the woman, I had stood with coming up in the elevator more than once—months before meeting her (such is the intimacy of apartment houses)—hearing the elevator coming apart until the current super told me one day not to worry, it was the slack in the cables rattling. But that day, it rattled like wind in a house and Maureen, whose name I didn't know, had a spray of Baby's Breath in a cone of green paper in one hand, a knapsack on her back, an odd sweet smell like a foreign food that could never go bad—and I said, "Baby's Breath, aren't they?" and Maureen smiled like a Midwestern girl and nodded but didn't say anything, perhaps feeling me too close or finding nothing in the way of words demanded of her at that instant. Baby's Breath delicate flourish of snowdrop flowers.

I wanted to hold her, just as I also wanted to hold her down or shut her up sometimes—oh damn me, did she really talk much except in dogmatic speeches at intervals? And later I wanted to hold her back, because she followed her beloved Leader but always went too far. To where she wasn't following her beloved Leader anymore, but herself, however you do that. Yet still purchased Baby's Breath, for that day in the elevator while she was going to see her beloved guide she was bearing those flowers for herself as well.

Later I heard that a group of workshop friends, some strong hilarious resourceful women who had long since seen that complaining in words establishes a historical record that can stand in place of doing something, planned a fairy-tale game of sorts which would subject the next man who entered that famous apartment to rape—"light rape," but overwhelming and thorough but "good" rape.

I did not ask what this would amount to, because I saw the apartment in question visited for so many hours a day of every week by the friends of the Leader. This person ran around doing neat somersaults usually with nothing on, listened like the most shrewdly attentive mother to the person behind the story, and made tea but had long since stopped making meals and bringing them out of that kitchen into her large, furnitureless salon.

Rape? I thought, participating in some distant part of my body. And imagined that Maureen was taking too far some trial balloon raised by our friend like Energy levels of a roomful of loving friends rapping or massaging—for that woman was *my* friend, too.

Rape? I thought. "Rape?" I said; "I don't believe it." "You're thinking just like a man, Luce," said Maureen. "Thanks," I said; "wouldn't our friend take that as a compliment?" Maureen blew up at me in some confusion and left me where I stood—not really on two feet the way you were supposed to stand, rather slouching a little on one hip, but frozen in my maturity by her exit.

For a few months, in those days of '76, the answer to the "power" question was money. As it still is, a year later, and was in the days of those great castle-women of Europe Maria di so-and-so, Marguerite of somewhere, who handled such power in their hilltown bastions with or without a consort that I would have worked for them in a minute, and gave orders with an ease that Maureen's Leader might approach only with humor, standing in her fantastic plastic boots at the advent of a taxi and ordering Maureen and Cliff—a curious assistant *he* was—to get into the cab first. Then the answer to the power question proved in other days quite steadily to be "Self-sexual," where even without a job's money or success (but don't assume you ever have one without the other) you can work on your body and be whatever you want to be sexually and find that the goddess was always in you (even, as I pointed out to Maureen, in that part of you that persisted in not knowing the goddess was inside you because where you're coming from is very important to where you wind up) (No, said Maureen, that was not correct because to dwell in where you came from was to get back into the past, and who cares if you thought when you were a kid that you didn't have dreams when you were asleep) (To which I responded that I didn't know where *that* was coming from but) (Maureen said it was some friend of a friend of our mutual friend the Leader who had told Maureen that she was convinced it was possible *not* to dream asleep but that something had to give somewhere and this man might have unusual powers flowing out of or into the void of those dreamless nights.) (Some such bull, I didn't say.) And yet a lot of outside information was making life quite interesting in those days of late '76, early '77 when I found myself loving Maureen, wanting to hold her, to rock her (which she liked), knowing though that I must also not lose myself in this love for her, loving the charm in how she talked the helpful, oversimplified dogmas of her guide, whose own attitudes seemed less extreme—who sometimes liked men, I mean; the Leader shrugged off her own rigidity about blocking the transverse colon and blocking the labyrinthine (my word) progress of the goddess in the circulation of the soul, or about the locked pelvis vis-à-vis our capacity to manufacture self-negative meat acids within our systems even when we were good upstanding vegetarians (though fruitarians—interestingly the position Maureen arrived at just before her departure—was going too far). Information, did I say? Its flow among us larded surely by mystical fictions put us more on the lookout for it. But the Leader, herself by various accounts one-sixteenth, one-eighth, and one-thirty-second Indian, had a list of women chiefs back in the seventeenth and eighteenth centuries and a goddess known as "Our Grandmother" who really had created the universe and had told the winds to treat Indian women as if they were the winds' sisters and if the women pulled their skirts up to their waists to frighten clouds away, the winds must not stare at their naked nethers; but the Leader had once humorously told of dreaming a reincarnation of herself as a Navachoor Prince who had actually met "Our Grandmother" and dickered with her about obtaining for men a standing with her like that she accorded women.

But what was happening? There was the Leader's career, shifting week to week—not so much in those public appearances and visiting workshops where she helped women to understand that they were not isolated or freaky or mean in their needs, as, rather, in projects that came and went, an article in a magazine here, a newspaper piece there, and of course misrepresentation as a sex fiend or female segregationist or male impersonator by the mainly male press even when the piece was by a woman. Shit, she said, she liked people.

And Maureen? Why what was the matter with me that I fell in love with that girl? that legionnaire, that nutritional scientist of the Great Change (let's not say "revolution" because the corporations go on pricing us up, up, into the echelons of their abstract intuition of American futures), that handmaiden of the Goddess whom I of all people (because the Leader was not available that day) had taken to the clinic where she had her first abortion (feminist in clarity as in its experimental source) and it went from her with that distantly gross plummet of flush, that explosion so that any person, man or woman, might be afraid, hearing it from the next room—as if something else got sucked out too, like your last ovary or your Little (i.e., lower) Heart or five laps of lower intestine, sucked out maybe more subtly as in a promising new trick of cataract-removal, and as scientifically as Maureen, at a swing controlled the accessibility of her ovaries by pleasure-committed breath-transcendence or a self-induced temporary infertility, *pill*-free of *course* but no diaphragm, which is not for beginners! Maureen? She left the bank, of course.

And she left her apartment (clean break, not even a legal sublet) in Greenwich Village, and now when you saw her in the elevator she was traveling to or from her own apartment, often from it to her Leader's with a large cloudy Mason jar or a wooden salad bowl home-covered with foil. She had given her Leader all her savings becoming thereby (I hoped for *her* sake) a partner in enterprises both multiplying and amalgamating under the Leader's name—therapeutic, media, even clothing.

Maureen became a leader of the building when the landlord had dragged his heels. There were interesting chips of the upper brick facing that had begun to fall down onto the street and sidewalk first thing in the morning and late in the afternoon and a newspaperman I had known some years before who had moved back into the building was reported to have told a fellow tenant who announced classical music on a small but surviving radio station who had told it to his wife's lawyer also living in the building who had told it to *his* wife, who told it to me in the incredible basement laundry (with its underwear-shredding dryer) and back to its *original* source (who told *my* source that it was better than what he had originally said) that the Housing Authority (postponing for a week its inspection visit) agreed with the landlord in the theory that, somewhere between those upper facings of the building and the sidewalk that was in danger of coming up to meet the aforementioned chips, the chips had become arrested in mid-air and would continue so until the landlord received word of Housing Authority action on the tenant report.

Also, the boiler had gushed oil, driving into the normally foodless laundry room two or three rats the size of large weasels. Maureen held a meeting, then another. I loved her. There were deranged ladies who had so little surface left in their anciently rent-controlled apartments they had to live on their upper walls or on the ceiling, and they came to one meeting or the other to ascertain whether they could be evicted, and one out of four of them was willing to withhold rent. Maureen retained a young woman lawyer we both knew who would not take a fee at first; and Maureen established an escrow account at the nearest branch of the giant bank until recently her employer. She had about one-quarter of the tenants with her.

Her Leader was for buying the building and turning it into a self-healing, self-supporting community; but the building was not for sale. The Leader promised that the following month she would begin withholding rent but had heard that our landlord had introduced rats into another building on the other side of town to get rid of his almost exclusively elderly female tenants. The radio announcer's wife's lawyer, commenting on the radio announcer's "rats the size of weasels," said weasels were what we *needed* since they *ate* rats. A leak days after a snowstorm descended down one "line" of apartments from the top floor to Maureen's and stained a magically colored Near-Eastern woven mat during the night and when her bathroom ceiling came down one afternoon while as if by the same token five tenant-complaint calls from unemployed elderly female tenants were recorded on her machine all while she was out picking up four crates of small, dark, non-toxically grown oranges shipped from her native Florida to an organic outlet practically next door to an Italian restaurant where our landlord was a known patron, she handed over the chairpersonhood to a young man with a rare dog on the second floor who checked security twice each night and had found the doorman once across the street at a deli waiting for a Western sandwich; and Maureen withdrew her escrow rentmoney and spent it on redecorating her bathroom and withdrew from the tenants' association at a time, incidentally, when a real estate broker living in the building had found out that two, maybe three apartments had been sold to their mainly absentee tenants through some loophole that did not entail co-oping the building or not as yet, and one of these new owners worked at a foundation housed uptown in a French Renaissance delight crazily encrusted with terra cotta mazes. Maureen was up front about all these things that she did.

As about organizing the messengers. When this unofficial union proved to include only one woman, a Cambodian aristocrat who did secretarial work on a hot typewriter and other business in a mainland Chinese haberdashery surprisingly near the aforementioned foundation plus her qualifying messenger stints on a hot bike that was less of a liability since serial numbers don't function in the bike-turnover world, Maureen wished the group well and excused herself just at a time when the original inspiration for this group of primarily retarded messengers, a black kid with amazingly large, out-of-control teeth, had discovered that he was being exploited by a man who had infiltrated a small theater group because he believed it was a front for some bloody escapade to do with Latin-American politics and the clandestine history of a middle-Atlantic newspaper family, and the black kid had tried in vain to get free of this entrepreneur, and did not speak easily but could communicate with Maureen.

The night she ended her affiliation with the messenger union, she and I sat all evening in my apartment. I was happy knowing she was content to sit and read. I looked up from my chair and she did not raise her eyes. She was reading, not meditating. And it was not just the book that kept her from looking up to meet my look. It was me. And at first I thought it was a me she took for granted as a sometime lover. Then I guessed she did not look up because she did not have quite enough faith that I had become the person she loved. I did not believe, like her Leader, that most men secretly wanted to wear garter belts and black silk stockings; I did not believe that the sins of the Catholic Church stained the glass at Chartres, I did not believe Saint Joan less or more a woman for having waged war, I did not believe that medication was a global male-doctors' plot, I did not believe that women ejaculate the same way as men, nor that a fruitarian diet lengthens a man's ejaculatory range if range is what one is after; I did not believe there was a Goddess but I did not say so to Maureen, in whose very body and feelings I sometimes felt myself so firmly lodged that I couldn't tell if I was stalled in some place of romance where to stay is to be nowhere, or was doubled or reincarnate in her, which I also would not announce to her except as an impersonal principle, and she agreed, convinced the miracle was open to anyone who could participate in the Goddess. Freedom is not sobriety but sobriety is freedom, the Leader had said after an all-night body-trip (with parallel— in her "case" multiple—orgasms for both but without penetration by her one-on-one visitor), an Irish monk touring American population centers in quest of funds for his remote foundation, trouble-shooting too: sobriety itself might mean no highs; but booze went down not up, and there were potential highs non-addictive-related, said the I-have-to-confess luminous and warm-hearted Leader to the workshop-ready Eirean—so the Irish certainly weren't *wrong* . . .

There came a night when Maureen and I were supposed to get together. I was so near her now that I entertained some insane idea of moving out of this building that I basically loved. I had sensed the day before that Maureen could call our evening off. I had so braced myself for this that, neck-knots, instep-tension, pelvic lock-cramp aside, I was worse off than if I had been a militant Lesbian nonetheless doctrinally devoted to no-attachments, which would be pretty hard in an already terrible world.

I had thought there was something between us besides the Void. Within twenty-four hours it was distance.

No response from Maureen's apartment. Phone, doorbell, housephone (though I did not tell the doorman who it was I was buzzing).

Meditation? I wondered. Something gentle. An unplanned fast. A sprouts study-weekend in Massachusetts with the Leader. But I received a call, then, from the Leader, which wasn't too strange but was part of what happened.

They had become too close, she said. Maureen had turned our mutual friend into a priestess or mother; and separation was indicated. She sat near me, her legs crossed, a sheen of body-glow lifting free from the curves of her excellent skin, the eyes friendly and attentive to me while it was she who spoke. Maureen had bonded. She had to go. She knew it but had to be told. She nodded and nodded, the Leader reported, all through the announcement, nodded and expressionlessly wept. There is a gap here—but who is it between? It must have been sad for both of them. She had been a sister-lover, then a mother to Maureen, who would always go purely too far like a scientist doing basic research around and around the clock. The Leader had been all things to Maureen, with whom she didn't like to, literally, "sleep," though spent many a night with Maureen in rap, and illuminated by the Goddess and her messages to all who had learned true history: which is feeling repressed underground to flow in circles or into others unknown to it (or them) maybe; the repression of feeling, hence fact, and invitation to addiction, hence imprisoning fantasy—a patterning of habit (the words mine or doubtless someone else's maybe—do I not make sense?—or not originally *any-one's*)—the escape from which (I'm boring my*self*) is both the periodic revolution in your life or, for the Leader, "hopefully" to find a habit of constant self-loving evolution (her words!) that is pattern each time until you almost see it, and right then it shifts: a drug analogy, I thought, as if the Leader was addicted to Change.

Maureen, I saw, had opened the door thinking to adventure into some earth of science, of agriculture, of healing; but at the last moment she turned around (if not back) for Grace Kimball, our Leader, a pretty well-known name by now. But she was asking—as she never asked of me—only to see Grace was still there. And she *was*. And in the same apartment that she and her ex had lived in until once upon a time she "left" *him*. And she is there, when Maureen turns. There like light. There, though, only to then say to the poor follower who thought she sought power, "I am not here for you. You were going out the door. That's good, dear. Really good."

"I gave you what you were able to ask for," she said one time—because (as I tried to tell her) I prefer body or deeper signals to voicing my heart-blood's Asking via the short-order sex-by-menu that turned honest lust into a strange fashion of honesty. "You gave me what you could," she concluded. As if I were that person she said the same thing to in a brownstone in Brooklyn when he invited her over to view from his windows those national celebrations in the harbor during the late summer of last year.

But I had found with her that I needn't be a cynic, and not even after she left me, having probably never been with me; for I had not even thought to be sour about prospects, life, and so forth, while I was for a period of months turned toward Maureen. What did the poet say?— Grace and her crowd do not trust old or new books of passion, they make up their own something or other. And what did the poet say? I know he was not my lover but I know some words of his all over me yet even as I set out to say them and am struck dumb and can only point to them because I have really and truly (believe me) come up to those words but as I say can only point to them, meeting them, and having made them mine, say them in my own way: so whatever I do I have the look of leaving. Living is leaving. For *work,* say!

Is that too sad to be anything but romantic-addictive-ultimately-sex-negative? I knew a prostitute who would not name her price ever, but would take what she was given. Is that Sex Negative or Sex Revolutionary? SN? or SR? Abbreviations recall the hospital newsletter I create each month.

I decided on a certain new type of workshop Grace Kimball told me she was starting. She said she would go back to the other workshops with regret because Maureen had helped her so much and often run them on her own, though some of the women said it wasn't the same as when Grace ran them.

Maureen had a mother in Florida. A father, too. She went to Florida and lived at about equal distances from her parents and from her brother, who was the most agreeable soul in the world and would sit with Maureen for hours, or do a yoga trip; they explored enema therapy by the book, by the machine (which might be like a Hollywood chocolate factory for all I know), and by Life/Sibling experience, and I heard through Grace that for a while it was nip and tuck whether Maureen would go into Enema professionally instead of that other amazing land of foot massage that made even me a believer right down to my toes through one of which a Japanese "sister" once divined that I had had a persistent kidney infection when I was younger and more vulnerable.

Maureen returned to me by parcel post my notebook, with all these things in it. She had always urged me to quit the hospital and write full-time.

I get abstract and vague. I didn't so much find something out as found myself *in* something. Well, there's a lot of this kind of talk going around these days and I kept it to myself.

You can't give me what I want, she said in the honesty of these recent days; but that's okay, Luce, she said. Was I a man or a woman to her?

What I never knew quite well enough even in the honesty of our arms freely finding each other was that her need was not for what she said: and my desire, if it had passed into her life easily and received, would have given her what she hadn't known she wanted or was it at that time a turning?—some slight curve of a long turning from that life she had found away from the mother who ruled without ruling and, I gathered but only from Grace's hearsay, did not much love Maureen but did not let her know; and turning from her life in New York—which had ensued upon her tour with the Peace Corps in South America in the late sixties (never talked about except as wonderful harsh landscape, and only if I insisted on Maureen sharing some information beyond the foreground of her abandoned banking "trip").

But her love for Grace became the power behind what we would discuss. And I could get puzzled—even by what Maureen said about my notebook when she sent it back—puzzled by having seen the Leader she followed in her and through her, when in fact that very visible Leader was between us: until I saw that it was me blocking the view and the view was of my future. And in the middle of one night, with Maureen's words working in me, working away by dark, I found myself imagining that man they had known of who was supposed to have never had a night dream (what was his name? it went unmentioned), while Grace advanced the theory—but I was not awake . . . I was dreaming pretty accurately stuff I already knew.

I had this letter from her. Not worth salvaging. From Maureen, that is.

I had a dream of being a merman. And in it, that man reappeared, who does not dream, and I thought I once knew him or his wife. I woke knowing it to be true. And that dreams are what they lead to.

Of my notebook, or the part I asked her to read, knowing she would read only that—she said, "Luce, you could see both sides. The man's and the woman's. In fact a million sides sometimes. That's a problem."

It occurred to me that she might not have read even what I had asked.

I pointed out to Grace Kimball that in wanting to be a "top," a business, a (God! a) vagina that is much more than a subtly hooded cock and its patient balls (lower extension of, i.e. shape of, outer lips), and claims to ejaculate, and in sashaying around like a boy trying to look like a man or whatever I am trying to say, Grace was further confusing what a woman is. She said I might be right, but so what?, she had seriously considered how she might have a child by Maureen. She laughed, then, and disappeared into her kitchen to bring me some tea. She was talking about the neglected asshole and how she would like to raise its status. She said she felt more comfortable with some gay men than some women she could name. She had a habit of listening that made you feel she was right there with you—closer still—beyond closeness—and eyes much warmer than all her absolute talk re:eye contact could do for me. She emerged with my mug, her warm, wonderfully healthy body some-how covered, though not by the mug and not by sweatpants or sporty camisole, not a stitch. ("Mother provider, hostess house-mouse, that's me!") She asked if I wanted to go into business with her. The phone was ringing and it was her mother hundreds of miles away, oh more than a thousand, who was speaking to Grace again after not speaking for several chilly months—and they were laughing and hollering—at least I assume her mother was, too.

One day, Maureen phoned me and I knew who it was before I stepped free of the blue jeans I was getting out of when the phone rang; and knowing who it was, I knew I would never be bloodless and so never without whatever was in that bloodstream, whatever smoke or worm or liquor of future. And taking the receiver and drawing it close to my ear and my mouth, I realized that I didn't see Maureen as a victim anymore.

THE CROW WOMAN

STEVE HELLER

Steve Heller grew up in Yukon, Oklahoma, where "The Crow Woman" is set. He now lives with his wife and two sons in Manhattan, Kansas, where he is Assistant Professor of English at Kansas State University. His first book of stories, *The Man Who Drank a Thousand Beers*, was published in 1984 by Chariton Review Press. This is his second appearance in the O. Henry collection.

Frank Kellerman was losing his son.

Losing him, Kellerman knew, as surely as the soft, breezy Oklahoma autumn of 1961 was hardening into winter. Losing him to something vague but sinister, a force Kellerman did not understand and, more importantly, could not control. Something he could not even see—except in the peculiar, disturbing behavior of his son.

At the age of twelve Curly seemed to have stopped growing, stopped maturing. Puberty was just around the corner, Kellerman knew, but instead of sprouting into an awkward, aggressive adolescent, Curly seemed to be frozen in childhood. In fact, as cold November winds began to blow from the north, sweeping over the plowed wheat fields just beyond Kellerman's five acres, stripping leaves off the maple and redbud trees, Curly seemed to be *regressing*—a word Kellerman had picked up from a psychologist Hugh Downs was interviewing on the *Today* show. *Regression,* the psychologist explained, meant going back, reverting to an earlier pattern of behavior. Kellerman stared over his morning coffee at the image on the small black and white TV resting on the kitchen counter. The psychologist was talking about some rats he kept in a box, but a moment after Kellerman heard the definition he leaped from his chair with the explosive energy of sudden recognition.

"That's *it!*" he cried to Babe. "That's what's happening to the boy—he's regressing."

"You make a better door than you do a window," Babe said, setting her cup on the table and leaning sideways to see around Kellerman to the maze the TV psychologist was pointing to with a stick.

Kellerman took a step to his left and heaved an impatient sigh. "Don't you *see?* Curly's going back—behaving like he did when he was younger."

Babe looked up at him and rolled her eyes. Babe was a plump woman in her late thirties, with a firm jaw and heavy bosom. Her expression and bearing conveyed a sense of weight, of an object immovable, out of proportion to her actual size. Rolling her eyes seemed to express something far more substantial, a great shifting of volume, like an ocean liner rising a few inches with a wave. Her slightest gesture had its effect on Kellerman, and often she could elate or dismiss him simply by raising an eyebrow. This time, however, she felt compelled to speak.

"The boy's not a rat, Frank."

Kellerman fell a step backward, as if the force of her words had struck him like a well-timed jab to the chin. "Nobody's calling him a rat," he sputtered, feeling slightly disoriented from the blow. "All I'm trying to do is find an explanation for the way the boy's been acting. The man on the TV's not talking about rats; he's talking about people."

In truth, Kellerman himself did not understand very much of what the psychologist was saying. Kellerman was an electrician on the building maintenance crew at the state capitol in Oklahoma City. It was a twenty-five-minute drive east to the capitol from Kellerman's five acres near the small farm town of Yukon. The day shift didn't start until eight, and Kellerman liked to have breakfast with his wife and son and catch the first few minutes of the *Today* show before starting off for work. Today was Friday and Curly wasn't up yet. Kellerman was going to be late—but that was the least of his problems.

Babe shook her head. "It's your problem more than his. You shouldn't make such a big deal out of it. The boy's all right; let things take their natural course."

"Natural course!" Kellerman glared at her. "The boy's talking to *birds*, goddamn it. Sparrows, crows, pigeons, hawks—I've see him."

Babe let out a long sigh. "He loves animals. He used to talk to them all the time."

Kellerman threw his hands up in the air. "That's what I *mean*, damn it. He used to do it, when he was six or seven. Now he's doing it again. It's the goddamn Crow Woman; I know it. Ever since I told him to stay away from her he's been regressing."

Babe shrugged in a way that told Kellerman the conversation was over.

She turned back toward the TV. Kellerman clenched his teeth, then crossed in front of Babe and headed toward Curly's bedroom.

He found Curly still buried under the covers, pretending to be sick. Kellerman yanked off the blanket and sheet.

"Rise and shine, son."

The boy drew his knees up under his chin and moaned, a pitiful, obviously faked moan. *Regression*, Kellerman thought, remembering the way Curly used to fake being sick to avoid the stern classroom of Mrs. Beauchamp, his fourth grade teacher. Curly was in the seventh grade now, and this was the fifth day in a row he'd pretended to be sick.

"Come on," Kellerman said sharply, but grabbed the boy's shoulders with gentle strength, shaking him just hard enough to let the boy know he wasn't buying any of it. "Come on, let's go."

"I don't feel good," Curly complained, but rolled slowly out of bed and started to pull on his blue jeans.

"Where's your pajamas?" Kellerman asked.

"I don't feel good in pajamas."

Another regression. When he was seven Curly used to claim his pajamas choked him, that he couldn't breathe inside the cotton. Babe had let him sleep in just his underwear for a year. On Curly's eighth birthday Kellerman had given him an official Mickey Mantle Little League baseball bat and pinstriped pajamas that looked like a real New York Yankee uniform. He'd slept in pajamas every night since then—until now.

Kellerman said nothing and watched the boy finish dressing. He didn't have to watch; he knew Babe would see to it Curly was dressed and fed in time to catch the school bus into Yukon, as she had every morning this week. He knew his wife and son were both waiting for him to leave for work, that the boy's "illness" was really a symptom of his father's presence, that everything would be all right as soon as Frank Kellerman stepped out the door. Curly would return home from school this afternoon feeling just fine, ready to run off and play down by the creek, where Kellerman had always—except for one regrettable time—left him alone. There would be no more talk of sickness until Monday morning, when Kellerman would once again try to get Curly up in time so the three of them could have breakfast together before he left for the capitol. No more talk of sickness, though the boy would be sure to avoid him all weekend, as he had for nearly a month now, since the day the boy changed.

Kellerman bit his lip as he watched Curly silently button his shirt. He still didn't understand *why* his son had changed, but he certainly knew *when.*

"What's bothering you, son?" Kellerman blurted. "Are you still mad at me about the Crow Woman?"

The boy looked at Kellerman blankly for a moment, then bent down to lace his tennis shoes. *Mad,* Kellerman knew, was too weak a word to describe what his son was probably feeling, but Kellerman didn't want to think about what the right word might be.

He sighed, then turned and left the room while Curly tied his shoes. "He's up," Kellerman said to Babe in the kitchen.

Babe nodded, then seeing Kellerman just standing there, looked up again. Her voice was soft. "It's not really so hard to understand, Frank. We're four miles north of town—there isn't another boy or girl Curly's age within two miles. You took away the only friend he had around here. His only playmate. It's natural he resents you for it."

Kellerman glared at her. "I don't want no sixty-year-old crazy woman thinks she's a *bird* playing with my boy! I had to do it—and you know it."

Babe blinked noncommittally. "You're just going to have to give him time to get over it."

Kellerman stared through the back screen door toward the brown, freshly plowed wheat fields that bordered his five acres. "Time? It's been a month now—how much more time does he need? And what am I supposed to do in the meantime—watch him talk to the goddamn birds in the trees?"

Babe shrugged. "I think the boy'll be all right."

Kellerman closed his eyes, then opened them. He nodded, grabbed his jacket off the counter beside the TV, and kicked open the screen door.

Babe called after him: "Don't you want some eggs or something?"

The yard was a luminous gold in the cool morning light, and quiet. Kellerman glared up at a line of black birds flying by overhead, then hurried on toward the car. The Hudson was parked on the gravel drive that curled around behind the two-story woodframe house. The only other structures on the property were Kellerman's five hundred gallon propane tank, which rested like a miniature submarine in dry dock about thirty feet north of the house, and an old one-room limestone schoolhouse that stood another fifty feet beyond the tank. The schoolhouse was his private workshop, the place he could go to work and forget his family problems and the bullshit he had to take at the capitol. The schoolhouse was his sanctuary; no one ever bothered him there—except the Crow Woman.

Before getting into the Hudson he searched the area around the schoolhouse with his eyes, checking the propane tank and the line of maple trees next to the fence that separated his five acres from Orville Zucha's wheat fields. He saw no sign of the Crow Woman and wondered hopefully if his latest threat had finally convinced Orville to lock the old loony bird away. He doubted it; threats had never worked in the past. Nothing had worked.

Kellerman shuddered as he remembered the very first time he had seen her: Ten years ago now, just a few weeks after he'd bought the place. He looked up and saw her peeking into the schoolhouse at him through the south window—her gray shrunken face cocked slightly, one black eye watching him like a scavenger bird eyeing a corpse. He jumped and nearly sliced his finger on the lawn mower blade he was sharpening. Before he could move again she puffed her chest and made a startling sound: a hoarse, moaning cry that sounded like something dying. It shook him like an unexpected peal of thunder. By the time he got outside she had vanished.

"You hear that?" he asked Babe when he reached the house.

Her back to him at the sink, she turned slowly, giving no sign of concern. Curly sat on the tile floor, playing with some blocks. "Hear what?" Babe said.

"That sound a minute ago."

"All I heard was a crow."

He called the police, as much for his own sanity as anything else. Big Bob Swanda was Chief of Police in Yukon in those days.

"The Zuchas should have warned you about Mabel before you bought that place," Swanda said. "You'd better have yourself a talk with Orville."

Kellerman's mouth opened slightly as he pulled the phone away from his ear and stared at the receiver. Orville Zucha had sold him the five acres, house and schoolhouse included, for two thousand dollars. Not a bad price in 1951. Orville was a big square-headed wheat farmer in blue overalls and a gray striped cap. He lived half a mile east, down a narrow dirt road, in one of the shabbiest houses around. Kellerman took him for a dumb Polack, and at two thousand the property seemed a steal.

"Mabel? Mabel who?" Kellerman barked into the phone. "*What* should Orville have told me?"

The voice on the phone sounded muffled, as if Bob Swanda were stifling a laugh. "Mabel Zucha," Swanda said finally. "Orville's mother. She's a sweet lady, really, 'cept for one thing—she thinks she's a bird."

Kellerman's lips parted again, and he remembered the rasping sound the old woman made at the window.

"A crow," Kellerman said.

"What?"

"Babe thought she made a noise like a crow."

"You could say that," Swanda agreed. "Fact is, folks around here call her the Crow Woman."

"Christ on a crutch. Why doesn't Orville put her in a home or something?"

"He keeps her locked in the house most of the time," Swanda said. "His wife looks out after Mabel while he's farming, but sometimes she gets out."

Kellerman sighed. "Well, fine. What's it all got to do with me?"

"Nothing—except you just bought her roost."

"Her what?"

"Her roost—the place she goes when she's on the wing, so to speak. You really don't know anything about Mabel?"

Kellerman bit the inside of his lower lip until it hurt. "I'm listening, ain't I?"

The police chief cleared his throat. "You ought to hear the whole story then. Call up Horace Loudermilk. He was there when most of it happened."

"When what happened?"

"That old schoolhouse of yours is over a hundred years old. Used to be Spring Creek School, only school in this part of the county. Lot of folks around here went to school there; used to be the only public building for miles. Well, Mabel was one of them. Her maiden name's Kolar. Parents come over from Bohemia; you know, the real place in Czechoslovakia. They made the run that opened up this part of the Indian Territory in eighty-nine. Had three boys, every one of them killed in the First World War. And Mabel. I don't know if it's true, but they say she was born on the first day of the century." Kellerman heard Swanda take a deep breath. "I don't know; maybe Mabel would have turned out different if any of her brothers had lived to take care of her. Ask Horace; he can tell you."

Horace Loudermilk was the unofficial historian for the town of Yukon. He lived on a farm just north of the Canadian River next to actor Dale Robertson's horse ranch, the Rocking R. *It was me named her the Crow*

Woman, Horace said when Kellerman called. *It was her eyes put me in mind of a crow—round and cold black, like you could see deep inside her head if you just looked close enough. But nobody did. Look her in the face and she'd stare you down with them black eyes like a crow eyeballin' you from a tree. I don't think she meant nothin' by it, but it made us boys uneasy. So we teased her with snakes and rats and dead armadillos. It was just our meanness made us do it. She was just a little bit of a girl, and we wanted to see her bawl, wanted to see them black eyes fill up with tears. Well, we teased her and teased her till she got jumpy like a ground squirrel and wouldn't look none of us in the eye no more—but I don't believe I ever did see her cry.*

Only boy let her alone was Hubert Zucha—and he was plain crazy. One day when he was twelve he decided he was a catfish—that's right, a catfish—jumped into the river and tried to feed right off the bottom. Took four of us to haul him up on a sand bar and pump out the mud water. Few years later, when it come time to go fight the Kaiser, all us boys old enough rode over to El Reno in Luke Kastl's hay wagon to join up. Only one the Army turned down was Hubert. I don't know what he done to cause it, but the sergeant said he wasn't puttin' no rifle in that boy's hands. So Hubert stayed home for the War. Bout the time most of us, the lucky ones, were just gettin' back from France, Hubert and Mabel got married.

No tellin' what attracted 'em to each other. They was both outcasts, so to speak. Only passion in Hubert's life was them pigeons he raised up in the loft of his parents' barn. Had a whole flock up there: white ones, gray ones, speckled ones, you name it. You could see a hundred or more circlin' round the barn of an evening. Hubert'd be up there with the pigeons; you could see him through the loft door, lettin' birds in an' out of the cages he'd built. I swear he'd stand in the doorway and toss pigeons up in the air one by one, then point an' wave like he was directin' each bird which way to go. They say he had some of them birds trained to fly all the way to El Reno and back.

Well, I'm glad I was back in time for the weddin'. The old Church of St. Francis burned down in the winter of eighteen, so they got married in the Spring Creek School. Half the town of Yukon was there. When the ceremony was over the two of them come outta that schoolhouse like a couple of chickens runnin' from a fox. Never seen a woman so scared in my life. Shakin' so bad I thought she'd tear right outta that weddin' dress, which was blue. First blue one I ever seen. They come down the steps all shimmyin' and shallyin' and then a funny thing happened. Hubert, who looked like a ghost most the time, took hisself a deep breath and got a little color in his cheeks. Then he grabbed Mabel by the hips and lifted her up like he was a strong man, which he wasn't, right up into the buggy —brand new shiny black piano box buggy he ordered special from the Studebaker Brothers. Oh, it was a sight, I tell you: Ribbed leather seats and a three-bow leather top; hickory cane wheels and steel tires. We still didn't have but three or four automobiles around Yukon then, so people appreciated a good buggy. Well, the moment Hubert sat Mabel down in that buggy she calmed down. I mean just dead quiet peaceful, sittin' there in that buggy with her arms folded in her lap just as calm as you please. I don't believe she ever actually looked at Hubert the whole time, just kept her eyes shinin' on the road ahead. It might of been the light reflectin' off the dress she was wearin', but I swear to God when they went past it looked to me like them black crow eyes of hers had turned blue.

They was fixin' to go when a couple ol' boys noticed the pigeon cages in the back of the buggy. It got quiet a moment and you could hear 'em cooin' plain as day. Later on when we was all talkin' about it, Ted Turch said Hubert had only his best flyers in them cages. Well, there wasn't time to say nothin' to Hubert about it, but just before Hubert cracked the whip over that big roan horse of his, Luke Kastl yells out "Where you headed?" Hubert looks back at him an' grins the biggest grin I ever saw an' says "We're going to the moon."

Well, afterward some of us were talkin' an' Ted Turch says he thought Hubert might of said "honeymoon." Well, I'm here to tell you he said "moon" clear as a bell.

Well, nobody thought much about Hubert and Mabel for a couple of days. Then Mabel's parents got a call from the sheriff down in Sulphur. Hubert's dead, he says. Fell off a cliff above the Wildhorse River. That's what he said at first. Later on it come out Hubert had took Mabel up on that cliff and then jumped. Why, nobody knows. But a couple of miners were fishin' down on the river an' seen him up on the edge of the cliff, lettin' birds outta cages. Birds flew all around in a circle above his head, like they was takin' their bearings. Then Hubert points up at somethin' way up in the sky—maybe it was the moon, I don't know—and starts flappin' his arms like they was wings. He kept flappin' an' the birds kept circlin'. Then he jumped. The miners swore he flapped his arms all the way down to the bottom. Birds circled around above the river for a while, then flew away. They found Mabel still sittin' in that buggy up on the cliff.

Sheriff brought Mabel home in that same buggy a couple days later.

Only instead of pigeons they had Hubert in a pine box lashed on the back.
We had a hell of a time gettin' Mabel outta the buggy; she hung onto that
seat like death. Didn't want to leave Hubert, I guess. Just when we
thought we had her calmed down, she got away from us and grabbed onto
one of the buggy wheels. Took us a good five minutes to pry her off. Sheriff
told her father it'd be ,a good idea to get rid of that buggy; it reminded
Mabel of too much.

Later on you could see it was more than grief, the change in her. The
shine had gone out of her eyes; they was black as a snake pit now, no life
at all in 'em. She didn't stare back at nobody now and didn't act jumpy
neither. Nothin' riled her now. Far as I know, she never talked to nobody
about what happened on that cliff. Not to the priest or nobody. Didn't
even go to the funeral—nobody could make her go. See her on the streets
of Yukon after that an' she'd take no notice of you, just go on her way. It
was like whatever was behind them eyes of hers died up there on that cliff.
But the worst of it was, we found out later she was pregnant. Naturally we
all thought she'd go away somewhere before her time come, but not Ma-
bel. She went about her business as usual just like before until the day
Orville was born.

I don't mind tellin' you we was all scared about what kind of mother
Mabel'd be. But we were wrong. She raised that boy herself, and, well, you
can see for yourself how Orville turned out. Mabel's parents died when
Orville was still little. Didn't surprise nobody the way they both went
within a few weeks of each other; they'd lost three boys in the War and
then Hubert. We worried about Mabel an' that boy all alone on the farm.
Well, we were wrong again. Mabel hired Luke Kastl and a couple more
boys to run the farm until Orville was old enough. They did OK right
through the Depression. Better'n most, anyway. Looked like things were
going to turn out all right for Mabel after all.

Then the next war come and Orville stayed home to run the farm. The
two of 'em come through that OK too. Fact, Orville got a medal from the
War Department for growing so much wheat to support our boys over in
Europe and the Pacific. Wears it every year in the Czech Festival Parade.
Well anyway, one day not long after VJ Day it got real hot, so hot the
locusts were crawlin' right outta their skins. Right in the heat of the day,
Mabel disappeared. Orville looked an' looked an' finally found her
standin' in the sun outside the old Spring Creek School, starin' into a
window. They'd closed up the school before the War, and Orville'd
bought up the five acres around it from the township an' built that house
you're livin' in now. He had in mind to tear that old schoolhouse down, I

believe. Well, when he called to Mabel she took no notice of him. Just kept starin' real intent-like into that window like she was lookin' for somethin'. Place was empty then; wasn't nothing in there to see. Well, before Orville could catch up to her, she turned away from the window an' run off down to the creek. Sight of her runnin' kind of froze him, I guess; he'd never seen her move fast like that before. By the time he got after her she'd disappeared in the trees. He looked an' looked—an' then he saw her. Up on one of them gully cliffs above the creek. Starin' up into the sky an' tremblin' all over like she'd spotted somethin' up there that scared her. But there wasn't nothin' in the sky but the sun. No clouds, no birds, not even a moon. From where he was down by the creek, Orville couldn't see her eyes, but they had to be burnin' from starin' up into that bright sun. Then you know what she did? Hooked her thumbs under her armpits an' started flappin' her arms like they was wings. Flappin' an' flappin' like she was gonna jump right off that cliff and fly away. Hot as it was that day, Orville froze like a icicle. Then she opened her mouth and made that sound. . . .

Now, ten years later, the sound echoed in Kellerman's ears as he drove on to work. The same sound he had heard that first day he saw the old woman watching him with her black crow eyes through the window of the schoolhouse. A sound that was many sounds: a laugh, a moan, a cry of pain. A hoarse, crow sound: *Haaa, haaa.*

At the capitol he settled into his usual routine—changing light bulbs, checking the new circuits in legislative bill drafting, keeping an eye on the main generator—and tried to put the sound out of his mind. It was no use. The sound followed him down the long arching hallway from the east entrance on the first level, all the way to the central rotunda, echoing up the tall cylinder, six full stories, from the big marble floor map of Oklahoma, up through the encircling balconies on each level, past the giant fourth-floor oil paintings of Will Rogers, Sequoya, and Robert S. Kerr, a hundred feet up to the top of the capitol dome, where the Great Seal of the State of Oklahoma was encased in leaded glass. The sound echoed through the capitol all day, following him from floor to floor, room to room, until he could stand it no longer.

He took off from work an hour early, at four o'clock, and hurried down the wide granite steps to the Hudson parked in the new asphalt lot next to the official Pride of Oklahoma oil derrick. He wanted to beat Curly home from school, wanted to meet the bus, greet his son with glove and ball, and maybe play some catch before dinner—the way they used to before the Crow Woman came between them.

Kellerman slammed the dashboard with his fist as he pulled out of the lot. The whole thing was his fault—he could see that now. The crazy woman had been pestering him for a decade, eyeballing him like a scavenger bird every time he went near the schoolhouse, making him feel like . . . like he didn't know what. He could have had her put away in Sunnyview or some other place where they locked up loony birds. Not that he hadn't *tried*—there was just no budging Orville on the point. And no forcing him either; Orville had too many friends in high places.

"My fault," Kellerman muttered as he pulled onto the highway. *Let the poor woman be,* Babe had always said. *She just watches you is all. What's the harm?*

"Harm?" Kellerman asked the road ahead. "No harm as long as it was just *me* the old bird brain was watching. It was different when she turned her crow eyes on my boy."

He had often warned Curly to be careful around Mrs. Zucha, that something had happened a long time ago to make things go wrong inside her head. Kellerman didn't make a big deal out of it, and Curly showed no special interest in the old woman until six weeks ago, the day Kellerman discovered her watching Curly for the first time. Kellerman gripped the wheel of the Hudson and chewed his lower lip as he remembered stepping out of the schoolhouse and seeing Mabel hiding behind the mulberry tree, watching Curly mow the grass around the propane tank. Kellerman was too far away to see the black crow look in her eyes, but the sight of her peeking around the tree trunk at his son gave him a chill.

She disappeared into the tall ripe wheat beyond the fence as soon as Kellerman stepped into view.

"Mrs. Zucha's been getting out again," he said to Curly as he approached the propane tank. "I'm going to have to call Orville; you let me know if she comes back."

To Kellerman's surprise, the boy spun around, letting the old wooden-handled push mower coast to a stop behind him, and he looked up at his father with angry eyes. "I knew she was there," Curly said. "She was just watchin'; that's all. What's wrong with that? Why you have to call Orville?"

Kellerman's lips parted in shock. "Son, that woman—"

"I know," Curly interrupted—and turned around, picked up the handle, and resumed mowing.

Kellerman stood motionless, watching the grass clippings spray up behind the churning blades. After a few minutes he went into the house and told Babe what the boy had said.

"Why should that surprise you?" Babe asked. "You think he should *like* the idea of keeping an old woman locked up?"

Kellerman decided to let it go. He said nothing to Orville this time, but kept an eye peeled for the Crow Woman. She seemed to disappear for the next couple of weeks, as if Orville had somehow received the message anyway. Good riddance, Kellerman thought, and looked forward to a few weeks of peace.

Then a month ago Curly was late for dinner, and Babe sent Kellerman out to look for him. "I think he's down by the creek," she said.

Kellerman was reluctant to look for him there, suspecting the boy had a secret place near the creek, a place where grown-ups were not welcome. One of Babe's jab-like glances sent Kellerman on his way.

Nearing the creek, he began calling Curly's name to give the boy a chance to come out without revealing his secret spot, if there was one. Kellerman heard his own voice echo along the banks, but received no answer. It was early October and the creek was dry. He looked along the wooded part first, past the sycamore and redbud trees, then wandered up the deep gully cut out by flash floods during the spring tornado season. From below, on the dry creekbed where he walked, the earth looked long dead, the red walls of the gully turning slowly brown, chipping and flaking away in the unseasonably hot sun. The sun bore down on him, radiating off the walls, and the sandy floor trapped the heat, burning through the soles of his shoes, making him hurry toward the promised relief of the shade trees where the gully flattened out beyond the last bend. Sweating dizzily, he had almost forgotten about Curly when he rounded a middle bend and looked up.

Fifteen feet above, on the edge of a gully cliff, he saw the Crow Woman. She stood in silence, staring up into the empty sky. She wore a long dress of faded, indistinguishable color reaching all the way to the ground. Despite the heat, a gray shawl wrapped around her shoulders like the furled wings of a bat. Kellerman gasped and stepped back out of sight, then peeked around the bend of the gully and watched.

For a long time she didn't move. Her black eyes stared intently at the bright sky overhead. Kellerman looked up, expecting to see a flight of birds, or maybe the moon, but the sky was empty. Then her mouth opened a little and worked up and down, silently, as if she were whispering something too soft to hear. Then she opened her arms, extending them to each side, slowly, until they were parallel with the edge of the cliff, the shawl spread open like wings.

Kellerman was afraid she was going to jump. No! he wanted to shout, but his mouth made no sound. A breeze came up, lifting the shawl, making the fringe flutter beneath her arms. Kellerman forced himself to look away—then spotted another figure: his small eyes intent, enraptured, silently watching the Crow Woman from the far end of the gully.

"Curly!"

Keller didn't mean to shout—the word burst from his lungs. The boy jumped, then stumbled, spilling onto the hot sand from his hiding place around the bend. He looked at Kellerman, then turned and ran, disappearing behind the red wall. Kellerman started to call after him, then swallowed his breath.

When he looked up, the Crow Woman had vanished.

Kellerman winced as he turned the Hudson off Highway 4 onto the Czech Hall Road into Yukon. The incident on the cliff had started the boy's regression, he decided. Of course he had forbidden Curly from going anywhere near the Crow Woman after that. He knew the boy wouldn't like it, but no son of his was going to play with crazy women who thought they could fly! Naturally, Babe took the boy's side: "He just feels sorry for her is all."

"Sorry my ass," Kellerman had countered. "That woman's spooky; you didn't see her spreading her wings like a buzzard up on that cliff."

That was a month ago. Since then Orville had harvested the wheat beyond Kellerman's back fence, and the autumn winds had turned cold. Curly had stayed away from the Crow Woman all right—but he'd also avoided his father, first claiming that since he had no one to play with he just wanted to be left alone. That was OK until Kellerman discovered him sitting under the mulberry tree, talking to a sparrow. *Who you talking to?* Kellerman had asked. The bird flew away as he approached. *Nobody,* Curly answered, and stared down at the ground until Kellerman walked on toward the schoolhouse. Inside, he looked out the window and saw Curly climbing the tree toward another sparrow on a higher branch. Kellerman held his breath as the boy climbed to within six feet of the bird—then sighed with relief as the bird flew off.

He decided to say nothing more about it to the boy, and hadn't, though in the month since the incident on the cliff Curly seemed to talk more to the birds in the trees than to his father. It'll pass, Kellerman had thought.

Then five days ago Curly started pretending to be sick in the morning.

This morning Kellerman discovered the boy had stopped wearing pajamas. Enough's enough, Kellerman thought now as he pulled the Hudson into the driveway. He wanted to make peace with his son by playing a little catch before they sat down to dinner. Fat chance, Kellerman admitted as he switched off the ignition. Curly hadn't touched a baseball in a month.

Getting out of the car, Kellerman had the strong impression the school bus had beaten him home. The back yard looked empty. "Where's the boy?" he practically shouted at Babe as he entered the kitchen—then hushed when he saw the look on her face. She was standing next to the window by the sink.

"He's talking to a skunk," she whispered and pointed through the glass.

Kellerman turned and looked back through the screen door. In a moment he saw them, next to the propane tank, which had blocked his view before. Boy and skunk faced each other about a yard apart. Curly sat cross-legged on the ground, whispering and holding out a piece of raw bacon. The skunk was twisted into a U with both ends facing Curly— nose sniffing cautiously at the meat, tail pointing straight up, ready to spray.

Kellerman watched the two figures and felt a chill. "See?" he whispered to Babe. "Regression."

"Oh, stop it, Frank," Babe whispered. "Just don't let him touch that thing."

Kellerman told her to calm down. Regression or not, the boy knew all about skunks. If he was fool enough to get close enough to one to get sprayed, then maybe this was the best way to learn his lesson. Babe looked at Kellerman and cringed. Kellerman watched the two figures by the tank and chewed his lip. Despite the erect tail, the skunk seemed more intrigued than angry—and appeared to be edging closer to the meat. The boy's eyes burned a brilliant white, lit with the same intensity Kellerman had seen in the gully. He suddenly realized the boy might get close enough to the skunk to be bitten.

"Hey!" Kellerman banged on the door frame as he yelled.

The skunk jumped, sprayed Curly, and ran into the field. Curly gagged and struck wildly at his face. Kellerman gasped, then ran to his son.

"You stupid, stupid!" Babe stammered a few minutes later, and struck Kellerman several times on the back as they rubbed Curly's face with wet soapy towels. The stench choked off the boy's sobs and made Kellerman's nose and eyes burn as if he were sniffing gasoline. He held his breath and tried to convince himself it would have been far worse if the skunk had gotten close enough to bite his son.

"I'm sorry," Kellerman moaned, but couldn't tell if the boy even heard him.

It took half the night to wash the worst part of the stink off. Kellerman winced as he watched Curly's face turn red and raw—dead, chafed skin peeling off in patches like a first-degree burn. "It'll be fine by Monday," Kellerman lied, and crept out of the bathroom.

Saturday morning Kellerman realized in shame that their roles had been reversed somehow—now *he* was lying and avoiding his son's eyes. Babe's unforgiving stare was almost as difficult to bear. *What are you going to do about this?* her eyes asked. He had no idea. Curly was even more remote now, hardly acknowledging Kellerman's existence. And when the boy did take note of him, it was with suspicion, as if there were always another angle, another shade of meaning in every word, movement, gesture. Kellerman chewed his lip and tried to think. He needed a lever, a point of common interest—like playing catch—to reach the boy. On Saturday afternoon he came up with an idea.

"Get in; we're going to town," he ordered both of them and held the door to the old GMC pickup.

"What for?" Babe asked as she climbed into the cab.

"We'll know when we get there," Kellerman answered and held the door open for Curly to climb in between them. The boy remained where he was, standing about six feet away, frowning at the truck. Kellerman waited. He had chosen the old GMC pickup because it was Curly's favorite to ride in. When he was five Curly pronounced GMC "Jimmie." *Hop up here in my lap and I'll let you steer Jimmie,* Kellerman used to say.

Now, his face red and peeling, Curly stared suspiciously at his father holding open the door. "Hop in," Kellerman said brightly. The boy glanced at Babe sitting quietly in the cab, then raced past Kellerman and climbed into the back of the pickup, settling down in the corner next to the spare tire. Kellerman choked off the groan in his throat and got in.

The ride into Yukon was silent. They stopped in front of Kroeger's Pet Shop. Babe looked over at Kellerman and sighed. "I appreciate what you're doing, but I don't think it'll work."

Probably right, Kellerman thought as they went in. He'd tried this tactic once before, when Curly was eight, bringing home a slobbering German Shepherd pup named Fritz. *What kind of boy doesn't like dogs?*

he reasoned. But Curly would have nothing to do with the pup, who wet the rug five times before Kellerman decided to keep him strictly in the garage. *I'd rather have a rat,* Curly said and refused to feed the pup. *You're forcing it on the boy,* Babe explained. *You should let him pick out his own pets.* Kellerman was bitter. *My old man wouldn't even let me have a dog,* he said. He was sure Curly would learn to love the pup in time, but after a week Fritz was run over by a hay truck.

Maybe Babe's right, Kellerman conceded now as they gawked at the newspaper-lined cages of howling, hissing, whimpering, pissing dogs, cats, turtles, geese, hamsters, and other stinking animals.

Got any skunks or rats? Kellerman almost asked old man Kroeger, but thought better of it. If the boy sees something he likes, fine. If not, I ain't saying a word. He almost said something when Curly stared for a long time into a tank containing piranha fish. Thank God it's not feeding time, Kellerman thought when the boy finally looked bored and moved on. All of the animals seemed to bore him, especially the yowling, scratching dogs. He passed cage after cage, barely glancing at the wet, eager noses pressed against the wire. At the end of the row was a single cage. Curly stopped in front of it and stared inside.

Casually, Kellerman moved over to the next aisle and began examining boxes of bird seed. Out of the corner of his eye he peered back at the cage. Inside was a ragged lump of brown fur. Kellerman pretended to read the back of a box of Hartz Mountain parakeet seed, waiting for Curly to move on. He didn't.

"What's in that last cage over there?" Kellerman whispered to old man Kroeger at the register. Babe was looking out the window, but he could tell she was listening.

Kroeger was a tan wrinkled old man with a face like a dried mud pie. "Golden basset hound," he said tonelessly.

"Dog?" Kellerman asked, raising his eyebrows.

"Practically pure bred." Kroeger was peeling 75¢ price tags off plastic bowls and sticking on tags that said $1.98.

"Dead or alive?" Kellerman said, looking back at the motionless lump in the cage.

"You couldn't afford a dead one," Kroeger said.

Kellerman walked back to where Curly was still standing in front of the cage. Up close Kellerman could see the basset hound looked just like Kroeger. "You like that dog?" he asked, trying not to sound hopeful.

Curly shrugged. "OK."

Kellerman looked down at the dog, who lay in a wrinkled heap with one eye open watching a bug crawl along the rim of an empty water dish. "This here dog chase cars?" Kellerman shouted back at Kroeger. "Guaranteed not to—legs too short." "Yeah, well what *does* he do?" "Drink beer. He prefers Budweiser, but he'll drink Coors if he has to." Kellerman looked back down at the dog, who lifted his head and gave him a droopy-eared look that reminded Kellerman of the winos in the Alley next to the old Colcord Hotel. "You sure this is the one you want, son?" Curly curled his fingers around the wire of the cage and nodded. A beer hound. Curly named him Boozer. The fence around their five acres consisted of only three wires, so the first thing Curly did was teach Boozer never to cross the road in front of the house alone. Kellerman watched him spend hours that first evening training the dog to be walked across, whipping him on the butt with a magazine whenever he tried to cross by himself. Now that's sense, Kellerman thought. Just before sundown they gave Boozer a pail of beer with his Kennel Ration. "Sonofabitch drinks like my old man," Kellerman remarked as they watched Boozer lap up the entire pail without coming up for air, then raise his head and lick the foam off his nose. Fifteen minutes later Boozer lay on his back in the grass, making gurgling noises and moving his legs back and forth like he was trying to walk upside down. Then he fell asleep.

"Well, I'll swan," Babe said, laughing on the porch.

"Not exactly Rin Tin Tin," Kellerman observed.

"He's better," Curly said.

Curly loved Boozer immediately, Kellerman noted with satisfaction and hope. Satisfaction that he had given the boy something that he liked; hope that it would somehow get them back on the right track. It was too early to tell. At least Curly was now playing with a real pet instead of talking to skunks and wild birds and crazy women. Kellerman was careful not to appear to take advantage of whatever feelings the dog might have awakened in his son. For his part, Curly remained distant all weekend, never inviting Kellerman to join in the games of chase and tug of war he played with Boozer. On Sunday afternoon, after Boozer appeared to be learning his lesson about the road, Curly took him hunting in the freshly plowed wheat fields down by the creek. Boozer was too short-legged to actually catch anything, so the two of them returned that evening empty handed except for the Daisy air rifle slung over Curly's shoulder and the cockle burrs stuck in Boozer's ears. Kellerman had given Curly the BB gun last summer. *I never had such a thing when I was growing up*, Kellerman said the day he handed the shiny black rifle to his son, but Curly had kept the gun in his closet, claiming he didn't like to shoot things. My son the apprentice monk, Kellerman had thought. He was glad the boy had finally changed his mind.

"I think you may have done something," Babe whispered in his ear as they crawled under the covers that night.

Kellerman nodded hopefully. "Tomorrow's the test," he whispered back—and turned to find Babe smiling at him.

On Monday morning Kellerman went to roust Curly out of bed—and discovered he was already at the breakfast table, eating a bowl of Wheaties. Boozer lay under the table, sniffing at Curly's sneakers. Now this is more like it, Kellerman thought, but said nothing as Babe handed him his coffee and turned up the volume on the *Today* show.

For the first time in weeks, Kellerman drove to work content.

The weather turned colder that week. The north wind stripped the last leaves off the maple trees in the back yard and covered the bare limbs with frost. As Kellerman pulled into the driveway each evening he could see Orville in the distance, plowing the field beyond the fence with his John Deere. Each evening Kellerman hoped Curly and Boozer would be waiting on the back porch or snuggled warm in the kitchen to greet him. But he was disappointed. Every afternoon after school Curly disappeared with Boozer and the BB gun. The first couple of days Kellerman let it go. Wednesday afternoon he began to complain. "Just once I'd like to come home to my family when my family's home," he said to Babe, hoping she'd take the hint.

"The boy's got his own way, Frank," she countered, though her eyes looked softer this time.

Thursday afternoon the boy and dog were gone as usual. Kellerman glared at Babe, then turned around and went back out the door to look for them.

As he crossed the plowed field to the wooded area down by the creek he began to have second thoughts. So the boy has his own private time with his dog—what's wrong with that? Now you're going to horn in on it. Why? Because it doesn't include *you.*

He had almost talked himself into going back when he spotted them. They were just ahead, moving through the dry brush around the redbud trees, heading for the creek. Without thinking about it, he decided to hang back and follow them.

He crept along fifty yards behind, watching Boozer lead the way, sniffing and scratching through the dead brush. Probably buried his empty Budweiser cans down here, Kellerman thought as he peeked through the redbud trees. Curly was right behind, air rifle braced against his chest, trying to move quietly through the brush but snapping twigs and catching limbs across the face. As hunters they were pathetic, Kellerman judged. Birds, rabbits, and chipmunks heard Boozer thrashing long before he was aware of them. When he managed to catch a scent he would rear up and bellow, scaring off everything within a hundred yards. Whenever a lazy sparrow would actually take wing at close range, Curly would line up the shot but never fire. Kellerman wondered if the BB gun was really loaded.

He lost them when the dry gullies leading into the creek began to branch out into the pasture beyond. He started to turn back when he heard Boozer woofing and baying at something farther up. Beerbelly's finally cornered something, he thought, and hurried on up the gully to see. He rounded a bend and saw the Crow Woman on the edge of the cliff.

Kellerman froze. Curly was on the cliff with her, only a few feet away. They faced each other, squatting about six feet from the edge, flapping their arms and making laughing, crow-like sounds. Boozer trotted nervously around them, barking and whining and trying to join in. Kellerman had no sense of time, no idea how long he stood on the dry creek bed looking up through the steam of his breath at the sight above him. He saw, felt only the image before him: The idiot woman and his son, facing each other, two gross mockeries of birds, flapping their arms like wings, cawing, staring into each other's eyes and seeing God knows what, while the whining dog bounded around and around them. And then, in a flash that nearly knocked him flat, Kellerman recognized what was taking place—saw Curly spread his arms wide and hold them steady like the wings of a hawk gliding above a field, saw the Crow Woman spread her own arms an instant later, her gray shawl lifting with the breeze. *She was imitating him.*

"Curly!"

The cry was involuntary. He yelled without thinking, without meaning anything. If he had been thinking, he would have kept silent. The sound of his voice startled the woman more than the boy. She jumped, took a couple of flapping hops, trying to right herself—and stepped over the edge. Her long dress caught the wind like lifting wings, holding her a moment in mid air like a great bird beginning to soar—the dress blew over her head and she dropped like a sky diver whose chute had failed.

The cliff was about twenty feet high at the point she fell, and Kellerman felt more than heard the smack of her brittle body on the sand floor of the creek. The impact flattened her into a splotch of indistinguishable color on the sand. She lay silent, unmoving, the dress covering her like a shroud. Kellerman raised his eyes to the cliff. Curly stood looking down at the Crow Woman, his eyes glazed over, seeing and not seeing the image before him, like a blind clerk Kellerman had once seen drop a porcelain statuette of Will Rogers on the marble floor in front of the Bureau of the Handicapped Booth in the capitol. The statuette had shattered with the explosive pop of a lightbulb. The blind man remained standing over the spot of impact, arms still extended, clenching and unclenching his fists, as if time could somehow be reversed and he could find again in the empty space before him the fragile object that had slipped through his grasp. On the cliff above Kellerman now, Curly's hands dangled helplessly at his sides, fingers quivering in faint spasms. Next to him Boozer peered over the edge, ears half lifted, half drooping in futile attention to the mute figure lying on the sand. Boozer wrinkled his nose and sniffed the air, then began to whine.

"She's OK," Kellerman yelled suddenly.

Even before Curly's stunned eyes turned toward him, Kellerman knew what he had done. "She's OK," he repeated, as if saying the words could make them true. He moved toward her with a will that was not will, a hope that was not hope. Fear thrust him toward her like the brute reflex of a cornered animal—but slowly, the air around him had grown suddenly thick and heavy, resisting him like water. He had never seen her close up. When finally he stood breathless and trembling over her still body, the first thing he noticed was insignificant, ridiculous: The dress she wore was blue. Or once was blue; age had left only a hint, a memory of color. He didn't wonder about it, for lying there in a rippled splatter on the sand she looked chillingly bird-like. Like a chicken hawk dashed to earth, knocked out of the clear sky by a farmer's shotgun. He saw no blood, no steamed breath rising from her lips in the cold air. The profile of her bird face displayed the rigid contortions and contradictory slackness of death: Her eyes pinched shut from opposing pressures of earth and twisted shoulders; her beak-like mouth opened slightly, allowing a gray tongue to spill out, coated with speckles of sand. She must have weighed all of eighty pounds, a wreckage of hollow broken bones.

Then she moved. Her head twisted slowly upward and her eyes cracked open, looking up at Kellerman with a cold black light. In the eerie suspense of the moment her stirring did not really surprise him. What he saw in her eyes did. He expected only the dumb, stricken look of a wild bird brought to earth. But as she looked up at him the impenetrable blackness in her eyes seemed to dissolve for a moment into soft blue. And something else—a look that startled, bewildered, and finally terrified him: A soft blue look of intimacy, trust. He knew instantly he would never understand that look—nor the word that issued faint but unmistakable from her cracked lips:

"Hubert."

The name shook Kellerman to his bones.

But before he could say anything, before he could even consider his reaction—for the sake of an injured woman—consider whether or not he should say and do nothing, just pretend, for the moment at least, that he was indeed Hubert, was indeed her long-dead husband (long dead *crazy* man who thought he was a catfish, then a bird) come back to this world from a better one—before he could even consider this, the soft blue look in her eyes vanished. Her eyes returned to black, and she was dead.

Trembling, Kellerman looked up at the cliff. Curly had disappeared. Boozer stared down at the body on the creekbed, then lifted his head toward the gray sky and began to howl.

Kellerman looked up. Staring down at him like a pale ghost was a full moon.

"I want you to know I don't consider what happened your fault, Frank." Orville Zucha sat on Kellerman's sofa, his John Deere cap crumpled in his lap.

It was Friday morning, following a night Kellerman wanted desperately to forget. Curly was still in bed. Kellerman had tried to get him up half an hour ago. *I'm sick,* Curly had said, and pulled the covers tightly around his neck. Kellerman was afraid to pull them off, afraid to discover the boy had shed his pajamas once again. He left Curly in bed.

"I appreciate your coming over to tell me that, Orville," Kellerman said. I wish you'd tell the boy, he wanted to add, but didn't.

"Nope," Orville said, twisting the cap in his fists. "You warned me for ten years something like this might happen. I guess I always knew it could."

"You want some coffee?" Babe asked.

"Nope," Orville shook his square head and rose to his feet. "That's all I come for."

Kellerman stood. "Sorry it happened."

Orville shrugged and opened the front door. He pulled on his cap and turned back to Kellerman. "I 'preciate your puttin' up with Mama all these years."

Kellerman felt his face turn bright red.

Orville's eyes were moist. "That old woman was crazy, but I loved her. I wished I could of been a bird so I could of told her."

Kellerman swallowed and started to say something, but Orville was out the door.

In the kitchen a few minutes later Babe laid her hand on Kellerman's shoulder. "I just looked in on Curly," she said softly, then paused for a moment. "Maybe you were right all along, Frank. We've got to do something to help him."

"Something," Kellerman said, and headed out the door.

He thought about it all day as he replaced light bulbs and monitored power gauges. What could they do? Despite all his thoughts about regression, Kellerman didn't really think much of psychology. The problem seemed bigger than that somehow.

Driving home that evening, he tried to think of something to say to Curly. *It's nobody's fault, son,* was the best he could come up with, and he knew it wouldn't do.

"Where is he?" Kellerman asked Babe when he stepped through the kitchen door.

"He's over on the south side of the house, playing with Boozer. I let him stay home from school today," she added.

Kellerman nodded and stepped over to the side window next to the refrigerator. Through the glass he saw the two of them, boy and dog, playing a silent game of tug of war with a rag. He had intended to rap on the glass and call Curly inside. The silent fury of the boy's tugging stopped him. He realized the game was not a game but a release. He did not interrupt.

He decided to speak to the boy after dinner, but when Babe cleared the dishes away, Kellerman discovered his mind was a blank. He opened his mouth to speak as the boy got up from the table, but no words came out. Curly looked him in the eye for an instant before heading back to his bedroom.

"In the morning," Kellerman promised Babe. "I'll talk to him in the morning."

"Tomorrow morning's the funeral," Babe reminded him.

"I know."

He awoke suddenly in the night.

"What? What?" he cried, and threw off the blankets.

"It's Boozer," Babe said wearily. "He's howling. Go see what's the matter with him."

Aroooooo. The mournful sound filled the house as Kellerman got out of bed and padded down the dark hallway toward the kitchen. In the moonlight he saw Boozer with his paws up on the sink, howling out the back window. Kellerman flipped on the light. In the brightness he could see the dog trembling.

"It's only the moon, boy," Kellerman said.

Boozer paid no attention. He howled once more, then dropped down on all fours, panting heavily, as if he had just run a great distance. Large drops of sweat dripped off his nose, spotting the floor. Kellerman whispered softly to him, but the dog appeared not to hear. A few moments later Boozer's ears lifted and he looked around the room, around and through Kellerman, as if he were not there.

Suddenly Boozer ran past Kellerman into the dark hallway.

"Where you going?" Kellerman called after him, then spotted two eyes watching from the dark hall. "Curly?" he said. The dog and the eyes vanished. A moment later he heard the door to Curly's bedroom click shut.

At breakfast on Saturday morning Kellerman felt himself trembling. It wasn't from trying to talk to the boy across the table, though the words still hadn't come, and Babe was beginning to look at him sharply. It was the idea of going to the Crow Woman's funeral that frightened him. His fear made no sense, he knew, but he couldn't help it. He was afraid she would make that sound—the hideous, moaning crow sound—and sit up in the casket and open her eyes (which eyes—black or soft blue?) and see him. See *who?* he asked himself. Frank Kellerman, the man who had scared her off a cliff? Or Hubert, who wanted her to fly?

He thought he understood now why Mabel had watched him all these years. But why had she picked him out to be Hubert? Just because he worked in the old schoolhouse? He looked nothing like Hubert—old man Loudermilk had shown him pictures of a tall, skinny, round-eyed boy with skin the color of bleached sand. The Man in the Moon, old man Loudermilk called him. Kellerman was short, swarthy, and squinty-eyed. Why pick *him?*

He tried to put the fear out of his mind by talking to Curly. "I want you to understand something, son," he began. "What happened to Mrs.

Zucha was nobody's fault. Not mine, not yours. She was old and it was her time." Kellerman noticed Curly was trembling too, then realized the boy had never been to a funeral. "There's nothing strange or scary about a funeral," Kellerman said. "It's just a time to show your respect, that's all. Your mother and I will be right there beside you. After we get home we'll have a talk."

Curly looked up at Kellerman and his eyes seemed to soften. Kellerman wanted to reach out and hug him, but was afraid the boy would back away. Don't push, he warned himself. A moment later Curly got up and went to his room. Babe came over and stood next to Kellerman; he took her hand. "Let's get ready," he said.

The funeral turned out to be uneventful. To Kellerman's relief, the Catholic funeral mass required a closed casket. Half of Yukon was there, including most of the old-timers like Horace Loudermilk and Bob Swanda. Kellerman knew some of them would go down to the *Los Angeles Gardens* afterward to swap Crow Woman stories. He wanted no part of it. Nor could he bear to look straight at Orville, whose honest, square head bowed like a tilting brick as he knelt in the first pew. Throughout the mass Kellerman kept an eye on Curly. The boy seemed to bear up pretty well, Kellerman decided, though he did notice Curly seemed unnaturally stiff, as if he were holding something in. Kellerman had expected the boy to cry, maybe make a scene, and was glad he didn't.

Boozer greeted them at the back door, bounding into Curly's arms. Kellerman tossed his coat on a chair and heaved a great sigh. Now that they were home, he felt less urgent about talking to Curly. He decided to talk to the boy after dinner, after he'd had a chance to figure out what needed to be said.

After dinner he was still sorting things out. *Idiot*, he thought. Just tell the boy what you want him to know. But what was that? That his father still loved him after taking away his only playmate, after what happened with the skunk, after what happened in the gully? It was true—why was it so hard to say?

The evening air was turning cold, but the three of them decided to take Boozer out back to play. Boozer was especially playful this evening, bounding after balls and rolling on the crisp lawn. Whatever had set him to howling the night before was obviously long gone. Later they sat on the porch and watched Boozer lap up his pail of Budweiser, foam bubbling up his snout. Kellerman smiled, though he'd seen this sight many times before. Babe and Curly were smiling too, watching the dog, and Kellerman was grateful—grateful for a rare moment when each of them felt the same way about something. A few minutes later they were all laughing out loud as Boozer tried to walk, right-side up this time, after finishing his beer. It was hilarious, watching him stagger around the back yard on three, then two legs, dragging his butt over the grass. Curly tried to help him keep his balance, lifting his rear end and trying to keep his back legs vertical. It was no use. "Nice try, Rin Tin," Kellerman said when Boozer finally gave up and rolled over on his back to sleep. Boozer always slept for at least an hour after taking his brew. As the sky darkened Curly went inside to watch television; Babe started the dishes. Kellerman remained on the porch, watching the lights of Oklahoma City begin to glow on the eastern horizon, feeling more content than he had in weeks. He didn't notice Boozer roll groggily to his feet and head for the road.

The Coca-Cola truck wound up in the ditch, bottles stuck in the earth like stubby knives. "I swerved to miss him," the driver swore. "But he came right at me."

"I'll bet, you blind bastard." Only the absurd knowledge that it was the *dog* who had been drunk kept Kellerman from grabbing the driver by the throat. Curly looked at the body in the ditch and said nothing.

They buried Boozer under the mulberry tree. Kellerman dug the hole and filled it. Curly stood off to one side, by himself, staring at the hole. When he had finished filling the hole, Kellerman dropped the shovel and stood there.

"We'll get another dog," Babe said in her strongest voice. "You can pick one out tomorrow."

Curly stared off toward the west, where the last glow of the sunset was fading into gray.

"It's OK to cry," Babe said. Curly looked down at his feet. Babe turned to Kellerman. "Tell him, Frank."

Father and son looked at each other. The boy's eyes were round and white in the twilight. "Well, *say* something," Babe urged.

Kellerman's lips trembled. He opened his mouth half an inch, but nothing came out. A few moments later Curly walked past him toward the house.

Babe watched him go, then shook her head and sighed. "Don't worry; he'll get over it," she said softly to Kellerman, and laid her hand on his shoulder. Kellerman pulled away and looked at her with wild eyes.

Late that night a sound woke Babe from a fitful sleep.
"Frank?"

She rolled over to find his half of the bed empty. "Frank?" she repeated, louder this time, and sat up in bed. The sound—low, mournful —echoed again. She leaped out of bed and flipped on the light. "Frank! Curly!"

No answer. She grabbed her robe and ran into the hallway toward Curly's room. The boy's bed was empty, the covers thrown back. At the foot of the bed his pajamas lay in a heap.

"Curly!" she shouted, and ran back through the house. In the kitchen she heard the sound again—it was coming from outside.

"Curly! Frank! Where are you?"

She could see nothing through the window. She took a deep breath and opened the back door. A cold wind stabbed her through the screen and she pulled her robe tight. Squinting, she brushed windblown hair out of her eyes and searched the dark yard.

A moment later the sound echoed again. She turned toward it—and gasped.

There, next to the mulberry tree, she saw them: two dim, shivering silhouettes in the moonlight. Her husband and son, standing naked, clutching each other chest to chin like frightened lovers—their heads tilted up toward the cold gray moon, their mouths open wide, moonlit steam rising from their lips like ghosts, releasing the sound, howling the moon out of the sky.

ABOUT BOSTON

WARD JUST

Ward Just, born in Michigan City, Indiana, in 1935, is the author of
six novels and two collections of short stories.

Beth was talking and I was listening. She said, "This was years ago. I was
having a little tryst. On a Thursday, in New York, in the afternoon. He
telephoned: 'Is it this Thursday or next?' I told him it was never, if he
couldn't remember the *week*. Well." She laughed. "It makes your point
about letters. Never would've happened if we'd written letters because
you write something and you remember it. Don't you?"

"Usually," I said.

"There isn't a record of anything anymore, it's just telephone calls and
bad memory."

"I've got a filing cabinet full of letters," I said, "and most of them are
from ten years ago and more. People wrote a lot in the sixties, maybe
they wanted a record of what they thought. There was a lot to think
about, and it seemed a natural thing to do, write a letter to a friend, what
with everything that was going on."

"I wonder if they're afraid," she said.

"No written record? No," I said. "They don't have the time. They
won't make the time and there aren't so many surprises now, thanks to
the sixties. We're surprised-out. They don't write and they don't read
either."

"That one read," she said, referring to the man in the tryst. "He read
all the time—history, biography. Sports books, linebackers' memoirs, the
strategy of the full-court press." She lowered her voice. "And politics."

"Well," I said. I knew who it was now.

"But he didn't know the week." She lit a cigarette, staring at the
match a moment before depositing it, just so, in the ashtray. "You always
wrote letters."

I smiled. "A few close friends."

She smiled back. "Where do you think we should begin?"

"Not at the beginning."

"No, you know that as well as I do."

I said, "Probably better."

"Not better," she said.

"I don't know if I'm the man—"

"No," she said firmly. She stared at me across the room, then turned to look out the window. It was dusk, and the dying sun caught the middle windows of the Hancock tower, turning them a brilliant, wavy orange. In profile, with her sharp features and her short black hair, she looked like a schoolgirl. She said, "You're the man, all right. I want you to do it. I'd feel a lot more comfortable, we've known each other so long. Even now, after all this time, we don't have to finish sentences. It'd be hard for me, talking about it to a stranger."

"Sometimes that's easiest," I said.

"Not for me it isn't."

"All right," I said at last. "But if at any time it gets awkward for you—" I was half hoping she'd reconsider. But she waved her hand in a gesture of dismissal, subject closed. She was sitting on the couch in the corner of my office, and now she rose to stand at the window and watch the last of the sun reflected on the windows of the Hancock. A Mondrian among Turners, she had called it, its blue mirrors a new physics in the Back Bay. And who cared if in the beginning its windows popped out like so many ill-fitting contact lenses. The Hancock governed everything around it, Boston's past reflected in Boston's future. And it was miraculous that in the cascade of falling glass the casualties were so few.

I watched her: at that angle and in the last of the light her features softened and she was no longer a schoolgirl. I checked my watch, then rang my assistant and said she could lock up; we were through for the day. I fetched a yellow legal pad and a pen and sat in the leather chair, facing Beth. She was at the window, fussing with the cord of the venetian blind. She turned suddenly, with a movement so abrupt that I dropped my pad; the blind dropped with a crash. There had always been something violent and unpredictable in her behavior. But now she only smiled winningly, nodded at the sideboard, and asked for a drink before we got down to business.

I have practiced law in the Back Bay for almost twenty-five years. After Yale I came to Boston with the naïve idea of entering politics. The city had a rowdy quality I liked; it reminded me of Chicago, a city of neighborhoods, which wasn't ready for reform. But since I am a lapsed Catholic, neither Irish nor Italian, neither Yankee nor Democrat nor rich, I quickly understood that for me there were no politics in Boston. Chicago is astronomically remote from New England, and it was of no interest to anyone that I had been around politicians most of my life and knew the code. My grandfather had been, briefly, a congressman from the suburbs of Cook County, and I knew how to pull strings. But in Boston my antecedents precluded everything but good-government committees and the United Way.

Beth and I were engaged then, and Boston seemed less daunting than New York, perhaps because she knew it so intimately; it was her town as Chicago was mine. I rented an apartment in the North End and for the first few months we were happy enough, I with my new job and she with her volunteer work at the Mass. General. We broke off the engagement after six months—the usual reasons—and I looked up to find myself behind the lines in enemy territory. I had misjudged Boston's formality and its network of tribal loyalties and had joined Hamlin & White, one of the old State Street firms. I assumed that H,W—as it had been known for a hundred years—was politically connected. An easy error to make, for the firm was counsel to Boston's largest bank and handled the wills and trusts of a number of prominent Brahmin Republicans, and old Hamlin had once been lieutenant governor of Massachusetts. In Chicago that would have spelled political, but in Boston it only spelled probate. There were thirty men in the firm, large for Boston in those days. The six senior men were Hamlin and Hamlin Junior and White III, and Chelm, Warner, and Diuguid. Among the associates were three or four recognizable Mayflower names. The six senior men were all physically large, well over six feet tall and in conspicuous good health, by which I mean ruddy complexions and a propensity to roughhouse. They all had full heads of hair, even old Hamlin, who was then eighty. Their talk was full of the jargon of sailing and golf, and in their company I felt the worst sort of provincial rube.

Of course I was an experiment—a balding, unathletic Yale man from Chicago, of middling height, of no particular provenance, and booksmart. I was no one's cousin and no one's ex-roommate. But I was engaged to a Boston girl and I had been first in my class at Yale and the interview with Hamlin Junior had gone well. All of them in the firm spoke in that hard, open-mouthed bray peculiar to Massachusetts males of the upper classes. The exception was Hamlin Junior, who mumbled. When it was clear, after two years, that their experiment had failed—or had not, at any event, succeeded brilliantly—it was Hamlin Junior who informed me. He called me into his dark-brown office late one afternoon, poured me a sherry, and rambled for half an hour before he got to the point, which was that I was an excellent lawyer mumble mumble damned able litigator mumble mumble but the firm has its own personality, New England salt sort of thing ha-ha mumble sometimes strange to an outsider but it's the way we've always done things mumble question of style and suitability, sometimes tedious but can't be helped wish you the best you're a damned able trial man, and of course you've a place here so long's you want though in fairness I wanted mumble make it known that you wouldn't be in the first foursome as it were mumble mumble. Just one question, I've always wondered: 'S really true that you wanted to go into politics here?

It was my first professional failure, and in my anger and frustration I put it down to simple snobbery. I did not fit into their clubs, and I hated the North Shore and was not adept at games. I was never seen "around" during the winter or on the Cape or the Islands or in Maine in the summer. I spent my vacations in Europe, and most weekends I went to New York, exactly as I did when I was at law school in New Haven. New York remains the center of my social life. Also, I was a bachelor. Since the breakup of my engagement, I had become an aggressive bachelor. Beth was bitter and I suspected her of spreading unflattering stories. Of course this was not true, but in my humiliation I believed that it was and that as a consequence the six senior men had me down as homosexual. In addition, I was a hard drinker in a firm of hard drinkers though unlike them I never had whiskey on my breath in the morning and I never called in sick with Monday grippe. I could never join in the hilarious retelling of locker-room misadventures. They drank and joked. I drank and didn't joke.

When I left H,W, I opened an office with another disgruntled provincial—he was from Buffalo, even farther down the scale of things than Chicago—half expecting to fail but determined not to and wondering what on earth I would do and where I would go, now that I'd been drummed out of my chosen city: blackballed. Young litigators are not as a rule peripatetic: you begin in a certain city and remain there; you are a member of the bar, you know the system, you build friendships and a clientele and a reputation. Looking back on it, Deshais and I took a terrible risk. But we worked hard and prospered, and now there are twenty lawyers in our firm, which we have perversely designed to resemble a squad of infantry in a World War II propaganda movie: Irish,

Italians, Jews, three blacks in the past ten years, one Brahmin, Deshais, and me. Of course we are always quarreling; ours is not a friendly, clubby firm. In 1974, we bought a private house, a handsome brownstone, in the Back Bay, only two blocks from my apartment on Commonwealth Avenue. This is so convenient, such an agreeable way to live—it is my standard explanation to my New York friends who ask why I remain here —that we decided not to expand the firm because it would require a larger building and all of us love the brownstone, even the younger associates who must commute from Wayland or Milton. Sometimes I think it is the brownstone and the brownstone alone that holds the firm together.

I suppose it is obvious that I have no affection for this spoiled city and its noisy inhabitants. It is an indolent city. It is racist to the bone and in obvious political decline and like any declining city is by turns peevish and arrogant. It is a city without civility or civic spirit, or Jews. The Jews, with their prodigious energies, have tucked themselves away in Brook-line, as the old aristocrats, with their memories and trust funds, are on the lam on the North Shore. Remaining are the resentful Irish and the furious blacks. Meanwhile, the tenured theory class issues its pronounce-ments from the safety of Cambridge, confident that no authority will take serious notice. So the city of Boston closes in on itself, conceited, petulant, idle, and broke.

I observe this from a particular vantage point. To my surprise, I have become a divorce lawyer. The first cases I tried after joining forces with Deshais were complicated divorce actions. They were women referred to me by Hamlin Junior, cases considered—I think he used the word "fraught"—too mumble "fraught" for H,W. In Chicago we used the word "messy," though all this was a long time ago; now they are tidy and without fault. However, then as now there was pulling and hauling over the money. Hamlin Junior admired my trial work and believed me dis-creet and respectable enough to represent in the first instance his cousin and in the second a dear friend of his wife's. He said that he hoped the matter of the cousin would be handled quietly, meaning without a lengthy trial and without publicity, but that if the case went to trial he wanted her represented by a lawyer ahem who was long off the tee. You know what it is you must do? he asked. I nodded. At that time divorces were purchased; you bought a judge for the afternoon. Happily, the cousin was disposed of in conference, quietly and very expensively for her husband. The success of that case caused Hamlin Junior to send me the second woman, whose disposition was not quite so quiet. Fraught it certainly was, and even more expensive.

I was suddenly inside the bedroom, hearing stories the obverse of those I had heard after hours at H,W. The view from the bedroom was different from the view from the locker room. It was as if a light-bulb joke had been turned around and told from the point of view of the bulb. Hundred-watt Mazda shocks WASP couple! I discovered that I had a way with women in trouble. That is precisely because I do not pretend to understand them, as a number of my colleagues insist that they "understand women." But I do listen. I listen very carefully, and then I ask questions and listen again. Then they ask me questions and I am still listening hard, and when I offer my answers they are brief and as precise as I can make them. And I never, never overpromise. No woman has ever rebuked me with "But you *said*, and now you've broken your word."

The cousin and the wife's friend were satisfied and told Hamlin Junior, who said nothing to his colleagues. He seemed to regard me as the new chic restaurant in town, undiscovered and therefore underpriced; it would become popular soon enough, but meanwhile the food would continue excellent and the service attentive and the bill modest. For years he referred clients and friends to me, and I always accepted them even when they were routine cases and I had to trim my fees. And when Hamlin Junior died, I went to his funeral, and was not at all startled to see so many familiar female faces crowding the pews.

My divorce business was the beginning, and there was a collateral benefit—no, bonanza. I learned how money flows in Boston, and where; which were the rivers and which were the tributaries and which were the underground streams. Over the years, I have examined hundreds of trusts and discovered a multiformity of hidden assets, liquid and solid, floating and stationary, lettered and numbered, aboveground and below. The trusts are of breathtaking ingenuity, the product of the flintiest minds in Massachusetts, and of course facilitated over the years by a willing legislature. And what has fascinated me from the beginning is this: The trust that was originally devised to avoid taxes or to punish a recalcitrant child or to siphon income or to "protect" an unworldly widow or to reach beyond the grave to control the direction of a business or a fortune or a marriage can fall apart when faced with the circumstances of the present, an aggrieved client, and a determined attorney.

This is not the sort of legal practice I planned, but it is what I have. Much of what I have discovered in divorce proceedings I have replicated in my trust work, adding a twist here and there to avoid unraveling by someone like me, sometime in the future. Wills and trusts are now a substantial part of my business, since I have access to the flintiest minds in Massachusetts. Turn, and turn about. However, it is a risible anomaly of the upper classes of Boston that the estates have grown smaller and the trusts absurdly complex—Alcatraz to hold juvenile delinquents.

So one way and another I am in the business of guaranteeing the future. A trust, like a marriage, is a way of getting a purchase on the future. That is what I tell my clients, especially the women; women have a faith in the future that men, as a rule, do not. I am careful to tell my clients that although that is the objective, it almost never works; or it does not work in the way they intend it to work. It is all too difficult reading the past, without trying to read the future as well. It is my view that men, at least, understand this, having, as a rule, a sense of irony and proportion. At any event, this is my seat at the Boston opera. It is lucrative and fascinating work. There was no compelling reason, therefore, not to listen to the complaint of Beth Earle Doran Greer, my former fiancée.

She said quietly, "It's finished."

I said nothing.

She described their last year together, the two vacations and the month at Edgartown, happy for the most part. They had one child, a boy, now at boarding school. It had been a durable marriage, fifteen years; the first one had lasted less than a year, and she had assumed that despite various troubles this one would endure. Then last Wednesday he said he was leaving her and his lawyer would be in touch.

"Has he?"

"No," she said.

"Who is he?"

She named a State Street lawyer whom I knew by reputation. He was an excellent lawyer. I was silent again, waiting for her to continue.

"Frank didn't say anything more than that."

"Do you know where he is?"

"I think he's at the farm." I waited again, letting the expression on my face do the work. There were two questions. Is he alone? Do you want him back? She said again, "It's finished." Then, the answer to the other question: "There is no one else." I looked at her, my face in neutral. She said, "Hard as that may be to understand."

Not believe, *understand;* a pointed distinction. I nodded, taking her at her word. It was hard, her husband was a great bon vivant.

"That's what he says, and I believe him. His sister called me to say that there isn't anybody else, but I didn't need her to tell me. Believe me, I know the signs. There isn't a sign I don't know and can't see a mile away, and he doesn't show any of them. Five years ago—that was something else. But she's married and not around anymore, and that's over and done with. And besides, if there was someone else he'd tell me. It'd be like him."

I nodded again and made a show of writing on my pad.

"And there isn't anyone else with me either."

"Well," I said, and smiled.

"Is it a first?"

I laughed quietly. "Not a first," I said. "Maybe a second."

She laughed, and lit a cigarette. "You were afraid it would be another cliché, she would be twenty and just out of Radcliffe. Meanwhile, I would've taken up with the garage mechanic or the gamekeeper. Or Frank's best friend; they tell me that's chic now." She looked at me sideways and clucked. "You know me better than that. Clichés aren't my style."

I said, "I never knew you at all."

"Yes, you did," she said quickly. I said nothing. "You always listened, in those days you were a very good listener. And you're a good listener now."

"The secret of my success," I said. But I knew my smile was getting thinner.

"The mouthpiece who listens," she said. "That's what Nora told me, when she was singing your praises. Really, she did go on. Do they fall in love with you, like you're supposed to do with a psychiatrist?"

Nora was a client I'd represented in an action several years before, a referral from Hamlin Junior. She was a great friend of Beth's but a difficult woman and an impossible client. I said, "No."

"It was a pretty good marriage," she said after a moment's pause. "You'd think, fifteen years . . ." I leaned forward, listening. Presently, in order to focus the conversation, I would ask the first important question: What is it that you want me to do now? For the moment, though, I wanted to hear more. I have never regarded myself as a marriage counselor, but it is always wise to know the emotional state of your client. So far, Beth seemed admirably rational and composed, almost cold-blooded. I wondered if she had ever consulted a psychiatrist, then decided she probably hadn't. There was something impersonal about her locution "like you're supposed to." She said abruptly, "How did you get into this work? It's so unlike you. Remember the stories you told me about your grandfather and his friend? The relationship they had, and how that was the kind of lawyer you wanted to be?"

I remembered all right, but I was surprised that she did. My grandfather and I were very close, and when I was a youngster we lunched together every Saturday. My father drove me to the old man's office, in an unincorporated area of Cook County, near Blue Island. I'd take the elevator to the fourth floor, the building dark and silent on Saturday morning. My grandfather was always courteous and formal, treating me as he would treat an important adult. On Saturday mornings my grandfather met with Tom. Tom was his lawyer. I was too young to know exactly what they were talking about, though as I look back on it, their conversation was in a private language. There was a "matter" that needed "handling," or "a man"—perhaps "sound," perhaps "a screwball"—who had to be "turned." Often there was a sum of money involved—three, four, fi' thousand dollars. These questions would be discussed sparely, long pauses between sentences. Then, as a signal that the conversation was near its end, my grandfather would say, "Now this is what I want to do," and his voice would fall. Tom would lean close to the old man, listening hard; I never saw him make a note. Then, "Now you figure out how I can do it." And Tom would nod, thinking, his face disappearing into the collar of his enormous camel's-hair coat. He never removed the coat, and he sat with his gray fedora in both hands, between his knees, turning it like the steering wheel of a car. When he finished thinking, he would rise and approach me and gravely shake hands. Then he would offer me a piece of licorice from the strand he kept in his coat, the candy furry with camel's hair. He pressed it on me until I accepted. I can remember him saying good-bye to my grandfather and, halting at the door, smiling slightly and winking. Tom would exit whistling, and more often than not my grandfather would make a telephone call, perhaps two, speaking inaudibly into the receiver. Finally, rumbling in his basso profundo, he would make the ritual call to the Chicago Athletic Club to reserve his usual table for two, "myself and my young associate."

In those days children were not allowed in the men's bar, so we ate in the main dining room, a huge chamber with high ceilings and a spectacular view of the lakefront. We sat at a table by the window, and on a clear day we could see Gary and Michigan City to the southeast. Long-hulled ore boats were smudges on the horizon. Once, during the war, we saw a pocket aircraft carrier, a training vessel for Navy pilots stationed at Great Lakes. The old man would wave his hand in the direction of the lake and speak of the Midwest as an ancient must have spoken of the Fertile Crescent: the center of the world, a homogeneous, God-fearing, hardworking *region*, its interior position protecting it from its numerous enemies. With a sweep of his hand he signified the noble lake and the curtain of smoke that hung over Gary's furnaces, thundering even on Saturdays. Industry, he'd say, *heavy* industry working at one hundred percent of capacity. Chicagoland, foundry to the world. His business was politics, he said; and his politics was business. "We can't let them take it away from us, all this . . ."

When the old man died, Tom was his principal pallbearer. It was a large funeral; the governor was present with his suite, along with a score or more of lesser politicians. Tom was dry-eyed, but I knew he was grieving. At the end of it he came over to me and shook my hand, solemnly as always, and said, "Your grandfather was one of the finest men who ever lived, a great friend, a great Republican, a great American, and a great client." I thought that an extraordinary inventory and was about to say so when he gripped my arm and exclaimed, "You ever need help of any kind, you come to me. That man and I . . ." He pointed at my grandfather's casket, still aboveground under its green canopy, then tucked his chin into the camel's hair. "We've been through the mill, fought every day of our lives. I don't know what will happen without him." He waved dispiritedly at the gravestones around us, stones as far as the eye could see, and lowered his voice so that I had to bend close to hear. "The world won't be the same without him," Tom said. "The Midwest's going to hell."

Tom died a few years later, without my having had a chance to take him up on his offer. But from my earliest days in that fourth-floor office I knew I would be a lawyer. I wanted to be Tom to someone great, and prevent the world from going to hell. Tom was a man who listened carefully to a complex problem, sifting and weighing possibilities. Then, settled and secure in his own mind, he figured a way to get from here to there. It was only an idiosyncrasy of our legal system that the route was never a straight line.

"I mean," she said brightly, leaning forward on the couch, "listening to a bunch of hysterical women with their busted marriages, that wasn't what I expected at all."

"They are not always hysterical," I said, "and some of them are men."

"And you never married," she said.

That was not true, but I let it pass.

"No," she said, rapping her knuckles on the coffee table. "You *were*

married. I heard that, a long time ago. I heard that you were married, a
whirlwind romance in Europe, but then it broke up right away."

"That's right," I said.

"She was French."

"English," I said.

"And there were no children."

"No," I said. We were silent while I walked to the sideboard, made a
drink for myself, and refilled hers.

"Do you remember how we used to talk, that place on Hanover Street
we used to go to, all that pasta and grappa? I practiced my Italian on
them. Always the last ones out the door, running down Hanover Street
to that awful place you had on—where was it?"

"North Street," I said.

"North Street. We'd get to dinner and then we'd go to your place and
you'd take me back to Newton in your red Chevrolet. Three, four o'clock
in the morning. I don't know how you got any work done, the hours we
kept."

I nodded, remembering.

"And of course when I heard you'd been sacked at H,W, I didn't
know what to think, except that it was for the best." She paused.
"Which I could've told you if you'd asked." I handed her the highball
and sat down, resuming my lawyerly posture, legs crossed, the pad in my
lap. "Do you ever think about your grandfather? Or what would've happened if you'd gone back to Chicago instead of following me here?
Whether you'd've gone into politics, like him?"

"I didn't follow you," I said. "We came together. It was where we
intended to live, together."

"Whatever." She took a long swallow of her drink. "Chicago's such a
different place from Boston, all that prairie. Boston's close and settled
and old, so charming." I listened, tapping the pencil on my legal pad. It
was dark now. At night the city seemed less close and settled. The cars in
the street outside were bumper to bumper, honking. There was a snarl at
the intersection, one car double-parked and another stalled. A car door
slammed and there were angry shouts. She looked at me, smiling. "I
don't want anything particular from him."

I made a note on my pad.

"I have plenty of money; so does he. Isn't that the modern way? No
punitive damages?" She hesitated. "So there won't be any great opportu-
nity to delve into the assets. And Frank's trust. Or mine."

I ignored that. "Of course there's little Frank."

She looked at me with the hint of a malicious grin. "How did you know his name?"

"Because I follow your every movement," I said, with as much sarcasm as I could muster. "For Christ's sake, Beth. I don't know how I know his name. People like Frank Greer always name their children after themselves."

"Don't get belligerent," she said. "A more devoted father—" she began and then broke off.

"Yes," I said.

"—he's devoted to little Frank." She hesitated, staring out the window for a long moment. She was holding her glass with both hands, in her lap. She said, "What was the name of that man, your grandfather's lawyer?"

"Tom," I said.

"God, yes," she said, laughing lightly. "Tom, one of those sturdy midwestern names."

"I think," I said evenly, "I think Tom is a fairly common name. I think it is common even in Boston."

She laughed again, hugely amused. "God, yes, it's common."

I glared at her, not at all surprised that she remembered which buttons worked and which didn't. Beth had an elephant's memory for any man's soft spots. Why Tom was one of mine was not so easily explained; Beth would have one explanation, I another. But of course she remembered. My background was always a source of tension between us, no doubt because my own attitude was ambiguous. She found my grandfather and Tom . . . quaint. They were colorful provincials, far from her Boston milieu, and she condescended to them exactly as certain English condescend to Australians.

"It's a riot," she said.

"So," I said quietly, glancing at my watch. "What is it that you want me to do now?"

"A quick, clean divorce," she said. "Joint custody for little Frank, though it's understood he lives with me. Nothing changes hands, we leave with what we brought, *status quo ante*. I take my pictures, he takes his shotguns. Except, naturally, the house in Beverly. It's mine anyway, though for convenience it's in both our names. He understands that."

"What about the farm?"

"We split that, fifty-fifty."

"Uh-huh," I said.

"Is it always this easy?"

"We don't know how easy it'll be," I said carefully. "Until I talk to his lawyer. Maybe it won't be easy at all. It depends on what he thinks his grievances are."

"He hasn't got any."

"Well," I said.

"So it'll be easy," she said, beginning to cry.

We had agreed to go to dinner after meeting in my office. I proposed the Ritz; she countered with a French restaurant I had never heard of. She insisted, Boylston Street nouvelle cuisine, and I acceded, not without complaint. I told her about a client, a newspaperman who came to me every six years for his divorce. The newspaperman said that the nouvelle cuisine reminded him of the nouveau journalisme—a colorful plate, agreeably subtle, wonderfully presented with inspired combinations, and underdone. The portions were small, every dish had a separate sauce, and you were hungry when you finished. A triumph of style over substance.

She listened patiently, distracted.

I was trying to make her laugh. "But I can get a New York strip here, which they'll call an entrecôte, and there isn't a lot you can do to ruin a steak. Though they will try."

"You haven't changed," she said bleakly.

"Yes, I have," I said. "In the old days I would've been as excited about this place as you are. I'd know the names of the specialties of the house and of the chef. In the old days I was as al dente as the veggies. But not anymore." I glanced sourly around the room. The colors were pastel, various tints of yellow, even to a limp jonquil in the center of each table, all of it illuminated by candles thin as pencils and a dozen wee chandeliers overhead. It was very feminine and not crowded; expensive restaurants rarely were in Boston now; the money was running out.

"I'm sorry about the tears," she said.

I said, "Don't be."

"I knew I was going to bawl when I made that remark about Tom and you reacted."

"Yes," I said. I'd known it too.

"It made me sad. It reminded me of when we were breaking up and all the arguments we had."

I smiled gamely. "I was al dente then, and I broke easily." I knew what she was leading up to, and I didn't want it. When the waiter arrived I ordered whiskey for us both, waiting for the little superior sneer and feeling vaguely disappointed when he smiled pleasantly and flounced off. I started to tell her a story but she cut me off, as I knew she would.

"It reminded me of that ghastly dinner and how awful everything was afterward."

I muttered something noncommittal, but the expression on her face told me she wanted more, so I said it was over and forgotten, part of the buried past, etcetera. Like hell. We had argued about the restaurant that night, as we had tonight, except I won and we went to the Union Oyster House. My parents were in town, my father ostensibly on business; in fact they were in Boston to meet Beth. The dinner did not go well from the beginning; the restaurant was crowded and the service indifferent. My parents didn't seem to care, but Beth was irritated—"The Union Oyster Tourist Trap"—and that in turn put me on edge, or perhaps it was the other way around. Halfway through dinner, I suspect in an effort to salvage things, my father shyly handed Beth a wrapped package. It was a bracelet he had selected himself; even my mother didn't know about it. It was so unlike him, and such a sweet gesture, tears jumped to my eyes. Even before she opened it, I knew it would not be right. Beth had a particular taste in jewelry and as a consequence rarely wore any. I hoped she could disguise her feelings, but as it happened she giggled. And did not put the bracelet on, but hurried it into her purse, after leaning over the table and kissing my father. He did not fail to notice the bracelet rushed out of sight. Probably he didn't miss the giggle, either. In the manner of families, after a suitable silent interval my father and I commenced to quarrel. On the surface it was a quarrel about businessmen and professional men, but actually it had to do with the merits of the East and the merits of the Midwest and my father's knowledge that I had rejected the values of his region. The Midwest asserted its claims early, and if you had a restless nature you left. It forced you to leave; there were no halfway measures in the heartland, at that time a province as surely as Franche-Comté or Castile, an interior region pressed by the culture of the coasts, defensive, suspicious, and claustrophobic. When I left I tried to explain to him that a New Yorker's restlessness or ambition could take him to Washington as a Bostonian's could take him to New York, the one city representing power and the other money. No midwesterner, making the momentous decision to leave home, would go from Chicago to Cleveland or from Minneapolis to Kansas City. These places are around the corner from one another. The Midwest is the same wherever you go, the towns larger or smaller but the culture identical. Leaving the Midwest, one perforce rejects the Midwest and its values; its sense of inferiority—so I felt then—prevented any return. In some way it had failed. What sound reason could there be for leaving God's country, the very soul of the nation, to live and work on the cluttered margins? It had failed you and you had failed it, whoring after glitter. My father's chivalry did not allow him to blame "that girl" publicly, but I knew that privately he did. Too much—too much Boston, too much money, too determined, too self-possessed. He hated to think that his son—flesh of my flesh, blood of my blood!—could be led out of Chicagoland by a woman. The image I imagine it brought to his mind was of an ox dumbly plodding down a road, supervised by a young woman lightly flicking its withers with a stick. That ghastly dinner!

"The thing is." She smiled wanly, back in the present now: that is, her own life, and what she had made of it. "It's so—*tiresome.* I know the marriage is over, it's probably been finished for years. But starting over again. I don't want to start over again. I haven't the energy." She sighed. "He's said for years that he's got to find himself. He's forty-eight years old and he's lost and now he wants to be found. And I'm sure he will be."

"Usually it's the other way around," I said. "These days, it's the women who want to find themselves. Or get lost, one or the other."

"Frank has a feminine side." I nodded, thinking of Frank Greer as a pastel. Frank in lime-green and white, cool and pretty as a gin and tonic. "But the point isn't Frank," Beth said. "It's me. I don't want to start over again. I started over again once and that didn't work and then I started over again and it was fun for a while and then it was a routine, like everything else. I like the routine. And I was younger then."

I did not quite follow that, so I said, "I know."

"Liar," she said. "How could you? You've never been married."

"Beth," I said.

She looked at me irritably. "That doesn't count. You've got to be married for at least five years before it's a marriage. And there have to be children, or at least a child. Otherwise it's just shacking up and you can get out of it as easily and painlessly as you got into it, which from the sound of yours was pretty easy and painless."

I looked away while the waiter set down our drinks and, with a flourish, the menus.

"How long ago was it?"

"Almost twenty years ago," I said.

"Where is she now?"

I shrugged. I had no idea. When she left me she went back to London. I heard she had a job there; then, a few years ago, I heard she was living in France, married, with children. Then I heard she was no longer in France but somewhere else on the Continent, unmarried now.

"That's what I mean," she said. "You don't even know where she *is.*"

"Well," I said. "She knows where I am."

"What was her name?"

"Rachel," I said.

Beth thought a moment. "Was she Jewish?"

"Yes," I said.

Beth made a little sound, but did not comment. The amused look on her face said that my father must have found Rachel even more unsuitable than Beth. As it happened, she was right, but it had nothing to do with Rachel's Jewishness. She was a foreigner with pronounced political opinions. "And you like living alone," Beth said.

"At first I hated it," I said. "But I like it now and I can't imagine living any other way. It's what I do, live alone. You get married, I don't. Everyone I know gets married and almost everyone I know gets divorced."

"Well, you see it from the outside."

"It's close enough," I said.

"Yes, but it's not *real.*" She glanced left into Boylston Street. It was snowing, and only a few pedestrians were about, bending into the wind. She shivered when she looked at the stiff-legged pedestrians, their movements so spiritless and numb against the concrete of the sidewalk, the sight bleaker still by contrast with the pale monochrome and the fragrance of the restaurant. Outside was a dark, malicious, European winter, Prague perhaps, or Moscow. "We might've made it," she said tentatively, still looking out the window.

I said nothing. She was dead wrong about that.

She sat with her chin in her hand, staring into the blowing snow. "But we were so different, and you were so bad."

The waiter was hovering and I turned to ask him the specialties of the day. They were a tiny bird en croûte, a fish soufflé, and a vegetable ensemble. Beth was silent, inspecting the menu; she had slipped on a pair of half-glasses for this chore. I ordered a dozen oysters and an entrecôte, medium well. I knew that if I ordered it medium well I had a fair chance of getting it medium rare. Then I ordered a baked potato and a Caesar salad and another drink. The waiter caught something in my tone and courteously suggested that medium well was excessive. I said all right, if he would promise a true medium rare. Beth ordered a fish I never heard of and called for the wine list. The waiter seemed much happier dealing with Beth than with me. They conferred over the wine list for a few moments, and then he left.

She said, "You're always so defensive."

"I don't like these places, I told you that." I heard the Boston whine in my voice and retreated a step. "The waiter's okay."

"You never did like them," she said. "But at least *before* . . ." She shook her head, exasperated.

"Before, what?" I asked.

"At least you were a provincial, there was an excuse."

I pulled at my drink, irritated. But when I saw her smiling slyly I had to laugh. Nothing had changed, though we had not seen each other in fifteen years and had not spoken in twenty. The occasion fifteen years ago was a wedding reception. I saw her standing in a corner talking to Frank Greer. She was recently divorced from Doran. I was about to approach to say hello; then I saw the expression on her face and withdrew. She and Greer were in another world, oblivious of the uproar around them, and I recognized the expression: it was the one I thought was reserved for me. Now, looking at her across the restaurant table, it was as if we had never been apart, as if our attitudes were frozen in aspic. We were still like a divided legislature, forever arguing over the economy, social policy, the defense budget, and the cuisine in the Senate dining room. The same arguments, conducted in the same terms; the same old struggle for control of our future. Her prejudice, my pride.

"You have to tell me one thing." She turned to inspect the bottle the waiter presented, raising her head so she could see through the half-glasses. She touched the label of the wine with her fingernails and said yes, it was fine, excellent really, and then, turning, her head still raised, she assured me that I would find it drinkable, since it came from a splendid little chateau vineyard near the Wisconsin Dells. The waiter looked at her dubiously and asked whether he should open it now and put it on ice, and she said yes, of course, she wanted it so cold she'd need her mittens to pour it. I was laughing and thinking how attractive she was, a woman whose humor improved with age, if she would just let up a little on the other. Also, I was waiting for the "one thing" I would have to tell her.

I said, "You're a damn funny woman."

"I have good material," she said.

"Not always," I replied.

"The one thing," she said, "that I can't figure out. Never could figure out. Why did you stay here? This isn't your kind of town at all, never was. It's so circumspect, and sure of itself. I'm surprised you didn't go back to Chicago after you were canned by H,W."

"I like collapsing civilizations," I said. "I'm a connoisseur of collapse and systems breakdown and bankruptcy—moral, ethical, and financial. So Boston is perfect." I thought of the town where I grew up, so secure and prosperous then, so down-at-heel now, the foundry old, exhausted, incidental, and off the subject. We lived in Chicago's muscular shadow and were thankful for it, before the world went to hell. "And I wasn't about to be run out of town by people like that," I added truculently.

"So it was spite," she said.

"Not spite," I said equably. "Inertia."

"And you're still spending weekends in New York?"

I nodded. Not as often now as in the past, though.

"Weird life you lead," she said.

I said, "What's so weird about it?"

"Weekdays here, weekends in New York. And you still have your flat near the brownstone, the same one?"

I looked at her with feigned surprise. "How did you know about my flat?"

"For God's sake," she said. "Nora's a friend of mine."

It was never easy to score a point on Beth Earle. I said, "I've had it for almost twenty years. And I'll have it for twenty more. It's my Panama Canal. I bought it, I paid for it, it's mine, and I intend to keep it."

She shook her head, smiling ruefully. She said that she had lived in half a dozen houses over the years and remembered each one down to the smallest detail: the color of the tile in the bathroom and the shape of the clothes closet in the bedroom. She and Doran had lived in Provincetown for a year, and then had moved to Gloucester. That was when Doran was trying to paint. Then, after Doran, she lived alone in Marblehead. When she was married to Frank Greer they went to New York, then returned to Boston; he owned an apartment on Beacon Hill. They lived alone there for two years, and then moved to Beverly—her idea; she was tired of the city. She counted these places on her fingers. "Six," she said. "And all this time, you've been in the same place in the Back Bay." She was leaning across the table, and now she looked up. The waiter placed a small salad in front of her and the oysters in front of me. The oysters were Cotuits. She signaled for the wine and said that "Monsieur" would taste. She told the waiter I was a distinguished gourmet, much sought after as a taster, and that my wine cellar in Michigan City was the envy of the region. She gave the impression that the restaurant was lucky to have me as a patron. The waiter shot me a sharp look and poured the wine into my glass. I pronounced it fine. Actually, I said it was "swell," and then, gargling heartily, "dandy." I gave Beth one of the oysters and insisted that she eat it the way it was meant to be eaten, naked out of the shell, without catsup or horseradish. She sucked it up, and then leaned across the table once again. "Don't you miss them, the arguments? The struggle, always rubbing off someone else? The fights, the friction—?"

I laughed loudly. "Miss them to death," I said.

We finished the bottle of white, and ordered a bottle of red; she said she preferred red with fish. I suspected that that was a concession to my entrecôte, which at any event was rare and bloody. She continued to press, gently at first, then with vehemence. She was trying to work out her life and thought that somehow I was a clue to it. At last she demanded that I describe my days in Boston. She wanted to know how I lived, the details, "the quotidian." I was reluctant to do this, having lived privately for so many years. Also, there was very little to describe. I had fallen into the bachelor habit of total predictability. Except to travel to the airport and the courts, I seldom left the Back Bay. My terrain was bordered by the Public Garden and the Ritz, Storrow Drive, Newbury Street, the brownstone where I worked and Commonwealth Avenue where I lived. I walked to work, lunched at the Ritz, took a stroll in the Garden, returned to the brownstone, and at seven or so went home. People I knew tended to live in the Back Bay or on the Hill, so if I went out in the evening I walked. Each year it became easier not to leave the apartment; I needed an exceptional reason to do so. I liked my work and worked hard at it.

She listened avidly, but did not comment. The waiter came to clear the table and offer dessert. We declined, ordering coffee and cognac.

"What kind of car do you have?" she asked suddenly.

I said I didn't own one.

"What kind of car does she own?"

I looked at her: Who?

"Your secretary," she said. "I hear you have a relationship with your secretary."

"She's been my assistant for a very long time," I said.

"Her car," Beth said.

I said, "A Mercedes."

"Well," she said.

"Well, what?"

"Well, nothing," she said. "Except so do I."

"Two cheers for the Krauts," I said.

"Is she a nice woman?"

I laughed. "Yes," I said. "Very. And very able."

"She approves of the arrangement."

"Beth," I said.

Beth said, "I wonder what she gets out of it?"

"She won't ever have to get divorced," I said. "That's one thing she gets out of it."

"Was she the woman in the outer office?"

"Probably," I said.

Beth was silent a moment, toying with her coffee cup. There was only one other couple left in the restaurant, and they were preparing to leave. "You were always secretive," she said.

"You were not exactly an open book."

She ignored that. "It's not an attractive trait, being secretive. It leaves you wide open."

For what? I wondered. I looked at her closely, uncertain whether it was she talking or the wine. We were both tight, but her voice had an edge that had not been there before. I poured more coffee, wondering whether I should ask the question that had been in my mind for the past hour. I knew I would not like the answer, whatever it was, but I was curious. Being with her again, I began to remember things I had not thought of in years; it was as if the two decades were no greater distance than the width of the table, and I had only to lean across the space and take her hand to be twenty-five again. The evening had already been very unsettling and strange; no reason, I thought, not to make it stranger still.

I said quietly, "How was I so bad?"

"You never let go," she said. "You just hung on for dear life."

"Right," I said. I had no idea what she was talking about.

"Our plans," she began.

"Depended on me letting go?"

She shrugged. "You tried to fit in and you never did."

"In Boston," I said.

She moved her head, yes and no; apparently the point was a subtle one. "I didn't want to come back here and you insisted. I was depending on you to take me away, or at least make an independent life. You never understood that I had always been on the outs with my family."

I stifled an urge to object. I had never wanted to come to Boston. It was where she lived. It was her town, not mine. Glorious Boston, cradle of the Revolution. I had no intrinsic interest in Boston, I only wanted to leave the Midwest. Boston was as good a city as any, and she lived there—

"You were such a damn good *listener*." She bit the word off, as if it were an obscenity. "Better than you are now, and you're pretty good now. Not so good at talking, though. You listened so well a woman forgot that you never talked yourself, never let on what it was *that was on your mind*. Not one of your strong points, talking."

"Beth," I said evenly. She waited, but I said nothing more; there was nothing more to say anyhow, and I knew the silence would irritate her.

"And it was obvious it would never work; we never got grounded here. And it was obvious you never would, you could never let go of your damned prairie *complexe d'infériorité*. And as a result you were"—she sought the correct word—*"louche."*

"I am not André Malraux," I said. "What the hell does that mean?"

"It means secretive," she said. "And something more. Furtive."

"Thanks," I said.

"It's a mystery to me why I'm still here. Not so great a mystery as you, but mystery enough. You had to lead the way, though, and you didn't. And I knew H,W was a mistake."

"It was your uncle who suggested it," I said.

"After you asked him," she said.

"At your urging," I said.

"When it looked like you wouldn't land anything and I was tired of the griping."

"You were the one who was nervous," I said.

"I didn't care where we lived," she said. "That was the point you never got." Her voice rose, and I saw the waiter turn and say something to the maître d'. The other couple had left and we were alone in the restaurant. Outside, a police car sped by, its lights blazing, but without sirens. The officer in the passenger seat was white-haired and fat, and he was smoking a cigar. It had stopped snowing but the wind was fierce, blowing debris and rattling windows. The police car had disappeared. I motioned to the waiter for the check. But Beth was far from finished.

"So I married Doran."

"And I didn't marry anybody."

"You married Rachel."

"According to you, Rachel doesn't count."

"Neither did Doran."

The waiter brought the check and I automatically reached for my wallet. She said loudly, "No," and I looked at her, momentarily confused. I had forgotten it was her treat. I had become so absorbed in the past; always when we had been together, I had paid, and it seemed cheap of me to let her pay now. But that was what she wanted and I had agreed to it. She had the check in her hand and was inspecting it for errors. Then, satisfied, she pushed it aside along with a credit card. She exhaled softly and turned to look out the window.

She said quietly, talking to the window, "Do you think it will be easy?"

"I don't know," I said.

"Please," she said. She said it hesitantly, as if the word were unfamiliar. "Just tell me what you think. I won't hold you to it, if you're wrong."

"His lawyer," I began.

"Please," she said again, more forcefully.

"You're asking me for assurances that I can't give. I don't know."

"Just a guess," she said. "In your line of work you must make guesses all the time. Make one now, between us. Between friends."

"Well, then," I said. "No."

"The first one was easy."

"Maybe this will be too," I said.

"But you don't think so."

"No," I said. I knew Frank Greer.

She said, "You're a peach." She put on her glasses.

I did not reply to that.

"I mean it," she said.

Apparently she did, for she looked at me and smiled warmly.

"I have disrupted your life."

I shook my head, No.

"Yes, I have. That's what I do sometimes, disrupt the lives of men."

There was so much to say to that, and so little to be gained. I lit a cigarette, listening.

With a quick movement she pushed the half-glasses over her forehead and into her hair, all business. "Get in touch with him tomorrow. Can you do that?"

"Sure," I said.

"And let me know what he says, right away."

"Yes," I said.

"I don't think it's going to be so tough."

"I hope you're right," I said.

"But I've always been an optimist where men are concerned."

I smiled and touched her hand. I looked at her closely, remembering her as a young woman; I knew her now and I knew her then, but there was nothing in between. That was undiscovered territory. I saw the difficulties ahead. They were big as mountains, Annapurna-sized difficulties, a long slog at high altitudes, defending Beth. I took my hand away and said, "You can bail out any time you want, if this gets difficult or awkward. I know it isn't easy. I can put you in touch with any one of a dozen—" She stared at me for a long moment. In the candlelight her face seemed to flush. Suddenly I knew she was murderously angry.

"I think you're right," she said.

"Look," I began.

"Reluctant lawyers are worse than useless." She took off her glasses and put them in her purse. When she snapped the purse shut it sounded like a pistol shot.

"I'll call you tomorrow," I said. I knew that I had handled it badly, but there was no retreat now.

She stood up and the waiter swung into position, helping her with her chair and bowing prettily from the waist.

Outside on Boylston Street the wind was still blowing, and the street was empty except for two cabs at the curb. We stood a moment on the sidewalk, not speaking. She stood with her head turned away, and I thought for a moment she was crying. But when she turned her head I saw the set of her jaw. She was too angry to cry. She began to walk up the street, and I followed. The wind off the Atlantic was vicious. I thought of it as originating in Scotland or Scandinavia, but of course that was wrong. Didn't the wind blow from west to east? This one probably originated in the upper Midwest or Canada. It had a prairie feel to it. We both walked unsteadily with our heads tucked into our coat collars. I thought of Tom and his camel's-hair coat. At Arlington Street she stopped and fumbled for her keys, and then resumed the march. A beggar was at our heels, asking for money. I turned, apprehensive, but he was a sweet-faced drunk. I gave him a dollar and he ambled off. Her car was parked across the street from the Ritz, a green Mercedes convertible with her initials in gold on the door. The car gleamed in the harsh white light of the streetlamps. She stooped to unlock the door, and when she opened it the smell of leather, warm and inviting, spilled into the frigid street. I held the door for her, but she did not get in. She stood looking

at me, her face expressionless. She started to say something, but changed
her mind. She threw her purse into the back seat and the next thing I
knew I was reeling backward, then slipping on an icy patch and falling.
Her fist had come out of nowhere and caught me under the right eye.
Sprawled on the sidewalk, speechless, I watched her get into the car and
drive away. The smell of leather remained in my vicinity.

The doorman at the Ritz had seen all of it, and now he hurried across
Arlington Street. He helped me up, muttering and fussing, but despite
his best intentions he could not help smiling. He kept his face half
turned away so I would not see. Of course he knew me; I was a regular in
the bar and the café.

Damn woman, I said. She could go ten with Marvin Hagler.

He thought it all right then to laugh.

Not like the old days, I said.

Packed quite a punch, did she, sir? Ha-ha.

I leaned against the iron fence and collected my wits.

Anything broken? he asked.

I didn't think so. I moved my legs and arms, touched my eye. It was
tender but there was no blood. I knew I would have a shiner and wondered how I would explain that at the office.

Let's get you into the bar, he said. A brandy—

No. I shook my head painfully and reached for my wallet. The doorman waited, his face slightly averted as before. I found a five, then
thought better of it and gave him a twenty. He didn't have to be told
that twenty dollars bought silence. He tucked the money away in his vest
and tipped his hat, frowning solicitously.

You wait here one minute, he said. I'll fetch a cab.

No need, I replied. Prefer to walk. I live nearby.

I know, he said, looking at me doubtfully. Then, noticing he had
customers under the hotel canopy, he hurried back across the street. I
watched him go, assuring the people with a casual wave of his hand that
the disturbance was a private matter, minor and entirely under control.

I moved away too, conscious of being watched and realizing that I was
very tight. I was breathing hard and could smell my cognac breath. I felt
my eye beginning to puff and I knew that I would have bruises on my
backside. I decided to take a long way home and walked through the iron
gate into the Garden. There was no one about, but the place was filthy,
papers blowing everywhere and ash cans stuffed to overflowing. The
flurries had left a residue of gray snow. I passed a potato-faced George
Washington on horseback on my way along the path to the statue facing

Marlborough Street. This was my favorite. Atop the column a physician cradled an unconscious patient, "to commemorate the discovery that the inhaling of ether causes insensibility to pain. First proved to the world at the Mass. General Hospital." It was a pretty little Victorian sculpture. On the plinth someone had scrawled *Up the I.R.A.* in red paint.

I exited at the Beacon Street side. A cab paused, but I waved him on. I labored painfully down Beacon to Clarendon and over to Commonwealth, my shoes scuffing little shards of blue glass, hard and bright as diamonds; this was window glass from the automobiles vandalized nightly. While I waited at the light a large American sedan pulled up next to me, its fender grazing my leg, two men and a woman staring menacingly out the side windows. I took a step backward, and the sedan sped through the red light, trailing rock music and laughter. Tires squealed as the car accelerated, wheeling right on Newbury.

My flat was only a few blocks away. I walked down the deserted mall, my eyes up and watchful. Leafless trees leaned over the walkway, their twisted branches grotesque against the night sky. I walked carefully, for there was ice and dog shit everywhere. The old-fashioned streetlights, truly handsome in daytime, were useless now. It was all so familiar; I had walked down this mall every day for twenty years. Twenty years ago, when there was no danger after dark, Rachel and I took long strolls on summer evenings trying to reach an understanding, and failing. I remembered her musical voice and her accent; when she was distressed she spoke rapidly, but always with perfect diction. I looked up, searching for my living-room window. I was light-headed now and stumbling, but I knew I was close. The Hancock was to my left, as big as a mountain and as sheer, looming like some futuristic religious icon over the low, crabbed sprawl of the Back Bay. I leaned against a tree, out of breath. There was only a little way now; I could see the light in the window. My right eye was almost closed, and my vision blurred. The wind bit into my face, sending huge tears running down my cheeks. I hunched my shoulders against the wind and struggled on, through the empty streets of the city I hated so.

SISTER

TOBIAS WOLFF

Tobias Wolff is a native of the state of Washington. His short fiction
has appeared in *Antaeus*, the *Atlantic*, *Esquire*, *TriQuarterly*, *Vanity
Fair*, and many other magazines, reviews, and anthologies in this country and abroad. His first collection, *In the Garden of the North American Martyrs* (Ecco, 1981), received the St. Lawrence Award for Fiction. "Sister" is part of a new collection, *Desert Breakdown*, to be
published by Houghton Mifflin in the fall of 1985. Tobias Wolff
teaches at Syracuse University.

There was a park at the bottom of the hill. Now that the leaves were
down Marty could see the exercise stations and part of a tennis court
from her kitchen window, through a web of black branches. She took
another donut from the box on the table and ate it slowly, watching the
people at the exercise stations: two men and a woman. The woman was
doing leg-raisers. The men were just standing there. Though the day was
cold one of the men had taken his shirt off, and even from this distance
Marty was struck by the deep brown color of his skin. You hardly ever
saw great tans like that on people around here, not even in summer. He
had come from somewhere else.

She went into the bedroom and put on a running suit and an old pair
of Adidas. The seams were giving out but her other pair was new and
their whiteness made her feet look big. She took off her glasses and put
her contacts in. Tears welled up under the lenses. For a few moments she
lost her image in the mirror; then it returned and she saw the excitement
in her face, the eagerness. Whoa, she thought. She sat there for a while,
feeling the steady thump of the stereo in the apartment overhead. Then
she rolled a joint and stuck it in the pocket of her sweatshirt.

A dog barked at Marty as she walked down the hallway. It barked at
her every time she passed its door and it always took her by surprise,
making her heart clench and then pound wildly. The dog was a big
shepherd whose owners were gone all the time and never took it out. She

could hear its feet scrabbling and see its nose pushed under the door. "Easy," she said, "easy there," but it kept trying to get at her and Marty heard it barking all the way down the corridor, until she reached the door and stepped outside.

It was late afternoon and cold, so cold she could see her breath. As always on Sunday the street was dead quiet, except for the skittering of leaves on the sidewalk as the breeze swept through them and ruffled the cold-looking pools of water from last night's rain. With the trees bare the sky seemed vast. Two dark clouds drifted overhead, and in the far distance an angle of geese flew across the sky. Honkers, her brother called them. Right now he and his buddies would be banging away at them from one of the marshes outside town. By nightfall they'd all be drunk. She smiled, thinking of that.

Marty did a couple of knee-bends and headed toward the park, forcing herself to walk against the urge she felt to run. She considered taking a couple of hits off the joint in her pocket but decided against it. She didn't want to lose her edge.

The woman she'd seen at the exercise station was gone, but the two men were still there. Marty held back, did a few more knee-bends and watched some boys playing football on the field behind the tennis courts. They couldn't have been more than ten or eleven but they moved like men, hunching up their shoulders and shaking their wrists as they jogged back to the huddle, grunting when they came off the line as if their bodies were big and weighty. You could tell that in their heads they had a whole stadium of people watching them. It tickled her. Marty watched them run several plays, then she walked over to the exercise stations.

When she got there she had a shock. Marty recognized one of the men, and she was so afraid that he would recognize her that she almost turned around and went home. He was a regular at the Kon-Tiki. A few weeks earlier he had taken notice of Marty and they'd matched daiquiris for a couple of hours and things looked pretty good. Then she went out to the car to get this book she'd been describing to him, a book about Edgar Cayce and reincarnation, and when she got back he was sitting on the other side of the room with someone else. He hadn't left anything for the drinks, so she got stuck with the bar bill. And her lighter was missing. The man's name was Jack. When she saw him leaning against the chin-up station she didn't know what to do. She wanted to vanish right into the ground.

But he seemed not to remember her. In fact, he was the one who said hello. "Hey there," he said.

She smiled at him. Then she looked at the tan one and said, "Hi."
He didn't answer. His eyes moved over her for a moment, and he
looked away. He'd put on a warm-up jacket with a hood, but left the
zipper open nearly to his waist. His chest was covered with little curls of
glistening golden hair. The other one, Jack, had on faded army fatigues
with dark patches where the insignia had been removed. He needed a
shave. He was holding a quart bottle of beer.

The two men had been talking when she walked up but now they
were silent. Marty felt them watching her as she did her stretches. They
had been talking about sex, she was sure of that. What they'd been
saying was still in the air somehow, with the ripe smell of wet leaves and
the rainsoaked earth. She took a deep breath.

Then she said, "You didn't get that tan around here." She kept rocking back and forth on her knuckles but looked up at him.

"You bet your buns I didn't," he said. "The only thing you get around
here is arthritis." He pulled the zipper of his jacket up and down.
"Hawaii. Waikiki Beach."

"Waikiki," Jack said. "Bikini-watching capital of the world."

"Brother, you speak true," the tan one said. "They've got this special
breed over there that they raise just to walk back and forth in front of
you. They ought to parachute about fifty of them into Russia. Those old
farts in the Kremlin would go out of their skulls. We could just walk in
and take the place over."

"They could drop a couple on this place while they're at it," Jack said.

"Amen." The tan one nodded. "Make it four—two apiece."

"Aloha," Marty said. She rolled over on her back and raised her feet a
few inches off the ground. She held them there for a moment, then
lowered them. "That's all the Hawaiian I know," she said. "Aloha and
Maui Zowie. They grow some killer weed over there."

"For sure," the tan one said. "It's God's country, sister, and that's a
fact."

Jack walked up closer. "I know you from somewhere," he said.

Oh no, Marty thought. She smiled at him. "Maybe," she said.
"What's your name?"

"Bill," he said.

Right, Marty wanted to say. You bet, Jack.

Jack looked down at her. "What's yours?"

She raised her feet again. "Elizabeth."

"Elizabeth," he repeated, slowly, so that it struck Marty how beautiful the name was. *Fairfield*, she almost added, but she hesitated, and the moment passed.

"I guess not," he said.

She lowered her feet and sat up. "A lot of people look like me."

He nodded.

Just then something flew past Marty's head. She jerked to one side and threw her hands up in front of her face. "Jesus," she said.

"Sorry!" someone shouted.

"Goddam frisbees," Jack said.

"It's all right," Marty told him, and waved at the man who'd thrown it. She turned and waved again at another man some distance behind her, who was wiping the frisbee on his shirt. He waved back.

"Frisbee freaks," Jack said. "I'm sick of them." He lifted the bottle and drank from it, then held it out to Marty. "Go on," he told her.

She took a swig. "There's more than beer in here," she said.

Jack shrugged.

"What's in here?" she asked.

"Secret formula," he answered. "Go for two. You're behind."

Marty looked at the bottle, then drank again and passed it to the other man. Even his fingers were brown. He wore a thick wedding band and a gold chain-linked bracelet. She held on to the bottle for an extra moment, long enough for him to notice, and give her a look; then she let go. The hood of his jacket fell back as he tilted his head to drink. Marty saw that he was nearly bald. He had parted his hair just above one ear and swept it sideways to cover the skin on top, which was even darker than the rest of him.

"What's your name?" she asked.

Jack answered for him. "His name is Jack," he said.

The tan one laughed. "Brother," he said, "you are too much."

"You aren't from around here," she said. "I would have seen you."

He shook his head. "I was running and I ended up here."

Jack said, "Don't hog the fuel, Jack," and made a drinking motion with his hand.

The tan one nodded. He took a long pull and wiped his mouth and passed the bottle to Jack.

Marty stood and brushed off her warm-ups. "Hawaii," she said. "I've always wanted to go to Hawaii. Just kick back for about three weeks. Check out the volcanoes. Do some mai tais."

"Get leis," Jack said.

All three of them laughed.

"Well," she said. She touched her toes a couple of times.

Jack kept laughing.

"Hawaii's amazing," said the other man. "Anything goes."

"Stop talking about Hawaii," Jack said. "It makes me cold."

"Me too," Marty said. She rubbed her hands together. "I'm always cold. When I come back, I just hope I come back as a native of someplace warm."

"Right," Jack said, but there was something in his voice that made her look over at him. He was studying her. She could tell that he was trying to place her again, trying to recall where he'd met her. She wished she hadn't made that remark about coming back. That was what had set him off. She wasn't even sure she actually believed it—believed that she was going to return as a different entity later on, someone new and different. She had serious doubts, sometimes. But at other times she thought it had to be true; this couldn't be everything.

"So," she said, "do you guys know each other?"

Jack stared at her a moment longer, then nodded. "All our lives," he said.

The tan one shook his head and laughed. "Too much," he said.

"We're inseparable," Jack said. "Aren't we, Jack?"

The tan one laughed again.

"Is that right?" Marty asked him. "Are you inseparable?"

He pulled the zipper of his jacket up and down, hiding and then revealing the golden hairs on his chest though not in a conscious way. His cheeks puffed out and his brow thickened just above his eyes, so that his face seemed heavier. Marty could see that he was thinking. Finally he looked at her and said, "I guess we are. For the time being."

"That's fine," she said. "That's all right." That was all right, she thought. She could call Jill, Jill was always up for a party, and if Jill was out or had company then she'd think of something else. It would work out.

"Okay," she said, but before she could say anything else someone yelled "Heads up!" and they all looked around. The frisbee was coming straight at them. Marty felt her body tighten. "Got it," she said, and balanced herself for the catch. Suddenly the breeze gusted and the frisbee seemed to stop cold, a quivering red line, and then it jerked upwards and flew over their heads and past them. She ran after it, one arm raised, gathering herself to jump, but it stayed just out of reach and finally she gave up.

The frisbee flew a short distance farther, then fell to the sidewalk and skidded halfway across the street. Marty scooped it up and flipped it back into the park. She stood there, wanting to laugh but completely out of breath. Too much weed, she thought. She put her hands on her knees and rocked back and forth. It was quiet. Then, from up the hill, she heard a low rumble that grew steadily louder and a few seconds later a big white car came around the corner. Its tires squealed and then went silent as the car slid through a long sheet of water lying in the road. It was moving sideways in her direction. She watched it come. The car cleared the water and the tires began to squeal again but it kept sliding, and Marty saw the faces inside getting bigger and bigger. There was a girl staring at her from the front window. The girl's mouth was open, her arms braced against the dashboard. Then the tires caught and the car shot forward, so close that Marty could have reached out and touched the girl's cheek as they went past.

The car fish-tailed down the street. It ran a stop sign at the corner and turned left back up the hill, coughing out bursts of black exhaust.

Marty turned toward the park and saw the two men looking at her. They were looking at her as if they had seen her naked, and that was how she felt—naked. She had nearly been killed and now she was an embarrassment, like someone in need. She wasn't welcome in the park.

Marty crossed the street and started up the hill toward her apartment building. She felt as if she were floating, as if there were nothing to her. She passed a gray cat curled up on the hood of a car. There was smoke on the breeze and the smell of decay. It seemed to Marty that she drifted with the smoke through the yellow light, over the dull grass and the brown clumps of leaves. In the park behind her a boy called football signals, his voice perfectly distinct in the thin cold air.

She climbed the steps to the building but did not go inside. She knew that the dog would bark at her, and she didn't think she could handle that right now.

She sat on the steps. From somewhere nearby a bird cried out in a hoarse ratcheting voice like chain being jerked through a pulley. Marty did some breathing exercises to get steady, to quiet the fluttering sensation in her shoulders and knees, but she could not calm herself. A few minutes ago she had nearly been killed and now there was nobody to talk to about it, to see how afraid she was and tell her not to worry, that it was over now. That she was still alive. That everything was going to be all right.

At this moment, sitting here, Marty understood that there was never going to be anyone to tell her these things. She had no idea why this should be so; it was just something she knew. There was no need for her to make a fool of herself again.

The sun was going down. Marty couldn't see it from where she sat, but the windows of the house across the street had turned crimson, and the breeze was colder. A broken kite flapped in a tree. Marty fingered the joint in her pocket but left it there; she felt empty and clean, and did not want to lose the feeling.

She watched the sky darken. Her brother and his friends would be coming off the marsh about now, flushed with cold and drink, their dogs running ahead through the reeds and the tall grass. When they reach the car they'll compare birds and pass the bottle around, and after the bottle is empty they will head for the nearest bar. Do boilermakers. Stuff themselves with pickled eggs and jerky. Throw dice from a leather cup. And outside in the car the dogs will be waiting, ears pricked for the least sound, sometimes whimpering to themselves but mostly silent, tense, and still, watching the bright door the men have closed behind them.

HOLDING ON

GLORIA NORRIS

This story marks Gloria Norris's third appearance in the O. Henry
Collection. She was born in Holcomb, Mississippi, and has worked as a
writer and editor in New Orleans, Chicago, and New York. Her first
novel, *Looking for Bobby*, will be published this year by Knopf.

The woman who started it all was a Mrs. Filburton. Mrs. Arkin met this
remarkable person while visiting her sister Beulah in the Delta. Mrs.
Arkin had packed her battered old suitcase and left Pinola on the Grey-
hound bus as her first act of defiance against Mr. Arkin. He didn't see
why he should be expected to cook for himself for a week. He never had
in thirty-eight years of marriage.

But Mrs. Arkin found the courage to oppose him because she knew
she was, after all the years of thinking so, truly at the end of her rope.
And the only thing in the world that would relieve her would be not to
see Mr. Arkin for a week, not to see his bachelor brother L.B., and, most
of all, not to see L.B.'s dogs lying around her front yard. The dogs were
one of the heaviest crosses she had had to bear in life.

The truth was—it hit her one morning while she stood cleaning her
rimless glasses, her shoulders sagging—that she had never had one single
thing she wanted in all her fifty-four years. Not one single thing that she
had wanted and set out to get and gotten. All her life she had tried her
best to be good and, when things didn't work out as she wanted, she held
on and prayed they would, somehow, someday. But it struck her that
morning, looking at one of L.B.'s hounds stretched on her front steps,
that all she was doing was holding on, not ever going one step forward.

So to have a perfect stranger like Mrs. Filburton change her life was
the last thing she expected. Later she came to believe that God arranged
it all from the moment she stepped off the bus in Belzoni. Because that
very afternoon Beulah, who was the most dependable nurse in town, left
her to answer an emergency call from the hospital. Mrs. Arkin was all

alone when the two visitors arrived out of the blue—the old lady who lived next door and her visiting daughter.

The visit started off by giving her the shock of her life. As she opened Beulah's front door, a woman's voice brayed, "Now don't hide that whiskey bottle we caught you with, just pass it around!" Raucous laughter followed as the younger woman steered her mother through the door. The old lady was dressed in a neat black dress. She trembled on her cane from St. Vitus's dance, and, despite coils of hearing aid, couldn't hear thunder. Mrs. Arkin was sure she was a sweet old lady—providing you were used to invalid old folks as she was, having cared for twelve years for Mr. Arkin's ancient father, who spit tobacco juice on her clean floors, and for a penniless Arkin aunt who never showed a speck of gratitude. But Mrs. Arkin quickly saw that the daughter was common as dirt. She was dressed in red shorts that exposed white middle-aged legs crisscrossed by lumpy varicose veins. She had hennaed hair and pencilled-on eyebrows black as the ace of spades. And to Mrs. Arkin's horror the woman pushed right by her and plunked herself down on Beulah's couch while puffing a Pall Mall, letting the ash fall on the carpet.

As the visit wore on, Mrs. Filburton's hoarse voice strained at the ceiling while she talked without pause about problems with her colon and about her daughter's three beautiful and unbelievably smart children and the big two-story Jackson house this daughter lived in, with the latest and best of everything.

She moved on finally to tell about a father of ten children in her hometown who just last week fell into a vat of boiling peanut oil at the peanut mill. "Burned to a crisp, like a potato chip," Mrs. Filburton pronounced grimly. She *was* lively company, Mrs. Arkin had to admit.

The next day Beulah went off to the hospital, again neglecting her own sister. Being alone in the strange house on the flat Delta made Mrs. Arkin so blue she was actually relieved to look through the side window and see Mrs. Filburton's red shorts zigzagging toward her through Beulah's rose beds. She was by herself this time.

For the first two hours Mrs. Filburton told about all the troubles that had been caused by her three separate husbands, none of whom had enough get-up-and-go and one of whom had an artificial stomach. Warmed by this talk, Mrs. Arkin blurted out her own troubles. "Now that my children are grown and gone, and Mr. Arkin is always worrying about his job managing the cotton gin . . . Well, I'd just like to have work of my own, but what can a lady do?"

What she couldn't put into words was that in her whole life no one had thought she deserved one moment of happiness. L.B.'s dogs had been given the run of her yard and dug up every one of the rosebushes she lovingly set out. L.B. and the old father and aunt had eaten Mrs. Arkin's meals day in and day out without a single thank-you. And during all their years together Mr. Arkin had regarded her as a fencepost: deaf, dumb, and there to serve.

Mrs. Filburton lit a fresh Pall Mall from her butt. "Why I can see that you're just like any woman without an independent income. Under *his* thumb. Why don't you open your own cafe? Now, don't laugh. I sold mine last year, and if I had it to do over, I'd hold onto that cafe."

Puffing out blue smoke, Mrs. Filburton rasped on: "Let me tell you this, cafes all over Missippi are gonna *get rich*. Because we're gonna have tourists crawling out of the woodwork. I know that for a fact—one of my high-up friends that's a governor's colonel told me that the governor himself is determined to make northerners aware of all the lovely things we got for them to come see. Why he's already got a public relations firm in New York City talking up the Natchez pilgrimage and the Gulf Coast and Vicksburg. Vicksburg's lucky—they got all those Yankee graves. And they're going to make Miss Hospitality a girl that will *work* to attract tourists," Mrs. Filburton continued, suddenly angry, "since you know Miss Hospitality has never been anything more than a *title* for a society girl to put in her engagement write-up. Oh, I nearly died of the unfairness when my beautiful Lula lost in '52 to a *bowlegged* banker's daughter!"

Mrs. Arkin wished she would get back to the cafe business, but she murmured, "What a shame."

"Now they're going to make it a fair contest, where the prettiest girl will win it, although my Lula didn't and is still perfectly happy, thank you, married to a Jitney Jungle manager with three of the most beautiful children you ever saw."

Mrs. Filburton launched back into cafes. "They're getting ready for the tourists by building roads all over. And you know what highway building means to cafes?"

"Why no."

"It means they'll be swamped with bidness. The crews will come, and they eat like horses—and I mean they eat three times a day, plus a afternoon break for coffee and pie. Oh, I promise you, cafe owners are gonna be rich!"

With a habitual gesture, crossing an arm across her chest and apologetically fingering her collarbone, Mrs. Arkin said that she could cook well enough, but she knew nothing about running a business.

Mrs. Filburton snorted with laughter. "There's nothing so complicated about running a bidness. That's just another idea men have to make theirselves important!" They both laughed, Mrs. Arkin harder than she had in years. She had listened to Mr. Arkin's business problems over the years, and, though she never dared say so, she had often thought a little common sense could have prevented him from having them in the first place.

As the week wore on, Mrs. Arkin's hopes rose as they hadn't in years. And one afternoon, sitting on Beulah's guest bed, lacing up her stout Natural Bridge shoes, Mrs. Arkin was as stricken as if an angel had landed on her bedpost. She suddenly realized the sheer coincidence of her and Mrs. Filburton being at the same spot at the same time. Mrs. Arkin's heart fluttered like a bird's wing. She realized that God was answering her prayers of a lifetime by sending Mrs. Filburton with the cafe idea. Although no one ever even asked her to make change at church suppers, she knew now that God was working to turn her into a financially independent woman, with her own bank account.

By the time her week was up, Mrs. Arkin had made her plans with Mrs. Filburton. She would convert a small vacant house in her own side yard into a cafe, where she could serve dinner at noon to the construction crews, and Coca-Cola and pie in the afternoon to ladies. She would hire a good colored woman she knew to help her, and Ruby Ella's son, Rufus, would be engaged to do the dishes.

Mrs. Filburton thought much bigger, roaring off in her cigarette voice about which wholesale grocers would let you run a bill, how to price items for a profit and fire waitresses, how to avoid Social Security benefits for employees. And, really, this breathtaking talk was what gave Mrs. Arkin confidence for the first time in her life. She tried to store the feeling within herself, bracing herself to face the blistering opposition she would find when she returned to Pinola and told Mr. Arkin of her great plan.

For a week he refused to speak of the matter at all, resting on his first reaction of satiric laughter. But Mrs. Arkin had become crafty as a new religious convert pledged to win over a sinner. She continued to pass along tidbits of Filburton bait, and after two weeks she could tell his resistance was actually breaking down. It was Duncan Hines that broke him.

As Mr. Arkin blundered noisily through the house checking the locks for the night, Mrs. Arkin suddenly remembered what Mrs. Filburton described as "a cafe's sure-fire ticket to success." But she waited until breakfast to bring it up. Mr. Arkin, a fat man with a steady appetite, was at his most congenial at meals.

"There's a man named Duncan Hines," she began, as Mr. Arkin bent over his plate of ham and eggs, "who comes around to cafes and eats, and if he likes it, you get a sign that says he recommends your cafe."

Mr. Arkin said nothing, but she could tell he was listening because he was only chewing, not putting anything more in his mouth. "And when you have that sign up that says Duncan Hines recommends your place, anybody going by will know you have a good cafe and they'll stop and give you business."

Slowly Mr. Arkin buttered three fresh biscuits and thickly spread them with fig preserves. "Not only people coming by," she added, "Duncan Hines puts out a book with the names of cafes he recommends and people traveling make it a point to go by those cafes and eat."

"Just on his say-so?" Mr. Arkin demanded.

"Just on his say-so," Mrs. Arkin answered confidently.

Unbelievably the day came when the cafe was opened. As soon as Mr. Arkin had given in, won by the notion of free Hines advertising, Mrs. Arkin made arrangements with such frenzy that Mr. Arkin said if she didn't stop running around like a chicken with its head cut off she was likely to drop dead with a heart attack. But though she worked from the moment she got up until far past her bedtime, supervising the renovation of the old house in her side yard and making lists of recipes, she was too excited to notice if she was tired.

The cafe was the first thing she had had just like she wanted it. It was a square room fronted by a door and a large glass window on which she carefully painted MRS. ARKIN's CAFE. There were four oilclothed tables alongside the counter, which had a hinged flap that opened up for her to go through. Behind the counter were her stove and icebox on either side of the side door. L.B.'s dogs parked themselves outside her side door, as though studying how to ruin it. But even they couldn't dim her satisfaction.

A few weeks after the opening, Mrs. Arkin wrote Mrs. Filburton a postcard: "Thanks to your kind help, I am operating my cafe in Pinola. Business is fine." This last statement was untrue, but Mrs. Arkin thought anything else might sound like a reproach. Her only regular diner was a toothless old bachelor who came by for dinner on alternate Mondays when his welfare check arrived at the post office. A lady or two might drop by in the afternoon for a Coke. But most days the only diners were she and Mr. Arkin, Ruby Ella, and Rufus.

Mrs. Arkin remained excited and happy as a bride-to-be. Very soon the road work would progress within driving distance of Pinola, and she expected to be swamped with business. And by the time the crews worked past Pinola, the road would be nearly complete and the tourists would be coming through. She thought about these future customers so many times that she could hardly believe it when the first stage—the patronage of the construction crews—fell through.

This happened, as she explained to Mr. Arkin, who was sitting at the empty counter finishing his dinner, through no fault in her reasoning. There was no way in the world she could have foreseen that Pinola's bootlegger, P. T. Whitney, would see the potential in her business and set up his own cafe across the railroad tracks, with his brassy daughter as the cook-waitress. "Besides," Mrs. Arkin said with unaccustomed spirit, "if the construction men would just as soon eat some slop cooked by P.T.'s daughter as long as she serves it switching her behind, I don't want them for customers."

Mr. Arkin pushed away his second helping of rice pudding and said tauntingly, sucking a tooth, "If you're so ticky about who your customers are, you should be satisfied—here you are feeding the same fine old customer you've been cooking for for thirty-eight years."

Mr. Arkin also deviled her by reporting daily the crowd of hungry construction workers crowding down at P.T.'s cafe on the wrong side of the tracks. And in the still afternoons she was forced to see P.T. slowly cruise in his pickup past her deserted cafe to check out her lack of customers. A man who inspired respect, if not admiration, he had shot six men dead, several of them in the back, bitten off the thumbs of three men in fistfights, and, in a recent to-do over a stolen hog, knuckled out the eye of a strong boy half his age. A short bald man who wore khakis and eye-magnifying glasses greasy with thumbprints, he had a big belly that hung over his pants like a melon under his shirt. The pants hung precariously below on his skinny hipbones, his armpits were perpetually darkened, and he smelled yards away of sweat.

But Mrs. Arkin's faith in God rescued her. For three more months she kept up her faith that when the construction men were gone forever from Pinola and the tourists—families that would want good food— made up the town's cafe trade, she would show the bootlegger he couldn't steal her idea and get away with it forever. She expected to watch him go out of business.

Meanwhile she let Ruby Ella go and she cashed the last one of her government postal bonds left by her great-aunt Emma. When the highway was completed and the construction men gone, she threw herself with fresh energy into making each day's meal a feast, expecting every morning a carload of tourists that would be the first trickle of the avalanche. But four months passed and the only stopovers from the new road were occasional salesmen she never saw again.

More and more Mrs. Arkin got the feeling that somewhere along the line a mistake had been made. She became so angry, thinking of the time after time the reward of her efforts had been delayed, that she considered closing the cafe. Whenever a carefully prepared dish went uneaten, she might have done this if it had not been for Mr. Arkin. He daily reminded her that he had been against the cafe from the first minute. So she held on, still hoping for the best.

One quiet afternoon, with the sun over the railroad tracks reflecting only the tangled shadows of chair legs on the cafe's shiny clean linoleum, she looked up at the sound of a car. The car, strange to her, had a New York license plate on the front of its silver grillwork, and her heart began to pound.

Two young men and a girl got out, squinting in the direction of the cafe. As they came inside the front screened door, Mrs. Arkin gasped.

All three of the Yankee tourists were dressed in blue jeans, shirts with the tails hanging out, and thong sandals with dirty toes sticking out. The girl had little slitty brown eyes and greasy dark braids over each shoulder, and for a horrified second Mrs. Arkin thought she was an Indian until she saw the paleness of the girl's face, colorless without rouge or lipstick. The young men were thin and they slouched down, kept from collapsing entirely only by some invisible support in their lower chests.

Both men had beards and long hair, and they looked over the cafe motionlessly, barely moving their eyes—like goats about to butt, Mrs. Arkin thought—then drifted until they sank into the cane chairs at the table farthest from the front door.

She advanced toward them, beaming as if they were her own long-lost children restored to life.

"Je-suz," said the dark-bearded man looking around, "when's the next lynching?"

He talked in such a hard Yankee accent that Mrs. Arkin could hardly make out what he was saying. They were all three wearing denim work clothes like tenant farmers—the most faded worn-thin jeans imaginable. But their jeans had extra decorations, like silver studs running down the sides of the legs, and the girl's blue shirt, unbuttoned shamefully low to expose the rims of her breasts, was sewn with red flowers. In an instant Mrs. Arkin saw through their obvious disguise. They must not be ordinary tourists but Duncan Hines representatives, sent to test the Arkin cafe. Praise God! Her very first real customers and they would be in a position to bring more to her. Now was the big moment of her life, if only she could do everything right!

Mrs. Arkin snatched off her hairnet and put menus before them and rushed to bring icewater and silverware. In between, she hollered out the side door where Rufus was sleeping stretched out on newspapers in the shade to get himself inside, ready to wash dishes. Since there was nothing to wash, the truth was she wanted an audience for her triumph.

"Well, well, well," she said brightly as she laid menus around, "I guess you boys must be growing beards for your town centennial someplace. Whereabouts are you from?"

The three looked blankly up at her, and, seeing their unfriendly Yankee faces, Mrs. Arkin shivered. The dark-bearded man who had spoken had thick kinky hair of a kind she had never seen on a white man. It stood out around his head in a halo of black snakes and swept like volcano lava down the sides of his face, down the back of his neck, and parted in the front of his neck only briefly before rushing on over his chest. He had big arm muscles and wore leather wristlets buckled tight around each hairy wrist.

The girl suddenly giggled.

"Linda," said the redheaded boy, "are you laughing about such a serious matter? Didn't you know Lennie was celebrating the hundredth birthday of his hometown, the picturesque old town of Queens, home of one million bourgeois, including his parents, the dry-cleaners Silverstein?"

Linda dropped her face into her hands in glee. The redhead laughed with her until they both choked. Lennie glared at them.

"All right, you jackoffs, you want to eat or you wanna make me mad? You wanna tell Grandma here what you want to eat, or you wanna go without eating? I'm telling ya, I'm getting to New Orleans before midnight." He sounded as though it was his burden in life to give orders because he was so much smarter.

"I urge you to try our fried chicken, sir, it'll be fresh-fried."

Linda turned her slitty eyes at Mrs. Arkin and said in a nasal voice,

"Oh no, Grandma, I'd rather have some, like, corned beef. You got that?"

Mrs. Arkin felt her heart contract apprehensively. She'd never heard of that.

"Why . . . ah . . . no."

"How about some pastrami on rye?"

"Well, we . . . uh . . . don't have that, whatever it is."

"Bagel and lox?"

"I'm sorry, no."

All three now fell over their china plates laughing. The redheaded one straightened at last, spread some tobaccolike substance on a cigarette tissue, rolled it, and looked around for a match. Mrs. Arkin called back to the kitchen, "Rufus . . . get a match in here for our customers." Flustered, she spoke in a commanding shout. Rufus came through the open flap carrying the big box of kitchen matches. Mrs. Arkin hissed, "No . . . no . . . the little crystal glass of matches, Rufus."

"Aha . . ." said Lennie. "What do we have here? Is Grandma an oppressor? Is this a racist cafe we've stopped at, Markie and Linda?"

They giggled, but Lennie cut them off. "Awright, jackoffs, shut your face. And hold that stuff until we get to New Orleans. You want to run into some state trooper schmuck with that stuff?"

Rufus, dumbstruck as Lot's wife turned to a pillar of salt, held the kitchen box of matches before this trio apparition, unable to move forward or backward. Markie reached out and plucked a match from the box, struck it on the side, held rigidly by Rufus, and lighted up. A sweet odor permeated the Arkin cafe.

"May I suggest the fried chicken, sir?" Mrs. Arkin said.

"Awright, awright, bring us three fried chickens," said Lennie.

Mrs. Arkin rushed to her stove, whisked the floured chicken from the icebox, and began to cook as though her life depended on it.

Rufus had skittered back behind the counter, but Lennie called him back. "Hey, come over here."

Rufus ambled over, walking bent forward so it would look like he was moving fast but in fact shuffling as slow as possible. He was short, and skinny as a beanpole in his bright chartreuse pants and red shirt, his brown forearms sticking out below the short shirtsleeves like brown twigs. Mrs. Arkin had known him from the age of two weeks when Ruby Ella brought him to the house nearly dead with colic. Mrs. Arkin took one look at the tiny twisted face, like a dying brown leaf, and called Dr. Hill. Mrs. Arkin and Ruby Ella spent the next week taking turns giving

Dr. Hill's paregoric and carrying the baby in their arms, pressed to the warmth of their bodies, until the dried leaf slowly uncurled, started to suck its bottle, and stopped crying.

Since then Rufus had grown up to be like any other nigra, but Mrs. Arkin could not forget the curled little leaf he had been. He looked frightened at the visitors, his eyes rolling.

"How much money you make here?" demanded the black-bearded man.

Rufus jumped. "Don't make no money, just eats." Mrs. Arkin could have speared him with her red-handled turning fork at this revelation. She had paid him as long as she could afford to.

The young red-bearded one spoke up now. "Eats is all you get, huh?" He had an undemanding redhead's face that did not ask to be remembered. Small light-blue eyes fringed with blond lashes and pink lips too big for the eyes. He was younger than the other two, and his red beard looked like a toy doctor's beard stuck on a child's face. He grinned through it in a silly way, puffing on the sweet-smelling cigarette.

"You know what Markie here gets just for an allowance?" demanded Lennie. "A hundred fifty dollars a week. But then his old man pulls down four hundred thousand a year from his box factory on Long Island, and he feels guilty because he wouldn't let little Markie study the cello like he wanted to."

Markie squirmed and looked—properly, thought Mrs. Arkin—embarrassed at this bragging on his fortune.

"Now, Linda, her daddy is a divorce lawyer, a bomber, and he pulls down two hundred thousand a year from all that marital discord. And he gives little Linda three hundred a week because she's daddy's little girl."

Linda blew out the smoke from the cigarette, narrowing her slitty little eyes and tossing her braids forward over her unbuttoned shirt. Mrs. Arkin looked up from her frying chicken and decided that, whatever her daddy made, Linda acted like a sharecropper.

"And you live off us both," snapped Linda, and Lennie glared at her.

"Whatcha doing with that ax back there against the wall?" asked the redheaded one.

Nervously Mrs. Arkin considered calling Rufus away. He was certainly not a feature of the Arkin cafe, and she did not want him creeping into *her* review. And of course now after getting over his fright at the visitors he was in his element. In another minute he'd be showing off.

"That *aks!*" Rufus crowed. "That aks for Mr. Blue!"

"Is he the law around here?" Lennie demanded.

"Mr. Blue, he sure the law around here!" Rufus brayed a huge laugh, and the visitors looked in awe at Rufus's strong yellow teeth opened before them, serried and perfect as a lion's.

"There he sit!" Rufus pointed dramatically, sure of his audience now, to the side door where L.B.'s pack of hungry hounds sat pressing their wet black noses and scrabbling at the cross-hatching of the screen. In the center, regally unmoving amidst the hounds, sat the scourge of Mrs. Arkin's rose beds, a bluetick hound with infinitely wise amber eyes, waiting confidently for the day's pleasures. The other common brown- and black-spotted dogs struggled to get to the screen door through the pack, each dog working his way to the front but holding his place only for seconds until others scrabbled over his shoulders. None of them disturbed Mr. Blue in the center.

"You use that ax on the dog?" asked Lennie, for the first time not speaking as though he were giving them all orders.

"Yessah. Mr. Blue like his Co-Cola, he do, so once a day Miz Arkin, she pour Co-Cola in a Dixie cup, and I push em out of the way with that aks and give it to Mr. Blue, and I use that aks to keep the others off while he drink it."

Lennie turned to his friends. "Jesuz, no wonder the NAACP got rid of whites. Here you got a black kid can hardly spell his name and he's sporting around with the whites' dogs giving them Cokes. Who can even understand what he's saying? But I think I got it—you leave out the main verbs."

Lennie turned back to Rufus. "You-out-of-here-someday?"

But before Rufus could embarrass Mrs. Arkin any further, another unexpected visitor pulled his muddy pickup in front of the cafe. The sun was clouding up as it sank behind the railroad track, which stretched straight as a board along the main street of Pinola. The sun silhouetted in the pickup's back window two rifles, a Franchi rimfire auto-loader for squirrels and a Mannlicher Safari, designed for shooting elephants in Africa.

P. T. Whitney came in bold as brass, his pistol popped into his belt. "How-do, Miz Arkin," he said politely. "How-do, Rufus," he added, looking the visitors over slowly like a herd of elephants that had miraculously appeared in Pinola. "Well, well, I see you got customers from out of town," he said, obviously bursting with curiosity. He must have seen their license plate.

Taking the table between the visitors and the front door, P.T. turned a cane chair backwards and lazily straddled it, as though he were settling down on his own front porch. The sun at this moment disappeared behind a moving wall of ugly thunderclouds. The threat of rain made the air heavy. Mrs. Arkin had to breathe harder, as though she had sunk suddenly into an ocean.

"Yew boys from New York City?" P.T. drawled. His eyes set on Linda's open shirtfront like a cat sighting a fat bird.

"What's it to you?" Lennie tossed over his shoulder like he was spitting. Mrs. Arkin wanted to rush over and shake him. *Watch out! It's P.T. you're spitting at!* The roll of thunder overhead echoed Mrs. Arkin's own thundering heartbeats.

"Sir, how far to New Orleans?" the redheaded one cut in, polite as could be, and Mrs. Arkin allowed herself to breathe out. Here was a placator like herself, the type that always saved the day.

"Rufus, how far to New Awlins?" growled P.T., arresting Rufus who had been sidestepping to the flap at the first sign of white folks' trouble.

"I be guessing 400 miles, Mr. P.T.," Rufus quavered. P.T. shot a quick, satisfied look at Linda. She could see from the way this nigger jumped to his word that P.T. was a big man hereabouts.

"Guess you all got some driving to do," P.T. said, not able to take his stare from the girl's nipples. "But I guess you got something to smoke to keep you going."

"You the sheriff around here or something?" demanded Lennie, turning slowly to P.T. for the first time with a withering stare, as though it was his habit to order sheriffs around too.

The first green flash of lightning forked over the darkening sky outside the cafe. Placating in the only way she could think of, Mrs. Arkin yanked up the hot chicken from her skillet, dumped it onto a plate, and rushed to P.T., carrying a long-stemmed goblet of ice tea. In the cheerful voice of a church hostess she cried, "Here, P.T., try my fresh-fried chicken."

At this point the two placators, Markie and Mrs. Arkin, might still have stopped the trouble. The thunderclouds that wrapped Pinola in their darkness might have spewed down their rain and passed on in ten minutes as Mississippi thunderstorms do, leaving the cafe occupants just as they were. But Lennie didn't allow that.

"Hey," he snarled at Mrs. Arkin, "how come he got served before us? We were here first!"

Rufus's mouth fell open, his teeth bared in fear. Mrs. Arkin held her turning fork in midair and couldn't help squeezing her eyes shut in prayer.

But P.T. didn't jump up and seize Lennie by the throat. Grinning, he only cocked his head at Linda and piped in a fake girl's voice, "Well, sugar, maybe you better line up with me to get good service." His voice dropped back to its usual commanding growl. "All kind of service you ain't been gitting. You come over here and sit by me."

Linda stuck her small pink chin in the air and tossed her braids over her shoulders. "You stupid old hillbilly, I wouldn't sit by you if you were the last man on earth."

P.T.'s face twisted like a man who's accidentally swallowed a whole chili pepper. He turned redder than a ham. His mouth untwisting and suddenly opening, he flung the silverware to the floor and howled like Mr. Blue, a howl that shook the glasses on the tables.

Lennie jumped up, his hair vibrating like live snakes. He grabbed Linda up and slung her toward P.T. "You little asshole, get over there and sit down like he says and shut up!"

With his muddy high-topped work shoe P.T. shoved out a cane chair, and when Linda sank wide-eyed into it, his big red hand snaked out and locked around her tiny forearm.

Markie half-rose. "N-n-nooo, Linda, come back."

Lennie seized him by the collar and dragged him back. "Shut up, I got a plan. Let me talk, I'll get us out of here. You don't and I won't answer for you."

He waited till Markie sat down, then he marched back toward P.T., twisting the armband on his left wrist. "Listen, P.T.," he said in a voice so compelling and deep that Mrs. Arkin and Rufus leaned toward it as though to the Sunday preacher on the radio. "I'm going to let you in on a secret."

Lennie waited for P.T. to look up, but P.T. was grinning again, his nose inching closer to Linda's low shirtfront. She looked back at him like a five-year-old who has been told her mother has died. Such things, her frightened brown eyes said, could not happen to her.

Lennie blared on in his loud voice. "We are from New York and we are on our way to New Orleans. But we're not ordinary tourists. We're working for an organization, a *powerful* organization."

P.T. dipped his nose right into Linda's shirtfront, holding her tight in his big red hand.

"You want to know the name of our organization?" Lennie shot out. "The FBI!"

"Not from Duncan Hines?" Mrs. Arkin whispered, gripping a dishtowel.

"Oh, the FBI." P.T. shifted in disgust, leaning back to look at Lennie

with his big red face and greasy glasses shining. "I've seed that teevee
program. *The FBI in peace and war.* They drive those little Pintos. I
wouldn't give a nigger a Pinto."

"The fucking FBI you're fooling with!" Lennie screamed in a terrible
threatening voice. "You lay a hand on her or him or me, and you'll have
the whole FBI down on you!"

"Who's talking about her or him, we'll just go one on one," P.T.
shouted back. He smashed his ice-tea goblet into a jagged spear on the
table and threw the table down before him, smashing dishes on the floor.
"I'm going to cut you good, boy." He crouched over his glass spear and
stalked Lennie.

"The ax, get the ax!" Markie shouted, running to the back wall where
Rufus was plastered, frozen in fear.

Lennie ran back and yanked the heavy ax down from its hooks, then
suddenly grabbed Rufus by the neck. Pushing Rufus ahead of him and
hiding behind him as though he was a shield, he swung the big ax in his
left hand and advanced on P.T.

Quick as an attack dog, P.T. lunged left, right, nicking Lennie on each
arm with his glass spear, drawing blood and cackling at it.

Lennie raised the ax high and swung it down toward the middle of
P.T.'s skull. P.T. sidestepped and the ax sank into the floor with a thud.
But before Lennie could raise it, P.T. seized the handle.

They struggled silently for the ax, the muscles in their arms bulging.
Lennie threw Rufus aside on the floor to use his right hand, but P.T.
held on to his spear and used only one powerful arm. Veins swelling, they
battled for thirty seconds; then P.T. yanked the ax from Lennie and
threw it easily back over his head. The ax sailed through Mrs. Arkin's
front window, shattering the glass and letting in a gale of rain.

Grinning again, P.T. raised his glass spear high over Lennie's chest.
Lennie stumbled back a step. "No," he gasped, his face chalky white.
Then he seized Rufus from the floor and held the boy before him.

"You want this nigger to die with you?" P.T. screamed.

"I ain't no FBI, Mr. P.T.," Rufus pleaded.

"Please God, take the cafe," Mrs. Arkin prayed. "Just don't let P.T.
kill Rufus. Save Rufus first and them second if You will."

Thunder suddenly rent the air as though the sky was a giant bedsheet
and someone had ripped it apart. Everyone froze except Mrs. Arkin, who
marched from behind the counter, her mild gray eyes burning behind
her glasses. What was happening was worse even than Mr. Arkin's slow
destruction of her love, worse than L.B.'s dogs digging up her rose beds,

worse than the ingratitude of the invalids. In the thunder's crack she saw things she had never seen in her whole life, and she knew what she must do.

"You let Rufus go, you P.T." She shook the fork at him. "You let him and them go or you'll never live another happy day."

P.T. reached out and pulled Rufus from Lennie. Rufus ran out the side door, leaving it blowing open in the rain.

The dogs spotted the chance of a lifetime. Dripping wet, they plunged into the warm cafe and dived between people's legs, rattling their long chains like Attila the Hun's hordes. Hemmed in by the dogs, P.T. pulled his pistol from his belt and aimed at Lennie's heart. But Mr. Blue, his chain swinging aloft like a runaway chain-gang prisoner's, broke across P.T. and dashed toward the front door. The flying chain hit P.T.'s shins like a crowbar, and he fell, his shot singing out and shattering a glass jar of sugar.

Stunned, Lennie gazed down at his fallen opponent among the milling dogs. Markie grabbed Linda's arm and dragged her through the front door, Mr. Blue at their heels. They plunged into the car. As the motor roared, P.T., shouting curses, grabbed through the dogs for his pistol, and Lennie sprang back to life. He sprinted through the door, caught the car racing backwards, flung open a door. The car tires squealed as the car raced forwards and Lennie jumped inside. The Yankees disappeared in the wall of rain.

Alone, Mrs. Arkin looked around her wrecked cafe. She shook her head in pure fury at P.T., who was hobbling out to his pickup. Maybe if P.T. hadn't barged in, her cafe might have made a go of it. But she shook her head, remembering what she had realized during that rip of thunder. She went to the front door and locked it. Then she took the broom out from behind the icebox and began sweeping up the broken glass and blood. She would not let herself cry.

The last rays of sunlight had broken through after the thunderstorm. The old bachelor shuffled up and shook the door, but Mrs. Arkin waved her hand at him to go away, and went on sweeping. What she realized was that people like P.T. and Lennie didn't give a hoot about being good themselves, but they knew what went on in other people's heads and how to use that to their own advantage. But people like herself, they knew so little about P.T.'s kind of people, not pee-doodle, and when they ran up against that kind they ran smack into trouble.

That was what was heartbreaking. She had tried just this once to break out and do something in her life, and she had held on and held on through the long months. But all the time it was too late. P.T. can have the cafe trade, she muttered to herself. The old man kept rattling the door, but she went on sweeping without looking up. Holding on would be a kind of losing. The Arkin cafe was closed.

HOMEWORK

PETER CAMERON

Peter Cameron grew up in Pompton Plains, New Jersey. He now works
for a land-conservation organization in New York City.

My dog, Keds, was sitting outside of the A. & P. last Thursday when he
got smashed by some kid pushing a shopping cart. At first we thought he
just had a broken leg, but later we found out he was bleeding inside.
Every time he opened his mouth, blood would seep out like dull red
words in a bad silent dream.

Every night before my sister goes to her job she washes her hair in the
kitchen sink with beer and mayonnaise and eggs. Sometimes I sit at the
table and watch the mixture dribble down her white back. She boils a
pot of water on the stove at the same time; when she is finished with her
hair, she steams her face. She wants so badly to be beautiful.

I am trying to solve complicated algebraic problems I have set for
myself. Since I started cutting school last Friday, the one thing I miss is
homework. Find the value for n. Will it be a whole number? It is never a
whole number. It is always a fraction.

"Will you get me a towel?" my sister asks. She turns her face toward
me and clutches her hair to the top of her head. The sprayer hose slithers
into its hole next to the faucet.

I hand her a dish towel. "No," she says. "A bath towel. Don't be
stupid."

In the bathroom, my mother is watering her plants. She has arranged
them in the tub and turned the shower on. She sits on the toilet lid and
watches. It smells like outdoors in the bathroom.

I hand my sister the towel and watch her wrap it round her head. She
takes the cover off the pot of boiling water and drops lemon slices in.
Then she lowers her face into the steam.

This is the problem I have set for myself:

$$\frac{245\ (n + 17)}{34} = 396\ (n - 45)$$

$$n =$$

Wednesday, I stand outside the high-school gym doors. Inside, students are lined up doing calisthenics. It's snowing, and prematurely dark, and I can watch without being seen.

"Well," my father says when I get home. He is standing in the garage testing the automatic door. Every time a plane flies overhead, the door opens or closes, so my father is trying to fix it. "Have you changed your mind about school?" he asks me.

I lock my bicycle to a pole. This infuriates my father, who doesn't believe in locking things up in his own house. He pretends not to notice. I wipe the thin stripe of snow off the fenders with my middle finger. It is hard to ride a bike in the snow. This afternoon on my way home from the high school I fell off, and I lay in the snowy road with my bike on top of me. It felt warm.

"We're going to get another dog," my father says.

"It's not that," I say. I wish everyone would stop talking about dogs. I can't tell how sad I really am about Keds versus how sad I am in general. If I don't keep these things separate, I feel as if I'm betraying Keds.

"Then what is it?" my father says.

"It's nothing," I say.

My father nods. He is very good about bringing things up and then letting them drop. A lot gets dropped. He presses the button on the automatic control. The door slides down its oiled tracks and falls shut. It's dark in the garage. My father presses the button again and the door opens, and we both look outside at the snow falling in the driveway, as if in those few seconds the world might have changed.

My mother has forgotten to call me for dinner, and when I confront her with this she tells me that she did, but that I was sleeping. She is loading the dishwasher. My sister is standing at the counter, listening, and separating eggs for her shampoo.

"What can I get you?" my mother asks. "Would you like a meat-loaf sandwich?"

"No," I say. I open the refrigerator and survey its illuminated contents. "Could I have some scrambled eggs?"

"O.K.," says my mother. She comes and stands beside me and puts her hand on top of mine on the door handle. There are no eggs in the refrigerator. "Oh," my mother says; then, "Julie?"

"What?" my sister says.

"Did you take the last eggs?"

"I guess so," my sister says. "I don't know."

"Forget it," I say. "I won't have eggs."

"No," my mother says. "Julie doesn't need them in her shampoo. That's not what I bought them for."

"I do," my sister says. "It's a formula. It doesn't work without the eggs. I need the protein."

"I don't want eggs," I say. "I don't want anything." I go into my bedroom.

My mother comes in and stands looking out the window. The snow has turned to rain. "You're not the only one who is unhappy about this," she says.

"About what?" I say. I am sitting on my unmade bed. If I pick up my room, my mother will make my bed: that's the deal. I didn't pick up my room this morning.

"About Keds," she says. "I'm unhappy too. But it doesn't stop me from going to school."

"You don't go to school," I say.

"You know what I mean," my mother says. She turns around and looks at my room, and begins to pick things off the floor.

"Don't do that," I say. "Stop."

My mother drops the dirty clothes in an exaggerated gesture of defeat. She almost—almost—throws them on the floor. The way she holds her hands accentuates their emptiness. "If you're not going to go to school," she says, "the least you can do is clean your room."

In the algebra word problems, a boat sails down a river while a jeep drives along the bank. Which will reach the capital first? If a plane flies at a certain speed from Boulder to Oklahoma City and then at a different speed from Oklahoma City to Detroit, how many cups of coffee can the stewardess serve, assuming she is unable to serve during the first and last ten minutes of each flight? How many times can a man ride the elevator to the top of the Empire State Building while his wife climbs the stairs, given that the woman travels one stair slower each flight? And if the man jumps up while the elevator is going down, which is moving— the man, the woman, the elevator, or the snow falling outside?

The next Monday I get up and make preparations for going to school. I can tell at the breakfast table that my mother is afraid to acknowledge them for fear it won't be true. I haven't gotten up before ten o'clock in a week. My mother makes me French toast. I sit at the table and write the note excusing me for my absence. I am eighteen, an adult, and thus able to excuse myself from school. This is what my note says:

> DEAR MR. KELLY [my homeroom teacher]:
> Please excuse my absence February 17–24. I was unhappy and did not feel able to attend school.
>
> Sincerely,
> MICHAEL PECHETTI

This is the exact format my mother used when she wrote my notes, only she always said, "Michael was home with a sore throat," or "Michael was home with a bad cold." The colds that prevented me from going to school were always bad colds.

My mother watches me write the note but doesn't ask to see it. I leave it on the kitchen table when I go to the bathroom, and when I come back to get it I know she has read it. She is washing the bowl she dipped the French toast into. Before, she would let Keds lick it clean. He liked eggs.

In Spanish class we are seeing a film on flamenco dancers. The screen wouldn't pull down, so it is being projected on the blackboard, which is green and cloudy with erased chalk. It looks a little as if the women are sick, and dancing in Heaven. Suddenly the little phone on the wall buzzes.

Mrs. Smitts, the teacher, gets up to answer it, and then walks over to me. She puts her hand on my shoulder and leans her face close to mine. It is dark in the room. "Miguel," Mrs. Smitts whispers, *"Tienes que ir a la oficina de* guidance."

"What?" I say.

She leans closer, and her hair blocks the dancers. Despite the clicking castanets and the roomful of students, there is something intimate about this moment. *"Tienes que ir a la oficina de* guidance," she repeats slowly. Then, "You must go to the guidance office. Now. *Vaya."*

My guidance counsellor, Mrs. Dietrich, used to be a history teacher, but she couldn't take it anymore, so she was moved into guidance. On her immaculate desk is a calendar blotter with "LUNCH" written across the middle of every box, including Saturday and Sunday. The only other things on the desk are an empty photo cube and my letter to Mr. Kelly. I sit down, and she shows me the letter as if I haven't yet read it. I reread it.

"Did you write this?" she asks.

I nod affirmatively. I can tell Mrs. Dietrich is especially nervous about this interview. Our meetings are always charged with tension. At the last one, when I was selecting my second-semester courses, she started to laugh hysterically when I said I wanted to take Boys' Home Ec. Now every time I see her in the halls she stops me and asks me how I'm doing in Boys' Home Ec. It's the only course of mine she remembers.

I hand the note back to her and say, "I wrote it this morning," as if this clarified things.

"This morning?"

"At breakfast," I say.

"Do you think this is an acceptable excuse?" Mrs. Dietrich asks. "For missing more than a week of school?"

"I'm sure it isn't," I say.

"Then why did you write it?"

Because it is the truth, I start to say. It is. But somehow I know that saying this will make me more unhappy. It might make me cry. "I've been doing homework," I say.

"That's fine," Mrs. Dietrich says, "but it's not the point. The point is, to graduate you have to attend school for a hundred and eighty days, or have legitimate excuses for the days you've missed. That's the point. Do you want to graduate?"

"Yes," I say.

"Of course you do," Mrs. Dietrich says.

She crumples my note and tries to throw it into the wastepaper basket but misses. We both look for a second at the note lying on the floor, and then I get up and throw it away. The only other thing in her wastepaper basket is a banana peel. I can picture her eating a banana in her tiny office. This, too, makes me sad.

"Sit down," Mrs. Dietrich says.

I sit down.

"I understand your dog died. Do you want to talk about that?"

"No," I say.

"Is that what you're so unhappy about?" she says. "Or is there something else?"

I almost mention the banana peel in her wastebasket, but I don't. "No," I say. "It's just my dog."

Mrs. Dietrich thinks for a moment. I can tell she is embarrassed to be talking about a dead dog. She would be more comfortable if it were a parent or a sibling.

"I don't want to talk about it," I repeat.

She opens her desk drawer and takes out a pad of hall passes. She begins to write one out for me. She has beautiful handwriting. I think of her learning to write beautifully as a child and then growing up to be a guidance counsellor, and this makes me unhappy.

"Mr. Neuman is willing to overlook this matter," she says. Mr. Neuman is the principal. "Of course, you will have to make up all the work you've missed. Can you do that?"

"Yes," I say.

Mrs. Dietrich tears the pass from the pad and hands it to me. Our hands touch. "You'll get over this," she says. "Believe me, you will."

My sister works until midnight at the Photo-Matica. It's a tiny booth in the middle of the A. & P. parking lot. People drive up and leave their film and come back the next day for the pictures. My sister wears a uniform that makes her look like a counterperson in a fast-food restaurant. Sometimes at night when I'm sick of being at home I walk downtown and sit in the booth with her.

There's a machine in the booth that looks like a printing press, only snapshots ride down a conveyor belt and fall into a bin and then disappear. The machine gives the illusion that your photographs are being developed on the spot. It's a fake. The same fifty photographs roll through over and over, and my sister says nobody notices, because everyone in town is taking the same pictures. She opens up the envelopes and looks at them.

Before I go into the booth, I buy cigarettes in the A. & P. It is open twenty-four hours a day, and I love it late at night. It is big and bright and empty. The checkout girl sits on her counter swinging her legs. The Muzak plays "If Ever I Would Leave You." Before I buy the cigarettes, I walk up and down the aisles. Everything looks good to eat, and the things that aren't edible look good in their own way. The detergent aisle is colorful and clean-smelling.

My sister is listening to the radio and polishing her nails when I get to the booth. It is almost time to close.

"I hear you went to school today," she says.

"Yeah."

"How was it?" she asks. She looks at her nails, which are so long it's frightening.

"It was O.K.," I say. "We made chili dogs in Home Ec."

"So are you over it all?"

I look at the pictures riding down the conveyor belt. I know the order practically by heart: graduation, graduation, birthday, mountains, baby, baby, new car, bride, bride and groom, house . . . "I guess so," I say.

"Good," says my sister. "It was getting to be a little much." She puts her tiny brush back in the bottle, capping it. She shows me her nails. They're an odd brown shade. "Cinnamon," she says. "It's an earth color." She looks out at the parking lot. A boy is collecting the abandoned shopping carts, forming a long silver train, which he noses back toward the store. I can tell he is singing by the way his mouth moves.

"That's where we found Keds," my sister says, pointing to the Salvation Army bin.

When I went out to buy cigarettes, Keds would follow me. I hung out down here at night before he died. I was unhappy then, too. That's what no one understands. I named him Keds because he was all white with big black feet and it looked as if he had high-top sneakers on. My mother wanted to name him Bootie. Bootie is a cat's name. It's a dumb name for a dog.

"It's a good thing you weren't here when we found him," my sister says. "You would have gone crazy."

I'm not really listening. It's all nonsense. I'm working on a new problem: Find the value for n such that n plus everything else in your life makes you feel all right. What would n equal? Solve for n.

TAKING A CHANCE ON JACK

ILENE RAYMOND

Ilene Raymond was born in 1954 and grew up in Wallingford, Pennsylvania. She is a graduate of Brandeis University and the Iowa Writers Workshop. Her short stories have appeared in *Mademoiselle* and *Playgirl* magazines. She lives with her husband, Jeff Rush, also a writer, in State College, Pennsylvania, where she teaches fiction writing at Pennsylvania State University and is at work on her first novel.

Nina walks the three blocks from the subway to her house, thinking of Jack. All day long, as she sits checking copy for the Federal Register, she deliberately blocks Jack from her mind. But the second she shuts her office door behind her, says good-night to Merrilee and starts down the 12 flights of stairs, a step she takes to keep fat from collecting on her thighs, Jack pops into her mind. Even after six years of marriage he still has the power to wipe everything else from the inside of her head and leave her with nothing but him.

If Jack knew how much time she spent thinking about him, he would be surprised. He would tell her to stop, that things would improve on their own with time. Yet ever since Jack was fired from his public relations firm a year ago, all he does is sit around the house tending his plants and fish. On occasion he drops a résumé into the mail. She wonders if he ever means to work again. All of Nina's girlfriends tell her that she is crazy to put up with such behavior, but she defends Jack, tells them he is looking for a job and that a job is hard to find.

"Not *that* hard," says Amelia. Nina has lunch with Amelia twice a week at Woodward & Lothrop. They have had lunch together on Tuesdays and Fridays for three years. For two-and-a-half years, Amelia has dominated the conversation. She is 30 years old and has been married three times. Her first husband was her high school math teacher. Her second was a law student named Craig who dropped out of law school after the first year to play minor-league softball. They never fought. Even when she got angry with him, he refused to argue. If Amelia was particularly furious, she would walk into the kitchen and punch thumbtacks into the pasteboard wall. When they left their apartment, the wall looked like a bad case of chicken pox. Amelia said, "All marriages leave scars."

Amelia's third marriage is on its fifth month, and she is still in bliss. Nina is happy for her friend, but has learned to weigh her advice.

"Practice makes perfect," Amelia tells her, stern.

"You've got to shop around to get the right fit," Amelia instructs.

Nina lets herself into the apartment. Jack is singing to the transistor radio propped against the kitchen window. He is making Chinese food. On Thursday nights he watches a Chinese cooking class on public TV and on Friday nights he always practices the newest lesson. Since he has been unemployed, Jack has developed such hobbies. A tankful of tropical fish—kissing fish and electric elephant fish—swim circles in their living room. African violets line the bookshelves beneath eerie purple light. He has reorganized the kitchen, color coding the cabinets for dishes, pots, utensils. Nina can't find anything in her own kitchen anymore, but she thinks that if it keeps Jack busy and makes him feel useful, it's okay with her.

"Sweetie pie," Jack calls from the kitchen. Oil sizzles in the wok, his knife jumps along the cutting board. She walks in and kisses him on the back of his neck.

"How was your day?" he asks.

"Slow." She knew he would ask this question. He has asked this question for 365 days now. She would like to change the subject, to have him talk about himself, to tell her what he is feeling. It bothers her that he doesn't seem to mind that he hasn't found a job in a year. His unemployment checks ran out six months ago and her own salary as an editorial assistant is stretched far too thin. They gave up movies in March; her lunches with Amelia are next. Amelia and Timmy, her new husband, asked them to go skiing over Christmas, but the car payments are overdue. Not to mention their dwindling bank account. Yet she worries about putting too much pressure on Jack.

Jack rubs two jalapeño peppers with thumb and index finger, springing tiny golden coins from the red casing. She studies him. His skin is rosy. He has lost weight. He stirs broccoli and snow peas into the oil, then lifts the lid on the pot of steaming brown rice. Setting dishes on the table, he arranges chopsticks and wineglasses. He reminds her of the housewives in the soap commercials. He has become the perfect hausfrau. He shops every day.

She has a vision of him carting a basket on his arm filled with loaves of crusty brown breads and creamy cheeses. The liquor store where he buys wine is on the corner. The tropical fish shop is two blocks away. There is a florist for plant fertilizer on Wisconsin Avenue. Jack has become the nurturer, while she is just another fish or plant waiting to be fed. She realizes that in a year Jack has not had the need to go beyond the four-block radius of their house. She watches him closely, to see if she can spot any changes. He looks up from his set table and grins.

"Let's eat," he says.

After Jack clears the table, she sits in the living room, reading the *Post*, while he does the dishes. At lunch Amelia had said, "You're a young woman. You deserve more than that." When they finished eating their salads, Amelia walked Nina down to the lingerie department and made her select three teddy outfits of filmy black lace. In the dressing room she inspected Nina intently, making her model them front and back, selecting the one that cut the highest across her thighs and the lowest across her breasts.

"Open his eyes with that, I'll bet," Amelia said, waving her credit card at the counter. Nina blushed as the saleswoman handed her the package, and Amelia laughed. After her second divorce, Amelia offered Nina her wardrobe of negligees from her first and second marriages, saying that they carried too many memories. She spilled them from a cardboard box: red lace, peach silk, pale blue net with ivory straps. Nina thanked her but didn't accept them. There was something wrong, she thought, about making love or sleeping or brushing your teeth in someone else's nightgown. It was too intimate, too exposed. She and Jack haven't made love in at least three months. They tried for a while, but it just wasn't right between them.

Amelia talks in detail about positions and postures. She tells Nina how she and Tim have made love at least three times a day since the first day they met in Kansas City. They met in the Hyatt Regency hotel lobby, when Amelia was working as a troubleshooter for the Internal Revenue Service. Tim was separated then. Amelia wasn't. Tim has a four-year-old daughter. The little girl is coming to spend next summer with them. The thought makes Amelia nervous.

"I don't know how to act around children," she says. "It's not like I'm a mother, you know."

"Amelia's little stepdaughter is coming to visit," Nina calls to the kitchen. She thinks it's good therapy for Jack to hear about the world. She gets no reply. The water is running in the sink. She walks to the kitchen doorway, still holding the newspaper.

"Amelia says that she and Tim are happy. She thinks this is the real thing." Still no answer. Jack is over the sink, arms up to the elbows in bubbles. She tiptoes behind him, meaning to take him by surprise, but then sees that his face is wet. He is crying, standing there in the kitchen, tears running down his face. He turns to look at her and she sees his eyes are red and swollen. The radio plays a Rolling Stones song and Nina is possessed by a need to run. She doesn't want to think about Jack anymore.

Pushing the teddy set into her arms, Amelia had said, "You have to keep men on their toes, otherwise they get bored."

Nina turns and goes out the front door, leaving Jack behind.

A wind blows across Twenty-fifth Street, stirring trash and leaves. Nina walks toward Pennsylvania Avenue, at first not certain where she is headed. She passes old men on stoops, sharing a bottle of wine in a paper bag, spitting and smoking. She walks across the avenue and into a corner bar. The first person she spots is Leon, an editor from work. He is sitting across a table from a busty blonde with large violet eyes and pink lips. Leon is married with four children and when Nina walks in he bends his head, then changes his mind, looks up, and smiles right at her.

"Nina," he says. He holds out his hand. "Come join us." He doesn't introduce the woman. Nina smiles at him, hoping her smile says, I won't give you away, and shakes her head no.

"I'm going to sit at the bar," she says. She orders a vodka tonic, then walks to the pay phone and puts two dimes in the slot. Amelia answers on the fifth ring.

"I'll be right there, honey," Amelia says. Her breathing is hurried, off. "I can't say I'm surprised."

Nina returns to the bar to wait for Amelia. Her heart beats hard behind her chest wall. She wants to call Jack, but won't give in. It's time for him to stand on his own feet, she thinks. She finishes her drink and orders another. She's tired of supporting him. Her anger expands into a bubble, painful to touch.

As she is about to order her third vodka, a young man, no more than 22 or 23 years of age, sits down on the barstool beside her. He lifts three olives from a beaker behind the counter and lines them in a row along the bar.

Nina watches him. He must have been desperate to pick her from among all the obviously single young women at the bar. That isn't positive thinking, though. Amelia said positive thinking was essential. It brought you out of yourself. Amelia said that if you wanted to be attractive to men, you should walk around thinking sexy thoughts. It made you glow. She had read that in a magazine. They taught it to airline stewardesses. Nina shuts her eyes. All she can see is Jack.

"Guess which one had an unhappy childhood," the young man next to her says. Nina turns. He points to the olives. "Okay," he says, when he receives no answer, "let's talk music." Slipping a cigarette from Nina's pack on the bar, he slides it between his fingers. "Don't you find Elvis Costello's voice the perfect expression of rage in our time?" He has a cleft in his chin and a dimple in his left cheek when he smiles. Nina ignores him. He stops smiling.

"Somedays I think I'm turning into my mother." He trades her cigarette for a cocktail swizzler. "Too neurotic, Sam," he admonishes himself. He studies the swizzler, then leans toward Nina. "The survival shelter is in the basement," he says. "We don't have to touch or anything."

Nina searches the bar. Amelia is still not there. Leon is kissing the blonde's fingernails one by one. On his desk at work sits a photograph of his four little girls: Katy, Christine, Lilli and Suzanne. His wife, Connie, gave the office a Halloween party last year, wearing her old Girl Scout uniform from fifth grade, which still fit. Leon came as a diver from the Chappaquiddick Bridge, wearing goggles and flippers and a button that read: "I'm Dead for Ted." The little girls paraded in Connie's old prom gowns and high heels. They ran up and down the stairs giggling at the adults in Hawaiian grass skirts and false noses. "I feel my life passing before my eyes," Connie confessed to Nina as they watched the pale pink and yellow skirts of her dresses flutter through the bars of the banister.

Nina isn't ready to go home. She wants to wait for Amelia. But the young man seems unbalanced, a little hysterical, ready to go off, and she's not in the mood to take on another set of problems. Opening her pocketbook, she motions to the bartender for her check.

"Okay," the young man sighs. "I'll tell you." He points the swizzle stick at the middle olive. "If you guessed olive number two, you were wrong. He's off to law school. Straight *A*'s. Well adjusted." Nina concentrates on counting change for her drinks. She leaves a tip. The young man doesn't stop talking.

"Number one, now," he continues. "She's an M.B.A. Harvard, of course. Procter & Gamble, Lever Brothers, they all want her." He moves his attention from the olives to Nina's eyes, then back to the olives. Even she has to admit: He has persistence. And a certain charm.

"Not impressed by money," he decides of Nina, talking to the bar. She shrugs her coat onto her shoulders. "Very healthy. Not to mention unusual."

For the last time, Nina looks for Amelia. She lifts up her pocketbook. The young man abandons the olives and watches her. His eyes are a dark green. Amelia's men were always dark and sensual. They approached her in shadowed hotel lobbies and crowded dining rooms, with offers of candlelit dinners and unlimited expense accounts. Temptations were everywhere, Amelia claimed, if you knew where to look for them. Her lovers brought her perfumes bearing names of famous designers and sent flowers from exotic cities. *She* went out *one* night of her six-year marriage and got an olive nut. Nina begins to laugh. She laughs until even Sam, who she is certain is crazy, starts to look nervous. Removing her coat, she drops her pocketbook to the floor and orders a Scotch. A fresh cigarette in hand, she turns to Sam.

"It's number three, right?" she asks.

Sam doesn't respond at first. Then he grins. The dimple resurfaces. "Nope," he replies. "It's olive number four. A very dark horse." He plucks olive number four from the top of the olive beaker, then sweeps the well-educated olives over the counter to the floor.

"Nothing personal," he says to Nina and leans toward her. "But could I pay for that drink?"

Over the past hour and a half, Sam has told Nina that he once played piccolo with the Juilliard String Quartet, that he is a vegetarian by birth and that he is studying for his C.P.A. exam. She decides to believe the last and forgive the rest. After her second Scotch, she excuses herself and walks to the pay phone, where she dials Amelia's number. It rings four times before Nina hangs up.

Sam is folding a piece of newspaper left on the bar into a paper hat. "No one wears hats anymore," he complains as Nina sits down. He pinches the peak into a sharp point. "My father wears a hat every day to work," he says. He works closely and carefully, reminding Nina of a small child. He considers the paper hat before him, thoughtful.

"My father *is* a hat," he muses. "A Stetson in the fast lane." He shoots a quick grin at Nina.

Nina is watching, but not listening. She is wondering why she didn't want Amelia to answer the phone.

"God, women are hard these days," Sam says. He stops working with the hat and looks at Nina. "One bad joke and"—he snaps his fingers before her eyes—"a guy doesn't stand a chance."

Nina smiles at him. "Not true," she says. She reaches into her pocket and pulls out a tissue. Feathering the tissue into shredded ribbons, she fastens it to the brim of the paper hat. Once you could tell a lot about a person by signals like hats, she thinks: Firemen wore red helmets; businessmen wore fedoras. Or rings: Women and men wore wedding bands and went home with their husbands and wives. She considers Amelia and Leon. She does not think of Jack. And then it hits her: For the first time in a year, she is not discussing Amelia's love life; she is not thinking about Jack's unemployment. It is like a vacation.

"All of Paris is clamoring for my designs," Sam whispers into Nina's ear. "But I refuse to do ready-to-wear." He lowers the hat onto Nina's head, considers the fit, then tilts the hat until the feather of tissue obscures her vision. "You've got to take certain risks to get ahead of the pack," he says, and putting his hand at her waist, leads her to the dance floor where other couples waltz to the jukebox that plays by the stairs. Amelia is probably caught on the Metro. Or maybe she isn't coming at all. Nina leans into Sam's arms, letting him support her weight.

The lights are dim. Leon passes and throws Nina a sly, all-knowing look. Touché, Leon, Nina whispers to herself. She doesn't care. Safe in Sam's embrace, she sways to the music. Sam is taller than Jack and to meet his height she dances on her toes. It makes her feel like a little girl. Under the camouflage of hat, she shuts her eyes. A year and a half ago, before Jack lost his job, they talked about having a child. They were at Rehoboth Beach in July, and Jack, tanned and smelling of coconut oil, woke her from a catnap with kisses and said, "Let's tempt fate," but she shook her head no and refused to forget her diaphragm.

Amelia taught: "No babies. One, they ruin your legs forever, and two, you'll never get anyplace with a kid hanging around your neck like a stone."

Nina moves back in Sam's arms. His eyes glow. His lips are a minute away from a kiss. She leans in, reaching her face toward his.

An unfamiliar hand grasps Nina's shoulder. A stubby girl with large black eyes and a fat twist of braid cuts in. She regards Sam with obvious ownership. Sam shrugs and says, "Ticket to ride, miss?" The girl glides Sam to a dark corner in the back of the room.

A night on the town for my young friend, Nina thinks, standing on the dance floor alone. She sways to the music, staying with her own thoughts, trying to imagine what it would be like now if she had gotten pregnant. She rubs her stomach. She imagines a baby's fine hair, the new eyes surrendering to light. She feels the child borne from her body, turning her inside out. Crouching to the floor, she looks to see if the child is a boy or a girl, but finds only the paper hat, fallen from her head.

"Lady." A man who has been standing beside the bar since she first entered is at her side. "Lady, you drunk?"

Nina looks at the hat, then at the man. Tears block her vision. She accepts the man's extended hand and he leads her to the bar.

"Set her up, Frankie," the man says to the bartender. He regards Nina, then Sam across the room.

"There's lots of fish in the sea, dearie," he observes.

The woman who has been sitting beside him, in a three-piece suit and ragged fingernails, lets out a sharp laugh. "Good Lord," she says. "I don't know where you store those pearls, Clyde."

Nina stares into her drink. Alone, she calms. Amelia is definitely not on her way. Nina's reason for waiting is gone.

"You need a taxi?" Clyde calls to her as she heads for the door. Nina shakes her head no.

"I know my way home," she says, and steps into the night.

Outside, headlights strobe Pennsylvania Avenue, illuminating St. Stephen's Church. Taking off her high heels, she runs her shoes along the iron grillwork fence surrounding Columbia Hospital. At Rehoboth Beach, she and Jack necked in an iron-grilled gazebo under a full orange moon. "Corny but sweet," Sam would say. "Très sensual," said Amelia.

In the living room, Jack is asleep on the sofa, one leg dropping off the edge to the carpet. The blue square of the television set lights the corner. The fish swim in clouds of bubbles and algae. The African violets shimmer beneath their purple halo. Jack's hands cup his crotch.

Moving as quietly as she is able, Nina perches beside her sleeping husband. She strokes his hair, holding her breath. He'd never know how close she'd come to kissing Sam. He wasn't ever going to know. Amelia either. Nina stares at his ruffled hair, his parted lips. She shuts her eyes and remembers the first night they made love, outside in a park near Philadelphia. The sky was gray-pink, and when they finished, Jack grabbed his chest and said, "Does your heart ever hurt?" and Nina, sure that those were Jack's last words, planted a kiss so immediate and unthinking and heartfelt onto his lips that later he said he was certain that she had brought him back to life.

Of course, Jack wasn't dying, but at that moment she had known that if he had died she might not have wanted to live and decided right then and there and without thinking at all that she was going to take a chance with Jack.

Nina puts her hand into her pocketbook and draws out the paper bag containing the teddy set. The rustling wakes Jack. He shifts. He smells like sleep.

"Would you look at this?" she asks him. He sits up and blinks, adjusting his eyes to the light.

THE AXE, THE AXE, THE AXE

ERIC WILSON

Eric Wilson studied under a Fulbright Grant at the Free University of Berlin before returning to Stanford for a Ph.D. in Germanic languages. He has taught German at UCLA and Pomona College. Since 1973 he has worked as a freelance writer and translator. His stories have appeared in the *Massachusetts Review, Epoch,* and *Carolina Quarterly,* and his opinion pieces in the Los Angeles *Times.* He lives in Santa Monica, California, and teaches fiction writing at the UCLA Extension.

The whole time I was at Stanford, Eisenhower was in the White House. The opening freshman mixer, with no scintilla of irony, was called a Jolly-Up. Things that were great were "bitching." In contrast to high school slang, at Stanford the "g" was now clearly pronounced; it made you feel as if you had finally put away childish things.

If anyone on campus ever smoked marijuana in those days I never heard of it. Tom Lehrer sang with spirited glee of the Old Dope Peddler and it sounded roguish and surreal. Student hangouts down Alpine Road would be raided periodically by the Alcoholic Beverage Commission—a zealous band of "ABC boys" storming Zott's or Mama Garcia's in search of fake IDs, while minors hurled a flurry of Dixie cups out the windows and the air was awash with unlawful beer. In Budapest teenagers were throwing Molotov cocktails and sloshing gasoline into the air as tanks opened fire: but Sandor and the revolution didn't burst into my world until a year later, when I was a sophomore.

A consummate Stanford prank—such as an all-out and as-yet-unretaliated attack with water balloons—was a "bitching R.F." There were a lot of R.F.s in those days, since with no co-ed housing the guys lived in a perpetual locker-room atmosphere. Sororities were not allowed, and the girls' dorms had lockable front doors and sentinel housemothers. They would page your date from a switchboard while you stood around listening to someone play Greensleeves on the lobby piano. The girls were locked in at 10:30 on weeknights; they could get a limited number of sign-outs until midnight, but they usually hoarded these for dates—or the hope of dates—with fraternity men.

Freshmen couldn't go through rush until after Christmas or move into a fraternity house until sophomore year. As a frosh you *had* to live on campus and in a dormitory. My first roommate in Norton Hall was a stolid jock from Watsonville who said either "No shit?" or "Jeez Louise!" to everything you told him. After only a few weeks Larry decided he'd much rather room down the hall with The Jolly Green Giant, a towering P.E. major whose real name was Roland. The Green Giant had been rooming with a straight-arrow pre-med named Douglas, and one night while Doug was out booking for an anatomy test, a floor R.F. was swept into action: all Larry's stuff—down to the bedding—was moved out of our room and all Doug's things were moved in. When the library closed and Doug came back to Norton, Larry and The Green Giant dispatched him down to me and his new room. Douglas just shrugged his shoulders and mumbled, "Hope you can sleep with the lights on." He sat down to continue booking and by the end of the year I had learned to sleep with a pillow wrapped around my head and not suffocate.

Douglas would have looked callow even for a high school kid. He wore white bucks as smooth as his face and not only ironed his jockey shorts, he folded them into neat little rectangles before putting them away. One day it occurred to me that *I* always started all the conversations between us—laconic and innocuous as they might be. I decided to leave the next opening line to Douglas.

And waited.

His silent treatment was particularly disturbing since I wasn't sure: was Douglas rejecting me simply because he was the cream-faced loon that he was, or was it because of my eye? Unilateral external strabismus. I remember I could say this even before we moved to Pacific Palisades, so that meant at least before I was five. My left eye goes slightly to the left, and with light blue eyes the dark errant pupil is particularly noticeable. When I was growing up I was never certain whether people were put off by the fact I couldn't look them straight in the eye, or whether they failed to notice this and just didn't like me.

I was never much good at small talk, but rooming with someone who made *no* talk was unnerving. I had been uncomfortable enough with Larry's incessant "Jeez Louise!" and his entourage of jocks, but being alone with Douglas soon grew unbearable. When Doug's mother in Walnut Creek called to invite me home for Thanksgiving, I accepted with a double relief: I wouldn't be abandoned in the dining hall on a holiday; and Douglas would be forced to speak to me now. But when that Thursday arrived, Doug still hadn't broken the silence. Mid-afternoon we both showered, put on suits and ties (Doug adding his own indomitable blend of Listerine and Old Spice), and then Doug followed me mutely down to my car. In transit he gave me a few sparse directions ("Take Dumbarton Bridge, then go north on 21 up past Danville"); and that was it. In fact, his last words to me *ever* were, "I *said:* pass the mince pie." But Doug's mother was already chattering as she greeted us on the front porch. I felt like Rosencrantz *and* Guildenstern, but even Hamlet was soon lost in the shuffle and the Queen herself put on the play. Periodically during the evening she would interrupt herself to exclaim, "Douglas, why didn't you *tell* us Greg was so interesting? You *must* bring him home with you more often!" Only later did it occur to me that Doug didn't have a car.

I had an old faded-beige Chevy station wagon that had been my parents' and had wallpaper that was supposed to look like wood. One Saturday, on the spur of the moment, Larry and The Green Giant and six of their buddies asked me to go with them to Half Moon Bay—and then they all piled into my car. They stayed on the beach playing bridge even by bonfire in the dark (I've never been able to play any sort of game), and I sat shivering wrapped in a blanket, my trunks still wet and gritty under my jeans.

Laurel was decorously bemused by the Chevy, especially the fading wallpaper. I had met her during a dinner exchange (sending a floor of Arbol Hall girls over to Norton helped keep down the food fights) and we started dating. I couldn't believe she would actually go out with me. But she had sat *next* to me at dinner, rather than across from me, so she wouldn't have seen the nonalignment of my eyes, at least not as a first impression. Laurel was from Boston and said "warter" for water, wore her hair in an elegant ash-blond duck-tail and was majoring in Chemistry.

The problem was that until you joined a fraternity there was no place you could go to be alone with a girl. You *could* go to the Cactus Gardens and park; but you didn't usually go to the Cactus Gardens unless you were going to go all the way. I didn't want to give Laurel the wrong idea about me—at least prematurely—so weeknights that left coffee dates at Stickney's: starched waitresses with sparkly glasses, refilling your cup until you sloshed.

One Saturday night I drove Laurel into the City to see Maria Schell in *Die letzte Brücke.* In high school I had been an exchange student in

Berlin, and had picked up German in spite of myself. (I arrived without knowing a word, but the mother of the family I stayed with grabbed my arm the first day, pointed at the sky and proclaimed: *"Gregor, der Himmel ist blau!"* I looked up and realized that it *was*. I just kept on absorbing things, and by the time I left Berlin I could say *ikke dette kieke mal* as well as any kid on the *Strasse.)* But Laurel didn't believe I could actually understand the film without looking at the subtitles. French, perhaps, but German? Nobody spoke *German.* Driving back down Bayshore she insisted we speak French. Laurel spoke French and I tossed in every Gallic filler I could think of, relying most heavily on *pour ainsi dire* and *pas que je sache.* Then I remembered La Fontaine's fables and began telling her of *loups* and *cigognes* and *chauves-souris,* and finally even the *grenouilles* who demanded a king. By the time we hit Palm Drive Laurel was fully assuaged.

It was only 11:30 and we still had time to join the Arbol Hall ritual. You would stand somewhere in the shadows (people tight up against the building as if it were raining) and make out until just before it turned midnight. You had to keep looking at your watch over your date's shoulder so you wouldn't miss lock-out; but you couldn't stop making out, say, at five minutes to twelve or it would look as if you'd lost interest or gotten into a fight. Then right at midnight couples would emerge from all directions of the darkness and a mob, trying to look casual, would stream up the steps to the front door.

The next time I took Laurel to a foreign movie it was *The Seventh Seal.* On the way back she asked me what it had meant. I hesitated and then ventured that the film might have been a parody. I had sat there watching the gloom, waiting for the real meaning—any meaning—to hit me. But the only thing I could think of was that the film was a joke: playing chess with the devil in all that murk had to be making fun of something. "It's symbolic," Laurel said firmly, looking straight ahead while I drove. "It all *means* something. You're the English major, you're supposed to know what it is."

"All right. I think the devil symbolizes a moose. If there had been any decent lighting you'd have seen the outline of antlers under all those robes."

"That's not the devil playing chess with the Knight," Laurel informed me, crossing her arms. "It's Death. Even I know *that* much." She thought for a while and then chided: "You should at least be able to recognize Death."

When we got back to Arbol it was only a quarter to twelve, but Laurel wanted to go straight in. We never had another date after that. Every time I called, her roommate came on the phone and said Laurel was out studying. She never returned any of my calls, and I finally gave up, figuring she had met somebody else.

I found I could study best in an empty classroom over at Cubberly. Sometimes I'd just sit in a corner of the floor, leaning up against the wall with a book in my lap. Why did Neanderthal man do his animal paintings so far inside the caves? Why did Prufrock wear his trousers rolled? Why did pink snapdragons have red offspring? The thing I liked about Introduction to Biology was that there were definite answers. One white, two pink, and one red. Mendel could be grasped, but not the mermaids singing, each to each.

Robbie, one of the guys in the dorm, had a brother who was a grad student and would buy beer for us. You couldn't take alcohol back to your rooms in the dorm, so we'd have to drive out into the hills and sit in the wallpapered Chevy and drink in the dark. We'd bring along multiple six-packs and get shit-faced just for the sake of getting shit-faced. John Buford, who'd been in Bremen when I was in Berlin, would start out wanting to talk about something serious like Cardinal Mindszenty's being freed, but Roger Steiner would tell about a guy at his high school who'd gotten a dose of the clap and Nick Pedersen would interrupt to say you couldn't ever just talk about the clap, it always had to be a *dose* of the clap just like it was always a *pride* of lions, that was the unit of measurement. I said it wasn't "air" it was "rrrr," to rrrrr is human, people kept saying it wrong. Robbie felt that twat was more onomatopoetic than snatch, things would gradually get out of hand, and sometimes we'd start to sing "Oh it's beer, beer, beer, that makes you want to cheer, on the farm, on The Farm. . . ." Once we even broke into the axe yell, although that was supposed to be evoked only during the Big Game with Cal and even then only when the cheerleaders deemed it an absolute last resort. During freshman orientation week they were going to teach us the axe yell in Mem Aud, just so we'd know it and be ready when the time came, but then one of the cheerleaders (I suspect now that this was all carefully rehearsed) suddenly tried to stop the others, it was *sacrilege* to do The Axe even to teach it because it wasn't really the Big Game and the Big Crunch, but the others pleaded with him, just this *once*, and while they were still arguing there came this groundswell filling the auditorium, Robbie and Nick Pedersen would usually lurch into it after the third or fourth beer, Give 'em the axe, the axe, the axe, give 'em the axe, the axe, the axe, give 'em the axe, Christ, it went on

like that forever, we'd keep screwing up, everybody off on his own like
some kind of round song, the neck, the axe, give 'em the axe, *where?*
Right in the neck, the neck, the neck, right in the neck, the axe, the
neck, right in the neck, right in the axe, the neck, the axe, right in the
neck, *there!* Right about this point Roger Steiner would lean out the
window and start barfing; it was the same color as the wallpaper so it
didn't really matter. Tom Callison was always so cheerful in the dorm,
but whenever he got shit-faced with us in the hills he'd just sit there in
the second back seat of the Chevy and start to cry. Once the crying
started, that was it, he wouldn't stop the rest of the evening. Nick would
usually put his arm around him and ask softly, "Hey, Callison babes,
what is it?" But Tom would just turn his head away and keep sobbing.

We went through rush at the start of winter quarter, right after
Christmas vacation. The guys in the fraternity houses wore slacks and
crew-neck sweaters and looked really self-assured and (to use the word of
the fifties) "studly." They'd serve you some bright red punch but give
you a stage-wink to indicate that there'd be a lot of the real stuff once
you were in the house—kegs of beer in the basement and suds at dawn
on Saturdays and life would be just one big R.F. They kept talking about
the "brothers" as if they really meant it, and they had files of all the tests
going back to God knows when. Their rooms looked like something left
over from a ransacking that had to stay like that until the police photog-
raphers were done. No Doz scattered around and capless tubes of zit
cream and dented tennis-ball cans used as ashtrays dumped over Kings-
ton Trio albums, paperbacks of *Gatsby* and *Great Expectations* and *Les
silences du colonel Bramble* broken-spined and spilling their pages. Most
of the beds were in ragged sleeping porches upstairs, with screens but no
windows and on the wall a yellow metal octagon said HUMP.

A lot of the fraternity guys were pinned and they had their girls on
hand in tight sweaters to pass out cookies and make name tags for the
open houses. Laurel was a hostess at the Phi Delt house and she wrote
GREG KIRTLAND with round letters in turquoise ink and then, taking hold
of his arm, asked whether I'd had a chance yet to meet Buzz. Buzz, she
told me, giving him a squeeze, had been Chairman of the Big Game
Bonfire, maybe I remembered. Buzz looked me right in the eye, or rather
right in my strong eye, and then back and forth between them, establishing beyond a doubt that you couldn't look into both of them at once.

There were only a couple of us on the floor who didn't pledge. Tom
Callison had already decided to leave Stanford at the end of the year, but
he got a lot of bids anyway. Nick Pedersen joined an eating club, which

was supposed to be an intellectual alternative to fraternities, and the club members had a special dorm of their own. Douglas also joined an eating club, but it was one of the "dorky" eating clubs and almost worse than not joining anything at all.

From winter quarter on, almost everything was fraternity- or eating-club-oriented, and the dorm-centered activities such as dinner exchanges between Norton and Arbol fell pretty much by the wayside. I went up to the City by myself to see *The Seventh Seal* again, but it was opaque from beginning to end. And I still couldn't figure out Douglas' unbroken silence; it gnawed at me like a continual reproach. For what? I kept wondering. *For what?*

But at least Douglas never turned violent like Robbie's roommate. Dave Donovan was a tennis player who had recently been diagnosed as having diabetes. He had become sullen and withdrawn, and one day Robbie came back from lunch to find everything on Donovan's side of the room knocked over, ripped apart or smashed to pieces. Donovan disappeared for the next week and a half; and on top of all the mess he left behind, Donovan had completely covered up his medicine-chest mirror with masking tape. Even after he finally came back and remained subdued for the rest of the year, Donovan was adamant on this one point: no one was *ever* to try to unmask the mirror.

Spring quarter I had a new English teacher and started getting B's instead of A's, even though I had been editor of my high school paper. Miss Middlemoss had a fixation about the "terrible gaiety" of Edith Sitwell and had once actually visited the offices of *The New Yorker*. She was alarmed that I found neither *Tristram Shandy* enormously comic nor *Heart of Darkness* enormously deep and said that having a "serviceable expository style" wasn't going to do me much good if I kept missing the point. Why couldn't I learn to get beneath the surface of things and interpret? For our final we were supposed to imagine that Joseph Conrad, Pirandello, George Eliot, and C. P. Snow had gotten together, and we were to write down a dialogue of what they said. I was tempted to write that they all sat around in the dark and played chess with a moose, but I didn't want to screw up my grade point average. Before I handed in my blue book, however, I scribbled boldly on the back cover, "Mistah Kirtland, he dead," and switched my major to Business Administration the next day.

If you didn't get asked to pledge a house and you didn't want to live off campus (living by myself in Palo Alto or Menlo Park seemed to me like banishment), you ended up in Sturges Hall. The place was pretty much of a joke and the humor magazine, *The Chaparral,* was always making barbs about how only fraternity rejects lived there. The *Chappy* had a parody of the social calendar, This Shell in a Monthnut (sometimes it was This Nut in a Monthshell), and right after "Dynamiting of Hoover Tower" they listed "Fall Rush Party, Sturges."

As I carried in the first load of stuff from the station wagon, I saw my name neatly typed on the card on the door, along with SANDOR RAGALYI. He hadn't shown up yet, and when I called home to tell my folks I'd arrived safely I spelled the name for them, adding I figured he'd probably be an exchange student and that would be something to look forward to. After a long silence on the phone my father said, ". . . Yes, but what color is he?" I didn't understand at first. "What if he's from Africa?" my father persisted. "What will happen if he's a *Negro?*"

My mother on the other phone started telling me about how people judge you by the company you keep, and you can't detach yourself all that successfully from a roommate, and what would that do to my social life? "Besides," she went on, "if you're going to go through fall rush what will you do if he wants to come *with* you? How are you ever going to get into a fraternity if you show up with a—"

Sandor had escaped during the Hungarian uprising the year before. He was tall and frail with shoulders hunched as if in fear. He had a pale complexion, pained dark eyes, and beautiful thick dark hair that looked like a velvet cap. In contrast to all the flattops that year, Sandor's hair was all the more striking. He smiled a lot, but in a leery, disoriented way. In the dorm he wore grandfatherly leather bedroom slippers which he apparently had thought to bring with him even in the midst of the revolution. The guys on the floor called him the Freedom Fighter, half joking, half in awe, but every time they said this Sandor would wince. A rumor got started that he had been in jail for political activities and had managed to break out, although Sandor refused to discuss this.

Sandor was oblivious, of course, to the fact that he had landed among such an oddball lot. There weren't any Sturges Hall jocks, and the grad student who was our R.A.—fondly referred to as Mother McAllister— used to lead floor meetings pretending he was a WAC drill sergeant. There was perhaps more than a routine feyness and familiarity among a number of the Sturges guys, but at the time I just chalked up their mannerisms to their being turkeys in general. They treated both Sandor and me as if we were from another world; and with respect. And they had the highest grade point average on campus.

Sandor's hands were extraordinarily fine; his fingers had the elongated reverence of an El Greco. When the Sturges guys—who were always very gentle with Sandor—routinely asked him whether he played the piano, he would whisper that no, he did not. He would hide his hands behind his back and stare down at his slippers, rigid with shame.

When we were alone, Sandor almost always spoke German with me, which he knew far better than English. And what elegant German it was! Sandor spoke in the blurred, trilled, faded grandeur of the Austro-Hungarian Empire and called me by my Magyar name, Gergely, even in German. He never wanted to talk about the revolution, but one night I found him staring straight ahead with an odd detached look in his dark eyes: bodies of Russian soldiers, he explained, were lying beside burnt-out tanks and armored cars and overturned trucks; men in white coats were going from corpse to corpse sprinkling snow-white lime, and the dead gradually began to look like cold marble statues. Small boys ran around in the rubble collecting bullets.

I introduced Sandor to the tradition of the Sunday Night Flicks: after a weekend of study you could walk over to Mem Aud and see films like *The Man Who Knew Too Much* and sing along with Doris Day belting out *Que será, será* in that harrowing denouement. One Sunday while we were waiting in line at the flicks I met Rubybell, who had gone by herself. She was quick to explain she had been named for a wealthy, childless Aunt Rubybell who felt that the whole namesake thing had been a cheap ploy to get at her money (it was) and had left everything to Sweet Briar College. Rubybell had smooth pale skin, rich blue eyes, and a throaty voice as deep as the red lacquer of her nails. In the free association of her conversation, I remember, she told us right there in line that her father had lost his foot in Rio; he had been in the diplomatic service and fallen afoul of a streetcar. She agreed to go out with me even though I was a Sturges Hall turkey.

Rubybell—over coffee at Stickney's—said she had never met anyone until Sandor who could truly be described as "abject." Should she try to fix him up with a girlfriend of hers? But Sandor whispered to me no, please, he would feel far too ill at ease. And for all the cordiality—even tenderness—he received, Sandor's depression was becoming helplessly resolute. No one knew quite what to do. Mother McAllister tried to cheer him up one night in the dining hall by doing impersonations of Tragic Heroines: Isadora Duncan flamboyantly being yanked to her death by that long, beautiful scarf; Virginia Woolf walking slowly, stead-fastly into the pond ("her ravelled sleeve of hair billowing out onto the water");—and F.D.R. ("inching agonizingly forward in 'her' wheel-chair"). Gerald Weintraub tried to incorporate Sandor into the main-stream of things by teaching him slang: things that Stanford men were wont to say such as "Did you plank her?" "Don't go apeshit!" and "How's your old wazoo?" But when Sandor formed these words in the reluctant blur of his accent, he sounded like an exiled prince forced to turn brigand. Gerald took us into his room to share some marzipan he had gotten from home and to play for us *The Unicorn, the Gorgon and the Manticore*. Mother McAllister loved the music and sang along with the libretto, but Sandor merely looked bleak. Back in our own room, lying in our beds in the dark, I asked him to teach me Hungarian. I still remember the first lesson began with *köszönöm* (thank you) and ended with *nem értem* (I don't understand).

The next day several members of the Catholic Church, which had sponsored Sandor, dropped by the room to ask if it wouldn't be advisable for him to get a tutor. Sandor sent them politely away, but confided to me he was not making his grades and that meant he might forfeit his scholarship. At this point I was taking both econ and chemistry—the Hawley-Smoot Tariff and exogenously given money supplies vying with mole fractions, volatile solutes, and supersaturations—and doing wretch-edly myself. To make matters worse, I was also doing poorly in German. I had merely wanted to keep up with the language, but we were having to read Schiller's *Kabale und Liebe*, a seething *Sturm und Drang* play that ran from frivolous roguishnesses to fissures rending the infinity of the universe. Amidst an incontinence of dashes and exclamation marks the characters came right out and *said* they were raving. Young Ferdi-nand gnawed at the seams of the bourgeois world and screamed he could never, ever love the Countess.

John Buford was in the same German class, and he and I would try to outdo each other in imitations of Ferdinand. John had pledged Sigma Nu, but would have lunch with me at Sturges on Saturdays when their cook had the day off. They were one of the more civil fraternity houses, all things considered, and one day it occurred to him I might be inter-ested: he could invite me over to the house and I could meet some of the brothers. After all, I hadn't tried Sigma Nu the first time around, had I? And, well. . . . He looked nervously over at the next table where Mother McAllister was anticly pretending to be a manticore. I told John thank you but no thank you. I didn't tell him that I couldn't bear to be rejected again.

There was a Sturges dance in the lounge and I took Rubybell. I was worried about how the guys would react to her name, but Mother McAllister, when I introduced them, merely said *"Enchanté!"* and kissed her hand. I think he was impressed I had brought a girl at all. Rubybell and I danced to the music of someone's hi-fi, slowly, holding each other closely, and I realized that one of the things I liked about her was the fact she seemed to take me seriously.

Between records we went to get some more punch—Gerald must have slipped in a whole bottle of vodka—and I asked her whether she had ever seen *The Seventh Seal.* I felt comfortable enough around Rubybell to admit that, to tell the truth, I wasn't quite sure what all of it meant. *"Meant?"* she asked, taken aback. Then she laughed her deep, throaty laugh, exhaling a swirl of sensual blue smoke: "It was *bullshit,* that's what it meant!" She ran her hand playfully over the top of my head, over the bristly flattop I kept rigid with a thick pink wax. "Look at Sandor's hair," she told me. "My God it's sexy. Greg, really, why don't you let your hair grow out . . . ?"

After I had taken Rubybell back to her dorm, I returned to find Sandor sitting on his bed waiting up for me. He spoke more softly than usual, so that I had to sit down next to him to hear him at all. The Soviets were threatening to do something to his mother if he didn't go back to Budapest. After he had come to America he hadn't received a single letter from her; he wasn't even certain she was still alive. He had asked his teachers if he could write his blue books in Hungarian and they had all laughed at first and then, realizing he was serious, said it was out of the question. He broke into muffled sobs: trucks were in flames in the rubble of the streets; someone was arranging a wreath of autumn leaves over a decomposing corpse; a boy had scrambled on top of a tank: when the turret opened, he dropped in a grenade just before the soldiers started to fire. Sandor looked at me in an unbearable terror.

And then he began to brighten. In fact, for the first time since I had known him, Sandor seemed downright jolly. In the dining hall he even made a point of going up to Gerald Weintraub and asking straight out: "How's your old wazoo?" It was wonderful seeing Sandor in such high spirits, even if they were a bit bizarre. Finally he seemed to be a part of things; his passivity and fear were replaced by a sense of confidence and purpose. He no longer hunched. Even the impending midterms no longer seemed to overwhelm him. If he studied diligently, he would pass;

it was as simple as that. But he would need some uninterrupted time with his books. What was I going to be doing on Saturday morning? I would be over at Cubberly, sitting in a corner with my books. Would I go directly to the dining hall from there? It seemed important to him, so I promised I would. Then I wouldn't be back in the room before one o'clock? *Nem, nem,* I told him in Hungarian, definitely not.

After lunch I knocked circumspectly and waited a while before entering the room. But Sandor was gone and there was no trace of him. In a way I was glad, since Cubberly was starting to get crowded on weekends and I found this distracting. I sat down cross-legged on top of my bed with my books piled around me, steeling myself for an all-afternoon cram session.

If you lower the vapor pressure of the solvent in a dissolved solute, this would be proportional to the mole fraction of the solute in an ideal solution. Oh shit oh shit oh shit. She has seen my entire soul—and she felt nothing? Felt nothing but the triumph of her guile? You tell me she swooned—oh deceit—but cannot coquettes swoon? For changes in the amount demanded that respond to changes in price are changes in the amount demanded and *not* changes in "demand." Hence there is no change or shift in the demand schedule (see Figure 2-7) and it is only as a short-cut term that we refer to "demand." Ha! Emilie! No, proud unhappy creature, you may shame me but never revile me! Magnanimity alone shall be my guide! Raoult's law holds true only for an *ideal* solution, from solute mole fraction zero to—

The tremor was relatively mild, but I thought automatically: Would this be the Big One? I guess that's what Californians always think when they sense an incipient earthquake. But when I felt the bed with the palms of my hands, everything was completely still. Now if this same consumer who has just bought milk for 25¢ a quart subsequently finds that down the block milk is selling for only 20¢ a quart, according to Table 4-6 she—I felt it again, a jolt to the bed, pushing upward on the springs. And then another jolt to the springs. The wind was blowing in the open windows. Had someone—as an odd joke—climbed in the window and was now hiding under the bed, waiting to leap out at me?

The face must have slid out jaggedly along the floor before it actually came up at me. Sandor was an eerie white in contrast to the dark dried curds of blood that had spattered out from the slash on his neck, drenching his white shirt and a towel he had dragged out with him, his usual tentative porcelain smile jammed into a leer as he started to go into convulsions. The next thing I am aware of I am on the floor in Gerald's

room, Mother McAllister is wrapping me snugly in a dark gray blanket
and holding me down firmly, tightening the blanket around my arms and
shoulders. This is without sound and in slow motion. Sandor is also
wrapped in a blanket up to his chin, his head thrashing from side to side,
but sometimes he's on a stretcher down the corridors of the med center
and sometimes they're putting him in the back seat of the station wagon,
but how can I see this while they're holding me down on Gerald's floor?

When I open my eyes I'm still wrapped up in blankets. I'm in a room
with a dozen or so beds, a sterile room in an old house. It's dark outside
and the dim electric light is a translucent blue. The other guys are
restless but I feel . . . snug-as-a-bug-in-a-rug. I try to say this aloud to
Mother McAllister leaning down over me but he's not there after all and
I can't talk, I can't move. The blankets are up to my chin and there is no
sound even though the guys are roughhousing around, someone's getting
walloped with a pillow. The sound comes on when a girl in white arrives
to quiet them down. There's teasing back and forth, Bonnie, give us a
back-rub, huh, how 'bout it, pretty please? They've got their pajama tops
off and Bonnie is kneading wide freckled shoulders with the pungence of
alcohol. Me next, Bonnie, me next they're all shouting but I can't say a
word. Hey, Terry wants a front-rub, do Terry next, come on, do Terry, do
Terry, he's lying on his back on the bed next to mine, bare-chested with
his arms folded behind his head, sandy hair in his eyes, do Terry they call
out, Bonnie moves in between our beds, one play all the way, hey hey,
one play all the way the guys chant, Bonnie moves down massaging, then
there's a hush, I stare at the ceiling in the cold blue light and there
comes a whoop in unison, me next, Bonnie me next, hooligans, Christ,
another woman in white, absolute *hooligans,* Bonnie's out the door, the
lot of you, why if you big galoots don't settle down—

By the time they released me from the convalescent home, there was
no hope of my ever passing chemistry; I dropped the class, which gave
me only 12 units. The Dean interceded for me in German, asking that I
be allowed to take an incomplete. Mother McAllister said it would be
left up to me as to whether I wanted a new roommate or to be by myself.

I wanted to be by myself. Every night before going to bed, like old
maids in cartoons, I looked under the bed. Under the other bed—now
starkly vacant—and inside both wardrobes, pushing back shirts and jack-
ets on hangers. My compulsive nightly ritual was humiliating, even
though no one was there to see me. I don't remember actually screaming
in my dreams, but Mother McAllister and sometimes Gerald Weintraub
would be sitting on the bed next to me telling me it was all right.

Mother McAllister said not to worry about what anybody else thought. Once I remember waking up crying uncontrollably and Mother McAllister held my head in his lap and said that would do me good, just go ahead and cry.

For the most part things went on as they had been before, except that I dropped Business Administration and was without a major again. Business had sounded so unremittingly practical, and it seemed foolish to declare "undeclared" just as I was trying to get my life squared away. Rubybell talked me into growing my hair out, long like a poet's, but she got on my nerves because she kept trying to "soothe" me. She would keep saying "after what you've been through," as if now I were some kind of psycho. I was glad she wasn't with me the night I was driving the station wagon down Harrison Avenue and thought I heard a noise from the second back seat. After Sandor, I had become so uneasy about being shut in with the unhappenable the *next* time it happened that as a reflex action I just bolted out the front door and into the open, scraping hell out of myself on the pavement. I must have thrown the car into neutral, anyway it came to a stop halfway up a curb. I sat beside the car on the grass for a long time with my knees pulled up to my chin until finally a policeman stopped to see if I were drunk or hurt and that broke the spell.

Winter quarter it rained almost non-stop and I started studying in the reading room of Hoover Tower since it was relatively free from undergraduates. Every afternoon an older woman in a gray dress and orange beads would sit across the table from me reading Russian newspapers that smelled like sawdust. I'd take breaks by riding the elevator up to the wet observation deck and looking out at the red tile roofs and rolling hills turning darkly lush and the pewter-colored bay out in the distance. Sometimes I would sit in the window ledge of a deserted biology lecture room and listen to it rain until dusk. I didn't take the Palo Alto *Times* and so I didn't see the article until John Buford brought it over to show me. Sandor had made so much progress after the shock treatments that they had given him ground privileges. With his belt he had hanged himself from a tree.

My folks would call me at least once a week and my father's refrain had become Well what *are* you going to major in? You can't reject everything just because you don't like it, the world's *full* of people who do things they don't like, that's what growing up is all about. My mother, on the other phone, would shush him and say I'm sure Greg knows what he's doing, don't you dear?

Then the note came from the fraternity—Dad's old house at Michigan State—inviting me over for dinner. So Dad had finally started to push my being a legacy, even though as far back as high school I had made him promise he would never do this. I certainly wasn't going to go through with it now—hey, Skip/Chip/Biff/Bucky, meet old Greg here from Sturges Hall—c'mon, Greg, step up a little closer and gobble for the fans. But then I decided I *would* go through with it. In the long run it would be the best way to shut Dad up.

The first guy I ran into when I got to the house was Terry Lindquist. I thought he looked familiar somehow, but he knew it had been in the convalescent home when we all had the Asian flu together, and just because I had been there he had it in his head that I was one hell of a bitching guy. He introduced me around to all the "bros" and at dinner we traded nudges about what a tough chick Bonnie had been and goddam he didn't think she'd really *do* it, Jesus was that ever bitching. After dinner when they pulled out some Cutty Sark Terry told me quite honestly he hadn't realized that *I* was Greg Kirtland, the name hadn't clicked, hell, word had gone around the house that I was just another Sturges Hall yo-yo being served up as the booby prize. Jeez Louise, had I heard that they finally caught old Bonnie going down on a Zete right in the middle of breakfast?

I didn't move into the fraternity house until the next fall. Even when I did, they never seemed to figure out that I didn't fit in. They'd talk about getting shit-faced and getting laid and we'd go out en masse to the home games and inject vodka into oranges and throw frozen gremlins around and after the card stunts we'd be the first ones to start flinging bright cardboard squares down at the cheerleaders even though they'd yell Hey you assholes, those could fucking blind somebody. I started working on the staff of the *Stanford Daily* and Terry said every house needed at least one brain and he guessed I was theirs. He said I even *looked* intellectual, what with my hair and my—, but he stopped before he said eyes. At their first party I was fixed up with a tough chick whose mystique was enhanced by the fact she was taking a course in something called existentialism. They said with her I was sure to score, and on one of the rumpled beds in the sleeping porch I did. I took Rubybell on a few coffee dates but never dared bring her around to the house: and only partially because of her name. The new diversion that fall was a freshman nympho named Elsbeth. When the bros could get hold of her they'd run her over to the house and take turns planking her on top of the pool table while everyone else stood around watching. Sometimes I'd walk into the poolroom not realizing it was an Elsbeth night and feel the same way I had felt in the freshman dorm where the toilet stalls didn't have any doors.

I learned to steer clear of Elsbeth, but Sandor was less predictable. The next time he appeared his face finally did crack and blood was streaming out from his nose and the gash in his neck, the police had even confiscated *my* razor and never returned it but Sandor had still found a way, Gergely, Gergely, he has bad breath and El Greco hands grab at my shoulders and shake me and shake me and all I can do is scream, I jerk up in bed, the light's in my eyes and the guys standing there in the sleeping porch are staring in disbelief; Terry in his jacket with the big red S looks stricken. Brad, finally, breaks the silence: "Hey, Kirtland, it's no big deal. We just thought you might want to go out with us for a late-night pizza. You know?"

I didn't try to explain. I just said quietly it's okay, you guys go ahead. The next morning Terry came up to me in front of the bookstore, giving me a rough playful yank as he put his arm around me. "Hey, fellah, you're really some joker, you know that? I mean, you really scared the bejesus out of us. I gather you were royally pissed we woke you up so late, but *Christ . . . !*"

I got to worrying about what I'd say the next time I did something like that. But as it turned out, that was the last time I ever dreamed about Sandor. Some deadening mechanism in my mind—I am chagrined at the egocentricity of self-preservation—took over. Sandor's memory has become remote, and the scene from under the bed could just as well have been a drive-in movie I caught a glimpse of going past on the freeway. I kept on living in the house, and became more dogged than ever in my efforts to do everything the other guys did—short of Elsbeth. It wasn't long before the *Daily* started giving me regular front-page bylines, and the editor wanted me to branch out from the basic who-what-when stuff and try some features or reviews. I never did, though; I just stuck to reporting exactly what happened, and left the interpreting —the meaning of things—to others. For all her terrible gaiety, I was convinced that old Miss Middlemoss had been right about me. *Tristram Shandy* might really *be* enormously comic. And *Heart of Darkness* enormously deep.

THE SEASONS

JOYCE CAROL OATES

Joyce Carol Oates is the author of a number of volumes of short stories, including *Last Days* (1984) and *A Sentimental Education* (1980). Her most recent novel is *Solstice* (1985). She lives in Princeton, New Jersey, where she teaches at the university and co-edits *The Ontario Review*.

Joy, who is now twenty-six years old, is waiting to conceive *as if by accident* a child with the man she loves. This will be irrefutable proof, she reasons, that she loves him and that they must marry. Though she has not believed in God for perhaps thirteen years she reasons too that conceiving a child in her special circumstances will be a sign of some kind, natural and healthy in effect but supernatural in origin. Her thoughts on the subject are kept secret from her lover Christopher but she suspects that he understands and concurs—he has developed such uncanny powers of intuition he sometimes knows what she is going to say before she says it. Frequently he reads her thoughts and announces them playfully, even in the presence of others. (Christopher is a playwright and his head is aswirl, he says, with dialogue. Stray floating dialogue. Aleatory sounds. So perhaps it is altogether natural that he can hear Joy's thoughts even when she doesn't intend to speak them aloud. Also, he loves her very much and certainly would marry her if she had his baby.) Only the accidental is truly significant in Joy's imagination because it is all that remains of grace and all she remembers of "grace" is that an elderly Catholic novelist, a woman friend of her mother's, told her when she was twelve years old that grace is a direct visitation of God, *unwilled by man*. ("There is nothing we can do to deserve grace," the elderly woman told Joy, who was rather frightened at the time and anxious to escape. "It is a gift from God that not even the most impassioned prayer can guarantee.") Apart from the small circle of friends of Joy's parents in Minneapolis no one ever seemed to have heard of this particular Catholic novelist so with the passage of years Joy stopped mentioning her. She has never brought up the name to Christopher, for instance, and isn't even certain at the present time that she remembers it correctly.

It is on a blowy and hazardous December evening, the day following the first snowfall of the season, that Christopher and Joy discover the starving kittens on a country road in northern New Jersey and bring them home to the Schankers' place in Millgate. (The Schankers are in Italy and Christopher and Joy are house-sitting for them. This is the third house in which they have lived since they met the previous January.) They are just returning from New York City, from a disappointing workshop production of a play Christopher's staged in an unheated studio near St. Mark's Square, and Christopher's head is so flooded with thoughts that he doesn't see the kittens by the roadside until Joy cries out excitedly for him to stop. By this time it is nearly one o'clock in the morning and Christopher has been driving non-stop for two hours and he couldn't have said whether he was exhausted by the strain of night-driving or by the fresh wound of his play so crudely mangled—so *eerily* mangled it wasn't his any longer; or whether, in fact, he is on the brink of a bout of heart-thumping exhilaration, and will be awake the rest of the night while Joy sleeps. (When Joy is exhausted she falls into bed and sleeps at once. This is a talent Christopher associates with his childhood, now long past, and tries not to resent in Joy.)

Christopher has become dazed and near-mesmerized by the long drive and when Joy seizes his arm and tells him to stop the car he hits the brakes at once, without question. Is it an animal? A deer? Has he hit something? For most of his thirty-two years he has lived in cities and he hasn't entirely adapted to life in the country. As soon as dusk falls, in fact, he is besieged by ghostly figures of white-tailed deer running toward the road and preparing to leap into his windshield. ("By the time you see a deer," someone has warned him, "it's usually too late to avoid hitting it.") But though Christopher has seen a depressing number of dead deer along the roadsides—some of them so uncannily beautiful even in death it's difficult to believe they have been injured—he hasn't had an accident yet, or even a near-accident.

Joy brings the kittens into the car, exclaiming over them: Look at the poor things, the poor starving things, they've been abandoned, someone has dumped them here, someone has left them here to die: and Christopher's heart is won at once. The kittens are no more than a week old,

mewing and squeaking, clearly ravenous with hunger, and far too imma-
ture to be frightened. White with gray markings, short-haired, with
plaintive little faces and watery eyes and stubby tails: How could anyone
do such a thing!—how could anyone be so cruel! Joy is saying as the
livelier of the two climbs up her arm, mewing loudly, and evidently
looking for milk. How can people be such monsters! Joy is saying passion-
ately.

So they have no choice but to bring the kittens home with them and
adopt them. The Schankers had had a cat, an obese Siamese, but the
poor creature had died of old age a few weeks after Christopher and Joy
moved in. The cat's death had upset Joy but the Schankers had told
them they didn't really expect it to be living when they returned from
Italy since it was twenty-one years old, a remarkable age for a cat, and
quite old enough considering its irascible temper. "What should we do if
it dies suddenly?" Christopher asked. He has never owned a pet and
knows nothing about cats, only that Siamese are extraordinarily intelligent. "Bury it out somewhere in the woods," Mr. Schanker told him.

In the past ten or twelve years Christopher has been involved with a
number of young women but he has never loved anyone as much as he
loves Joy. She is nearly his height, slim-hipped, beautiful and melancholy
and given to long brooding silences, with wild crimped chestnut-red hair
and a very pale complexion. Even when her skin is slightly blemished or
when a knife-blade of a frown appears between her eyebrows she is
remarkably attractive: Christopher thinks of her, with a tinge of resentment, as commandingly attractive. Her voice is soft and vague and sometimes trails off into silence, and her eyes have a queer ghostly-gray quality
as if nothing is precisely *there* for her. "Do you love me?" Christopher
asked when they first began living together and he'd follow her about the
house, into the unfamiliar rooms, anxious that she might disappear, "Do
you really love me?" he asked, and Joy would stare at him, baffled, as if
she were frightened of giving the wrong answer. Sometimes she drew
away from him, saying: "I wish you wouldn't look at me like that. I don't
like it when people look at me, like that."

Christopher cannot now clearly remember several of the women with
whom he was involved, but he knows that he imagined he was in love at
the time, but was deluded. It angers him to realize he was deluded, but
there you are. He has a romantic, easily excitable imagination.

When he sees Joy hugging the kittens, exclaiming over them, kneeling
on the kitchen floor and feeding them milk in a saucer, tears streaming

down her cheeks, he realizes suddenly that he doesn't know her at all. He has often worried that Joy is vague and unfocussed and superficial in her emotions, that he is fated to love her more than she loves him—he couldn't have predicted the intensity of her concern for these pathetic little animals. And if they don't survive the night? If in fact they are already dying?

"Why are you crying, Joy?" Christopher asks uneasily. When she doesn't look up he repeats his question in a louder voice: he is standing crouched over her and the kittens, still in his leather jacket and boots, wearing his gloves.

Joy has been susceptible to strange experiences for as long as she can remember. Once, as a child of nine, she was running in her grandmother's house as she was forbidden to do, through an arched doorway and along a stretch of sun-spangled carpet—it seemed significant, that the carpet was sun-spangled at the time—when something happened, and the next thing she knew, she was being lifted from the floor. Both her parents were frightened that she had fainted but her grandmother said curtly: "Women in our family always faint." So it is, Joy does not mind fainting.

Shortly after Joy moved in with Christopher, in a small stone-and-stucco house overlooking the Raritan River—the Rutgers professor of Asian Studies who owned it was travelling at the time—she was breaking eggs in the kitchen when a misshapen yolk streaked with blood slipped out of a shell: and she screamed for Christopher to come. "It's an embryo," she said, shielding her eyes like a child, "it's a living thing—I didn't mean to kill it—." Christopher was amazed that Joy could be so upset but he disposed of the offending egg—in fact, the entire bowl of eggs—and sat with Joy in the darkened living room for nearly an hour, hugging her, and comforting her, and telling her how much he loved her. Joy kept repeating that she hadn't meant to kill the embryo and Christopher kept repeating that she *hadn't* killed it, so far as he knew, so why didn't she simply forget about it? Joy buried her face in his neck and shivered. But she hadn't fainted.

Not long before they brought the kittens home she *had* fainted, at a rowdy informal party given by friends in Newark. Conversation had turned to open heart surgery and to the implanting of artificial hearts, and Joy had gone dead-white, and tried to get to her feet, but succeeded only in crashing heavily against a glass-topped table. Afterward, driving home, Christopher silently reached over to take her hand and squeeze it hard. Joy was a little drunk by this time and feeling unaccountably happy, as if she had narrowly avoided a terrible experience. She said: "You'd never want to marry a woman who breaks tables." It struck them both as hilarious at the time, they laughed, fairly snorting with laughter, for much of the drive home. The next morning Joy remembered the laughter but not its cause.

Must laughter have a cause, she wondered,—when you are in love, and all the world is perfect?

Joy and Christopher sit in bed, playing with the kittens and thinking up names. It's remarkable how quickly, within a matter of hours, the kittens have been restored to life. Their stomachs are round and tight and full to bursting. Their tawny eyes, black slots at the centers, are bright and guileless. So far Christopher can determine the smaller of the two is a female, the other a male, emboldened and really quite amazing in his fearlessness. Both are white with odd splotched gunmetal-gray markings on their heads and sides; their tails are gray with neat white tips. There is something clownish about the markings—the kittens have a fey asymmetrical look—Christopher even wonders if they might be slightly misshapen, their tails are so stubby, their heads so large for their bodies. Joy says they are beautiful and not at all misshapen: they are probably only a few days old.

Heloise and Abelard. Yin and Yang. Hamlet and Ophelia. And what was Heathcliff's lover's name? Cathy? Catherine? And there is John Thomas and Lady Jane. When Christopher suggests Peppermint and Red Zinger, Joy is offended, even angered. "You don't take anything seriously," she says in a whisper. Poor Christopher is astounded: hasn't he, of the two of them, always taken things too seriously?

The kittens, taken to a vet in Millgate, are discovered to be both males, so their names become Heathcliff and Rochester. For a long while, until Rochester grows discernibly more husky than Heathcliff, it is difficult to tell one from the other. By then Christopher and Joy have moved from the Schankers' house and are occupying, for a token rent of $100 a month, a studio apartment in a converted carriage-house a few miles north of Princeton. Christopher's play, revised for the fifth time, is going to be produced by the Houston Repertory in New York City—or so he seems to have been promised.

Joy is studying macramé and pottery. And then modern dance. And acting. And French conversation; she's a delightful mimic and languages have always been easy for her initially. She begins a ten-week course in computer programming but drops out after a few classes. She begins a six-week course in the techniques of real estate but soon drops out because her nature is violated by the idea of focussing so crudely and deliberately upon *selling*, and *making money*, and *competing with other persons.*

She takes most of her courses at Mercer Community College where she has a job in the library. Then she gets a better-paying job at Western Electric as a receptionist where she is much admired for her beauty, her clever clothes, her air of perfectly modulated calm. Even when she is nervous or anxious she gives no sign, her face is a cosmetic mask, her voice is controlled. She has learned to employ a "telephone voice" most of the time.

The years, Joy thinks. The seasons.

Sometimes it seems to her that she has been waiting to conceive a child with the man she loves for a very long time: that they have grown old together yet are still waiting for their lives to begin. Also, certain problems have arisen. Such as: Christopher is often too distracted with worry about his career to make love to her. Such as: she has lost so much weight without quite noticing it, her menstrual periods are erratic and widely spaced, does that mean she might be temporarily infertile?— "infertile" being a blunt neutral term that frequently assaults her when she isn't adequately busy.

Joy has only to close her eyes and (for instance) she is nine years old again running along her grandmother's hall, from the front foyer that smelled of floor wax to the old dining room, and then they are lifting her and staring into her face. But is the child's face really *hers? And those faces—are they theirs?* Do they (now) belong to anyone at all?

"Why do you think such disturbing things?—can't you help yourself?" Christopher asks one day, watching her closely. Joy smooths the wrinkles from her forehead. She isn't certain she has spoken aloud. "If only you'd trust in me," Christopher says, burying his warm face in her hair, "if only you'd allow me to siphon off those poisonous thoughts."

He is embracing her so tightly she can scarcely breathe. She imagines her ribs are about to crack but of course they don't.

One overcast Saturday Heathcliff and Rochester are driven off to the vet's for their distemper shots and their "neutering" operations, which are evidently so painless (a local anesthetic is administered) they are running and tumbling about the house a few hours later, and eating as hungrily as ever. There is something so refreshingly comic about pets!—good-natured healthy non-pedigree pets. Both Christopher and Joy speak amusingly of their twin cats to friends, Joy is always retrieving from one pocket or another coupons for cat food she has forgotten to "redeem" at the A & P, Christopher is always picking white cat hairs off his trousers. Within a year both cats have acquired distinct habits and mannerisms and ways of calling attention to themselves. Rochester, for instance, is always hungry no matter how often he is fed. Whenever Christopher or Joy goes near the refrigerator Rochester is immediately underfoot, mewing plaintively, and nudging with his head. Heathcliff prefers affection. In fact he has become oppressively affectionate—jumping onto Christopher's desk, purring loudly, making frantic kneading movements with his claws against Christopher's sleeves. Sometimes he is so grateful for Christopher's absent-minded attention he drools onto Christopher's papers. "For Christ's sake," Christopher shouts, "haven't you been weaned?"

When Joy is sick with a prolonged and debilitating case of the flu it is Rochester who lies with her in bed, sleeping contentedly for hours, and Heathcliff who cuddles up against her on the living room sofa. (At this time Joy and Christopher are renting a small house owned by a professor of American history at Princeton. Joy draws up an ambitious reading program for herself based upon the professor's immense library and spends much of the winter dozing over books with titles like *Blacks of the Old South, Union Officer and the Reconstruction, American Slave and American Master.*)

Christopher's play opens to guardedly enthusiastic reviews and most nights the little theatre is filled; unfortunately the play is booked for a three-week limited engagement only, and plans to produce it elsewhere never quite materialize. Christopher is gratified, however: he believes he has been baptized, he has proven himself—despite the strain and exhaustion of the past year he hasn't broken down. (The play is even nominated for a Drama Critics Award.)

He begins work immediately on a longer and more ambitious play set in 1950, "the legendary year of his birth." Joy is caught up in his excitement and speaks proudly of him to friends. He *is* a genius, she has known it all along, he isn't like other men. . . . Christopher and Joy are photographed for an admiring article in a local New Jersey paper, Playwright Christopher Flynn and his companion Joy Stephens seated side by side on a sofa, their hands tightly clasped, a white cat sprawled languidly across their laps. Christopher Flynn holds himself rather stiffly for the photograph, his deep-set eyes narrowed as if in suspicion, or simple shyness; his close-cropped head appears to be a few shades lighter than his hair. He isn't a handsome man but he exudes an unquestioning air of authority. His companion Joy Stephens, however, is a dreamily beautiful young woman with a sad, sweet, rather haunting smile. Her name in the caption beneath the photograph is "Joy Stehpns."

A feverish momentum carries Christopher through the long quiet seemingly interminable workdays at home while Joy is away, at Western Electric or at one of her classes. (She has recently enrolled in a course in silk-screening at the community college.) He writes from seven-thirty in the morning until one o'clock in the afternoon, then from approximately four o'clock until dinner. Often he writes in the evenings as well, locked away in the room designated as his study. Sometimes the day's work has so exhilarated or distressed him, or he has consumed too many cups of coffee, or swallowed too many amphetamine tablets (not obtained illicitly —but given to him by a friend of his who has a prescription), so that he ends up writing during the night as well. Joy worries over his "pitiless consuming of himself" but she provides most of his meals and keeps herself and the cats out of his way. Perhaps she will sleep with the middle-aged executive at Western Electric who takes her to lunch frequently. Perhaps she will quit her job and see about establishing a permanent household. Or—since she is becoming quite absorbed in silk-screening—perhaps she will become an artist of sorts, after all. Her twenty-eighth birthday is drawing near.

Christopher is invited to have a drink with Mrs. Schanker in New York City, at one of the splendid new midtown hotels. He has not thought of her in a very long time and is mildly surprised to discover how youthful she is, for a woman in her late forties. Her hair is fashionably curly, her make-up is flawless. Why has she invited him for a drink? What is the purpose? So Christopher wonders while Mrs. Schanker talks and smiles and occasionally touches his arm. Evidently Mr. Schanker is seriously ill: but she is coy about actually naming the disease, or the organs it is ravaging. Christopher is at a loss for words. He says: "I'm sorry to hear that. . . . I'm sorry to hear that." (Lately it has come to

Christopher's attention that a number of acquaintances of his and Joy's, and people he has known since college, have been taken seriously ill; or have actually died. But Joy insists that these events are accidental and not related to one another.)

Mrs. Schanker has several martinis and keeps muddling Joy's name. She embarrasses Christopher by asking if they plan to have a family someday, if they plan to get married. She asks about Christopher's new play and nods gravely when Christopher explains that he can't discuss his work—it makes him too tense. Twice, or is it three times, she asks about the kittens—"those darling white foundling kittens of yours"—and Christopher explains laughingly that they are hardly kittens any longer. (Both are solid, husky, muscular cats, fully mature, with insatiable appetites for both food and affection. Rochester is so heavy that Joy staggers when she carries him, he has become a household joke, his nickname "Tank." Poor Heathcliff has developed a "fat pouch"—a loose flaccid hunk of flesh that hangs down from his lower abdomen and swings when he trots, making him look pregnant. The vet says it's similar to a hernia in a human being, it isn't a health problem at all, both Heathcliff and Rochester are in superb physical condition. But, perhaps, slightly overweight.)

Mrs. Schanker reminisces about "Domino"—Christopher believes the name is "Domino"—and gradually it develops that she is speaking of the fat old cranky rheumy-eyed Siamese who died shortly after Christopher and Joy took responsibility of him. Christopher wants to joke that *that* had been a clever trick of the Schankers—to dump a dying cat on him because they hadn't the hardness of heart to have the poor thing put to sleep. But he senses this would be an inappropriate remark.

Some days afterward he realizes that Mrs. Schanker had (perhaps) wanted to initiate a love affair with him. Or the semblance of one. In fact, their meeting itself was a kind of love affair in embryo, a surrogate for the real thing, whatever the "real thing" is. He tells Joy about the meeting and the odd awkward conversation but he doesn't tell her about the miniature love affair. He muddles Mrs. Schanker's first name, which Joy insists is either "Lizzie" or "Bobbie."

Joy has become a vegetarian and has taken up membership in an Animal Rights organization in Philadelphia. For much of an elated week she is certain *though she does not hint of it to Christopher* that she is pregnant: but her condition turns out to be a false alarm. (She is furious with her gynecologist, who keeps insisting that salt water retention isn't unusual or particularly abnormal: hence Joy's swollen breast and stomach, and the sensitivity of her skin. "But I have never had this condition before!" Joy says angrily. Her voice rises to such a shrill pitch, the doctor's assisting nurse approaches Joy as if to comfort her, or restrain her. "It has never happened to me before, I don't even know what you're talking about!" Joy cries. "I think you're lying!")

One day while Christopher is in the city Joy does a forbidden thing, poking about in his study, scanning drafts and notes for his new play. It frightens her that she is living with a genius. Or with a man who believes himself a genius. It frightens her to discover that the play, though set three decades before, is clearly about Christopher and herself. Despite the fragmentary nature of the scenes and the messy scrawled writing Joy is able to piece together a narrative that relates to her own. She is "Lilly," a somnambulist of "uncommon beauty" who has no center to her life, no focus, no identity. But it is said of her, admiringly, by her lover "Alexander," that she is soulless and therefore cannot be injured. (Alexander defines himself as a "romantic cynic" who can be injured by virtually anyone and anything.) Lilly is vague, superficial, charming in a childish manner, she has a habit of allowing her words to drift off into an inconclusive silence. By the end of the play Lilly will have become catatonic, and committed to a mental asylum: and Alexander will spend the rest of his life mourning his loss.

"His loss!—*his*," Joy murmurs.

She has been absent-mindedly scratching Heathcliff's head and now the burly cat scrambles over Christopher's desk, knocking papers about, nudging and butting against Joy, near-frantic with love.

One morning Christopher reappears in the kitchen just as Joy is about to leave for work and tells her, in a hoarse whisper, that he feels very strange. He doesn't feel like himself. He began work at seven-thirty but couldn't concentrate, his heart has been beating erratically, he has been thinking obsessively about. . . . (And here he recites a now-familiar litany of anxieties. Past failures and humiliations; probable failures and humiliations to come. And his fear that his father, who has a serious heart condition, will die. And an old high school friend of his recently killed himself in San Francisco, leaving no note behind. . . .)

"When things speed up their meanings are lost," Christopher says.

The words are so precisely enunciated, Joy knows they are words from his play.

"When things speed up their meanings are lost," Christopher says, staring at her. "But we can't live if meanings are lost. We aren't human . . . if meanings are lost."

"Yes," Joy says carefully.

Across a space of several yards she can feel the trembling in her lover's body. But she must leave for work: it has begun to rain hard and she will have to drive slowly. She is a shy, cautious driver.

As she is about to leave Christopher says abruptly: "You aren't in love with anyone else, are you?" Joy laughs, startled, but doesn't quite turn to him. He says: "Because you've always been happy with me. Before we met—I don't think you were happy, I think you were psychologically troubled. But you've always been happy with me."

"Yes," Joy says.

He kisses her goodbye. She feels him standing in the doorway and watching her until she is out of sight.

One evening after a dress rehearsal of Christopher's new play, an actor shows Joy the remarkably lifelike mask he wears during the final act to make him appear fifty years older than his age. "Feel this," he says, and Joy touches the rubber mask, so light, so delicate, it might be actual human skin. . . . She shivers, touching it.

On stage the actor is altogether convincing as an elderly dying man—haggard, hollow-eyed, ashen-faced. In person, smiling at Joy, he is a striking youngish man, no more than thirty-five. Joy hadn't known the technique of professional mask-making was so complex: the actor shows her not only the mask itself but the plaster mold of his face and a series of charcoal sketches. "Isn't it amazing? I frighten myself when I look in the mirror," the actor says fondly. He holds his elderly face up to his own, smiling at Joy, peering at her through the eye-holes.

One April night Christopher makes love to her for the first time in many weeks, or has it been months. He is agitated, panting, near-sobbing, but finally triumphant. Joy holds him tight and is passive and accommodating in his embrace; she isn't unfaithful to him by thinking of someone else. The years, she thinks. The seasons. Afterward she brushes his damp hair away from his forehead and makes a pretense of smoothing out the wrinkles.

He grips her tight, tight. He is trembling. He murmurs something about starting a baby at last, getting married. . . . When Joy doesn't reply he remains silent, his warm face burrowed against her neck, his ragged breath gradually growing rhythmic.

Shortly after they move to another house, a few miles north of Princeton, Rochester disappears and doesn't return for a full day and a night. But he does return, ravenously hungry. "A false alarm," Christopher says in a fond scolding voice.

Joy has enrolled in a six-week "mandala" course at the YW-YMCA, partly because her lover's wife is also enrolled in the course and she is curious about the woman. (But her curiosity is soon placated. Her lover's wife is in her early forties, slightly washed-out about the eyes but still pretty, wanly attractive, with a Virginia accent. Her manner is hopeful and zealous but she hasn't the talent for painting mandalas.)

The course is taught by a boisterous woman named Heloise who wears ankle-length gowns of coarse-woven fabric and a good deal of Navajo jewelry. She is an excellent teacher, however, filled with praise and enthusiasm, repeating many times each hour: "Free your innermost impulses, give vent to your *hidden* appetite for beauty and wholeness. . . ." She is particularly impressed with Joy's lavish mandalas which are painted in rainbow colors with no attempt at precision or symmetry. Often she rests her beringed hand on Joy's slender shoulder. "Fantasy is beauty, beauty is fantasy," she says huskily. She carries herself well for a woman of her size though sometimes her breathing is audible. There is a faint downy moustache on her upper lip.

One evening she singles out a mandala of Joy's for special praise. It is painted on a sheet of stiff construction paper measuring five feet by four but it looks even larger. Flamboyant fiery swaths of paint, peacock tails and cat eyes, heraldic cat figures suggestive of ancient Egyptian art. . . . Joy stands to one side, warm and flushed, her gaze veiled. Gradually she realizes that her lover's wife isn't in class that night and that she hasn't seen the woman for a while.

Christopher imagines that Joy is having a love affair though he has no proof and is too proud to quarry out proof. He has dreams in which he is clean-shaven and his face is a pink round baby's face, his skin so sensitive even the touch of air irritates it. Dear God, simply to be *looked at* in this condition!—he is filled with chagrin, self-loathing. He has worn a beard since the age of twenty-two and cannot imagine himself without one. In his dreams it is mixed up with his plays, his "career," the woman with whom he lives whose name, in his sleep, he has temporarily forgotten.

. . . When he wakes, however, it is to vast heart-pounding relief. He strokes his chin and his beard is still there. He reaches out beside him and Joy is still there, sleeping, or perhaps by now awake. Most nights the cats sleep in the bedroom, one on the bed and one beneath the bed, following an inflexible sort of protocol neither Christopher nor Joy can always predict, though they know it must not be violated.

Christopher reaches out in the dark, toward an inert white shape pressed against his thigh. Rochester?—or Heathcliff?—no matter.

Because it is the only pragmatic thing to do *at the present time* Joy arranges to have an abortion at a clinic in New Brunswick. Christopher drives her there, waits for her, comforts her, weeps quietly with her. For many days he hugs her at odd impulsive moments. It is a queer dream-like time—the ordinary laws of nature appear suspended—a whisper can be heard throughout the house, a sigh, a stifled sob, a clearing of the throat. Even the cats are anxious and aroused and easily spooked.

A friend of Joy's asks if the procedure is painless and Joy replies at once: "I don't remember."

Christopher's new play opens to warmly enthusiastic notices. It is acclaimed as "powerful," "haunting," "lyric," "poetic"; Christopher himself is acclaimed as a "startling new talent." However, the play is not a commercial success and closes after seven weeks: not a bad run, considering the inhospitable theatrical climate.

Consequently Christopher's plans to move to New York City, to sublet a friend's loft on Vandam Street, are suspended. Consequently he may be forced to accept a playwright-in-residence position—in fact it is quite an attractive position—at the University of Connecticut. Friends congratulate him and go away puzzled by his bitterness.

"It has become so degrading," Christopher tells Joy. "And I meant it to be so ennobling." He speaks with the melancholy precision of the leading man in his play.

One night, slightly high, he angrily corrects Joy's pronunciation of the word "pid-gin," which she has mispronounced charmingly in the past. (She pronounces it "pidgin," as it is spelled; or, alternately, "pig-din.")

When Joy does not defend herself he becomes angrier. He accuses her of treachery and "sustained deceit." He knows she is having a love affair with someone in Princeton. He knows the baby wasn't his—if, as he says sarcastically, *there was any baby at all.*

"What do you mean?" Joy says, staring at him.

"You know what I mean," Christopher says. Suddenly he is very drunk. Suddenly, though his thoughts have a razor-sharp precision, his words are incoherent and there is nothing to do but grab Joy and shake her so that her head and shoulders strike the wall. "You want to suck out my soul—I know you!—because you have no soul of your own," he says. Afterward they cry in each other's arms, and eventually fall asleep.

Christopher and Joy have decided to separate, for experimental purposes. So they inform their friends. Perhaps Joy will move out, to live for a while with her married sister in Wilmington. Or Christopher may move out, and rent a small apartment in New York.

Then again, one balmy day in late March, they decide that they will get married after all. And put an end to it.

Christopher rocks Joy in his arms and promises they will have another baby. That is, they will have a baby. He can accept the position in Connecticut and stay there for a few years at least. Perhaps they can buy a farm in the country. An old farmhouse. With a few acres. Aren't the old farms selling very cheaply in New England? Joy sobs, and clutches at him, and grinds herself against him almost convulsively, horribly: Christopher is a little repulsed by her passion. And her physical strength.

In June Christopher makes the decision to move out of their rented house: he has been unable to work for weeks. But he is so obsessed with Joy that he hears her footfall behind him, feels the static electricity of her hair brushing against him, dreams of her constantly. . . . He drinks too much, smokes too much dope with friends who aren't really friends, who don't care about his happiness or whether he and Joy get together again. He listens to bad advice. Cruel rumors. Inflammatory news. One night, driving past his former house, now Joy's house (which is to say, a house he is still renting but in which Joy lives alone), he sees an unfamiliar car in the driveway and knows it is Joy's lover and that *she had been betraying him for a very long time*. Still, he does not wish her dead or even injured. If he had a pistol he wouldn't circle the house to get a good shot through one of the windows, he isn't that kind of man, he is far too civilized. He doesn't even write that kind of play.

That was the night he woke in his car, in a parking lot behind a tavern on Highway 1, and had no idea what time it was or where he was or what had happened to him. He couldn't even remember passing out. But in the instant of waking he was suffused with a queer sense of elation because he remembered nothing. Nothing terrible had happened yet.

Or, alternately, everything had happened and he was still alive and why had he ever given a damn?

The telephone rings, rings. Joy picks it up and says carefully: "If you want to talk with me, Christopher, please talk to me. Don't do this, Christopher—" she says, and the line goes dead. Some days, Heathcliff and Rochester sleep for as many as twenty hours. (Though in different parts of the house. They rarely cuddle together or groom each other as they did as kittens: but Joy can't remember whether their estrangement was gradual or sudden.) Other days, they are skittish and forever underfoot, mewing to be fed.

Joy takes a bus to Wilmington, Delaware, to spend a weekend with her married sister Irene, whom she decides after all not to confide in— she doesn't want news of the abortion, or the middle-aged lover, or "Lilly" to get back to her mother. When she returned to Princeton it seems to her that the house has been broken into but she can't be certain. "Are you here, Christopher?" she calls out. She walks on tiptoe through the rooms, her heart beating oddly. "Christopher? Are you here? Please—" But no one answers.

Every scrap of dry cat food she left out has been devoured, and most of the water lapped up, but Heathcliff and Rochester show no interest in her return and when she tries to take him onto her lap Rochester shrinks away from her. She sits at the kitchen table, still in her raincoat, crying softly.

Christopher and Joy meet for coffee and Christopher tells her he misses her, he misses her and the cats, "and things the way they used to be." His eyes are lightly threaded with blood and his beard is grayer than Joy remembers. When she asks him if he wants to move back, however, he hesitates before saying he does. "You don't have to move back if you don't want to," Joy says, the faintest touch of irony in her voice. But Christopher says yes, yes he does, he *does* want to move back . . . except he's frightened of loving her too much.

Joy begins laughing, showing her perfect white teeth, narrowing her eyes to slits. After a moment or two Christopher lays his hand over hers as if to calm her. "People are looking at you," he whispers.

In the end it is decided that Christopher will move back, since he finds it impossible to work anywhere else; and that Joy will spend the month of September with her sister in Wilmington. (Christopher sus-

pects that she is really going to move in with her lover—if she has a lover
—but he's too proud to say anything. He doesn't love her any longer but
he is still vulnerable to her.)

When he telephones Joy in Wilmington, however, her sister tells him
carefully that Joy is out at the moment, or can't come to the phone, and
would he like to leave a message?—but he never does, he is sickened at
the thought of making a fool of himself, of saying the wrong thing. He is
also frightened of breaking down and weeping over the telephone while
Joy's sister (whom he has never met) listens on, embarrassed.

One day he decides to give up the house and move to New York City
after all. By delaying so long he lost the position at the University of
Connecticut but he has been promised a part-time teaching job at New
York University starting in January. What the hell, he thinks, excited, he
will start a new life, he has begun work on his most ambitious play yet,
he's only thirty-five years old. Perhaps, by the time he is thirty-six, he will
have been awarded a Pulitzer Prize.

Not that prizes mean anything to him, he thinks, as if making a point
to Joy, who is standing silently at the periphery of his vision.

He is ashamed to ask anyone he knows if they will take Heathcliff and
Rochester; and he is fearful of turning them over to the country animal
shelter—wouldn't they be put to sleep after a few days? The kindest
thing to do is drive them out into the country—the deep country, away
from busy roads—and give them their freedom. They are such strong
healthy alert creatures, they will have no trouble hunting their food.

So he coaxes them into separate cardboard cartons, and carries them
out to the car, and drives ten or twelve miles north and west of town,
into farming country. The poor things are so piteous in their yowling and
panting, such cowards, he doesn't know whether he should be angry with
them or stricken to the heart.

In a desolate area in Hunterdon County, on a curve in a narrow
unpaved road, Christopher stops the car and releases them. Heathcliff,
panting, bounds into the tall grass at once but Rochester is dazed and
must be urged to leave the car. (Poor "Tank" so panicked during the
jolting ride, he soiled the bottom of his cardboard carton. But no matter:
Christopher tosses both cartons into the ditch. He reasons that they
can't be traced back to him.)

Driving slowly and cautiously away he sees both cats in his rear-view
mirror, staring after him. Oversized, clumsy, dumb creatures, with such
blank unaccusing faces, simply staring after him. . . . Why don't they

protest as any dog would, why don't they run after the car? Can it all end so abruptly? Christopher's heart lurches, he feels sickened and betrayed. He slows the car, breaks to a stop. He tells himself that, if the kittens make the smallest gesture of reconciliation, he will take them back home.

SHE SHOULD HAVE DIED HEREAFTER

ROLAINE HOCHSTEIN

Rolaine Hochstein has published two novels, *Table 47* and *Stepping Out*, eighteen short stories, and scores of popular magazine articles. Born in Yonkers, New York, she was graduated from Syracuse University, and received her Master of Fine Arts degree from Columbia University in January 1985. She received a 1985 Fellowship for prose writing from the New Jersey State Council on the Arts. A longtime New Jersey resident, she is married and has three grown children. This is her second appearance in the O. Henry Awards anthology.

The last time I saw Sylvia was at the Theatre Marigny in Paris. She was seated down front with a lot of friends, but you could tell Sylvia apart from all the rest. She was in lavender silk pajamas with strands of lemon-and-lime-colored beads loose around her neck. I was in the balcony but I could see her clearly through my binoculars. I could see her blazing eyes and the fine, high-bridged nose that we had always known would be a mark of *distingué* as she got older. I could see the wide curves of her narrow lips and even the black mole beside her right nostril. Her hair curled like licks of flame though it would have to have been dyed by then. The men hummed around her and she listened to first one, then another, nodding, smiling, turning her long, slender hands. Her fingernails were painted lavender. I could hear her laughter all the way up in the balcony. The sound faded with the first rap of the cane . . .

I was up in the balcony with Big Bill, my husband, who was being very good to me. He couldn't understand why I would want to see a play in French. I hadn't spoken the language since my college days and these days if I tried to read a book in French, I could hardly get through it. Bill's French was worse than mine and I couldn't really blame him for wanting to leave after the first act.

The woman in purple pajamas was in the lobby. I got a close look at her as we walked out. She wasn't at all like Sylvia.

Sylvia was my childhood friend, two years older than I, but infinitely wiser, more subtle, more daring. She would never have noticed me but that we walked the same six blocks to public school. And what a walk it was! Walking to school with Sylvia was a ritual fraught with mystery and danger, the possibility of falling from ledges, of being attacked by wild dogs or seduced by witches whose backyards we stole through, whose porches we sneaked under. I hated it when Sylvia moved on to junior high and I had to walk the plain old route alone.

I caught up with her for only a year in junior high and then she was out again into high school. Maybe that's why we were never the kind of girlfriends who trade bathroom secrets. I never knew when she got her first bra, when she had her first period. It may be that we just skipped those years. But today when I hear young girls talking together—*do you like this one? . . . that one said . . . fingernails . . . pantyhose*—I wonder what happened to girlhoods like ours, life in stained-glass colors.

We came together again in high school with momentous discoveries. Her favorite opera was *Tosca.* Mine was *La Bohème.* "But of course Puccini," Sylvia said. She had grown tall and angular, bookish-looking but unbookishly limber, with near-sighted amber eyes. But of course we had interests in common. Had we not been nurtured almost in the same womb? Was it so strange we were both reading George Sand? Not everybody in that school ran for the subway and the City. We were a pair of oddballs but Sylvia didn't notice, or pretended not to, or really—as she told me she did—felt that the others were common little guttersnipes and wanted no part of them.

I was at her graduation because she had two tickets and her father was gone by then. I sat with her fat little black-veiled mother and watched Sylvia take every award on the program, including a full scholarship to a fine, all-girls' college. After college—Valedictorian again, French Prize, editor of the Yearbook, et cetera—she was snatched up for a job in a New York publishing company.

Nobody we knew worked in publishing. My father worked in an insurance office. Sylvia's had worked in a jewelry store. Mr. Shontz in the house between our houses was a retired policeman. But Sylvia seemed born to the literary life. Working days, in a long skirt and loose sweater, she took the train to Grand Central Station, walked down Lexington Avenue, turned in at a corner and climbed the dark, steep steps to the Dickensian offices of Bridge and Blackness. There she found all the acceptance she had lacked in high school.

In two weeks' time she seemed to be on close terms with everybody.

Having lunch with a seersucker David, whose mother was a famous actress. Taking brisk walks with a tweedy Peggy, who spoke five languages. She had stories about all of them: feuds, affairs, women who went home and put on men's trousers. That winter she wrote to me at college that the cookbook editor, a thin, stooped man, painfully deaf and surely past sixty, had taken to giving her single roses with a love poem wrapped around the stem.

Another of my depressing summers came and the only job I could find was as cashier at a loan company. I went to work on the grubby West Side subway, sweat and salami, and when I looked up to escape the faces, what did I see but lying carcards advertising my own company! Ads inviting happy loans; all I knew were the sad collections. The other cashiers hated me for using big words. One of them got me at the basin in the woman's room while I washed my hands. "You think you're so smart," she sneered at my face in the mirror, "but you're only a jerk." Sylvia was outraged when I told her, trying to make it funny. She wanted to get me in with the people at Bridge and Blackness. One day she telephoned me at work: "Be here Thursday," she whispered over the wire, "at precisely five-thirty. I've fixed it with Sardinius."

Mr. Sardinius was Sylvia's boss, the editor-in-chief. I knew him, through her, as a crusty old bachelor, girl-shy, hard on the help, but— Sylvia was convinced—with a heart of butter. I could hardly wait to meet him. I'd never seen an editor. I arrived in a summery dress with ruffles. The Bridge and Blackness women, coming downstairs as I ran up, wore dark tailored clothes and heeled shoes. But Sylvia introduced me with aplomb. Valued friend. Luminary at my college.

The place was dim and musty with bare wood floors, shelves on the walls, dark old wood, heavy desks. Mr. Sardinius had his own room behind the main office. His desk stood on a platform among a crowd of books. He was a biscuity-looking man with clipped white hair and sly little eyes taking curious little glances at me. (God knows what Sylvia had told him.) He managed a cut of a smile as we shook hands. Leaving the office, he walked behind, pulling one string after another to turn out the overhead lights. Five minutes later we were all downstairs at the bar of a residential hotel down the street, sitting on three bar stools, Mr. Sardinius in the middle.

Sardinius: Have you had ginger beer?
Me: Is it hard?
Sardinius: No. It's very easy.
(Chuckles from Sylvia.)

Sardinius (to barman): Give the young lady a ginger beer. Cock 'n' Bull.

(That was the brand name, Cock 'n' Bull. Every time he said it, he giggled.)

Sylvia (leaning forward so she could look him straight in the eye): Tell me, Mr. S., is it the name or the flavor you like so much?

Sardinius (shrewdly narrowing his eyes): I should think it was a bit of both.

(Roaring laughter from Sylvia.)

He turned suddenly to me and said, "Your girlfriend had me on ice, you know."

Sylvia confessed. She had wanted to go to Rockefeller Center, but Mr. S. had held out for the relative anonymity of Central Park. He had never skated before and didn't want to be seen making a fool of himself. "He wouldn't have been bad," Sylvia told me, "if only they'd given him the right size skates." As it was, his ankles had caved in and she and Peggy had had to hold him up.

"I say," Mr. Sardinius said, "how do you like the Cock 'n' Bull?"

I said it was snappier than ginger ale.

He said it was imported from England, as was his favorite newspaper supplement, Jack o' London. This seemed to be a very big joke.

"From England makes the difference. Right, Mr. S.?" Sylvia was smoking a cigarette with one of the complicated filter holders she had started to use to protect herself from cancer. I can see her now looking distinctly *art nouveau:* lambent eyes, bony nose, the mole, red hair in a tendriled mass.

"Ginger beer, can it make you drunk?" I asked Mr. Sardinius.

"Not me!" He stopped laughing long enough to fish his reading glasses out of his suit jacket pocket. But Sylvia caught the bill first and said it was her treat. Mr. Sardinius was allowed to pay the tip.

Later, when I got to know the Bridge and Blackness crowd that hung around Louie's on Sheridan Square, I learned that Old Sard was not always so affable and that, in fact, when caught in a mistake, he was not averse to blaming it on Sylvia. Only Sylvia could manage, somehow, to cover up for him and to save herself. "Your girlfriend here is a lot of woman," he told her that summer night before we left him at his subway entrance. I was standing right beside him. "Tell her," he told Sylvia, "to see us about a job when she gets out of that college of hers."

He never gave me a job though I know Sylvia did her best for me. It didn't matter. I met Big Bill during my senior year and after that jobs didn't matter much. Sylvia played the piano at our wedding. I think she was seeing Fred by that time, but he was not at the wedding.

I saw her once at an Upper West Side party. The guest of honor was a young woman who had just returned from hitchhiking around the world. There must have been a hundred people there, all looking as if they'd had adventures, too. I was there because Big Bill was there: he had a dinner appointment with his lawyer that night and the lawyer said we should all meet at the party; it would be so big nobody would know the difference. Bill was all for it: he goes out of his way to include me.

I spotted Sylvia at the end of the living room. She was slouched on a low-slung sofa, one arm stretched along the back, the other hand holding a martini with an olive. She was wearing a kind of green silk kaftan with gold embroidered designs and her hair was high up and rolled, the color of a croissant. She was clearly very comfortable at parties like this although they were just sidelights to the really important things she did. I thought she might be a sculptor with her strong hands and her sense of shaping things. That night she was just talking to a young man, who leaned close to catch every word. He was clean-featured and solidly built, not much older than Little Bill, who is now almost as tall as his father. You'd think what Sylvia had to tell him was going to change his life.

I didn't see Fred anyplace but that didn't surprise me. I knew Sylvia would never have married him, not when it came down to it. Bill gave me a sign from the door that it was time to go and, as I walked close by her, I saw, of course, that the woman wasn't Sylvia. Her speaking voice was harsh and the silly young man was saying *Yes* to everything.

The last time I saw Sylvia, her face was white as translucent china. Even the frames on her eyeglasses had blanched. Everything was white. The pillows. The sheets. The hospital walls. She was wearing a white, quilted bathrobe, long and skinny. It had grown too big for her. "Anorexia," she told me. "Overheard doctor. Lost no time. Wheedled nurse into smuggling me into library. Rapidly discovered definition."

She lifted her shoulders. The quilted robe flapped. "Much ado," she said with exquisite contempt. "Lack of appetite," she said. "I knew as much already."

"Still," I said, "it's an impressive way of putting it."

"True," she said. "And a very *firm* excuse for not finishing one's porridge."

She couldn't eat and her blood was turning white. Soon she would be lifted almost weightlessly into a white coffin and that would be the end of it.

Even as a child she was superior. Old photos show a smug little monkeyface amid tubular curls. In the street, between the rows of two-family houses, with stoops as grandstands, the other kids played Kick-the-Can—Jimmy Kelly, Edwin Sher, DeeDee Manzi, and me in my big-belly overalls and Dutch Boy haircut. I wore the toes off my shoes kicking cans and running into curbstones. Sylvia, sublimely solitary, sat on her graystone stoop, neat rump on one stone step, neat feet on the next step down, skirt discreetly pulled over her knees, reading a book, coloring, cutting.

I was drawn toward Sylvia's stoop, away from the hearty immediacies of Lolly Polansky and DeeDee Manzi. My mother was uneasy over this new friendship and she was right: Sylvia told me all the things my mother didn't want me to know. Where babies come from, for one. Sylvia and I played lascivious games: we were sheiks and abducted maidens under my mother's grand piano with the gold-tasseled piano shawl. We were witches on the roof of a house that slanted into the hill on the corner of our street. There we sat and told dark stories about the poor little rich boy who lived in the house and never came out without his nursemaid.

"Governess," Sylvia said. We stripped him bare and chopped him up into soup.

Once on the roof, Sylvia had a spell. Nothing could rouse her. I called her, shook her, pleaded with her, but she was immobile, eyes sealed shut. At last, as, weeping, I got up to go for help, she came to life again. "It was a daze," she said. "One of my dazes." She really *was* wicked. But it was exciting, even, in the spring, when violets came, to pick bunches of them for our mothers and for Mrs. Shontz, the wife of the policeman who lived next door to both of us.

Nothing about Sylvia was ordinary. Many times she explained that she was descended from aristocracy on both sides. Her father strode from the pages of American history. His family had built the West. He himself had been, Sylvia recited, a prospector, surveyor, actor, train engineer, prize fighter, and cowboy. Her mother had been a beauty, gently bred in South America, a Spanish orchid plucked by the Yankee adventurer. There was no competing with this: my parents were plain and my house was wide open. Her family lived behind lowered window shades. Her mother emerged from the graystone house no more than four times a year—a short, fat woman, always in a black coat and a feathered hat with a veil. She locked the door and hurried down the steps. She talked in a soft flutter of feathered syllables. When I came to the door to call for Sylvia, her mother was a scuffle of bedroom slippers.

"I must be in for dinner at precisely six o'clock," Sylvia told me haughtily. "Our clock is set by radio."

We ate supper in my house, and at whatever time I came in. "Our clock is electric," my mother comforted me. "That's accurate, too."

Sylvia's father's store was in the City. Even as a child, along with her Mickey Mouse watch, Sylvia wore a topaz ring, sometimes an amethyst. Hidden in the dark, cat-smelling house were boxes of silver spoons and cocktail forks, which Sylvia described but never showed. What I saw, on the rare occasions when I was allowed in, were foot-high piles of *Child Life* magazines, long rows of books, all the Nancy Drews, all the Louisa May Alcotts. Outside is what I remember most clearly, outside when the Mickey Mouse watch said five-to-six and we started for the train station. We'd run through the gate and catch Sylvia's father stepping off the train.

"Daddy! Daddy!" we'd both shriek and the two of us would jump on him like puppies. He was a big porterhouse steak of a man—long legs, deep chest, big jaw, red cheeks, tobacco-stained teeth in a big, manly smile. He'd drop his briefcase and yank us up, one in each arm. "Daddy! Daddy!" we'd shriek, hugging and kissing him. One of us would carry the briefcase and the other his newspaper. He had a springy walk and we'd walk with him, each of us holding one of his big, beefy hands.

Years later my own father, by then jowled, stooped, and extinguished as Sylvia's father would never be, mentioned Sylvia and was reminded of him. "A nice guy, the old man," my father said. "But an awful drunk. You knew that, didn't you?"

I didn't. "Owed everyone in town," my father said.

I saw Sylvia cry only once. During a college summer, she and I went to see a performance of *The Father*. It was my first Strindberg and appropriately played on a grim little stage in a dinky Greenwich Village playhouse. The captain has been oppressed unto madness by his man-hating wife. The aged nursemaid is called upon to slip a straitjacket around him. He is docile, unsuspecting, all the fight teased out of him. The audience hangs in pity as the nurse cajoles him with baby words from his childhood. I heard Sylvia laughing. I looked at her and saw she was in tears. Other people turned to look. She was sobbing. "Daddy! Daddy!" she cried out. She couldn't stop. I grabbed her arm and pulled her up from her seat. We squeezed past the people in the row and ran up the aisle, out of the theater.

Her father had been dead for years. We sat down in a coffeehouse and had a *cappuccino*. She said she didn't know what had come over her.

Sylvia wanted to be a great artist but I was not so dedicated. I turned myself inside out trying to be popular with boys. Sylvia, too, had an eye for the men, but she did not live in fear that she would be passed over. My young men tended to be a lot like me—my age, my kind of family, happy-go-lucky. Sylvia seemed to attract an altogether different lot, impossibilities mostly: a friend's father, a college professor, all much older, somber, out of the question, like Mr. Fox, the cookbook editor, who continued to send poems and make sheep's eyes at her. The men she would have liked did not come forward. The young David, for example, for all his good grooming and engaging conversation, remained friendly but no more. Sylvia wanted to marry, but marrying men were not attracted to big-nosed, intellectual young women, no matter how clever they were or how game.

Except for Fred.

When it was time for me to return to college after that last summer, she walked with me to the train station. We crossed the overpass to the far, citybound, side, went down the long stairway to the platform on which, the next day, she would wait for the train to take her to work. Waiting for my train, we stood across the tracks from the platform where her father used to swing down off the step from the train that brought him home. We were still full of talk when my train arrived, so Sylvia got on with me. She telephoned her mother from Grand Central Station when we got there and said she'd be back on the next train. Then we found my seat on the train to college and sat there talking until the conductor came and made Sylvia get off.

Fred had a long face, like a sad white horse. He was built small and didn't have much to say. He had bright blue eyes and loose red lips. He worshiped Sylvia, but he wasn't good enough for her. She said he was really very intelligent, but had been beaten down by a tyrannical father. I don't know where they met, but from the time they met Fred wouldn't leave her alone.

"I found a lump," Sylvia wrote to me not long after she started seeing Fred. "Nothing serious, though irksome at first." She described a riotous taxi ride to the wrong hospital. "It's safely out now," she wrote, "and has left a rather fascinating scar." Fred had been with her for the surgery.

I brought her earrings from New Hope. They looked like jade but were probably just expensive glass. They looked as wet as teardrops. I bought her the kind with posts for pierced ears, in the handmade jewelry store next to the handmade leather goods store and up the street from the place where they sell almost-perfect seconds of high-quality china. That's why we were there, Bill and I—to buy our china. "She'll never wear them," he said. "You're throwing out money." He was not being tight, just practical. He liked Sylvia a lot, in fact, better than my other friends. She had stayed overnight once in our newlywed apartment, slept like a spinal curvature on our semi-circular sectional sofa. She had not expected to stay, but it got too late to go home. She slept in her slip with one of Bill's shirts as a bathrobe. She borrowed some of my stockings to put up her hair in. She had brought a little jar of caviar that night; we ate it with eggs and onions. Sylvia was always poor and always had money to spend. I don't know how she did it.

"The nurses will steal them," Bill said. But I bought the earrings anyway. The extravagance comforted me. Sylvia would see the gift as a sign of my faith in her getting well. She loved green. The jewelry maker laid them on a satin pad in a little white box.

She sat high against the pillows as she opened it. All angles she was then. No swirls of *art nouveau*. "Rather bad news," she had told me, calling from the hospital. I vowed, after that call, that she would not have to comfort me again. At her bedside, I laughed, presenting my gift. "Mere baubles," I said. "Think nothing of it." Her eyes glowed with sad pleasure. She held the earrings out to the soft-moving nurse: "Did you ever see such depths of color?" "No, darling," the nurse said. "I never did." There were other visitors, always a crowd around the bed. Someone handed her an oval mother-of-pearl mirror. She put on the earrings: green teardrops. Her face was like the mirror frame. In the white light, her skin was iridescent, almost transparent. Her hair was still a dark coppery shade of red.

Usually my visits were short. Work. Bill. So much to do. But on that day I stayed late. The other visitors—even Fred—said goodnight. I stayed. Cherished friend. She kept the earrings on. She wanted to get out of bed. In the quilted robe, which was whiter than she, she walked with me to the bank of elevators. All the way down the long corridor, I matched slow steps to hers, and then we stood there, talking and laughing, while the elevators arrived, opened their doors, closed, and departed. We laughed about Old Sard, who had been up to see her the day before, wearing a knit cap she had made him for ice skating. We laughed over my sectional sofa, not made for sleeping on, and about Fred's fluttery mother, who had sent a box of candy creams. Sylvia didn't want me to leave that day. We stayed by the elevators, doors opening and closing, till the nurse came looking for her.

No one could have been more devoted than Fred. He came to see her morning and night. His job had something to do with airplanes, but he stayed on the ground. He was docked for being late in the morning, but his bosses understood that he would continue to be late. His determination to see Sylvia was so strong that he walked right past the hospital guards. He knew all the back entrances and service stairways. One day Sylvia was moved to another section. (Was it that nothing more could be done for her?) Fred was shot with panic when he saw the empty bed in her room. Long before visiting hours it was, too early for him to show himself and ask questions. Fred ran down the stairs and found the newspaper boy. He bought all the boy's newspapers and then went from room to room selling them until he found Sylvia, in a four-bed ward, in a curtained-off corner, attached to a bottle of liquid nourishment. Sylvia told me about it. She said Fred spent all his money on flowers for her.

At the funeral, he sat up front with Sylvia's mother and an uncle and aunt on her father's side, who had come down from Connecticut. After the brief service, Fred walked behind the coffin, supporting Sylvia's mother. Mr. and Mrs. Shontz were there and Mr. Sardinius. Neighbors. Teachers from her college. Friends from Bridge and Blackness. Friends from her French class. Friends I had seen before in her hospital room. Fred, in a black suit, with his bright blue eyes stained red from weeping, with his head bent as he guided Sylvia's mother, looked like someone who had been hired by the funeral home. On one of the few times I saw them together, Sylvia was wearing ballet shoes, ungainly flat-bottomed ballet slippers, that looked like plum skins on her feet. She wore them to be shorter than he was. At the funeral, people looked at Fred curiously. I heard people telling one another: "They were going to be married."

One day, not very long ago, I called Fred on the telephone. He lives in an apartment in Jackson Heights with his wife and children. I told him who I was and he remembered me. He was very matter-of-fact. He still works for his old company. Every Saturday morning, he takes his children to the park while his wife goes to the beauty parlor to get her hair shampooed and set. He also told me, in his flat voice, that Sylvia sometimes comes to him in his dreams. Before his marriage, he said, he asked for her approval. In his dream, she gave him her blessing.

THE MANGO COMMUNITY

JOSEPHINE JACOBSEN

Josephine Jacobsen served two terms as Poetry Consultant for the Library of Congress. She is the author of a collection of short stories, *A Walk with Raschid*, and her most recent book of poetry, *Chinese Insomniac*, was published in 1982 by the University of Pennsylvania Press. This is her fifth appearance in the O. Henry Awards. She lives in Baltimore, Maryland.

The Vice-Consul again looked at his shoes. He appeared not critical but, more annoying, embarrassed.

"Mrs. Jane Megan—yes, and Mr. Henry Sewell." He raised very pale blue eyes to Jane's, dropped them to his toecaps. "And Daniel. Daniel Megan. Fifteen? Is that right?"

"That's right," said Jane. She added, "Mr. Adams."

"And your purpose here was a vacation?" This time he got himself together and looked at her quite hard.

"Work," said Jane. "I'm a painter." His eyes flicked to her fingernails. "It's on my passport. Henry is a writer. A novelist."

If she had looked for him to say, "Oh, *that* Henry Sewell," she was wrong.

"Yes, well," said Mr. Adams moodily. "You see my position," he said rapidly but uncertainly. "I can't actually ask you to leave. I mean, there would have to be actual and manifest danger."

She hoped ardently that Harry would not appear, lugging fish and cristofine. He and Mr. Adams were, temperamentally, unsuited to a dialogue. Soothingly she said, "I think you've been very kind to come all the way out here. And I quite see your point. We'll think about it, we really will. But this business has been going on for weeks and weeks, and we leave, anyway, in a few months."

At last Mr. Adams looked cross. "Mrs. Megan, I've tried to explain that if you do insist on staying on under present circumstances," he stopped and repeated more loudly, "present circumstances, the U. S. Government simply cannot be responsible for your safety."

"I know that," she said hastily. "That's perfectly reasonable." (All the same, she thought, your problem is that I know, and I know you know, you'd try.) They had reached an impasse. Would it be like suborning a policeman to offer him a drink? "Could I offer you a cup of tea, or a drink before you leave?" Perhaps the tea decontaminated the invitation.

"You're very kind," he said primly. "I'm going to miss my plane if I'm not careful. Well, the other families in town to whom I've spoken have all agreed on the advisability of leaving." He looked at her, and his general disapproval was just diluted by a flash of friendliness. "I do wish you well, Mrs. Megan. You're really isolated here." ("Oh, there're people next door . . ." she protested; he ignored this.) "Perhaps you'll pass on to Mr. Sewell what I've said. And there's your son to consider."

The implied reproof made her say jauntily, "I'll keep that in mind." She put out her hand, and the Vice-Consul, unable to do less, shook it and restored it to her. "Good-bye, then," he said, and a minute later the jeep started too fast, kicking up sand.

In an attempt to sort out her mind, she sat down on the eroded planks of the porch steps and stared out over the beach to the mad palette of the Caribbean.

She felt she was muttering. When did it all *begin?* She thought that while it had been by laughter that she had first known her husband, it was by a hot and huffy argument, improbably conducted on the fringes of a cocktail party, that the threshold of intimacy had been crossed with Harry. Of all things, the Sermon on the Mount. And hadn't that argument, between a fresh divorcee and a stranger, across a sea and in another world, landed her right here, between Harry and the Vice-Consul?

Isolated by Harry's intensity, they had found themselves on ancient ground: overnight the world could be changed by passive resistance—unflagging, indomitable. To violence, the universal cheek turned, once and for all. In a flash of conviction, that evening Jane had come to believe what she still did, that Harry would let himself, in the proper cause, be martyred without so much as making a fist. Profoundly, this impressed her.

"All *right,*" she had said, draining the last drops of her martini, "say you're going to be murdered. You're going to be raped . . ." ("Less likely than you, there," he murmured.) "You turn the other cheek; and you *are.* But what do you do when someone else doesn't *want* to be

murdered? Turn their cheeks for them? It never tells you about *that,*"
she said bitterly.

Not then or later had he answered the question to her satisfaction.
Was it unanswerable? He never lost that inner assurance that she could
see captivating Dan. Undeviating programs are so dear to the young, she
thought meanly. But she knew it was more than that.

It was as though Dan had been waiting for Harry. Disconcertingly,
the classic case of preparing an adolescent for a resented stepfather reversed itself. Even early on, Jane became aware of a united front, a sort
of silent compact, in which Harry's need to proselytize and Dan's to be
stable were locked into a kind of dogged intimacy. Why this should
frighten her, she had no idea.

As she stared morosely ahead, here, loping jerk jerk along the beach,
came the three-legged dog. That dog. The most enchanting of the children who burst onto the sand even in this remote section, when school
was out—a liquid-eyed, gentle-faced charmer with the suavest voice—
flung stones at the lame dog. "She ogly! See how she go—so!" And he
hobbled, jerking. Entranced, doubled with laughter, the children
reached for sand, stones.

Through the sprays of magenta bougainvillea, the sky of Ste. Cecile
appeared as a mosaic—blue, green, lilac.

"Did he come?"

It was Harry who had come, noiseless on the sand.

"What kind of fish is *that?*"

"That is a turbot. Did he come?"

"Yes. He came. And went."

"And said?"

"And said we should leave."

"Had to leave?"

"No. He stopped short of that. If we're stuck and a coup breaks out,
he can't promise us help. You know, I think we *should* go," she added,
surprising herself. Did she think so? Politically, or personally?

Harry disappeared into the shadowy interior; a moment later he was
back. He sat down beside her, plucked off a sneaker, knocking out sand.

"What did you tell him?"

"That we'd think about it. That we really would."

"Very diplomatic. His own game."

He looked perfectly beautiful, sitting there pulling off his other
sneaker. The idealized beachcomber, the tropical poster.

"Look, Harry," she said, "I think we're getting in awfully deep."

She could feel the tightening. "How so?"

"Well, something *is* going to happen. We both know it; it's just *when*. We're isolated here. We're strangers—*really* strangers, I mean. It wouldn't be malice, but we'd just be in between."

"*You* look, my dear," he said in his inspirational, persuasive teacher's voice, his hand on her bare shoulder. "We came here for a year. The place is beautiful. The people are marvelous. I'm working, you're painting. Dan's happier than I've ever seen him. This guy is going to be thrown out eventually. In the most civilized way we'll ever encounter. That isn't something to make us run away. That's good."

"He's not going to be thrown out without a lot of people getting hurt."

"Jane, do you know, in a way it's the most impressive thing I've ever seen. They've lost their jobs, shut their shops, been spied on, pushed around, jailed, worse, much worse. Thugs in police uniforms have been sent after them, looting and smashing. The Barracudas are holding a cocked gun to their heads—and they *march!* That's what they do! No guns, no machetes—they just march and chant and pull in their belts!"

"Harry, I live here too."

"Well, sure. You know, too. But you don't seem to realize how amazing it is. They're forcing him out without a shot."

Here came the black-coral boy; heavily lame, he threw out his left leg in an immense arc, lurching. He had fallen from the top of a coconut palm. Jane had a wild vision of the three-legged dog at his heels. The boy had a small waist, broad gleaming shoulders, and an immense smile and lifted a hand to them. Now he angled across toward the Montroses' fence, lurching more heavily in the dry sand. Mrs. Montrose appeared at her gate, and they fell quietly into one of those dialogues of which Jane could not have understood a word. This, although the Montroses, in their sparse conversations with their American neighbors, spoke an English perfectly intelligible, if more musical and differently emphasized. The only time Jane had ever seen Mrs. Montrose laugh was when Jane had asked about "mongeese." But when Mrs. Montrose said "four sheeps" and "three mices," it seemed not so much funny as expressive— more mouse-like, more sheepish.

Far out in the daze of sun, she could see a red object—the Sunfish, and two dots, Alexis and Dan.

Harry got up, sneakers in hand. "We're not going to settle it this afternoon," he said. She saw that he had already settled it. Well. She could leave, and take Dan; but there were too many reasons why she would not.

Alone on the porch, she felt a tiny deflection in the heat. The sun had lowered by a fraction; the Sunfish, nearer, was defining itself.

Guns cocked at their heads, said Harry. Barracudas, recruited by Him from the dregs of this and other island jails. How men loved the sound of a cocked rifle: Ton-ton Macoute. Ku Klux Klan. Yet when she and Harry argued, in his domain of words she seemed evasive and cynical. I can't bear the writer in him. In his beginning was the word.

She found Harry's work disconcertingly superior to her own, but never, never his medium. On this tiny island she remained amazed at the progressive detail of her own sight; new shades of purple and rose appeared in the noon sea. She was stunned by the varieties of green: the serious glossy green of the breadfruit, the translucent green of the fringed plantain-blades, the trembling play of the flame trees, the palms' hard glitter. Green, what on earth was it? Behind their stilt-house and its path, behind the road, the hill rose in a Rousseau jungle. On its steep garden patches, in violent blues and reds and yellows, the dark distant figures moved in the dawn light when disoriented roosters and insomniac dogs at last fell silent.

Now here came Mr. Montrose out of the house, a hoe in one hand, machete in the other. In the mornings, astride the burro, his buttocks resting just before its tail, the huge balanced milk cans at his knees, he wore one day a yellow, the next a violet shirt and a ravelling straw hat. Now he wore only faded khaki shorts that blended with his identically colored skin.

Seeing her head turned toward him, he raised his machete slightly in a courteous but formal gesture. In six months they had not got much further than that. At first the Montroses had seemed friendly, though baffled and a bit nervous. But in exact proportion as Dan and Alexis had plunged into their intimacy, the Montroses had retreated into a pattern formal as an armor. Always greetings; now and then a sour-sop or a sapadillo from their tree, sent via Alexis; once, some cassava cakes made by Mrs. Montrose. Never an acceptance or an invitation.

Twice Jane, meeting Mrs. Montrose coming home from market, or carrying on her head the big wicker basket of clothes to the line stretched across the dusty yard, had rather timidly suggested a cup of tea. Mrs. Montrose had smiled, her teeth strong and white, while she dropped her eyes, saying nothing whatever. Jane instinctively knew this was not rudeness; it was the dilemma of someone unable to accept and not possessed of the formulas of refusal. Jane had thorough sympathy for this. Was Mrs. Montrose to say that she had an engagement for tea every day for six months?

Jane did not waste much time speculating as to whether all this was Mr. Montrose. But she knew, infallibly, that it had to do with Dan. She could see that Mr. Montrose, no fanatic, could not well forbid his son to associate with a next-door neighbor of almost the same age; but though he treated Dan with the same grave courtesy, Jane knew that he found Dan an extraordinary phenomenon, and feared and disliked the friendship. What was Dan doing here in the first place? Why was he not at school or at work? Why did he call his father Harry? How could his parents (did Mr. Montrose think they *were* his parents?) permit his tone in talking to them? When the Montrose family went to Mass on Sunday —Christabel and Eugenie-Marie in starched dresses and long white socks, Alexis in a crisp short-sleeved shirt, Mrs. Montrose in pond-lilies on red, and Mr. Montrose in dark trousers and a shirt of palmetto palms —their three neighbors could be prone on the beach, practically naked, Dan sulking at Alexis' departure (no cricket); or on the Sunfish; or Jane could have set off with her gear and Harry be rattling on his portable, stopping constantly to curse and bemoan his electric typewriter, useless in its corner.

Jane had had a solitary conversation with Mrs. Montrose. It had left her with a curious sense of warmth and communication, though it had led to nothing whatsoever.

Five or six weeks after the ménage's installation, Jane—possibly propelled by an inability to deal with the evasions of tropic green—had been driven in nostalgic defiance to a canvas of snow crystals. Three lit within the limits of the canvas, one disappeared in midpattern over the edge. On the black background they looked like stellar intentions.

Coming past in her royal walk, three coconuts in a small basket on her erect head, Mrs. Montrose had unwillingly but helplessly paused.

"What it is?" she said.

"They're snow crystals," said Jane shyly. "Flakes of snow," she added in response to the glance Mrs. Montrose had transferred to her face and back to the canvas.

To this Mrs. Montrose said nothing, and together they stared at the flakes, unmelting in the brutal sun. When Jane thought, we will drown in silence . . . , Mrs. Montrose said, her eyes still on the canvas, "You did see snow?"

"Oh yes. We have it often."

"It is whiter than sand?"

"Oh, much. When it first falls."

"It does lie on the ground? Right on the ground? You have walked on it? Right on over it?"

"Yes," said Jane. Suddenly envious she thought, I've never seen snow! They stood there for a minute, isolated and intimate. Then Mrs. Montrose gave her a small adventurous smile, bent, and cradled the basket in her arms. She raised one hand in the familiar sidelong gesture and, without looking back, went through her wooden gate, across the bare yard and up the steps into the house.

Jane repeated to herself, I don't think I've ever seen snow . . . , but she felt an exhilaration welling up inside her. She began cleaning her brushes, hissing a little song. Something wonderful had happened. What? Now we can't ever be strangers. She couldn't wait to tell Harry; but she never did. Because peace was his specialty, and she was not sure what kind of peace she had to talk about. Always Harry thought "community," but she knew sadly that he hadn't gained an inch on this sandy strip. "The mango community?" she had jeered once.

The Sunfish was right off the beach. It turned over, as usual, and Alexis and Dan, floundering in the water, pushed it in and dragged it up the sand. By now Dan was the same shade as Alexis. Christabel and Eugenie-Marie, like Mrs. Montrose, were mahogany dark.

Jane waved to the boys; they waved hastily back. Already they had the bats and the tennis ball out of the old beached and dissolving rowboat in which they were deposited each morning, shoved down from dogs and other marauders. There had been difficulties over those bats. The boys at first had played, like other children up the beach, with flat pieces of found wood; then one day Harry came back in the Minimoke with two cheap cricket bats. At once, Mr. Montrose had jibbed. Finally it had been diplomatically settled that while both bats were Dan's, Alexis had possession of one.

Now down the hard sand Alexis was running, releasing the straight-arm pitch. At first Jane had imagined that it was because Dan thought baseball as Alexis thought cricket, that Dan could never compare. Then, her trained eye taking in the motions, she saw that it would never change. Alexis ran, and pitched, and batted, as he swam, as he climbed a bare bole, as he dove, with a fluid power. Dan said proudly that Alexis was the best cricketer in his school. "He's going to get a scholarship somewhere—maybe Jamaica or Trinidad. He's going to be like V. Richard. He's going to be better," said Dan, carried away.

Oddly, it was Alexis, daily embroiled in their lives, who stopped Jane. She did, and she did not know him. Instantly, she had had a sense of almost intimacy—a drawing toward. Was it that of a painter? The marvelous texture of the skin, the head's perfection, the movement as worth watching as a secret dance, the quick deep luminous look? Though he smiled, he never laughed with her; but she could hear him; soft, irresistible convulsions, broken up, falling against the rowboat-skeleton, with Dan's staccato yelps.

After a while she began to understand that, the end of a long year come, she would never know Alexis. Separated, he and Dan would remember each other as part of the sun and sand and salt-wind, as in patches of light and happiness. She—and she thought, Harry—would be to Alexis figures come and gone, strange and not very interesting. She thought of the boys as a frieze against the sea.

As she went into the house, Jane could see through the window the peaceable kingdom: the water picking up red from the sun's angle, the red sailfish on the humped sand; on the gleaming edge, the boys against the sea.

There was Mr. Montrose, calling to Alexis to come now, come; and crossing to the back window she watched as Alexis rounded the house, crossed the lane and shot up the hill. She followed his blue trunks through layers of green; then here he came, the white goat trailing behind, stopping to snatch at a frond and jerking ahead. The green growth hid, revealed, hid, revealed them. The goat, shoved into its shed, let out its stammering vibration.

"What did you say to that guy?" Dan had come up behind her. His hair was still damp from sweat or sea water, the cricket bat was over his shoulder. "We saw his jeep when he left. What did you say to him?"

Conscious of a male alliance, she had begun to feel like a witness under interrogation. "I told him we'd think about what he said."

"Which was?" He had picked up Harry's mannerisms, his inflections.

"Which was that we should get out. Now."

Dan's face darkened, he leaned against the house wall. "Silly wimp," he said. "Petty official."

Amazed, Jane heard herself shouting on behalf of Mr. Adams.

"Dan! Don't be such an idiot! You know absolutely nothing about what's going to happen."

"Neither does he."

"Look, there's no use yelling at each other!" ("*I* wasn't yelling . . .")

said Dan.) "We'll just have to reach some sort of sensible decision. As a family," she piously added.

"Harry says He can't take the pressure much longer. He'll have to have elections like He promised. Now the teachers are out, they're going to have the kids march too."

She looked at him. "Not unless their parents are crazy. People disappear here, Dan. They just *disappear.*"

"No kid is going to disappear; He's got to pretend."

"All right, no child is going to disappear. But someone is going to get shot in public, not just in private. And when that starts . . ."

"Suppose Gandhi had said that? Suppose the people who lay down on the tracks . . ."

"Oh, go and wash *up!*" she said rudely. "I'm tired of being preached at."

A great beginning, she thought, for the family decision-making process. Why did discussions of peace inevitably produce fury? She put her hand on her fist and stared at the low sun; it was the top half of a blood orange, exactly touching sea level.

The first time she had seen Him was at close hand. She was walking down the real road, cautiously on the edge of the jagged cavity of its deep stone gutter, when the black big car, flying its small intense flag, had slid past her. Flanked by two burly figures, the face familiar from posters, under the military cap, the eyes invisible behind the ritual dark glasses, had stared straight ahead. A second car followed closely. That was when He was still playing for respectability, still the emerging statesman, the strong but just father of His island, paternal rather than fascist. There was, in the stance of the rigid chauffeur, the three faces expressionless behind their formality, the middle man's head advanced a little, like a dominant vulture, something which made everything suddenly real. That's what they've all looked like, she had thought, chilled.

She went in to the icebox. It was almost empty. Tomorrow, Saturday, was market day. By thinking of how much chance she would have to be alone tomorrow, she discovered the depth of her uncertainty. Was *she* the wimp? When she had arrived in Ste. Cecile, one question had loomed: marriage. It drew and repelled her. She desired, admired, probably loved Harry; she believed in his toughness, his kindness, the absolute quality of his integrity. Did it really matter that that integrity's expression sometimes frightened and infuriated her? He and Dan. She thought snidely, lucky devils! What bliss total commitment must be. How long was she going on this way, perhaps yes, perhaps no, perhaps leaving, perhaps staying? Alone with Harry the choice would be easy. It was Dan. But how on earth was Dan going to get hurt? Yet in moments she knew he would. He would throw a stone, he will yell at Him.

Then all at once, the thread of patience snapped. Tomorrow, away for hours and hours from the pressure of voices, of presences, for worse or better, she would harden her mushy mind. She felt like the heroine of an opera; she even said aloud, "I *am* Dan's mother . . ."

That evening they played Scrabble.

The light from the kerosene lamp enveloped them with—*mollesse*, she thought, a light unknown to the glare of a bulb: cheekbones, eyes, the faded, rather dirty shirts, took on a luminous look so that the three sat—man, woman and boy—untroubled, archetypal, in the light's soft pulse. Outside the sea hissed and hushed, hissed and hushed. A faint indeterminate calypso just touched their ears. The dogs answered each other, near, far up in the hills, bark bark bark. Bark. Bark bark. Already, a manic rooster crowed. This is peace. But she knew it to be armistice.

She was taking the Minimoke all the way to Bellemore to paint the new boat; they were building it there. Elevated, the spare ribs were still fresh-cut wood; the shape, bow, prow were there. It went very slowly. Somehow it was wonderful to see tree turn to skeleton, earthgrowth to marine intention; the ancient shape, near any sea, always. She must market first; when she came back, all the best fruit and vegetables would be gone. She was alarmed at how delight rose in her at the thought of being alone.

"Q on a triple," said Dan, and his face lit with just his father's look.

The rough sketch was all right, but the rudimentary painting was a disaster. She stopped, wiping her brushes, going into the bush to pee, then sitting on the frame of the inevitable wrecked rowboat, opening her thermos. But even after she decided just what was wrong, the painting balked. The magic of promise in the bare ribs, strong, complex, but still only a shape, was broken. All she had was a mathematical structure. Ah, but she had another structure, complete, in her mind; she knew she could hold to something, once given. She was going to stay.

Everything had been a risk. Mixing her life so deeply with Harry's resolute and single mind; pulling up stakes from friends and the full, competitive world of her work; being remote among people of a different race plunged in their own rough struggle. Either it was worth it or not. The mania that Dan would be shot, would be arrested, would be hurt in some preventable way, left her. Was hero-worship so dangerous? In a world of vicious enmities, was it so perilous if Dan saw Harry as pointing the path to light, to which there was one way only?

Her grandmother had used a palm-leaf fan; she hadn't seen one in years, Jane realized. Why had she thought of that pale yellow shine, so remote from its gusty green? Then her grandmother's dictum came, as though the lacquered fan had wafted it. In the inn of decision, the mind sleeps well. Now she entered, tired, rejoicing.

The nets, fishy-smelling, lay on the sand. Haul over, the racks of tiny fish dried in the sun. There was only an old man, grizzled and small, sitting on a log, his pipe out but clenched, his rheumy eyes meeting hers as she gathered up her load. He smiled. His teeth were intermittent, but from leathery lips he said, with the air of a host, "How are you, Mistress?"

At first she had naïvely winced at the address, then felt a fool for her assumption, when she discovered it to be pure Elizabethan courtesy, extended to the washerwoman, the goat-tender.

"Well," she said, meaning it. "Thank you, well." She dumped her gear in the Minimoke; there was the pile of fruit and vegetables. Uncertain, embarrassed, she lifted a mango.

"May I offer you this?" she formally asked. The old man removed his pipe. Screwing up his eyes, he considered. "What it is?" he asked; then, seeing, "Is it ripe?" he asked with interest. She stepped forward and handed it to him. He took it in his used-up hands, turning it. "It is ripe," he said. "My wife and I will eat it tonight. I will give it to she." He had not thanked her. It was as though they had collaborated on a logical action.

She climbed into the Minimoke and turned the key.

"You are from Cal-i-for-nia?" he called, his pipe in the air. They all asked her that. The movie nearest to him was a tin building at the other end of the island. But he asked the same question.

Cutting the wheel, she called back, "No. I come from Baltimore."

Disappointed by the useless name, he put his pipe back in his mouth and juggled the mango a little in his hands. He had lost interest.

The marketplace, when she turned into it, was empty. Boxes, stands deserted; shards of vegetables, a broken crate. Two Barracudas, lounging over rifles. A hot sick pang went through her. She tramped on the brakes and leaned out.

"What's happened to the market?" she called to the nearer policeman. He stared at her, less with hostility than contempt. He hefted his rifle. "That does be closed!" he called back.

"What's happened? Has something happened?" she shouted at him, but he only gave her a wide cold smile.

She saw now that in all directions the streets were empty. Along the sea wall, two more Barracudas strolled. A very old woman, bent, in bright blue, came out of the Catholic church a steep block uphill.

I mustn't drive too fast, she thought. Small pastel houses, wooden shacks shot by. Here came a whole lorry of Barracudas; forced to the edge of the steep stone gutter, she nearly lost control. Now she began to see a few people, in small groups, on the steps of houses, under the high porches.

They'd never do anything to Dan or Harry. Americans. Not unless there was fighting. And there isn't—look, there's a girl driving home two goats. But all the tension of weeks sang in her nerves. On her right she could see the beach flying past her. At the final turn the Minimoke rocked precariously, shot down the lane and fetched up in a shower of sand.

There was Harry, on the porch. He had his arms crossed and he stared at her. She could feel her blood drain.

"Where's Dan?"

"He's in his room."

"Is he all right? What's happened?"

"Of course he's all right," said Harry irascibly.

She had been gripping the wheel so hard she could scarcely straighten her fingers. "What's happened?" she said again. She couldn't decide whether Harry looked angry or exalted; at any rate, strange. At the steps, she cried again, "What's happened?"

"All hell," he said. "His goons broke up a march. A man got shot. Where are you going? Dan's door's locked." He grabbed her wrist. "Jane! Just sit down a minute, will you? Just ease off a little. I'll tell you all about everything. Sit *down* a minute."

But she was already knocking lightly at the door.

At once Dan's voice, keyed high, said, "Not now . . . Go away. Please, go away."

Harry had followed her. He passed her; at the cupboard he pulled out a bottle of Mount Gay, gathered two glasses.

"Dan's perfectly all right," he said. "Give him a little time. Come on out on the porch."

Like a knot in her gut, Jane could feel the anger swelling. "I take it there was a march." She followed Harry outside. He poured rum in each glass.

"Yes, there was a march," he said.

"You knew about it ahead of time?"

"Not really. Word gets around fast, you know."

"And I take it you marched?"

He held out the glass to her with a small friendly gesture, and she shook her head. "That's right."

"You took Dan?"

"I didn't 'take' Dan. He'd been planning to go."

"I told him he couldn't."

"Jane, a time comes when you can't make that stick."

Angrily she met his eyes; she saw then how badly he was shaken. Suddenly she felt exhausted. Nothing irrevocable had happened. She was undermined by Harry's face.

She took up the rejected glass and leaned against the rough railing, staring unseeingly at the Montroses' empty yard of dust.

"I can't fight about it now, Harry. But how could you, behind my back? Who was the man? Was he killed?"

"I don't know. Yes. The Barracudas were cracking heads, and he yanked away a police club. It wasn't behind your back. You just weren't here. You couldn't have stopped Dan. He's fifteen."

"*You* could!" she said in a flare of bitterness. She saw in Harry's face an odd mingling of the old stubborn glory and a curious timidity. But he said doggedly, "I wouldn't if I could have. He's old enough to have a conscience and a will, Jane. In three years he could be drafted. He's old enough to know what he believes."

"Was it the shooting?" Jane said uncertainly. "Did he see it?"

Something was unspoken. Harry turned the glass round and round. "No, actually he didn't."

"Then why . . . ?"

To her amazement she saw Harry's eyes blur with pain.

"It's Alexis."

"*Alexis!*"

He looked at her miserably.

"Alexis got hurt."

"*Alexis* was marching?"

"He came with Dan."

"They let him?"

"Mr. Montrose was on his route. I think his mother had walked into town. To the market."

"*You* let him?"

"For God's sake, Jane. I've no earthly power over Alexis. He scarcely believes I exist. I didn't want him to come."

"Wasn't he worth proselytizing?"

Harry did not answer that.

"What happened to him?"

"A policeman hit him in the head—but it wasn't that. He was knocked flying down into the gutter. You know what those are. He broke something in his back. We didn't even know. It was a madhouse and we were separated."

"How do you know now?"

"Dan and I went to look for him, and we couldn't find him. After we got back, the police came."

"Here?"

"To tell his parents. Montrose had just got back. He went off with the policeman, to the hospital. Dan tried to go, but Mr. Montrose . . . He was so upset he didn't know what he was saying," said Harry bleakly. "When Mrs. Montrose got back, I tried to drive her to the hospital but —for Christ's sake, Jane, how do you think *I* feel?"

"Well, how *do* you feel?" she said; and then the community of their misery stopped her. "How bad is it?"

"Dan and I went to the hospital. They'd left word we weren't to be allowed to see Alexis. It's pretty bad, I think. Of course, these doctors . . . The back is broken and there are some internal injuries—I don't think they're very positive about anything yet. At least, I don't see how they can be." His face looked pared, polished. Round and round he turned his emptied glass. She reached over and touched his shoulder, and in his eyes tears appeared, for whom she was not sure.

They stayed there, silent. The tide was coming in, pushing the curved bubbling fringe up over the high sand. A way down the beach they could just hear faint thin shouts; tiny shapes ran and pitched. Games had resumed.

At that moment two figures appeared, coming slowly down the path from the road: the Montroses. Ahead walked Mr. Montrose; a few paces behind came his wife. Without hesitation, without a glance, they passed through their gate, across the yard, up the steps to the house.

"I'm going over," said Jane.

"Wait till tomorrow," said Harry quickly. "Don't go right now."

"I *can't* wait," said Jane. "Don't you see? We can't just sit here—us here, them over there. We can't."

"Dan tried to say something to Mr. Montrose. I wish you'd wait."

"I can't." She stood up.

"Look," Harry said in a desperate whisper. "They can't tell really how bad it is yet. But it is bad. Leave them alone."

Jane went down the steps. She thought she had never walked so far as to the Montroses' gate. I won't just keep saying I'm sorry, I'm sorry. The house was silent. A small lizard darted by her toe. The cricket shouts just reached her ears. She knocked at the door.

As if he had been waiting behind it, Mr. Montrose stood before her. Her instant impression was of distance—the fierce remoteness in his gaze paralyzed her.

She said, "Mr. Montrose, I've just heard about Alexis. How bad is it?" she said. From a million miles, from a million years, the eyes watched her. At last he said, "The back is broke up. The hip too." Slowly, impersonally he added, "No way they can fix it right."

"They can't say that!" she cried, terrified. "This is just a tiny hospital. In Trinidad—please, *please* let us send him to Trinidad!"

The face changed so that Jane recoiled.

"You go to hell," said Mr. Montrose very slowly. "Where you is come from. Evil, evil, evil. All of you. Go home—if you do have one."

Behind his shoulder appeared Mrs. Montrose's head; her hand covered her mouth.

I can't move, thought Jane. I am here forever.

"You come here," said Mr. Montrose. "Why? Why you come? You are devils. Go where you come from. You are evil." Then he added with formality, "If you do stay here, you will die."

She couldn't tell if it were a threat or a statement. She looked behind him at Mrs. Montrose's face—it had a strange expression as though it were being pulled apart.

"I'm going," she said to the still figure towering over her. "We're going." With a huge effort she moved, turning. Then she stopped.

"Dan and Alexis are friends," she said.

At that, suddenly Mr. Montrose let out a kind of howl. "*He* should be there, in that place!" he shouted. "Never he should run again! Bad things will come to him, you have done it. You will see. Bad things."

Mrs. Montrose moved suddenly forward, but his right arm shot out pushing her back.

Halfway to her steps, Jane heard the door close.

The next morning while there was dew everywhere and the air was still fresh, Harry drove them to the airport. Dan sat in the back.

He had not spoken since late last night when he had found no shelter. "I won't go," he said then.

Jane, beyond tact, beyond persuasion, said, "You have to. I'm taking you home."

"I'm staying here," he said. "I'm staying with Harry."

"No, you're not, Dan," said Harry. They were down to raw statement. "I won't have you. You've got to go with your mother now."

"I won't go. How can you make me? Carry me? Call the Barracudas?"

"You can't stay right now, Dan," said Harry more gently. "How could you? Not here, not next door. Where?"

"I'll stay with the Montroses!" he cried. There was a small silence. Dan began to weep. Jane touched his hand but, as though she had burned it, he flinched. He gazed furiously at Harry. "You quit!" he said thickly. "The very first thing, you quit! You give up! You give me up! You tell me something, you make a big deal, and then you quit!"

"What's that?" said Jane quickly. "That was a knock."

"It wasn't a knock," said Harry. "It was someone on the porch."

They listened: dogs, dogs; and the sea. Harry got up and walked over to the door. He said over his shoulder, "If someone's here, just give me a chance to talk to them. Right?" At the door he raised his voice. "Yes?"

No voice answered. Harry turned the brown glazed handle and the door opened on the scented night. As it did so, something fell forward onto the floor and lay there shining a little: a cricket bat. They stared at it, its handle oiled with sweat, soaked in sun and salt. Then Dan darted over and snatched it up. He took it and went into his room. The bolt shot in its slot.

A few miles from the airport, dawn arrived. First the outline of tinged clouds, separate in their drift. Then a sort of enormous renovation of the sky—it cleared, produced a faint pure blue, gradually lit all the greens. On the edges of the road children appeared, with cans or bundles. A man overtaken in his loose barefoot stride raised a machete in greeting.

Jane was transfixed by the dailyness. Light would come just like this through the Montroses' red curtains; over Alexis, asleep or awake, announcing the day of hours, minutes, seconds. Of the first boats, and the sea's colors, and the sand. And in the afternoons, the rich fall of that blood orange, the yells and shouts and flat hard sound of the plank bats. Alexis would indeed remember his neighbors.

At the airport, the waves ran up almost to the runway. The tiny plane already sat there.

At the head of the narrow steps, the tall brown stewardess obstructed them, her voice bored and musical. Of course the cricket bat would not fit under any seat. Forbidden to frown, the stewardess smiled in annoyance. She took the bat gingerly and, carrying it before her, wedged it upright in the coat section.

Dan would not sit with her. But, like a damaging consolation, she knew that already, willing the opposite, he was fleeing—mutinous, looking back—but fleeing something he couldn't bear now, or change, ever.

Harry would be confirmed. Or not. How far he went, to them or from them, what happened, what became of everything, was part of the unfinished. Now he still hoped all things, money, doctors, something. The principle was sacrifice; but what of Harry now that Alexis had stolen it, to carry?

They vibrated violently. The tarmac slid toward them. There was the wheels' *chock*, a wing tilted and the few dark figures fell away.

They were over the sea and through the thick glass she saw the green bright land, valleys, dense hills, falling, falling, bright and small and smaller, in its particular shape, releasing them to the universal sky.

THE OTHER

JOHN UPDIKE

John Updike was born in Shillington, Pennsylvania, in 1932. He gradu-
ated from Harvard College and worked several years for *The New
Yorker*. Since 1957 he has lived in Massachusetts as a free-lance writer.
This is his tenth appearance in the O. Henry Prize Stories.

Rob Arnold met Priscilla Hunter at college in the fifties, and the fact
that she was a twin seemed to matter as little as the fact that she had
been raised as an Episcopalian and he as a Baptist. How blissfully little
did seem to matter in the fifties! Politics, religion, class—all beside the
point. Young lives then, once Eisenhower had settled for a draw in Korea
and McCarthy had self-destructed like a fairy-tale goblin, seemed to be
composed of timeless simplicities and old verities, of weather and works
of art on opposite sides of a museum wall, of ancient professors, arrogant
and scarcely audible from within the security of their tenure, lecturing
from yellowing notes upon Dante and Kant while in the tall windows at
their backs sunlight filtered through the feathery leaves of overarching
elms. In those days Harvard Yard was innocent of Dutch-elm disease.
And in those days a large and not laughable sexual territory existed
within the borders of virginity, where physical parts were fed to the
partner one at a time, beginning with the lips and hands. Strangely, Rob
and Priscilla had been traversing this territory for several weeks before
she confided to him that she was an identical twin. One of her breasts,
clothed in an angora sweater and the underlying stiffness of a brassiere,
was held in his hand at the time. Their faces were so close together that
he could smell the mentholated tobacco in the breath of her confession.
"Rob, I ought to tell you. I have a sister who looks just like me." Priscilla
seemed to think it slightly shameful, and in fact it was exciting.

Her twin, the other, was named Susan, and attended the University of
Chicago, though she, too, had been admitted to Radcliffe. Their parents
—two Minneapolis lawyers, the father a specialist in corporation law and

the mother in divorce and legal-aid work—had always encouraged the girls to be different; they had dressed them in different clothes from the start and had sent them to different private schools at an early age. A myth had been fostered in the family that Priscilla was the "artistic" one and Susan the more "practical" and "scientific," though to the twins themselves their interests and attitudes seemed close to identical. As children, they had succumbed simultaneously to the same diseases— chicken pox, mumps—and even when sent to different summer camps had a way, their conversations in September revealed, of undergoing the same trials and initiations. They learned to swim the same week, in widely separated lakes, and had let themselves be necked with in different forests. They fell in love with the same movie star (Montgomery Clift), had the same favorite song ("Two Loves Have I," as sung by Frankie Laine), and preferred the same Everly brother (Don, the darker and slicker-looking). Rob asked Priscilla if she missed her twin. She said, "No," but to have said otherwise might have been insulting, for she was lying entangled with him, mussed and overheated, in his fifth-floor room, with its single dormer window, in Winthrop House.

Rob was an only child, with a widowed mother, and asked, "What does it feel like, having a twin?"

Priscilla made a thoughtful mouth; prim little creases appeared in her pursed upper lip. "Nice," she answered, after a long pause that had dried the amorous moisture from her eyes. They were brown eyes, a delicious candy color, darker than caramel but paler than Hershey's kisses. "You have a backup, seeing the same things you do. A kind of insurance policy, in a funny way."

"Even when you're sent to different schools and all that?"

"That doesn't matter so much, it turns out. Suzie and I always knew we weren't the other and were going to have to lead different lives. It's just that when I'm with her there's so much less explaining to do. Maybe that's why I'm not much good at explaining things. Sorry," Priscilla said. Her face was still pink from the soft struggle they had been having on his bed.

"You're good enough," Rob said, and dropped the subject, for it had interrupted this slow journey they were making, bit by bit, into one another. He considered himself lucky to have landed her. She had, Priscilla, a lovely athletic figure, long-muscled and hippy and with wide sloping shoulders, yet narrowed to a fine firmness at the ankles and wrists; his pleasure at seeing her undressed at first disconcerted her in its intensity, and time passed before she could accept it as her due and, still a virgin, coolly give him, in his room, in the narrow space between his iron frame bed and standard oak desk, little one-woman "parades." Though they could not, for all those good fifties reasons (pregnancy, the social worth of female chastity), make love, he had talked her into this piece of display. She held her chin up bravely and slowly turned in mock-model style, showing all sides of herself; the sight was so glorious Rob had to avert his eyes, and saw how her bare feet, fresh from chilly boots and rimmed in pink, slowly pivoted on the oval rug of braided rags his mother had given him to make his room more cozy. When his minute of drinking in Priscilla was up, she would scramble, suddenly blushing and laughing at herself, into bed beside him, under rough blue blankets that Harvard issued in those days as if to soldiers or monks. They would try to read from the same book; they were taking a course together—Philosophy 10, Idealism from Plato to Whitehead.

Once she had told him that she was a twin, he could not forget it, or quite forgive her. The monstrous idea flirted at the back of his head that she was half a person; there was something withheld, something hollow-backed and tinny about the figure she cut in his mind even as their courtship proceeded smoothly toward marriage. He wanted to become a lawyer; she was doubly the daughter of lawyers and in all things ideal, given the inevitable small differences between two individuals. She had been raised rather rich and he rather poor. His drab and pious upbringing embarrassed him. He had felt indignantly drowned on that absurd day when, dressed in a sleazy white gown, he had submitted to the shock of immersion, tipped backward and all the way under by the murderous hands of a minister wearing hip waders; whereas Priscilla kept in her room like a girlhood Teddy bear the embossed prayer book given her upon confirmation and sometimes carried it, in white-gloved hands, to services at the pretty little Church of New Jerusalem across from the Busch-Reisinger. Both young people were for Stevenson in 1956, but she seemed secretly pleased when Eisenhower won again and Rob had wished Henry Wallace were still running. He wanted to become a lawyer for a perverse reason: to avenge his father. His father, not yet fifty when he died of Hodgkin's disease, in the days before chemotherapy, had been an auto mechanic who had borrowed heavily to open a garage of his own, and it had been lawyers—lawyers for the bank and other creditors—who had briskly, with perfect legality, administered the financial ruin and thwarted the dying man's attempts to divert money to his survivors. None of this at the time seemed to matter; what mattered was her beauty and his ardor and gratitude and her cool appraisal of the future value of his gratitude as she dazzlingly, with a silver poise faintly resembling cruelty, displayed herself to him. The fact of her being a twin put a halo around her form, a shimmer of duplication, a suggestion, curiously platonic, that there was, somewhere else, unseen, another version of this reality, this body.

Priscilla's parents lived in St. Paul, in a big, cream-colored, many-dormered house a few blocks from the gorge holding the Mississippi, which was not especially wide this far north. Though Rob several times travelled there to display himself, in his best clothes, to his prospective in-laws, he did not meet Susan until the wedding. She had always been away—on a package tour of Europe or waitressing in Southern California, a part of the world where she had been led by some of her racier U. of C. friends. When Rob met her at last, she had come from Santa Barbara to be Priscilla's maid of honor. Though it was early June and cool in Minnesota, she had a surfer's deep tan and a fluffy haircut short as a boy's. A stranger to the family might not have spotted her, amid the welter of siblings and cousins, as the bride's twin. But Rob had been long alerted, and as he clasped her warm hand the current of identity stunned him to wordlessness. Her face was Priscilla's down to the protruding, determined cut of her upper lip and the slightly sad droop of the lashes at the outside corners of her eyes. He reddened, and imagined that Susan did, though her manner with him was instantly ironical—bantering and languid in perhaps the West Coast manner. Enclosed within Priscilla's body, the coolness of a stranger seemed rude, even hostile. Rob noted what seemed to be a ray or two less of caramel in her irises, a smoother consistency of chocolate. These darker eyes made her seem more passionate, more impudent and flitting, as she moved through her old home with none of a bride's responsibilities. And Susan was, Rob thought, appraising her repeatedly through the social flurry, distinctly bigger, if only by a centimetre and an ounce.

His impressions, Priscilla told him when they were alone, were wrong: Susan had expected to like him and did, very much. And though she had been the firstborn, she had never been, as often happens, the stronger or heavier. Their heights and weights had always been precisely the same. Priscilla thought that, indeed, Suzie had lost some weight, chasing around with that creepy crowd of beach bums out there. Their parents were up in arms because she had announced her intention to do graduate work in art history at U.C.L.A., where there really wasn't any art, when there was that entire wonderful Chester Dale collection at the Art Institute, along with everything else in Chicago. Or why not go East, like Priscilla? Their parents had hoped Susan would become a physicist, or at least a psychologist. Rob liked hearing Priscilla, not normally much of an explainer, run on this way about her sister; being near her twin did seem to embolden her, to loosen her tongue. He enjoyed the tumble of an extensive, ambitious family, amid whose many branches his own mother, their guest for the weekend, seemed a wan, doomed graft. The big house was loaded with pale padded furniture and vacation souvenirs; his mother found a safe corner in a little-used library and worked at a needlepoint footstool cover she had brought from North Carolina.

In church, the twins, the one majestic in white tulle and the other rather mousy in mauve taffeta, were vividly distinguishable. Rob, however, standing at the altar in a daze of high Episcopalianism, the musk of incense in his nostrils and a gold-leafed panel of apostles flickering off to the side, had a disquieting thrill of confusion, as if the mocking-eyed maid of honor might be his intimate from Winthrop House days and the mysterious figure on their father's arm a woman virtually unknown to him, tanned and crop-haired beneath her veil and garland of florets. Susan's voice was just a grain or two the huskier, so he knew it was Priscilla who, in a shy, true voice, recited the archaic vows with him. At the reception, amid all the kissing, he kissed his sister-in-law and was startled at the awkwardly averted, rather stubbornly downcast cheek; Rob had reflexively expected Priscilla's habituated frontal ease. And when they danced, Susan was stiff in his arms. Yet none of this marred her fascination, the superior authenticity she enjoyed over the actual reality as the wedding night untidily proceeded through champagne and forced jollity to its trite, closeted climax. Susan was with them (her remembered stiffness, as if she and Rob had too much to say to dare a word, and her imagined slightly greater size and heft) during the botch of defloration, exciting him, urging him on through Priscilla's pain. Though he knew he had put an unfortunate crimp in this infant marriage, and had given his long-cherished ardor a bad name, he fell asleep with happy exhaustion, as if all his guilt were shifted onto the body of a twin of his own.

Rob was not accepted at Harvard Law School; but good-hearted Yale took him. It was all for the best, for if Cambridge in those years was the path to Washington, New Haven was closer to New York and Wall Street, where the real money was. After a few years in the city, the Arnolds settled in Greenwich and had children—a girl, a boy, and a girl.

Having married a La Jolla builder of million-dollar homes, Susan kept pace with a girl, a boy, and then another boy. This break in symmetry led them both, it seemed, to stop bearing children. Also, the Pill had come along and made birth control irresistible. Kennedy had been shot, and something called rock blasted from the radio however you twisted the dial. The twins, though, had their nests safely made. Susan's husband was named Jeb Herrera; he claimed descent from one of the old Spanish ranching families of Alta California, but in joking moods asserted that his great-great-grandfather had been a missionary's illegitimate son. He was a curly-haired, heavy, gracious, enthusiastic man, a bit too proclaimedly, for Rob's taste, in love with life. His small, even teeth looked piratical, when he smiled through the black curls of his beard. He was one of the first men Rob knew to wear a full beard and to own a computer—a tan metal box taller than a man, a freestanding broom closet that spat paper. Jeb had programmed it to respond to the children's questions with jokes in printout. His office was a made-over wharf shed where dozens shuffled paper beside canted windows full of the Pacific. None of his employees wore neckties. Though the twins, as they eased into matronhood, might still be mistaken for one another, there was no mistaking the husbands. Susan, it would appear, had the artistic taste, and Priscilla had bet on practicality. Rob had become a specialist in tax law, saw his name enrolled in the list of junior partners on the engraved firm stationery, and forgot about avenging his father.

The growing families visited back and forth; there was something concordant about the homes, though one was white clapboard set primly on watered green lawn, and the other was redwood and stucco wedged into a hillside where fat little cactuses intricate as snowflakes flourished among expensively transplanted rocks. Both houses were cheerful for children, with back stairs and big windows and a certain sporty airiness. The Arnolds had a long sun room with a Ping-Pong table and, above it on the second floor, a sleeping porch with a hammock. As soon as they could afford it, they crowded a composition tennis court into the space between the garage and the line fence, where the lawn had always been scruffy anyway and the vegetable garden had gone to weeds every July. The La Jolla house, which overlooked the fifteenth fairway of a golf course, shuffled indoors and out doors with its sliding glass doors and cantilevered deck and its family-sized hot tub out on the deck.

Rob first saw his wife's sister naked one warm evening in Christmas vacation when Susan let fall a large white towel behind her and slid her silent silhouette into this hot tub. Rob and his wife were already in, coping with the slithering, giggling bodies of their excited children; so the moment passed almost unnoticed amid the family tumble. Almost. Susan was distinctly not Priscilla; their skins had aged differently on the two different coasts. Priscilla's was dead pale this time of year, its summer tan long faded, whereas there was something thickened and delicately crinkled and permanently golden about Susan's. With an accustomed motion she had eased her weight from her buttocks into the steaming wide circle of water. Her expression looked solemn, dented by shadow. Rob remembered the same resolute, unfocussed expression on Priscilla's face in the days when she would grant him her little "parade" in the shadows of his narrow college room. Both sisters had brown eyes in deep sockets and noses that looked upturned, with long nostrils and sharp central dents in their upper lips. Both were wearing bangs that winter. Their heads and shoulders floated side by side; Susan's breasts seemed the whiter for the contrast with her year-round bathing-suit tan.

"How much do you do this sort of thing?" Priscilla asked her twin, a touch nervously, glancing toward Rob.

"Oh, now and then, with people you know, usually. You get used to it —it's a local custom. You sort of let yourself dissolve."

Yet she, too, gave Rob an alert glance. He had already passed into dissolution, his vapor of double love one with the heat, the steam, the abundant dinner wine, the scent of the eucalyptus trees brooding above the deck, the stars beyond them, the strangeness of this all being a few days before Christmas. Immersed, their bodies had become foreshortened stumps of flesh, comical blobs of mercury. Jeb appeared on the deck holding a naked baby—little Lucas—in one crooked arm and a fresh half gallon of Gallo Chablis in the other. Early in his thirties, Jeb had a pendulous belly. He descended to them like a hairy Neptune; the tub overflowed. When the water calmed, his penis drifted under Rob's eyes like a lead-colored fish swimming nowhere.

The families stopped travelling back and forth in complete units as the maturing children developed local attachments and summer jobs. The two oldest cousins, Karen and Rose, had been fast friends from the start, though there was no mistaking them for twins: Karen had become as washed-out and mild-faced a blonde as Rob's mother (now dead), and Rose was so dark that boys on the street catcalled to her in Spanish. The two older boys, Henry and Gabriel, made a more awkward matchup, the one burdened with all of Rob's allergies and a drowsy shyness all his own, and the other a macho little athlete with a wedge-shaped back and the unthinking cruelty of those whose bodies are perfectly connected to their wills. The girl and the boy that completed the sets, Jennifer and Lucas, claimed to detest each other, and, indeed, did squabble tediously, perhaps in defense against any notion that they would someday marry. The bigger the children became, the harder they pulled apart, and the more frayed the lines between their parents became. Once little Lucas became too big to hold in one arm and strike a pose with, Jeb's interest seemed to wander away from families and family get-togethers. There were late-night long-distance calls between the sisters, and secrets from the children.

Susan suddenly had more gray hair than Priscilla. Rob felt touched by her, and drawn in a new fashion, when she would visit them for a few weeks in the summer without Jeb, with perhaps an inscrutable Rose and a resentful Lucas in tow. More than once, Rob met the L.A. red-eye at LaGuardia and was kissed at the gate as if he were Susan's savior; there had been drunks on the plane, college kids, nobody could sleep, Lucas had insisted on watching a ghastly Jerry Lewis movie, Rose threw up over Nebraska somewhere, they had gone way north around some thunderheads, an old lech in an admiral's uniform kept trying to buy her drinks at three in the morning, my God, never again. As Rob gently swung the car up the summer-green curves of the Merritt Parkway, Susan nodded asleep, and seemed his wife. Priscilla's skin, too, now sagged in those defenseless puckers when she slept.

As a guest in their home, Susan slept on the upstairs porch. The swish of cars headed toward the railroad station, and the birds—so much more aggressive, she said, than those on the West Coast—awakened her too early; and then at night the Arnolds took her to too many parties. "How do you stand it?" she would ask her twin.

"Oh, it gets to be a habit. Try taking a nap in the afternoon. That's what I do."

"Jeb and I hardly go out at all anymore. We decided other people weren't helping our marriage." This was a clue, and far from the only one. There was a hungry boniness to her figure now. Like a sick person willing to try any cure, Susan drank only herbal tea—no caffeine, no alcohol—and ate as little meat as she politely could. Whereas Priscilla, who had once appeared so distinctly a centimetre smaller, now was relatively hefty. Broad of shoulder and hip, she moved through parties with a certain roll, a practiced cruiser who knew where the ports were—the confiding women and the unhappy men and the bar table in the corner. Sometimes after midnight Rob watched her undress in their bedroom and thought of all the Martinis and Manhattans, the celery sticks and devilled eggs that had gone into those haunches and upper arms.

"Other people don't help *it,*" was Priscilla's answer to Susan. "But they might do something for *you.* You, a woman. Aren't you a woman, or are you only a part of a marriage?" She had never forgiven him, Rob feared, for that unideal wedding night.

Poor Susan seemed a vision of chastity whom they would discover each morning at the breakfast table, frazzled after another night's poor sleep, her hair drooping onto the lapels of a borrowed bathrobe, her ascetic breakfast of grapefruit and granola long eaten, the *Times* scattered about her in pieces read with a desperate thoroughness. Rob wanted to urge bacon and waffles upon her, and to make up good news to counteract the bad news that had been turning her hair gray. Priscilla knew what it was, but was no good at explaining. "Jeb's a bastard," she would say simply in their bedroom. "He always was. My parents knew it, but what could they do? She had to get married, once I did. And all men are bastards, more or less."

"My, you've gotten tough. He was always very dear with the kids, I thought. At least when they were little. And he builds those million-dollar houses."

"Not so much anymore he doesn't," she said. As she pivoted on their plush carpet, yellow calluses showed at her heels.

"What do you mean?"

"Ask *her,* if you're so interested."

But he never could. He could no more have asked Susan to confide her private life than he could have tiptoed onto the sleeping porch and looked down at—what he held so clearly in his mind—his wife's very face, transposed into another, chastened existence, fragilely asleep in this alien house, this alien climate and time zone. So magical a stranger might awake under the pressure of his regard. He would have trespassed. He would have spoiled something he was saving.

The 1973–75 recession gave Jeb's tottering, overextended business the last push it needed; everything coming undone at once, the Herreras began to divorce amid the liquidation. When Susan visited them in the bicentennial year, it was as a single woman, her thinness now whittled to a certain point, a renewed availability. But not, of course, available to Rob; the collapse of one marriage made the other doubly precious.

As in other summers, Rob was touched by Susan's zeal with the children, ushering as many as could be captured onto the train and into the

city for a visit to the Museum of Natural History or to see the tall ships
that beautiful hazy July day. Rose was not with her; the girl had drawn
closer to her father in his distress, and was waitressing in a taco joint in
San Diego. And Karen, now stunning with her flaxen hair and pale
moonface above a slender body, was above everything except boys and
ballet. One Saturday while Priscilla stayed home, having contracted for a
lunch at the club with one of those similarly boozy women she called
"girlfriends," Rob accompanied Susan on an excursion she had cooked
up for the just barely willing Jennifer and Lucas, all the way to New
Haven to see the Beinecke Library, with its translucent marble and the
three Noguchis so marvelously toylike and monumental in their sunken
well. Rob had not seen these wonders himself; they had come to Yale
after his time. And he rather enjoyed these excursions with his sister-in-
law; all that old tumble of family life had fallen to them to perpetuate.
He let her drive his Mercedes and sat beside her, taking secret inventory
of all the minute ways in which she differed from Priscilla—the slight
extra sharpness to the thrust of her upper lip, the sea scallop of shallow
wrinkles the sun had engraved at the corner of her eye, the hair or two
more of bulk or wildness to her eyebrow on its crest of bone. The hair of
her head, once shorter, then grayer, was now dyed too even a dark
brown, with unnatural reddish lights. She turned to him for a second on
a long straightaway. "You've never asked about me and Jeb," she said.

"What was to ask? Things speak for themselves."

"I loved that about you," Susan pronounced. Her verb alarmed him;
"love" was a word he associated with the tacky sermons of his youth.
"It's been a nightmare for years," she went on, and he realized that she
was offering to present herself in a new way to him, as more than a
strange ghost behind a familiar mask. She was in a sense naked. But he,
after nearly two decades of playing the good husband, had discovered
affairs, and had fallen in love locally. The image of his mistress—she was
one of Priscilla's "girlfriends"—rose up, her head tipped back, her lipstick smeared, and deafened him to the woman he was with; without
hearing the words, he saw Susan's mouth, that distinctive complicated
mouth the sisters shared, making a pursy, careful expression, like a
schoolteacher emphasizing a crucial point.

Lucas, in the back seat, was listening and cried out, "Mom, stop
bitching about Dad to Uncle Rob—you do it to *everybody*!"

Jennifer said, "Oh listen to big man here, protecting his awful daddy,"
and there was a thump, and the girl sobbed in spite of her scorn.

"You make me barf, you know that?" Lucas told her, his own voice shakily full of tears. "You've always been the most god-awful germ, no kidding."

"Daddy," Jennifer said, with something of womanly aloofness. "This little spic just broke my arm."

The adult conversation was not resumed. Priscilla a few days later drove her sister back to LaGuardia, to begin a new life. Susan was planning to take her half of what money was left when the La Jolla house was sold and move with the two younger children to the Bay area and study ceramics at Berkeley.

"I told her she's crazy," Priscilla said to him. "There's nothing but gays in San Francisco."

"Maybe she's not as needful of male consolation as some."

"What's that supposed to mean? You're not above a little consolation yourself, from what I've been hearing."

"Easy, easy. The kids are upstairs."

"Karen isn't upstairs; she's in New York, letting that cradle robber she met at the club take her to the Alvin Ailey. Wake up. You know what your trouble has always been? You're an only child. You never loved me, you just loved the idea of sneaking into a family. You loved my family, the idea of there being so many of us, rich and Episcopalian and all that."

"I didn't need the Episcopalian so much. I thought I was going to sneeze all through the wedding. Incense, I couldn't believe it."

"You poor little Baptist boy. You know what my father said at the time? I've never told you this."

"Then don't."

"He said, 'He'll never fit in. He's a guttersnipe, Prissy.' "

"Wow. Did he really say 'guttersnipe'? And fit into what—the St. Paul Order of the Moose? Gee, I always rather liked him, too. Especially early in the mornings, when you could catch him sober."

"He *despised* you. But then Sue picked Jeb, and he was so much worse."

"That *was* lucky."

"He made you look good, it's a crazy fact."

"Yes, and you make Sue look good, so it evens out. Come on, let's save this for midnight. Here comes Henry."

But the boy, six feet tall suddenly, was wearing earphones plugged into a satchel-sized radio; on his way to the porch he gave his parents a glassy, oblivious smile.

Any smugness the Arnolds may have felt in relation to the Herreras' disasters lasted less than a year. An ingenious tax shelter Rob had directed a number of clients into was ruled invalid by the I.R.S., and these clients suddenly owed the government hundreds of thousands of dollars, including tens of thousands in penalties. Though they had been duly cautioned and no criminal offense was charged, the firm could not keep him; his divorce soon followed. One of the men Priscilla had been seeing had freed himself from his own wife and was prepared to take her on; Rob wondered what Priscilla did now, all hundred and fifty pounds of her, that was so wonderful. To think that he had started it all off with those formalized, chaste "parades."

She resettled with the children in Cos Cob. Having fouled his professional nest in the East, Rob accepted with gratitude the offer of a former colleague to join a firm in Los Angeles, as less than a junior partner. He had always been happy on their visits to Southern California and, though a one-bedroom condo in Westwood wasn't a redwood house overlooking a fairway in La Jolla, Old Man Hunter had been right: he fitted in better here. Southern California had a Baptist flavor that helped him heal. The people mostly came from small Midwestern towns, and there was a naïveté in even the sin—the naked acts in the bars and the painted little-girl hookers in jogging shorts along Hollywood Boulevard. The great stucco movie theatres of the thirties had been given over to X-rated films; freckle-faced young couples watched them holding hands and eating popcorn. In this city where sex was a kind of official currency, Rob made up for the fun he had missed while catching the train and raising the children in Greenwich, and evened the score with his former wife. Los Angeles was like that earlier immersion, at the age of religious decision, which coincided with puberty; that bullying big hand had shoved him under and he had come up feeling, as well as indignant, cleansed and born again.

One day downtown on the escalator from Figueroa Street up to the Bonaventure, he found himself riding behind a vivid black-haired girl whom he slowly recognized as his niece, Rose. He touched her naked shoulder and bought her a drink in the lobby lounge, amid all the noisy, curving pools. Rose was all of twenty-four now; he could hardly believe it. She told him her father had a job as foreman for another builder and had bought himself a stinkpot and kept taking weekend runs into Mexico; his dope-snorting friends that kept putting a move on her drove her crazy, so she had split. Now she worked as a salesgirl in a failing imported-leather-goods shop in the underground Arco Plaza while her chances of becoming an actress became geometrically smaller with each passing year. These days, she explained, if you haven't got your face somewhere by the time you're nineteen you're *finito*. And indeed, Rob thought, her face was unsubtle for a career of pretense; framed by a poodle cut of tight black curls, it had too much of Jeb's raw hopefulness, a shiny candor somehow coarse. Rob was excited by this disappointed young beauty, but women her age, with their round breasts and enormous pure eye whites, rather frightened him, like machines that are too new and expensive. He asked about her mother, and was given Susan's address. "She's doing real well," Rose warned him.

An exchange of letters followed; Susan's handwriting was a touch rounder than Priscilla's, but with the same "g"s that looked like "s"s and "t"s that had lost their crossings, like hats blown off by the wind. One autumn Saturday, he flew up to the Bay area. Three hundred miles of coast were cloudless and the hills had put on their inflammable tawny summer coats, that golden color the Californian loves as a New Englander loves the scarlet of turning maples. Berkeley looked surprisingly like Cambridge, once you ascended out of Oakland's slough: big homes built by a species of the middle class that had migrated elsewhere, and Xeroxed protest posters in many colors pasted to mailboxes and tacked to trees. Susan lived in the second-floor-back of a great yellow house that, but for its flaking paint and improvised outside stairways, reminded him of her ancestral home in St. Paul. She had been watching for him, and they kissed awkwardly halfway up her access stairs.

The apartment was dominated by old photos of her children and by examples of her own ceramics—crusty, oddly lovely things, with a preponderance of turquoise and muddy orange in the glazes. She was even selling a few, at a shop a friend of hers ran in Sausalito. A female friend. And she taught part time at a private elementary school. And still took classes—the other students called her Granny, but she loved them; their notions of what mattered were so utterly different from what ours were at that age. All this came out in a rapid voice, with a diffident stabbing of hands and a way of pushing her hair back from her ears as if to improve her hearing. Something in her manner implied that this was a slightly tiresome duty he had invented for them. He was an old relative, a page from the past. She was thinner than ever and had let her hair go back to gray, no longer just streaked but solidly gray, hanging down past the shoulders of a russet wool turtleneck sweater such as men wear in Scotch ads. He had never seen Priscilla look like this. In tight, spattered jeans and bare feet, Susan's skinniness was exciting; he wanted to seize her before she dwindled away entirely.

She took him for a drive, in her Mazda, just as if they still had children to entertain together. The golden slashed hills interwoven with ocean and lagoons, the curving paths full of cyclists and joggers and young parents with infants in backpacks looked idyllic, a vision of the future, an enchanted land not of perpetual summer, as where he lived, but of eternal spring. She had put on spike heels with her jeans and a vest of sheepskin patches over her sweater, and these additions made her startlingly stylish. They went out to eat at a local place where tabbouleh followed artichoke soup. Unlike most couples on a first date, they had no lack of things to talk about. Reminiscence shied away from old grievances and turned to the six children, their varying and still uncertain fates; fates seemed so much slower to shape up than when they had been young. Priscilla was hardly mentioned. As the evening wore on, Priscilla became an immense hole in their talk, a kind of cave they were dwelling in, while their voices slurred and their table candle flickered. Was it that Susan was trying to spare him acknowledging what had been, after all, a great marital defeat; or was Rob trying not to cast upon her a shadow of comparison, an onus of being half a person? She took him back to her apartment; indeed, he had not arranged for anywhere else to go.

Suzie kicked off her shoes and turned on an electric heater and dragged a magnum of Gallo from the refrigerator. She was tired; he liked that, since he was, too, as though they had been pulling at the same load in tandem all these years. They sat on the floor, on opposite sides of a glass coffee table in whose surface her face was mirrored—the swinging witchy hair, the deep eye sockets and thoughtful upper lip. "You've come a long way," she announced, in that voice which had once struck him as huskier than another but that in this room felt as fragile as the pots blushing turquoise on the shelves.

"How do you mean?"

"To see me. *Do* you see me? *Me,* I mean."

"Who else? I've always liked you. Loved, should I say? Or would that be too much?"

"I think it would. Things between us have always been . . ."

"Complicated," Rob finished.

"Exactly. I don't want to be just a way of correcting a mistake."

He thought a long time, so long her face became anxious, before answering, "Why not?" He knew that most people, including Susan, had more options than he, but he had faith that in an affluent nation a need, honestly confessed, has a good chance of being met.

This being the eighties, she was nervous about herpes, and even after his reassurances was still nervous. She asked him to hold off for a while, until she really felt trust. Meanwhile, there were things they *could* do. Seeing her undress and move self-consciously, chin up, through a little parade in the room, he thought her majestic, for being nearly skeletal. Plato was wrong; what is is absolute. The delay Susan imposed, the distances between them that could not be quickly changed, helped Rob grasp the blissful truth that she was only another woman.

MAGAZINES CONSULTED

The Agni Review, P.O. Box 229, Cambridge, Mass. 02238

Amazing Science Fiction Stories, P.O. Box 110, Lake Geneva, Wisc. 53147

Antaeus, Ecco Press, 1 West 30th Street, New York, N.Y. 10001

Antietam Review, 33 West Washington Street, Hagerstown, Md. 21740

The Antioch Review, P.O. Box 148, Yellow Springs, Ohio 45387

Apalachee Quarterly, P.O. Box 20106, Tallahassee, Fla. 32304

Arizona Quarterly, University of Arizona, Tucson, Ariz. 85721

Ascent, Department of English, University of Illinois, Urbana, Ill. 61801

Asimov's Science Fiction Magazine, Davis Publications, 380 Lexington Avenue, New York, N.Y. 10017

The Atlantic, 8 Arlington Street, Boston, Mass. 02116

Bennington Review, Bennington College, Bennington, Vt. 05201

The Black Warrior Review, P.O. Box 2936, University, Ala. 34586

The Brooklyn College Alumni Literary Review, Brooklyn College Alumni Association, Brooklyn, N.Y. 11201

Buffalo Spree, 4511 Harlem Road, P.O. Box 38, Buffalo, N.Y. 14226

California Oranges, P.O. Box 421, Cazadero, Calif. 95421

California Quarterly, 100 Sproul Hall, University of California, Davis, Calif. 95616

Canadian Fiction Magazine, P.O. Box 46422, Station G. Vancouver, B.C., Canada V6R 4G7

Canard Anthology, Canard Foundation, P.O. Box 8207, La Jolla, Calif. 92038

Carolina Quarterly, Greenlaw Hall 066-A, University of North Carolina, Chapel Hill, N.C. 27514

The Chariton Review, The Division of Language and Literature, Northeast Missouri State University, Kirksville, Mo. 63501

Chicago Review, 970 East 58th Street, Box C, University of Chicago, Chicago, Ill. 60637

Christopher Street Magazine, 249 Broadway, New York, N.Y. 10007

Clockwatch Review, 737 Penbrook Way, Hartland, Wisc. 53021

Commentary, 165 East 56th Street, New York, N.Y. 10022

Confrontation, Department of English, Brooklyn Center of Long Island University, Brooklyn, N.Y. 11201

Cosmopolitan, 224 West 57th Street, New York, N.Y. 10019

Cottonwood Review, Box J, Kansas Union, University of Kansas, Lawrence, Kans. 66045

Crazyhorse, Department of English, University of Arkansas at Little Rock, Ark. 72204

Dark Horse, Box 9, Somerville, Mass. 02143

Denver Quarterly, Department of English, University of Denver, Denver, Colo. 80210

Descant, Texas Christian University, Department of English, Fort Worth, Tex. 76129

Ellery Queen's Mystery Magazine, 380 Lexington Avenue, New York, N.Y. 10017

Epoch, 254 Goldwyn Smith Hall, Cornell University, Ithaca, N.Y. 14853

Esquire, 488 Madison Avenue, New York, N.Y. 10022

Farmer's Market, P.O. Box 1272, Galesburg, Ill. 61401

Fiction, Department of English, The City College of New York, New York, N.Y. 10031

Fiction International, Department of English, St. Lawrence University, Canton, N.Y. 13617

Fiction Network, P.O. Box 5651, San Francisco, Calif. 94101

The Fiddlehead, The Observatory, University of New Brunswick, P.O. Box 4400, Fredericton, N.B., Canada E3B 5A3

Forum, Ball State University, Muncie, Ind. 47306

Four Quarters, La Salle University, Philadelphia, Pa. 19141

Gargoyle, P.O. Box 3567, Washington, D.C. 20007

Georgia Review, University of Georgia, Athens, Ga. 30602

Grain, Box 1154, Regina, Saskatchewan, Canada S4P 3B4

Grand Street, 50 Riverside Drive, New York, N.Y. 10024

Gray's Sporting Journal, 205 Willow Street, P.O. Box 2549, South Hamilton, Mass. 01982

Great River Review, 211 West 7th, Wirona, Minn. 55987

Green River Review, Box 56, University Center, Mich. 48710

The Greensboro Review, University of North Carolina, Greensboro, N.C. 27412

Guest Editor, 179 Duane Street, New York, N.Y. 10013

Harper's Magazine, 2 Park Avenue, New York, N.Y. 10016

Hawaii Review, Hemenway Hall, University of Hawaii, Honolulu, Hawaii 96822

The Hudson Review, 65 East 55th Street, New York, N.Y. 10022

Indiana Review, 316 N. Jordan Avenue, Bloomington, Ind. 47405

Iowa Review, EPB 453, University of Iowa, Iowa City, Iowa 52240

Kairos, c/o Mandell, 127 W. 15th Street, Apt. 3F, New York, N.Y. 10011

Kansas Quarterly, Department of English, Kansas State University, Manhattan, Kans. 66506

The Kenyon Review, Kenyon College, Gambier, Ohio 43022

Ladies' Home Journal, 641 Lexington Avenue, New York, N.Y. 10022

The Literary Review, Fairleigh Dickinson University, Teaneck, N.J. 07666

The Little Magazine, P.O. Box 78, Pleasantville, N.Y. 10570-0078

The Louisville Review, University of Louisville, Louisville, Ky. 40208

Mademoiselle, 350 Madison Avenue, New York, N.Y. 10017

Magical Blend, P.O. Box 11303, San Francisco, Calif. 94010

Malahat Review, University of Victoria, Victoria, B.C., Canada

The Massachusetts Review, Memorial Hall, University of Massachusetts, Amherst, Mass. 01002

McCall's, 230 Park Avenue, New York, N.Y. 10017

Memphis State Review, Department of English, Memphis, Tenn. 38152

Michigan Quarterly Review, 3032 Rackham Bldg., University of Michigan, Ann Arbor, Mich. 48109

Mid-American Review, 106 Hanna Hall, Bowling Green State University, Bowling Green, Ohio 43403

Midstream, 515 Park Avenue, New York, N.Y. 10022

The Missouri Review, Department of English, 231 Arts and Sciences, University of Missouri, Columbia, Mo. 65211

Mother Jones, 607 Market Street, San Francisco, Calif. 94105

New Directions, 80 Eighth Avenue, New York, N.Y. 10011

New England Review and Breadloaf Quarterly, Box 179, Hanover, N.H. 03755

New Letters, University of Missouri–Kansas City, Kansas City, Mo. 64110

New Mexico Humanities Review, The Editors, Box A, New Mexico Tech., Socorro, N.M. 57801

The New Renaissance, 9 Heath Road, Arlington, Mass. 02174

The New Republic, 1220 19th Street, New York, N.Y. 10036

The New Yorker, 25 West 43rd, New York, N.Y. 10036

Nit and Wit, Box 14685, Chicago, Ill. 60614

The North American Review, University of Northern Iowa, 1222 West 27th Street, Cedar Falls, Iowa 50613

Northeast Magazine, 179 Allyn Street, Suite 411, Hartford, Conn. 06103

Northwest Review, 129 French Hall, University of Oregon, Eugene, Ore. 97403

Ohio Journal, Department of English, Ohio State University, 164 West 17th Avenue, Columbus, Ohio 43210

The Ohio Review, Ellis Hall, Ohio University, Athens, Ohio 45701

Omni, 909 Third Avenue, New York, N.Y. 10022

The Ontario Review, 9 Honey Brook Drive, Princeton, N.J. 08540

The Paris Review, 45–39 171st Place, Flushing, N.Y. 11358

Partisan Review, 128 Bay State Road, Boston, Mass. 02215/552 Fifth Avenue, New York, N.Y. 10036

Perspective, Washington University, St. Louis, Mo. 63130

Phylon, 223 Chestnut Street, S.W., Atlanta, Ga. 30314

Playboy, 919 North Michigan Avenue, Chicago, Ill. 60611

Playgirl, 3420 Ocean Park Boulevard, Suite 3000, Santa Monica, Calif. 90405

Ploughshares, Box 529, Cambridge, Mass. 02139

Prairie Schooner, Andrews Hall, University of Nebraska, Lincoln, Nebr. 68588

Quarterly West, 312 Olpin Union, University of Utah, Salt Lake City, Utah 84112

Raritan, 165 College Avenue, New Brunswick, N.J. 08903

Redbook, 230 Park Avenue, New York, N.Y. 10017

Salamagundi, Skidmore College, Saratoga Springs, N.Y. 12866

San Francisco Focus, 500 8th Street, San Francisco, Calif. 94103

Seattle Review, Padelford Hall, GN-30, University of Washington, Seattle, Wa. 98185

The Seneca Review, P.O. Box 115, Hobart and William Smith College, Geneva, N.Y. 14456

Sequoia, Storke Student Publications Bldg., Stanford, Calif. 94305

Seventeen, 850 Third Avenue, New York, N.Y. 10022

Sewanee Review, University of the South, Sewanee, Tenn. 37375

Shankpainter, 24 Pearl Street, Provincetown, Mass. 02657

Shenandoah: The Washington and Lee University Review, Box 722, Lexington, Va. 24450

The South Carolina Review, Department of English, Clemson University, Clemson, S.C. 29631

South Dakota Review, Box 111, University Exchange, Vermillion, S.D. 57069

Southern Humanities Review, Auburn University, Auburn, Ala. 36830

The Southern Review, Drawer D, University Station, Baton Rouge, La. 70803

Southwest Review, Southern Methodist University Press, Dallas, Tex. 75275

The Spoon River Quarterly, P.O. Box 1443, Peoria, Ill. 61655

Stories, 14 Beacon Street, Boston, Mass. 02108

Story Quarterly, P.O. Box 1416, Northbrook, Ill. 60062

Take the North Fork, 417 Delaware, Kansas City, Mo. 64105

Tendril, Box 512, Green Harbor, Mass. 02041

The Texas Review, Department of English, Sam Houston University, Huntsville, Tex. 77341

This World, San Francisco Chronicle, 901 Mission Street, San Francisco, Calif. 94103

The Threepenny Review, P.O. Box 335, Berkeley, Calif. 94701

TriQuarterly, 1735 Benson Avenue, Evanston, Ill. 60201

Twilight Zone, 800 Second Avenue, New York, N.Y. 10017

University of Windsor Review, Department of English, University of Windsor, Windsor, Ont., Canada N9B 3P4

U.S. Catholic, 221 West Madison Street, Chicago, Ill. 60606

The Virginia Quarterly Review, University of Virginia, 1 West Range, Charlottesville, Va. 22903

Vogue, 350 Madison Avenue, New York, N.Y. 10017

Washington Review, Box 50132, Washington, D.C. 20004

The Washingtonian, 1828 L Street, N.W., Suite 200, Washington, D.C. 20036

Webster Review, Webster College, Webster Groves, Mo. 63119

West Coast Review, Simon Fraser University, Burnaby, B.C., Canada V58

Western Humanities Review, Bldg. 41, University of Utah, Salt Lake City, Utah 84112

Wind, RFD Route 1, Box 809, Pikeville, Ky.

Wittenberg Review of Literature and Art, Box 1, Recitation Hall, Wittenberg University, Springfield, Ohio 45501

Woman's Day, 1515 Broadway, New York, N.Y. 10036

Yale Review, 250 Church Street, 1902A Yale Station, New Haven, Conn. 06520

Yankee, Dublin, N.H. 03444